DESCEND

INTO

MADNESS

A Vampire Menage Duet

Maddison Cole

Dirty Talk Publishing

DISCLAIMER

The time has come literary lovers,
To talk of other things,
Of torment and triggers
and hostile (tea) parties -
Of smut-filled pages and sins.

So, if the steamy sea proves too hot
And only nightmares this will bring,
I caution you to retrace your steps
Before welcoming yourself in.

CONTENTS

CHAPTER 1

MAL

"Milk and sugar?" I ask Polly as I fix her a nice cup of tea. She doesn't answer so I leave it black and turn my attention to my own cup. A dainty addition to my China tea set, white with small pink flowers curling around the rim and a delicate handle. The type you can only use with your pinkie flicked outwards. That's the law. My jagged fingernails scrape on the miniature milk jug, I wince, then shudder.

They wouldn't irritate you if you'd just bite them short, a voice rolls around the back of my mind. Twitching my head violently to shake the voice out, I opt for singing a teatime song, instead of tumbling down the rabbit hole of proper etiquette.

> *How doth the little cup of tea*
> *Improve my shifting temperament*
> *And ease the waters of my insanity*
> *With every drop of peppermint!*

Tipping the teapot up, I continue to hum whilst Polly watches me work. Her painted eyes stare lifelessly, the condescending smirk stretching across her plastic face not wavering as we enjoy our morning together. Beyond the barred window, the sun is steadily traveling towards midday, but it's always 6pm somewhere. The perfect time for tea. Adding three cubes of sugar to my cup, the weight of Polly's red, wool hair proves too much, tilting her head to the side as the echo of a patronizing mutter reaches me.

"Did you have something to say there, Polly?" I dip my voice dangerously low, sending a tremor of warning through the air. Dropping my spoon against the fragile saucer with an ear-slitting clatter, a few sensible residents dive behind the sofas. Polly, though, that judgy bitch doesn't back down. A solid minute rolls by as our staring contest stretches on, until my eyelids burn and I have to snap them shut.

"That's it!" I scream, throwing her tea in her face. Not mine obviously because I'm not wasting a damn good tea on a whore like her. She's always doing this, every time I find my Zen and get most of the rec room to myself. As if I can't drown out the voices in my head long enough for a single tea party, my only companion needs to be on my back too.

"I *need* three fucking cubes of sugar to keep me sweet enough. I should be judging *you*, Miss Black-English-Breakfast-on-a-Sunday-Morn. Do you know who drinks black tea on a Sunday? Satan, you Devil worshiping bitch!" I narrow my eyes at Crazy Kurt kneeling by the window, gripping his rosary between his hands and muttering about redemption. I don't waste my time on such things, not after what I've seen and done. This time, I throw the whole tea pot at Polly and she flies from her extra-cushion I'd propped her up on. Regret giving her that extra comfort now, don't I?

Holding my own cup at a safe height, I throw my arm across the table's surface and the tea set I spent months unclogging shower drains for, smashes to the floor. The shattering ricochets through my tea-loving heart but there's no time to dwell on sentimentality now. The tablecloth goes next, fluttering over the smashed remains to hide them from view. Much better.

Flashing above the single entrance and accompanied by an alarm, a red light calls for the Bastards-in-Blue, as I like to call them. The door bursts open and I sit still, my chest heaving on ragged breaths. Today is not the day to find myself in isolation, stuck with nothing but my own thoughts. Tomorrow is free on my schedule though. Uniformed figures loom over the threshold, hitting me hard with a warning glare to calm the fuck down. Raising a steady hand, I take a refreshing sip of my sweet tea and sag my posture.

"I'm fine. It's all good," I lie. Nothing has been fine since I was a little girl. Since I was swallowed by a world of fantasy and the wonders of my wildest dreams. Since I returned to a life of mockery and disdain I seem destined to rot in.

Scowling at the mess Polly has made of my carefully orchestrated tea party, I see regret swirling in the gloopy paint-filled tears that trail down her face.

"Oh, don't start crying. You know how I get," I roll my eyes and reach for her. Trying to wipe away the tears with the hem of my light blue dress,

I manage to smudge it more until she's unrecognizable. Red and black coats her face in a spiralizing pattern, like a black hole embedded in the melted plastic. An attendant steps forward, hand braced on his baton as he anticipates my next flip out but I don't react. In fact, I prefer Polly this way.

"Time for your meds, Mal," a cheery voice breaks through the tension. Pushing her way through the crowded doorway, Nurse Suzie smiles her rose lips at me. Curtseying in her black pencil skirt and flat canvas shoes, I take one of the white pots from the tray in her hands. She winks at me as if we're best friends, and since she's one of the only people in this place I haven't attempted to kill at least once, I suppose she is. Swallowing the pills, I finish my tea before it goes cold. Another luxury I had to earn via manual labor - hot water.

"Why don't you head back to your room and fix yourself up? You have visitors waiting in reception," Nurse Suzie winks again before sauntering away to deliver meds to the others who are hiding behind sofas and under tables. Only Crazy Kurt is brave enough to remain out in the open when I'm present, but he's also stupid enough to believe any god will forgive the basement of dead prostitutes they found him sticking his dick into.

"Visitors?" I perk up and then scowl. "Lawyers, you mean." Fucking leachy assholes. The attorneys assigned to my case are determined to rehabilitate me, or at least convince a judge it is possible. I've made it more than clear I have no intentions of leaving this hospital but as long as my so-called family keep throwing money their way, they're relentless.

The attendant in the doorway, the same one who enjoys some electric baton play, jerks his head as if I don't have a choice. His harsh face would be rather handsome if it weren't for the thick scar sliced from his temple to cheek. Not the sexy kind of scar either - the bubbling kind of raw, pink flesh that hinders his left eye from opening properly. I should probably feel bad about that, but like I said - he enjoys using his electric baton far too much and even I have my limits. No means no, motherfucker.

Gripping Polly to my chest, I barge past him and the others hovering around, their observant eyes watching me too closely. Breaking into a bare-footed skip, I travel back to my room with my blonde mane of hair bouncing behind me. My room is all the way down the hall, the last one in the corner. It puts me at an equal distance from the rec room to the mess hall with the shower block just beyond. It's a long way to pad when naked and dripping wet but means I can get a snack on the way past. Everyone here has seen me in my birthday suit, yet there's not a single one of them I'd falter on stabbing in the eyes with a plastic fork if I catch them doing so.

Entering my room, I take intense pleasure in slamming the door shut like a moody child. I prop Polly on the end of my bed, if the skinny excuse of a mattress laid with itchy sheets can be called that. Beds may only be shelves for the body in shut down mode but waking with prickly hives everywhere takes the fun out of drifting between worlds behind the safety of my eyelids.

Peering in the polycarbonate mirror above my tiny sink, I wash my hands and wipe them over my face. My blue eyes appear hollow and shrouded in black circles, my skin rough from the cardboard version of a hand towel hanging on the rail. I pick up the large paddle hairbrush that had to be custom ordered for my mass of knots, and then chuck it down again. I like the wavy afro that seems to keep others at bay, and also graces my butt with a comforting caress. It's not like I have much else that is purely mine.

The blue dress clinging to my chest is stained with the inky blotches of Polly's face so I reach for a replica, fresh and folded on my bedside table. Standard issue at Charmsfield Institute.

Changing into a clean dress, smoothing down the miniscule blue checked pattern, I pinch it at the back to accentuate my curves. If I stand at a certain angle and squish my tits together with my elbows, I could pass for a Victoria Secret model. Too bad when I release the paper-like fabric, it springs back like a shapeless potato sack. Fuck it, this is as good as it gets.

Looks pretty good to me, the voice comes again and I roll my eyes. In the reflection of the mirror, a curved, toothy smile hangs over my shoulder, twisting in circles. I wave it away, cursing beneath my breath that there's nothing 'pretty good' about me. I'm fucking stunning and completely unhinged. It's my niche.

The smile lowers, disappearing beneath my bed and I follow it. Dropping onto my front, I watch it fade into the darkness over a bulky, rectangular shadow. It'll remain there, protecting my most valuable belongings. A secret I can't reveal, a possession I can't let be confiscated. Not if I want to return to Wonderland one day.

Dusting myself off and leaving my room, the attendant with the scar sticks close to my side. I don't bother with names when too many quit within days of starting, but I call this prick the Terminator because he just won't fuck off. He fancies himself as the future warden, controlling my fate with the swing of his baton but everyone has a boss. And I refuse to let him be mine.

Taking the lead, I force him to follow me through the resident hallways. All the bedrooms are identical, which is bullshit because I've definitely earned a premium membership by now and should be upgraded to a private penthouse suite. The doors are supposed to remain open during daylight hours, thanks to trialing a new 'open door policy' with a formal lock-in after eight, but I suspiciously find my door locked more often than not. I would have preferred it today so I didn't have to sit through a lawyer spiel. Talk about suicidal.

Creating a rectangle, Charmsfield Institute comprises of three levels. Ground floor is for the eyes of visitors and flashy politicians that come to gush over the advancement in their criminal rehabilitation facility. I've seen camera crews pull up the tarmac driveway, scoping the manicured gardens surrounding the property until catching a glimpse of my bare chest pressed against the glass of my bedroom window. They quickly disperse then.

The second floor is based on recreation and 'providing equal opportunities for all.' Even crazed murderers that the world would prefer to remain locked away and out of sight. And that leaves us on the top level, the best one for jumping to our deaths, if I could only master picking the locks to the windows and dislodge the exterior bars.

Dragging back the old-fashioned grate covering the elevator which came with the antique stately home, I wait for the Terminator to grace the mounted pad with an electronic key card. Sure, they couldn't replace the disintegrating showers, but keypads and motion sensored cameras, no problem. The retractable cord snaps the card back to his belt and would have done some damage if he'd had a dick to speak of.

The doors peel back, coaxing me into a shell of gold paneling and soft jazz leaking from invisible speakers. My toes scrunch against the freshly shampooed carpet, a lemon scent drifting to my nostrils.

"Ready, and go," I tell the Terminator as the doors close the two of us inside. Snatching the baton from his side, I raise it high and freeze with the blunt end an inch from his forehead, my stance open and posture filled with intent. The Terminator rolls his good eye, plucking the baton from my grip and placing it back into his belt. Still, I remain in position, my teeth gritted.

"Don't move or you'll ruin the fun," I grit through frozen teeth. Mocking me, he reclines on the railing, checking his nails.

Sighing miserably, I slump into a pissed-off, relaxed pose for when the doors reopen and we exit without an entourage. That trick has never been as good as the first time, when I had one of the newbies frozen in fear and security thought the cameras had glitched. A whole squad was braced outside the elevator when we arrived at the bottom and I laughed into the next day. To be honest, nothing entertains me around here anymore.

Rushing over to the white, secured door, I peer through the peekaboo window to spy the lobby beyond. An extension on the front of the building, complete with domed glass ceiling that fills the opulent interior with bursts of blinding light. It doesn't help that the waiting area furniture and half-moon reception desk are white too, accented by hints of gold from the chair legs to the specked countertop. The only color slicing through the entrance appears in gigantic potted plants, stretching higher than the revolving glass door exactly opposite.

"Come on," the Terminator nudges me when I linger too long. I don't move yet, waiting for the young receptionist to sense my presence and bat her long lashes my way. The instant our eyes meet, I squeal at the top of my lungs and hammer my fists on the glass.

She kindly joins my screaming symphony, clutching a hand to her pristine bloused chest as the Terminator drags me away. I chuckle to myself, giving up on walking for the rest of today and allow him to heave me along via his meaty arm hooked around my front. Only fools walk to their own death via boredom.

Long strips of light pass overhead, the hallway disinfected to high heaven of all bacteria and color. My nose tingles, my eyes longing for the dark corner of my cell. I mean, rehabilitation suite. Planting me down outside visiting room three, the Terminator receives a whispered message from a mousey woman who ducks back into the observation room next door.

"I don't know what sick game is being played here," the Terminator grunts, roughly yanking me to a halt when I try to enter the room anyway, "but try to keep it together."

I twist my head to look at him through the veil of my blonde hair. We've developed a strange relationship over the years to the point his asshole can almost always gauge my reactions, which is unacceptable. I need to up my game. Yet he's *never* stopped to warn me before.

With a quirk of my brow, I twist the door handle, waiting for him to press his key card to the pad with a sigh and let myself in. A pair of blonde heads swivel my way and the breath hitches in my lungs. Dropping their shades in freakish unison, vibrant green eyes spear me like twin daggers to the chest.

Aside from their perfectly styled quiffs and chiseled jaws, matching striped vests cling to their muscled bodies. The material is thin enough to see their nipples through and I can trace the ridges of their abs to where the table cuts off my view. Purple braces hook over their shoulders, drawing my attention to the only difference I can see in the pair. Their tattoos.

From shoulders to fingers, their arms are coated in ink. Swirling, black designs that bleed from one into the other without visible joins. I peer at the richly illustrated drawings, yet my attention keeps being brought back to their chests. In mirror image, each displays a suit of choice on their peck. One a red heart, the other a black spade.

Standing at the same time, I take a tentative step back into the now closed door. Whatever fucking prank is being played here, it twizzles my patience within a thread of snapping. I'm well aware of the walled mirror and the attendants behind watching closely for my reaction. These assholes aren't lawyers. They look more like fantastical strippers from my dreams and I'm not playing this game. The one furthest away braces his long fingers on the metal table, his voice sliding through the air like a melodic massage to my ears.

"Happy birthday, Alice."

A moment passes where I calculate the day and month before I utterly lose my shit. The nearest chair bounces off the impenetrable glass first. The table is flipped second. Reaching for the other chair by its legs, I wheel it around towards the fucker that dared to speak my trigger word, lining the metal up with his flawless face perfectly. He grabs it with ease, halting my assault and twisting it free just as the door bangs open for a second time today.

Without hesitation, the attendants rush in, wrenching my arms behind my back as I scream blue bloody murder. The sharp stab of a needle in my neck takes effect almost immediately, my legs giving out as my chest is slammed against the wall.

"Fucking condescending...prick," I heave, my vision swimming. "Thinks he's...funny." One of the blondes tiptoes into my eye line, tilting his head almost upside down to get one last curious look beneath my hair before the lights go out.

CHAPTER 2

MAL

I shoot upright with a gasp, my rise interrupted by the fastenings at my wrists. Yanking on the cuffs securing me to the bed, I shake my legs to find my ankles in the same predicament. *Again*.

Screaming at the fluorescent lights, I fuel every seed of anger into the noise. Someone thought they'd be funny and send me a pair of tweedled strippers on the birthday I was adamant to forget. Why would I want to celebrate another year of mockery, another year of living in a world that doesn't deserve me? Worst of all, turning twenty-seven only reminds me it's been twenty whole years since those in Wonderland forgot about me.

After my body is free from every shriek, howl and frenzied hissy-fit I can muster, I slump back against the unbelievably thin pillow. What even is this - a fucking leaf? Whose neck is this supposed to support? A man-sized playing card and nothing else.

Between the harsh lights, I settle for tracing the lines of the polyester tiles with my eyes, like a maze across the ceiling I can't get lost in. Up, right, down, left, just like the crow flies, muttering to myself all the while.

> *If I were to slide a needle*
> *Into my very eye,*
> *Would colors burst through the universe*
> *Or would only my vision die.*
> *If I were to ease a nail*
> *Into my very foot*
> *Would I hobble on a wobble*
> *Or would I, on a lean, stay put.*
> *These are the mysteries I wonder so*
> *Since meeting that old man I used to know,*
> *A-sitting on a gate oh so long ago.*

"*Contrariwise,*" a voice replies and it takes me a moment to realize it was neither the female voice that haunts me, or any of the other tones that tumbleweed through my head. "It is the blind who see the most, or the weak who never feel frail. Let's lop off your foot completely and see how you prevail."

Craning my neck, I hunt for the source of the voice and settle on the only corner shadow in the entire room. A darkened area behind an oversized hunk of brown leather that the shrink likes to recline in. You know the type – ankle perched on the knee, large notepad in his hands and a pen that he clickety click clicks whilst waiting for me to calm down.

Standing in unison, the two men hit me with that same stoic stare through their sunglasses. Probably a good idea with the beaming lights burning our retinas. The longer I look, the more of a difference I'm able to see in them. Beyond their shared appearance, simmering just beneath the surface, there's tension. More so in the one with the heart tatt, his jaw ticking against the bite of his clench, his shoulders a millimeter more squared – like that of a soldier.

Quirking my brow, I quickly glance at the camera attached to the top of the doorframe, noting the red light is missing and the hatch in the door is firmly closed. Very well.

Twisting my right wrist around, instead of bucking against the pull, I stretch over the bed railing and unbuckle the clasp attached to the metal frame. Once freed, I tackle my next wrist and ankles, and all the while, their attention never leaves my body. I *feel* them gawking. Their stares searing at my pasty white skin. Throwing my legs over the side of the bed, I cock my head and create a curtain of blonde around my face.

"Why were you lying there if you could free yourself?" the one with the heart tattoo asks sharply. Almost as if he's chastising me for being stupid. My brows hit my hairline and just like that, any minor fantasies I may have had on how I could play out this reunion are shattered.

"The doppelganger appears far too logical," I frown, swinging my legs back and forth. "So, the better question is, who *are* you?" He doesn't answer me and I wonder if he even knows the answer. Sighing, I roll my head on my shoulders. "Not everyone who appears trapped is in distress. Believe me when I say, I wouldn't remain somewhere I don't want to be."

The pair don't move, and I refuse to back down so that leaves the three of us locked in the stalemate atmosphere binding us. Whoever hired these strippers and permitted them access into the psych ward needs a pay rise. Not even my wet dreams could conquer such a perfect match to my memories, stripping the chubby young boys of their fat and elongating them into muscled men with sizable bulges behind their electric blue, skinny jeans. And the way they reach up to pluck off their glasses in utter unison, well I can't help but give them a slow clap. Good show fellas.

"Be that as it may, we've come to retrieve you," Red Heart continues, trapping me in the line of his emerald eyes. No, I can't call him that. I'll go for Tweedle-Dick. His brother who opts for a lazy bat of his lashes and breaks into a smirk can be Tweedle-Douche.

"The only place I'll be going with you two," I spear them with a wagging finger, "is a mausoleum, i.e., over my dead fucking body." I hop off the bed, twisting my spine with a satisfying crack in multiple places. Next, I bend over to touch my toes, giving my calves a good stretch to get the blood flow circulating properly. A trick I picked up when training myself to shake off the tranquilizers as quickly as possible before the shrink bored me to death.

"As intriguing as such a place sounds," Tweedle-Douche appears genuinely interested, "there's nowhere else you belong aside from Wonderlust." He has a softer edge to his voice, not as demanding. A soothing balm to spread across the lash of his brothers. Yet his words only serve to do the opposite.

"Okay, now you're just trying to piss me off. Did Lorina send you?" I bark and the twins spare each other a side glance. I knew it. My older sister was as much as a sarcastic sourpuss as our father, although it wasn't my childhood tales she decided to cash in on. Just a delusional sibling she could bully into adulthood and then even more so when she became a journalist in the national paper. She made her career mocking me, filling the headlines with witty puns and my face splashed all over the front page. So, I gave her something to really write about.

Storming over to the door, I bang my fist on the metal loudly. "Okie dokie, I'm done in here. I'm calm, settled and completely remorseful!" I shout to whichever guard is posted outside. "Take me back to my room and show these cheap strippers the exit!"

"There won't be a response," Tweedle-Douche says. "If you wish to be free, you'd only need to use the key."

"For the love of St. fucking Nicholas, I'll double whatever my sister's offering if you'll stop with the rhyming." I leave out the part where I have no access to my trust fund. "On me, it sounds hot and whimsical. Your efforts to be *him* are just embarrassing."

Spinning around, I see T-Douche has taken a step forward, his head tilted back towards the ceiling. I follow his eyeline to the lightbulb and shield my eyes to make out the silhouette of a key stuck to the tile directly beside it.

"Why the fuck would you put it up there?!"

"It wasn't us. It flew up there itself," Tweedle-Dick growls. The movement draws my attention to his throat and holy hell, my mouth waters. His green orbs flick up to the key and back again, a spike of alarm flashing at the way I lick my lips and close the distance between us. "See something you like?" he frowns.

"Apples," I nod, drool escaping the corner of my mouth. He swallows thickly again and there it is - the sharpest Adam's apple I've ever seen. Plump, round and juicy, right before my face. Luckily, my long legs don't put me at much of a disadvantage to his six or so feet, otherwise I'd have to climb him like a tree. Actually...that sounds kind of fun.

Launching myself at T-Dick, he stumbles back against the leather chair and drops over the arm. I clamber on top, clawing at his braces to draw him closer to my mouth. Tongue lolling out, the tip just graces his skin when the T-Douche hoists me off like I weigh nothing. His hands remain bunched in the back of my blue paper gown, holding me in place as his brother scrambles to his feet.

"Give it to me!" I yell, clawing for him. Damn, it's been way too long if going cavewoman is the only way I'll be getting laid around here. Or maybe it's because they look like *them*. The twins that appear in my dreams, the ones I've been praying might save me. Whatever it is, I'm committed. "I'm going to suck your Adam's apple dry!"

T-Douche hoists me back against his firm chest, his arms crisscrossing over my front as he incapacitates me. Pinned against his pinstripes, his woodsy scent washes over my senses. Not struggling as hard as I should, his nose works its way through my tangled hair and somehow, his hot lips are on my ear.

"Once we return to Wonderlust, you can suck anything you like on me," he groans low and dangerously. I still. My thighs clench, slickening instantly and I carelessly push back against him. Yeah, it's been way too long.

A curved smile appears in the air beyond T-Dick's confused expression, stretching its white teeth wider than ever before. Snapping to my senses, I buck out of the arms holding me and fold mine over my chest. Mostly because my nipples have hardened through the thin material and any future rubbing would just cause me to attack one of these poor professionals again.

"Wonderlust? Shouldn't it be Wonder*land*?" I roll my eyes, not buying into this stripper fairy-tale they must have practiced for weeks. Hell, maybe it's their whole niche.

"It was once, but not anymore. Lust is the only currency our world knows now," T-Dick answers, his voice grave. Holding my eye, he clicks his fingers and points up at the key, like a giddy up pony gesture. I growl at him, full on Bandersnatch-style.

"And how do you propose I get up there? Stand a-top your shoulders while you look up my dress?"

"Well," T-Douche chokes on his own voice and I peer over at him. "I'd borrowed this from the Lizard just in case, but your idea sounds much better." Reaching into the jean pocket that's too tight to fully fit his hand in, he begins to pull out a stick. It keeps coming, defying the laws of three-inch pockets and I have to wonder if the damn thing was actually strapped to his outer thigh. Plucking the last of the stick out, he holds it level in his open palm for me to peer at closer. Hang on, it's not a stick after all – but a miniscule wooden ladder that he throws on the ground and pushes me back a step before it balloons to full size.

Eyeballing the ladder, I kick the base with my bare foot and feel the very real agony of a stubbed toe. Okay, that was a little trippy. The drugs are clearly still in my system, causing powerful hallucinations. So powerful that when I firmly grip the timber, a splinter pokes straight into my skin and I curse.

Slapping away the hands that try to grab for me, noting the fleeting compassion in T-Douche's eyes, I climb the ladder until my face is close enough to the bulb to feel the heat radiating back. The key is wedged right in the fixture, causing me to burn the same splintered hand when trying to pluck it out.

The moment it's free, the key tries to shoot out of my grip with the power of a rocket. It tosses me back onto the bed, the cuffs rattling from impact while I struggle to maintain my hold. The metal in my palm is also scorching from the bulb, searing into my now splintered and burnt hand. Why does everything bad always happen in threes? Tossing me this way and that, I catch a glimpse of the twins just standing there, expressionless.

"Fancy helping?!" I grit out, forcing myself back to my feet. Neither move and I do what women do best. Handle it my damn self.

Grasping the key between my cleavage as it tries to shoot out in any direction possible, I slide one foot in front of the other until standing before the heavy fire door. Bending in half, I use my tits as support to navigate the key into the lock, my hands now blistered and angrily red. It slots inside and I cry in triumph, wiping at the sweat coating my forehead. Twisting the key, a deadened cu-clunk rings out, refusing to move. Narrowing my eyes, I try the handle and the door freely swings open.

"I said you'd only need to use the key. I never said the door was locked," T-Dick says, shoving past me. My mouth drops, my rage bubbling hotter than any external injuries I just sustained until I spot a pair of legs sprawled across the floor. Venturing into the hallway, the rest of the Terminator becomes visible, his eyelids closed over his protruding scar. The twins don't wait to see if I'm following, their legs moving in powerful, synchronized strides.

Peering from the dimmed hallway to the pitch-black sky beyond the barred windows, I start to piece together why it's so quiet out here. The inmates are all locked up cozy for the night and the guard's roster only calls for one patrolling attendant at a time.

Rushing to catch up, because what else am I going to do when adventure comes calling, I follow them all the way back to my room. I'd query how they knew where I resided, but since it's the only room with the door slightly ajar, I put it down to coincidence. T-Douche drops down on the bed, dislodging Polly while T-Dick paces around the small space, muttering to himself about mimsies and mome raths.

Propping a shoe in the doorway, because I don't want to be locked in with some strippers until I'm certain they don't have a fetish for flaying their audience and wearing their birthday suits as part of their act, I stand with my hip cocked.

"Okay so you want to take me somewhere? What's in it for me?"

"It's not so much a want," T-Dick grumbles, pausing his pacing to stare into my mirror, "as it is a *need*." He doesn't sound at all happy about that which only brings more questions but T-Douche is currently drawing my attention. Sitting cross-legged, he pulls Polly into his lap. Licking his thumbs, he begins to rework her face, shifting the curdled paint back to their origins. Lifeless, large eyes, thinly closed smile. Even the freckles fall back into place as he sits her on my pillow and strokes her down her red, wool hair.

"Here's how it's going to work," T-Dick sighs sharply, taking control where there seems to be none. "We're going to use this looking glass to portal you back to Wonderlust, and from there on, you'll need to do everything I say if you want a chance at survival. Our world isn't what it used to be and you'll do well to remember that."

"Is he always so charming?" I tilt my head towards T-Douche, yawning widely. As intended, it bristles every nerve in T-Dick's body and it only makes me ignore him more. The twin on the bed smirks at me, the shadows slipping into the cervices of his face like an old accomplice, giving the appeal of a hollowed-out skull.

"It's true we came to recover you, but I'm more of an advocate for free choice. Should you so wish to accompany us home, I'll do my best to assist you. And for the record, you never have to do anything Tweed says." For the first time, a slow, genuine smile hitches up the corners of his mouth.

"Tweed, huh? Better than Tweedle-Dick I suppose." I cock a brow at Tweed, finding the inner monster of this man's temper rising to the surface. It ripples against his creamy skin, shifting in the pulsating of his muscles while his eyes darken to a dangerous shade of army green. If he's trying to intimidate me, it won't work, but there's a high chance the air being sucked from the room will suffocate me before he finds that out. T-Douche stands, leveling a fist in his twin's jaw in one swift move neither of us see coming.

"That's enough," he spits, taking barely a moment to right himself. With a ping on his thumbs beneath his braces, the relaxed smile returns as if it never left and he spares me a small nod. "Since we're making introductions - I'm Cash. How do you do?" He briefly bows and misses how I scrunch up my nose. "Let's get this portal open so we can continue this conversation over a nice cup of tea. That sounds much more pleasant, wouldn't you agree Alice?"

My heel slams down on Cash's foot before I can clear the blood that floods my vision. Apparently, his unlaced boots have steel-toe caps and I just about manage to conceal the bolt of pain that shoots up my leg. Grunting into my bottom lip, I circle around to sit beside Polly. Don't look at me bitch, I scowl at her when she tries to mock me.

Blinking the red haze clear, neither of the twins seems surprised by my outburst. Turning their backs to me, I crane my neck to see Tweed pull a handful of glittery powder from his front pocket and blow it against the mirror. The powder sparkles as it rolls down the surface, tumbling freely into the sink and hairbrush below.

Bracing on low legs and bent arms, Tweed has a two-step run up before launching himself into the mirror. His face crunches against the wall beyond, his body crashing into the sink and cracking it into several large chunks of porcelain. Water sprays everywhere and I quickly snatch my hand soap, lathering up the bubbles to wash myself beneath the gown. Can't pass up a free shower. Cash's eyes trace the movements of my hands, making no move to aid his groaning brother or step out of the gushing spray.

"Want some?" I ask, offering out the bar of beeswax. His vibrant green eyes don't waver from mine for a second as his long fingers stretch out. Instead of taking the soap, he slides it up my arm, over my dress sleeve and round the back of my neck. The movement puts us chest to chest, his full lips just above my eye level. Soaping up my nape, I drop the bar with a thud on the ground, entranced how he uses the lubricant to circle my neck. His other hand joins, lathering my throat, his thumbs brushing the line of my jaw as he prepares to say something.

"What the bloody fuck-" Tweed curses, pushing himself up against the spray and holding a bloody nose. He slips and slides, using the grip on his twin's arm to fully regain his footing. The spell I was temporarily under snaps and I shove Cash's chest, forcing him to step back because I'm sure as shit not moving. No way, no how.

"Payback for the unlocked door," I shrug at Tweed, unable to find my laughter at both his broken nose and stupidity. "All the mirrors here are synthetic - as in, fake. They can't trust the inmates not to smash the glass and use it to hold an attendant hostage or cut out the middleman, so to speak, and just kill themselves with it." A note of disdain claims the twin's faces at that last option, a transient hint of grief that's locked down before I can grasp it.

The pair suddenly turn to each other, shouting at the top of their lungs. I can't decipher which words leave who's mouth but I catch the gist. *I told you it wouldn't work. She has to return. We can't force her. You'll do as I say. Your mum's an ostrich.* Pushing my way between them, I cover each of their faces with one of my blistered hands.

"Okay, okay! Jesus titty fucking Christ!" At my outburst, both twins stalk away to different sides of the room, crossing their arms and glaring at the other. Wow, mature much. Lengthening my spine, I take the role of the dripping wet, bossy matron.

"Look, I've got my own agenda here so a break-out would work in my favor. But I have two rules," I brush my hands over my tatted hair, now even more knotted with unrinsed bubbles. "Firstly, you'll do everything *I* say because somehow, I seem to be the only one capable of results, and secondly, don't ever, fucking never ever, say my trigger word."

"And that would be?" Cash asks, sitting forward on intrigue. Holding up a hand to prepare myself, a shudder rolls through my spine.

"A..." I gag on my own words, blurting it out as painlessly as I can muster. "Alice." Just the word on my own tongue makes my skin crawl, the memories of classmates screaming my birth name in mockery flaring to life in my head. I can hear their laughter, see their fingers all pointed at me.

The daughter of Lewis Carroll, as he liked to call himself. Not even his pen name prevented the ridicule when the illustrations of his beloved books were so clearly me. The girl that lost her mind and spent more time with counselors than in school, acting out every chance she got. But my father did teach me one thing. You can create any story you like when you take the narrative into your own hands. Several stab wounds to his chest and an insanity plea proved that.

"So, what should we call you?" Tweed's voice is sharp as a blade as he cuts through my trip down memory lane. Both twins are staring at me intently and I replace the easy-going smile I've learnt to master.

"How rude, I'm Malice," I hold out my hand. Cash accepts it, kissing the back with a lingering look. I bob my head. "Mal, for short."

"Tis a pleasure to meet you, Mal," Cash winks and I have to say, employed stripper or not, I'm rather smitten.

CHAPTER 3

MAL

D rawing my hands through the silky-smooth length of my hair, I bring it to my nose and inhale. Vanilla and raspberry fill all my senses until I can taste it on the back of my tongue and feel it seeping into my pores. The shower pounds onto my scalp, encasing me in the steamy throes of bliss. Cocooning myself like a caterpillar, I take my sweet time, preparing to emerge as a reformed, beautiful butterfly.

"I'm back!" a cheery voice skates through the midst and I know it's Cash. His shadow looms on the other side of the curtain for merely a second before whipping it back and presenting me with a fluffy towel. Not the kind the inmates are usually provided with, but the premium cotton ones which are reserved for the staff. I don't know how these twins became master sleuths but I'm not complaining. Knocking off the faucet, I accept the towel with a smile until my eyes settle on the folded blue and white checked dress on a nearby plastic chair. The one a guard will perch on to watch us shower. Perverts.

"I thought I said new clothing, like what the prissy receptionist wears," I growl. There's a puppy dog quality to Cash's lop-sided grin as he lifts the offensive garment, revealing the Terminator's belt underneath.

"What can I say? I prefer you in blue," he winks as his brother appears. Kneeling with his back to me, he lays out the items I sent him on a scavenger hunt for whilst reeling them off one by one. All the while, I drop my towel to dress, not concerned with Cash's eyes watching me with hawk-like accuracy.

"A pen run dry of ink, orange juice, a paperclip, a disposable toothbrush-" I bend over his back to grab for the brush and shove it in my mouth. The round, silicone ball unfurls and releases a minty substance that I gnaw, whisking my teeth towards freshness. "And the only book I could find in your room was this."

Holding up a thickly bound book I'd kept hidden beneath my bed, I pluck it from his grip and clutch it to my mildly damp chest beneath the paper dress I loathe. At least Cash thought to grab me some underwear, although his motives may have been skewed when plucking the lacy black set from someone's locker. I can't imagine who's, since everyone around here is too stuck up to floss their ass in a tiny G-string like this.

"Yeah, this is the only book they let me have as not to 'indulge my fantasies.' Plus side is, I can insult you as eloquently as this," I raise my fist to clear my throat and stand tall. "There is a perennial wooden structure in an unspecified location, who's solitary justification of existence is to supply the oxygen you squander." I beam at the narrowed glare over his shoulder.

"You must think you're real cute," Tweed mutters and I spin, whipping his face with the wet mop of my washed hair. Chocking in shock, Tweed rises to grip my hips, his fingers tight enough to leave a bruise. "I'm done playing, little girl. Tell me the plan so I can get the fuck out of here. The human world vexes me no end."

"Temper, temper, dear brother," Cash begins but I hold up a hand to signal I can handle this. Tiptoeing with the book clenched between us, because I don't want to be any closer to this patronizing mofo than necessary, I lean to whisper in his ear.

"If you're going to keep up this Tweedle façade, that'd make us the same age, *little boy*." Slamming my knee up into his balls, I rush to drop into the nearby chair to watch him writhe around in pain. Nothing like a decent midnight show. I'm almost surprised he toppled like a bowling pin; I'd have thought his bark had more bite than that. Cash kneels to scoop up the carefully placed items and twists to hand them over.

"Ready to get out of here?" he asks so obediently, remaining on one knee. Dictionary in my lap, I push the inkless pen behind my ear, sip on the orange juice and toy with the paperclip in my free hand. The shower was the most essential part of the plan because I have my best ideas in the shower and the scavenger hunt...well that was to provide enough time for said shower.

"Almost. There's just one more thing we need to do first," I declare. Tweed groans from the shower floor, re-dampening his striped vest that had mostly dried. "I can't go anywhere without my main man, Stan."

"Who the fuck is Stan?" Tweed uses the wall to stand, holding an arm around his middle. I roll my eyes at him because clearly, the boy doesn't listen.

"My main man," I repeat. Finishing the juice, I toss the bottle aside and push to stand when Cash's hand on my thigh halts me. Reaching into the back of his skinny jeans, he produces a pair of flat canvas shoes with a wicked smile. Ahh, so it's Nurse Suzie we've robbed of her lacy underwear. Never pegged her as the type, although pegging might be *her* forte at this rate. While I mentally commend myself for just shaving with Joanna's razor blade, hidden for suicidal purposes, Cash's tender fingers stroke down the length of my leg, hooking up the back of my ankle to ease the first shoe on.

"Think you've got your fairy tales mixed up," I comment, but let him do it anyway. Once he deems me ready, I stand clutching my dictionary and hitch up the belt tied at my waist. Leading the twins to the elevator, I use the Terminators key card to permit us access and crowd them into the corner beneath the camera. We pile out on level two just as an ear-splitting alarm tears the night in half.

"We've been rumbled, boys," I smile widely, my tongue hanging out of my mouth. The night security team bursts through the fire escape doors, opting to use the staircases in emergencies.

"Where's this Stan and why is he important?" Tweed asks as the first uniformed man runs at him, snapping out his baton. I recognize the guard from the butt-dimple lining his chin and for a brief second, I'm not sure who I want to prevail. Watching Tweed get knocked on his ass by Anus-Face might just become the new best moment of my life. Tweed doesn't even blink as he smashes his fist into the guard's chest with enough force to send him flying backwards. Ahh man. Bye, bye Butthead.

The next is already upon him while I stand gawking. The fluidity of his fight, the definition of his muscles. Gracefully, he unhooks his braces to give him free reign of movement and oh my mini milk. His braces are left to hang over thick thighs that are only enhanced by the tight jeans. His chest heaves as he knocks foe after foe on their asses. All of which I'm logging as imagery for the good ol' rub hub.

Tweed catches me gawking and I blush, returning to the question at hand. "He's my longest friend," I snap. "The only one who's ever believed my stories were real."

Tweed snarls as the guards continue coming. At one point, there's three on him and somehow, he hulk-blasts out and sends them all crashing into the nearest walls. Huh, I wonder if his ejaculation could shoot me across the room like that. Wait, shut up stupid brain, no I don't. Shaking my head and picking up my jaw from the floor, I remember the other part to his question. "Oh. Third door on the right."

Cash, who has been leaning against the window this entire time, bolts upright and takes off down the hall. I move to follow when an electric baton stabs into my side. I cry out, not having realized through the bodies flying everywhere, one had slipped past Tweed's barrier to get to me. Two can play at that game.

Unsheathing my own baton, I twist and duck, catching my attacker by surprise. Yeah, this bitch can fight back. His military-trained focus hangs on the club in my hand, as planned. The perfect decoy as I whip the inkless pen from behind my ear and stab him in the eye. Thumping my foot in his shin with a satisfying crack, I smack his head aside with the baton on the way down and jam the electronic end into his neck for good measure. By the time he's collapsed on the ground, the other guards take a reluctant step back and radio for extra help. That totally has everything to do with my awesome take down and is in no way related to the exhibition of mangled bodies at Tweed's feet.

Singing along with the siren blaring overhead, I skip over Cash, who's struggling with the locked door. Apparently, his pockets are big enough for a damn ladder, but not a lock-picking kit. *Beep*, my key card goes and he frowns at it as the door pops open of its own accord. Tweed keeps watch while we slip inside the darkness and I run to the desk at the back of the classroom.

"There's no one in here," my accomplice shouts over the alarm but I'm already placing down my book to straighten the paperclip. Looming over the two-tiered cage of slender white bars, I soothe Stan as his huge pupil-less eyes peer up at me from inside a bed of cotton wool. Pushing the paperclip inside the tiny lock he only has because Keith tried to eat him once, I hook the release in just the right way for it to pop open and I rush to open the cage.

"Hey buddy," I close my hands around my only friend. His nose tickles the key-shaped burn I've sustained and his little tongue scrapes over it in comfort. "I know, rough night," I agree. Pressing a kiss to the black diamond on his forehead amongst the coffee-brown fur, I ease him into my drying hair that's already beginning to frizz. The curls will bounce back in no time, appearing like I haven't washed them in a year. Stan's pink claws are rather chunky for his tiny size, which he proves by shifting across my scalp with light scratches. Finding a place to settle behind my ear, I grab my book and unhurriedly stroll out of the classroom.

"Well, where the fuck is he?" Tweed shouts back as a plucky guard charges forward, only to be hoisted and rolled over the twin's back. Landing heavily on the ground at my feet, Tweed slams his boot down on the man's chest, who immediately coughs up blood all over my shin. Thanks for that. Using the guy's mop of brown locks to wipe most of the blood off, I shift aside the hair by my ear for Tweed to see Stan nestled inside.

"We went through all this trouble for a rat?" he yells and I gasp, even though Cash strolls up with an easy-going smile.

"It really wasn't any trouble on my part," he muses while I'm stepping onto the guard, using him as a stool to confront Tweed eye to eye.

"He's not a rat, he's a sugar glider. And he's a damn sight handier to keep around than you." I prod him in the chest to emphasize my point and then stride on by, ignoring his mutterings about saving our asses.

Calling the elevator by key card once more, the twins manage to hurdle over the groaning bodies and enter just before another wave of guards breaches the stairwell door. Ours slide close on their bewildered faces and shocked bellows as I give them a friendly wave goodbye.

"Well, you've got your stupid rodent, so now what? No doubt we're going to use that card thingy on your belt and just walk out the front door. *How original.*" Tweed snarls while I hide the fact I need to quickly come up with a better plan. His green eyes swirl with shades of olive to lime in a hypnotizing manner that doesn't work on me. I'm too busy noticing the braces are still hanging either side of his denim-clad legs and the abs through his transparent vest are more prominent after use.

"The best exit doubles as an entrance," I shrug. It's blissfully quiet in here with the gentle croon of violins playing throughout. When the doors open though, a squad of pissed-off guards are already there and I balk. "You know what, why don't you take the lead on this," I murmur, stepping behind Tweed. He tosses me an asshole-ish smirk I hate even more than the hit to my femininity.

It's not that I *need* to hide behind a man or get them to fight my battles, but my faith in this escape is quickly waning. I have a cushy set-up here, tucked away from the sarcastic smirks and taunting tales. The guards tolerate me, the inmates fear me. Do I really want to give that up for a chance at escaping with a pair of very dedicated, method-acting strippers?

But then again, this is the calling I've been waiting for. The best chance I'll get to investigate what's hidden within the pages of the book clutched beneath my arm.

As Tweed shoves a hand into the opposite front pocket from before, he throws a mass of purple powder over the guards and turns to cover me from the explosion rocking through the lower level, I know my decision is firmly made. His woodsy scent of fresh mushroom and pine surges through my body, the firm touch of his palms pinning me against the wall doing wicked things to my lady parts. I've never fucked through an explosion before, but then I reach up and slap myself. Stupid Mal, they're strippers - not prostitutes. Although the jealous spark in Cash's watchful eyes tells me they possibly could be and I'll just bill it all to my sister's credit card.

"Move," Tweed snaps, breaking through my gyrating against his leg. He doesn't give me an option, hoisting my arms upwards until I'm thrown over his shoulder, ass in the air. Tossing my book to Cash, I bark at him to guard it with his life.

Everything else is a blur as Cash snatches the key card from my waist and I'm jostled around, my eyes trained on the curve of Tweed's butt. Who said a man could look so hot in a pair of electric blue skinny jeans? I didn't, so maybe he should take them off. I laugh mechanically to myself, my hands reaching out and retracting a few times as I battle with my self-will. He's a fucking strip-o-gram, not a new toy I can molest. We haven't even discussed safe words.

Do it, a voice coaxes in my ear. The smile is back, along with the faintest glow of slitted blue eyes as big as saucers. They dare me to, tricking my subconscious into thinking it might actually be here. Yet, I know it's all in my imagination because unlike the frustrating cat I once knew, the voice that's been speaking to me is distinctly female. Alas, thanks to the daily dose of antipsychotics that only work in reverse for someone who's not actually mentally and criminally insane, it's all in my head.

Tweed's arm tightens around my legs just before he lifts into the air and I take my chance. Clutching his butt cheeks, *for stability*, I make sure I feel every inch of the hardened globes as the shatter of a window echoes around us. The rounded muscles flex beneath my palms, just the right amount of squish covering his squat-induced oh-my-wows before he lands on his feet once more and takes off running into the night.

"You can let go now," a growl comes and looking up, I'm surprised to find it came from Cash. His face is hidden as the blinking red lights of Charmsfield Institute lend themselves to the backdrop. The alarm softens with the distance being put between us and the building – that or I'm slowly going deaf – as Tweed's boots eat up the earth at an impressive speed. Disappearing into the woods surrounding the institute's grounds, we become enveloped in darkness. Coated in shadow, lost to the night. The winter is blowing in on a frosted chill, stripping the trees of any leaves that may have softened the scratches outstretched branches lash us with.

"Over there," Cash (I think) says, although he's moved like a whippet to be somewhere up ahead. I lie limply, bobbing up and down as the breeze filters up my dress until Tweed finally skids to a halt. Twisting back, I don't see anything worth noting, other than both sets of eyes either side of me being trained on my exposed ass. Turns out that breeze has flapped the paper-like material up my back and left me completely exposed in the black G-string that should be called a G-*sting*, because fucking ow! If I've ever wondered what flossing my arsehole felt like, now I know.

Tweed's turned head is practically touching me, the warmth of his breath reviving my left, frozen cheek. You could take an icepick to my bubbled behind and it'd shatter on impact. At the awkward angle, I'm stuck relying on my peripheral vision but it seems like Tweed leans in just that little bit more and through the icy numbness, I'm sure I feel the scrape of his teeth.

"If you mark her right now, I'll fucking kill you myself," Cash remarks. This isn't the twin I saw in the Institute. Amongst the shadows, his green eyes begin to glow like luminescent peas swimming in a bowl of burnt gravy. A growl is drawn through Tweed's chest beneath me and in the next second, my face is meeting the ground as I'm tossed aside without a single regard for poor Stan. He's been clinging to my scalp, his claws embedded so deeply, I'm sure I'm bleeding.

Shoving myself upright, my hands skid over the damp, fallen leaves I can hear rustling through my hair. So much for a fucking decent shower. The blue dress is coated with a thick layer of mud by the time I stand and turn to face the shadows bleeding into the moonless night, finding myself completely alone.

CHAPTER 4

MAL

Trekking on forever,
In this tulgey, darkened wood.
A trudge and grudge of canvas shoe
in clogged mud is never good.
On and on I travel
'til my feet are soaked through
And no doubt when I reach daylight

My toes will be frostbite blue.

Slapping myself to stop thinking in stanza-commentary mode, I come to rest by the next thick trunk I feel. An oak I'm guessing, as I rasp my knuckles on the bark and feel out the width. I had spent a lot of time napping by trees as a child - it's where my father reckoned I procured the 'silliest' of my ideas. I grit my teeth at the thought of him, my anger burning hot. If I had a knife, I'd kill him twice and be glad to see him rot.

"Arghhh!" I scream upwards, frightening a canopy full of birds on flippy flappy wings. Scratching at my eyes, I drop back, drawing labored breaths in and out. I'm rhyming again. Must be the drugs wearing off and my true nature settling back in. If anyone thought medicated Malice was looney, they don't want to meet sober me in a dark alley. That bitch be crazy.

Looking back the way I came - I think, I listen out for any unnatural sounds against the busy nightlife of the forest. Yet, just like earlier when I took a break sprawled across a low hanging branch, there's nothing. No pound of guards running to catch me. No twins filling my head with escape plans and running off as soon as their time being paid to entertain me is up.

Nothing except the sound of my back cracking at the uncomfortable angle I laid across that stupid wooden limb. This night seems like it's never going to end as I push myself onwards, wondering if it was even worth it. That brief touch of contact, the fleeting hunger-filled gazes. Worst of all, I've lost my book so now my reasons for leaving are mute.

This way, a voice whispers on the edge of my subconscious. I roll my eyes, knowing it wouldn't be long until this particular voice found me. Even in the pits of hell, I reckon I couldn't escape the figment of my imagination that tricks me into seeing a floating, toothy smile. And there it is, hovering in the distance, just to the right. The visual reminder no matter how bland my chosen prison is, I can't run from myself. My longing, my nightmares.

Beckoning me to follow, I brush a hand through the bird's nest sitting atop my head and give Stan a reassuring stroke. "If nothing else, I'm going to find you a decent home, buddy. One where someone won't try to eat you." The smile floats further away, spiraling all the while until the glint of a warm glow creates a halo around the grin. Just like that, it widens and fades, leaving me staring at a wooden cabin hiding between the folds of two, overhanging willows. Their snowy white ferns cascade down the roof's silhouette and fall over an extended porch which creaks beneath my muddy feet.

Dropping low, I crawl the rest of the way, only making the noises more prominent until I pop up to peer through a grime-coated window. A fire is burning over a stack of thickly chopped wood, filling the room with a homely atmosphere I can feel seeping into my bones, even from out here. Paneling ranging from the deepest mahoganies to the richest walnut coats the walls, leaving the furniture to add splashes of cream and mocha.

A half-filled glass of whiskey sits on the stripped and varnished maple coffee table, the cubes of ice almost fully melted away. Strewn over the back of the L-shaped sofa, there's a white jacket with the tell-tale logo printed over the breast pocket. This must be one of the guard's living quarters and judging by the book tossed onto the bear-skin rug, where Cash disappeared off to. Abandoning assholes or not, I have to retrieve my dictionary.

Following the porch that wraps all the way around the cabin's exterior, I creep through the back door which is helpfully unlocked. My main concern should be hunting for keys for the motorcycle glinting out the back window or hacking my family's accounts and relieving them of the fortune that's owed to me, but nah. Too much effort when the silky raspberry and vanilla home I'd made for Stan is now a tattered, stinky mess once again. What kind of friend leaves their bestie to reside in that?

Grabbing my book from the shaggy rug and darting up the stairs, I locate the bathroom through the process of elimination. Every door I open presents a bedroom, study, cupboard or sex dungeon. Intriguing - I may *cum* back to that last one, once I'm fresh as a daisy and looking to finger-blast some images out of my head. Transparent striped vests and braces, thick thighs and skinny jeans. Blonde hair, jaws cut from ice and glowing green eyes centered on me – just to name a few.

Standing outside the only remaining closed door, I brace my hand on the handle when a pleasured groan sounds from inside. I still, my heart halting in my chest as I listen carefully. It comes again. Shit, I got it wrong about the guards rushing off, but I've come this far and once I'd got the anticipation butterflies of a scorching hot shower fluttering around my tum tum, nothing can deter me. So instead, I hold out an open palm by my ear and coax Stan out with a low whistle. We've practiced this so often, it's another reason the Terminator gave for padlocking Stan's cage – I just refuse to believe him.

"Ready, Stan? Three, five, sixty-nine, attack!" Bursting through the door, my eyes don't have time to adjust as Stan flies from my open palm, extending his fur-coated wings to descend on his target. A roar leaves Tweed as soon as Stan makes contact with his reddened face, scratching like a sugar glider possessed as I stare on with morbid fascination and a hint of jealousy. I wanted to be the one to slice him to shreds after tossing me aside and going all Houdini.

Casting my eyes over the bigger picture, the realization he wasn't having a face painting party without me settles in. Red, glossy and potent, everywhere. Tweed shifts around his perch on the closed toilet, reaching out to drag down the shower curtain that concealed Cash, who's reclined in the bathtub. Head to feet, he's coated in what looks and smells like blood which he licks from his devilishly long finger. My mouth parts on instinct, those tingles in my lower belly taking on a life of their own. Oh, this is new.

"Get the fuck-" Tweed curses, desperately trying to grab for Stan who claws his way around the back of the blonde's head, "-off!" My main man here is like a ninja, putting those chunky claws and sharp little teeth to good use. Stepping forward to rescue my friend for his own sake, my soppy shoe skids out on a sheen of crimson and I stumble forward.

Cash's hand whips out for my wrist but the blood acts like a lubricant and doesn't help at all. Instead, I crash like a sexy tower of Jenga, slamming my head into Tweed's crotch.

"Lends a whole new meaning to giving head," I muster, once toppled aside. I don't know what titanium cock he has in those jeans but I rub my temple, sure I'll have a bruise.

"Why do you hate my dick so much?" Tweed groans, tilting sideways where I see Stan clutching onto the back of his hair for dear life. There's no escaping the blood now, a thick layer coating my back, dying my hair and clogging my throat. The coppery stench makes me gag and that's saying something. I'm no stranger to blood, death or a decaying body for that matter. Yet whatever went down here was nothing short of a massacre.

"So, this is where you guys went?" I ask, pushing myself upright after a few messy tries. "Abandoned me to..." I trail off as a foot catches my attention, tucked behind the base of the toilet. The oddest part are the gnaw marks along the ridge that makes it appear to have been *chewed* off. Not to mention - where the fuck is the rest of the body? My eyes slowly lift to a casual Cash, licking each finger with unhindered satisfaction. Ew, talk about the cat who got the cream.

"Sooooo," I nod slowly, "if you guys offer to eat me out, the answer is a resounding no."

"We'll see about that," Cash grins lazily, rolling his head to meet my gaze. Stan leaps for it then, landing on the ground to scamper through the bloody swimming pool and claw at my leg for salvation. I snatch him up as Tweed dives to the ground, his hands locking on my knees and a growl tearing through his throat. This close, it's easy to see which wounds Stan inflicted and where Tweed's pasty white skin is simply covered with someone else's blood. Mostly because the ragged scratches and chunks of skin peeling from his skull are oozing a congealed orange liquid that makes me cringe.

Before I safely tuck Stan back into the nest of my hair, I raise one finger towards my furry friend and smirk at Tweed's responding flinch. One point to team Malice. Stan pushes his padded paw to my finger, maintaining eye contact between Tweed's glowing green orbs and his beady black ones as we miniature high-five. What a legend.

"Next time that rat isn't under your protection, I'm tearing his tiny limbs from his tiny body and having a tiny barbeque with them," Tweed growls once more like a caged animal. Jeez, this guy could really use my dictionary if it weren't dropped back on the hallway floor.

"Well, I'd better get used to having him shit in my hair then," I quip back, my eyes sliding away for the briefest moment as I replay that last line back in my head.

Breaking the tension, Cash switches on the shower with his foot, projecting a spray of water directly over his horizontal body. His face becomes visible, his blonde hair rinsing free of color as he shimmies around in the tub. His clothes hit the bathroom floor with a slap a moment later, spraying Tweed and I in a fresh spray of blood. Tweed's eyes are still firmly on me, burning two emerald-shaped holes through my head.

As intriguing and alluring as those swirling spheres are, just beyond him, Cash stands in all his glory and my eyebrow hitches. What constricting, devil's denim were those skinny jeans created from to have vacuum-packed his boa so well? If I thought their zipped bulges were impressive, they have nothing on the monstrosity flopping between Cash's thighs. I'm certain as he turns, it winks at me, inviting my curious nature closer, if Tweed wasn't pinning me in place with the pressure on my legs. I pay it no mind, too concerned if Cash could give me blunt force trauma with that thing, lining me up like a croquet ball and swinging it against my head? Mouth open, of course.

The silky, bulbous tip shifts from view and the spell is broken, although Tweed knows. He can see my interest, sense the tremors shooting up my inner thighs to my Mary Magdalene. Either that, or he's just gripping me so tightly, my circulation is becoming compromised. The thought of becoming a double amputee before I'm thirty has me shoving him off, although the tantalizing warmth of his touch remains. That's what I get for liking it rough.

"Your turn," Cash tells no one in particular, exiting the bathtub with a wondrous view of his full, heavy balls and leaving the bathroom without a towel. After a beat, both Tweed and I shoot forwards, racing for the shower in what seems like an uphill slip and slide. Not even a game of twister has had limbs tangled so much but with plenty of shoving, kicking and dirty tactics, I manage to pull myself up on the ridge of the tub, using Tweed's face beneath my foot for a boost.

I thought tearing off my dress and jumping beneath the water would declare me the champion, but Tweed's body crushes against my back a moment later, smushing me into the tiles so he can steal the best part of the spray.

"Really think you can win in a fight against me?" he mocks in my ear. Stan shifts around the back of my scalp and leaps to the back of the tub. Clearly this isn't a fight he wants to be a part of, or he just doesn't like getting wet. Leaning over me to grab a body wash bottle from the plastic shelf, I wait for Tweed to lather up first, before shifting to wash his front. Then, with the inch of space between us, I spin.

"Oh, this is you winning? I'm confused because it was part of my plan all along to use you as a giant loofah." Shimmying my shoulders, I rub the black, lacey bra all over Tweed's chest. Whether from exertion or the quick twitch of his arm, my bra pings off and swirls around the drain. I'm not deterred, though, rubbing the length of my torso over Tweed's rock-hard abs. A strand of bubbles drips down his ribs until I scoop them up and fist my cleavage with it. Tweed's eyes plunge into the depths of dwindling seaweed, swirling and lost at sea. Slamming his hands into the wall behind me, and I mean *into* because I hear the tiles crack, the strained croak that leaves his sinful lips makes a bee line for my g-string.

"How about you get on your knees and I'll wash out the back of your throat too?" My eyes dip to the black boxers hugging his hips, the only piece of clothing he's left wearing. On cue, his dick jumps to wave at me and I lick my lips on instinct.

"My mouth happens to be minty fresh, thank you very much," I heave a breath over his face. "But I do have something that could use a good scrubbin'." Shoving the boxers down his thighs, I lift my leg and his arm automatically wraps around my ankle, pinning it to his shoulder in an open split. I'd have preferred his double to have been in here, since this asshole doesn't deserve the delight of my body, but cleanliness is key. All that separates us is the tiny slip of the G-string rubbing deliciously over my pussy as I use his dick for stability.

"Make sure to get in all the nooks and crannies," a wicked sweeping smile passes over his face and I do just that. Dropping his forehead to mine, not even Tweed can keep up the façade that this isn't affecting him. He's rock hard against my pussy, although I avoid eye contact with the steely monster in question. I can only imagine what cement-like cum might shoot out the end, blinding me instantly.

Bubbles tumble between us as he continues to pump more body wash into his hands and rub it over his chest – being careful not to lather up mine because that would be crossing the line. A groan leaks from his lips as I grind over him, making sure we're both clean enough to eat our dinners off of when his hands dive into my hair. Holy sweet mamba.

"Fuck yeah, just like that," I groan, grinding my hips harder. "Scrub a dub rub, getting squeaky clean in the tub." A dark chuckle is drawn from Tweed, a supportive thrust of his shaft aiding my clean clit cause.

His fingers massage my scalp, using the soap to wash every wisp of crusted blood from my blonde locks. I don't even have the heart to tell him about shampoo and conditioning etiquette. The pressure on my clit is glorious, the fabric creating a whole new dimension of oh-my-yes. Using his grip on my scalp, Tweed tilts my head at the right angle for his lips to hover over my pulse. My body stiffens, preparing to take this to the next level when a cough divides our lust-filled haze, swiftly snapping both of our heads to Cash.

"We ready to go?" The mirror-image to the man I'm using as a soapy sponge is standing in the doorway, my book in his hand. A pair of boots treads inside, uncaring of the blood still covering the bathroom floor. Black cargo trousers hang low on his hips, somehow appearing sexier than the skin-tight jeans of previous. The purple-striped tank top is back however, and I'm extremely thankful for that. Clinging to every ridge of his torso, it only takes one more roll of my clit over Tweed's solid shaft to spiral me over the edge. Tremors rack my body, only the grip of Tweed's hands encasing my head and nape keeping me upright. I rest against him like a pole, moaning through the pulsating waves rolling through my pussy. Fuck, I needed that.

"Who knew getting clean could be so fun?" I sigh, releasing my leg from Tweed's shoulder. I knew keeping up with my yoga routine would come in handy. Pushing Tweed a reluctant step back, I go to leave the tub before eyeing the blood on the floor. Mmmm, seems counterproductive when I've used Tweed like a whorey wash cloth. Bracing one foot on the tub, I give Cash a sharp nod and fling myself into the air.

"Catch meee!" Strong banded arms wrap around my slippery body and with a whistle, I watch Stan hop from the tub's edge to the back of the toilet, over the sink and sail into the safety of my hair. Even sopping wet, I bet it's nicer for him than remaining in Tweed's company. Dude can rub me into a climax whenever he wants, doesn't mean I need to like him.

Carrying me into the bedroom, Cash places me down gently before wrapping a towel around my middle. A matching outfit to his own, complete with boots has been laid across the bed for Tweed, beside what I suppose I'm expected to wear. A powdered blue dress in satin. Fuck no.

I don't care if the central panel is white, outlined with boning that would mold to my body. I don't care about the black sash that circles the middle, the uneven bump underneath hinting at a large bow, or how it ties into the ruffling beneath the skirt. *Nor*, do I give a fuck about white stockings, elbow gloves, oversized hair bow or sky-blue high heels.

"Dress quickly, the portal is nearly ready," Cash tells me, looking over his shoulder. I turn to see the wall distorting behind a sickly, yellow sheet of wallpaper. It rolls in waves, warping into what looks like the hollow outline of a face. When I take a step back, Cash is no longer there and I drop onto the edge of the mattress. My hand comes to rest on the satin, although my attention is set on the tunneled eyes boring out of the paper, a gaping mouth stretching and reaching for me. I somehow don't think I'm imagining this, since it's not my fantastical niche, and I'm not about to die in a fucking towel. Snatching up the clothes, I duck to the other side of the room to dress at a safe distance.

Once fully covered, I dart from the room, in search of the twins before that damn thing *consumes* me. The tearing of wallpaper follows me through the hallway, echoed by a roar that rocks the cabin on its wooden plinths. Gripping the railing on the staircase, Cash is jogging up to stop me from escaping completely. His eyes drag over my body with keen interest but there's no time for that apparently.

Crowding me back up the steps, I throw punches to his shoulders, not so sure about this anymore. I know what happened to me as a child was real and fuck what anyone else has to say about it. I also know I need to get back there and see if what I believe has any truth to it. On that thought, I snatch the dictionary from Cash's grip and hold it close. You're going nowhere. But surely there's an easier way than this. A rabbit hole surrounded by daisies, perhaps?

Wrapping an arm around my body, Cash carries me back along the hall and I note the bathroom door is wide now, the tub completely empty. Bloodied footsteps trail the cream carpet towards the bedroom door and as Cash kicks it in, there's Tweed.

"Oh wow," Cash halts, releasing a wolf whistle. "Suits you brother." I twist out of Cash's grip, taking in the sight before me in full detail. Never mind the face stretching from the wall, which is obviously a clown because that's not terrifying.

Standing with his legs at crooked angles, his toes crammed into the heels, Tweed's muscled chest heaves from inside the blue dress. I was right – the boning does do wonders for the figure, giving Tweed an hour-glass appearance models would kill for. Despite the scowl etched into his face, he's gone the whole mile, snow-white gloves over his manly hands, oversize bow in his hair and all. His eyes, though, are burning with fury.

"What? Cash told me to get dressed; he didn't specify into which outfit," I suppress a snigger.

"No one breathes a word of this," he growls and snatches my wrist. Tugging me into the heat of his body, his teeth snap out and grazes my cheek. "You'll regret ever crossing me once we get back."

"I don't think so somehow," I burst out laughing, right in his face. Nothing he does to me from here on out will make this any less the best moment of my life. The clown roars again, groaning until it halts mid-stretch, the protruding sharp teeth just inches from my face. White paint surrounds the bulging eyes, his lips enhanced with a vibrant red smile that stretches back to the ripped wallpaper. In his opened mouth, a black and white spiral begins to spin, making me dizzy when I stare into the never-ending curve for too long. Without warning, Tweed grabs me through the mesh of his vest and throws me inside.

I release a scream, tumbling down the clown's pie-hole. Like a curling slide, my body is tossed around until I'm vertical and falling at a snail's pace. Air plumps up my cargo trousers, giving me a natural parachute as objects float on by. Animal skeletons, jars containing who-knows-what but any that contain eyeballs all swivel to glare at me. A few teddies with glowing red eyes glide past, their mechanical voices singing my trigger word on repeat.

Alice. Alice. Alice.

Swimming my arms out to turn my back on them, not having the breath to meditate myself back to composure, I find a bookcase. It seems to be descending in time with me, giving a little wiggle in a 'bitch, fondle my shelves' kind of way. Running my finger over the mantel, the bookcase shudders and I smirk. We're all objects of pleasure; doesn't matter if you're made of wood, plastic or connective tissue. We're all just atoms, and atoms need a good rodgering sometimes.

Plucking out the spine of a book that catches my eye, I glance over the fuchsia pink cover, noting a badass chick holding a bat on a quad bike. Crushin' Candy? *Hmm, seems like my kind of read*, I muse with an upturned smile and tuck it into the overly large cargo pants pocket that isn't concealing my dictionary.

As soon as I accept the book, the bookshelf shoots upwards and I don't have time to wave goodbye as the tunnel opens up and I'm deposited from the sky. My fall speeds up and I slam into a pile of bones. Human, I'd presume from the sea of skulls cracking beneath my crash landing. *Malice, I don't think we're in Kansas anymore.* Two figures loom over me, blocking out the upturned crescent moon hanging beyond them like a lazy smile.

Hoisting me to my feet, any familiarity is lost in their shadowed faces. If anything, my presence would appear inconvenient to them, even though it's their fault I'm here. I blink rapidly and suddenly; I'm realizing tonight hasn't just been a fun escapade.

Unfortunately, Tweed has changed into a long trench coat made of...well, tweed. The collar is popped around his neck, his blonde hair ruffling in a balmy wind. Must be summer here, and definitely too warm for his heavy jacket or the sweater clinging to Cash. Holding out a hand for me to take, I stroke a hand over his arm and roll my eyes at the luxurious softened wool. Fucking 'cash'mere, as if their chosen names could be any more cliché.

"You know what," I tilt my head. "I'm starting to think you guys aren't strippers after all."

"Think again," Cash roughly turns me by the shoulders to see the flashing lights of a club, a heart around the entrance at odds with the spade-shaped windows. Pinned a-top the wavy roof, a neon flashing sign labels this establishment as Dirty Dee's. Well, shit.

CHAPTER 5

TWEED - THE DAY BEFORE MALICE'S RETURN

*T*he rattle of a sigh echoes in my chest. Limbs are piled on my body, constricting me to the heart-shaped bed and every passing second, my patience wears thinner. The cogs in my mind keep ticking, clicking, clacking against my skull. Stop wasting time little Tweedle, I tell myself in mockery. There's work to do.

Bolting upright, I ignore the feminine protests. Like the undead, adamant on reaping my soul, clawing hands trying to drag me back down into the mattress but I refuse to lie there any longer with my thoughts. Tonight was meant to be...I'm not even sure. An orchestrated plot for me to forget myself in the company of tits and pussies. But I can't forget the horrors I've seen, the man I've been forced to become.

The snap of a beak catches my wrist, the curl of a fox tail trying to lock around my ankle. Pushing myself upright, my nose wrinkles at the scent of sweat amongst the cesspit. I don't know if one of these females has sardine in her bloodline or if she just hasn't washed recently but I'm surprised I was able to withstand it this long. Striding from the honeymoon suite, I throw the door wide and come nose to snout with PB, my so-called servant. Shoving him out of my fucking face, I barge past despite his insistent oinking.

"S-sir," he calls, chasing me on swift trotters. "C-come back. The Queen requires you t-t-to complete the exercise." Stopping in my tracks, PB slams into my naked back. The brass buttons of his suit jacket scrape against my skin, the tag in his floppy ear knocking into the back of my head. He's rather tall for an upright piglet, despite being twenty-one this year. To be honest, when I pulled him from a rabbit hole in the woods, I didn't expect him to grow at all. But then the Queen punished my temporary lack of restraint by designating him to be my servant.

"I don't see the point of these exercises," I spin, fisting his red jacket in my hands. White hearts line the lapels and cuffs, in contrast to the white shirt with red hearts tucked underneath. The complete set with matching trousers had to be tailored specially for his lumpy figure.

Not receiving an answer beyond the twitchy grunts of his snout, I shove PB away and head for somewhere I can actually burn off some of the frustration riding me. I know what today is, and only the distraction of blood on my knuckles will suffice. Following the black and white checkered hallway, I leave the east wing of deluxe suites and take a winding staircase all the way down to the ground level. There's a distinct lack of chandeliers and velvet wallpaper present in the areas her majesty won't visit, giving me a reprieve of décor I much prefer. Cold stone, uneven crevices and the lack of fakery like an icy, fresh breath hitting my chest hard.

I enter through the back of the changing room adjoining the gym to the indoor pool, heading for the locker labeled with a 'T.' Digging out a pair of lightweight red shorts, shin guards and hand wraps, I begrudgingly slam the door closed. As much as I prefer skin to bone contact, the Queen would have my head if I presented myself covered in bruises today. Unlike most servants who have to remain out of view in the kitchens or slave quarters on the far side of the castle, PB stays with me every step of the way. Grabbing a rolled towel between his hoofed hands, he moves to open the door with his backside, squishing his curly tail against the glass.

"Well, look who decided to emerge from his honeymoon," Gryphon chortles, quickly followed by the involuntary "Hjckrrh!" he constantly makes. I don't know if the mismatch of his animal characteristics meant there was a misplaced wire in his head, or if he just has tourettes, but I've learnt to tune it out. Years locked in a cell will do that to a person.

"I wasn't on a fucking honeymoon and you know it," I growl, throwing a dumbbell at his head. A single beat of his powerful wings tosses him out of the target line, landing him close enough for me to see the humor in his piercing blue eyes. He can't smile around the curved brown beak stretching from his face but I've come to understand when he's joking through the painfully accurate lectures he delivers.

Appearing mostly man, his entire body is bound in a thick coat of beige fur that towers over my six feet. White feathers with brown tips protrude from his temples, matching the span of his huge wings and the colored tuft of fur at the end of his swaying lion's tail.

"Denying the inevitable is a foolish errand to distress yourself." Instead of answering Gryphon, I do what I came here for. Throwing my shoulder into *his gut with a powerful surge of my legs, I send us both flying into the closest wall.*

"S-Sir! Your h-h-hand wraps!" PB frets as I jump back up to my feet in a battle stance.

"Speak again and I'll be making h-h-ham wraps out of you," I shout back and hear the distinctive squeal of PB diving beneath the weight bench. The metal bar rattles with his quaking, distracting me long enough for the Gryphon's tail to lock around my knee. As he flies himself upright, I'm hoisted upside down and left swinging sporadically and cursing colorfully.

"You should be nice to him," Gryphon jerks his beak towards PB. "You know he's suffered as much as you and I. Hjckrrh!" Dropping me onto my face with his twitchy outburst, I scowl into PB's brown eyes from across the floor.

Grabbing for a hefty chain by the mirrored side of the gym, I use a burst of speed to whip the metal around Gryphon's wings and pull tight. He jerks before I've made it off his back, creating a hybrid rodeo for me to cling onto.

Bucking around the gym, equipment is sent flying into the walls, smashing the mirrors around PB's shuddering body. A few must slice his skin because the scent of bacon drifts through a bout of uncontrollable sneezing. Gryphon spans his wings out, shooting us upright for my back to slam into the ceiling. I rip out a handful of feathers at his temple, drawing a hiccupped roar from his beak.

We were sort-of friends for one brief moment in time, as well as cellmates. Somewhere between Gryphon losing his high-valued morals and me transforming into the monster I am today, but then the changes became too substantial and we went back to merely tolerating one another. Snaking his tail up my shorts, Gryphon takes it to the next level when he catches my balls in a vice-like grip and tugs, tears instantly bursting to life in my eyes.

"Tweed," a bark as sharp as a laser cuts through the air. Our movements halt to gaze upon the Queen's dog in the doorway. The mustache over his nose

resembles a broom which twitches in the direction of PB's trembling backside sticking out from the weight bench. "You've been summoned, and you know better than to keep her waiting," Broomdog barks harshly again and back tracks from the room, sweeping the floor with his face as he goes. The Queen isn't happy - story of my damn life.

Releasing Gryphon's chain at the same time he retracts his tail, I slide down from his back and drop onto my bare feet. Cupping my crotch, I struggle to walk and decide straight after the Queen is done also busting my balls - a cold bath is in order. Sensing the fight has officially finished, PB crawls out to pop up by my side, offering me the towel clutched between his hooves. A furry hand wraps around my bicep as I move to leave and I snarl right in Gryphon's beak.

"There's freedom to be found in captivity, if you'd only look."

"I don't have time for your riddles," I snap, wrenching my arm from his grip. His blue eyes sadden and a grief-stricken frown tugs at the sides of his large beak. I know that look. I've seen it a thousand times displayed on everyone I know who's foolishly mourning the loss of who I used to be. The soft-hearted, whimsical boy that was oblivious to how close to home the betrayal of backstabbers really was. Thank hearts that weakling has gone.

"Let's go PB, I need to change," I grumble, heading back to the locker room. A playing card is waiting there for me, a hanger hooked around his chubby wrist. I groan at the sight of it - a purple striped vest with matching braces attached to electric blue jeans. "Get fucked and get me something real to wear," I demand of the Two of Hearts, snarling at him to fetch my tweed jacket this instant.

"Queen's orders," he relays, a hint of fear in his black eyes. "You know what will happen if you don't." Adam's apple hidden within his red collar bobs and I shrug.

"Yeah, 'corse I do. Heads will roll, but it won't be mine. I'm too valuable to her." Striding from the locker room, I pass through the main lobby, out the rear doors and enter into the royal gardens. As always, the sun is shining over the luxurious castle, while rain pours and thunder rumbles beyond the ten-foot hedges that border the Queen's land. While the rest of Wonderlust goes to shit, we sit here awaiting the day we can fulfill the prophecy, and our wait is almost at an end.

Scanning the gardens, I see no trace of the Queen on her usual croquet pitch, but her pet Kitty is hanging around instead. Her actual name is Kitty, and she's a chinchilla Persian with black hair that malts fucking everywhere. As a kitten, I imagine the yellow eyes with black slits and smushed nose like she's been hit with a frying pan were considered cute, but since she's grown into a fully grown woman with a bushy tail, she just looks demented. And ugly as sin if you don't happen to have a furry fetish.

"Where is she?" I ask sharply on approach, not wanting this conversation to last. PB runs up behind me, the offensive outfit clutched between his hooves and sweat dripping from his brow. Kitty twists her face towards me, brushing her cheek against her shoulder.

"Who?" she plays dumb. Her huge eyes drag along the length of my body, taking particular interest in my abs and the V dipping into my shorts. Growling, I whip the purple striped vest from PB and drag it on, against all better judgment.

"Don't fuck with me. Where is the Queen?" Kitty licks the back of her hairy hand, lining up her bone mallet with the tiny mouse curled up on the grass. The mallet was a dodo at one point. Now it's just a skeleton frozen with a silent scream escaping its boney beak. Preparing to whack the mouse as far as possible, only to chase it afterwards, I bend and scoop up the rodent in one swift move.

"Bit late to start playing hero, Tweed," Kitty drawls lazily. "Give me back my lunch."

"I'm no fucking hero, and this here is my lunch." I shove the squeaking head of fur into my mouth and crunch down hard to put the pathetic thing out of its misery. Withdrawing my teeth, I suck the tiny body free of blood before tossing the leftover corpse to PB. His jaws snap loudly, a solid gulp finishing any protests Kitty could give. Chucking the bone mallet aside, she hisses in my face and I do it right back, baring my pointed incisors.

"You," she starts, stabbing a clawed finger into my chest just above the vest's neckline. "You always have to shit on everyone else's parade because you're not man enough to admit the only reason you won't accept a wife is because you want to fuck the queen!"

Opening my mouth to respond, the shift of movement in a nearby bush cuts off any reply I might have had. With a banshee shriek, flying from the foliage, a ninja dressed in black and red shoots high into the air, coming to land directly behind Kitty with a blade pressed to her throat. Wild amber eyes meet mine, crazed tomato-red hair whipping around her shoulders and a malicious smile curved on those crazed lips.

"If you think you know so much little puss, you'll know you've made your bed. No cream to lick, no tail to flick because you've cost yourself your head." With a jerk of her hand, she slices Kitty's throat wide and I jump back to miss the spray of blood that shoots in my direction. I'm not changing into this damn vest twice if it needs cleaning and I'd rather take a stake to my own heart than have to lick Kitty's blood from myself.

The royal pet buckles, dropping to the floor with yellow eyes bulged as the Queen screams for a chainsaw. The seven of hearts is happy to oblige her every wish, rushing a chainsaw out in one of his stubby hands. He tries to rev it up for her but considering the effort it takes to bring his hands even close to touching, she's already snatched it for herself. PB winces at the sight of the machine, worried the Queen will make him live up to his name - Pork Belly. One day, he's going to make a fine tea party spread but not until he's exhausted of all other uses.

By the time the Queen is done chopping up the beloved cat she grew up with, I've taken a seat on PB's back. He snorts from all-fours on the grass, his curled tail flicking in excitement that I'm letting him serve me. Wheeling those amber eyes my way, alight with pure fucked-up insanity, the Queen unzips her leather suit and steps out as a new woman.

The dress concealed beneath the catsuit bursts free in a skirt of frills, all black and red with a corseted bust. How she manages to appear so limber in not one, but two constricting outfits is beyond me but I gave up caring long ago. Whatever nonchalance and wonder I used to possess died a painful death not even I can revive from.

"Arabelle," I nod, rising to my feet. Her blood-spluttered grin widens as she acknowledges I'm the only one bold enough to call her by her birth name.

"Walk with me, little Tweed," she beckons, ignoring the foot height difference I have on her. Leading me towards a canopy of trees, PB remains back with the play card servant, wary of Arabelle's violent mood swings. The branches knot together overhead, creating the perfect shade from the sun that only beats down here. Outsiders may be jealous, but they haven't tried keeping an entire garden of red rose bushes alive during constant sunshine and no rainfall. Mind you, neither have I, but I've seen the pile of discarded heads of those who couldn't. We all have our burdens to bear.

Catching the corner of my eye, an upturned smile of perfectly white teeth glint in the rays that break free of the canopy. Reaching for the back of Arabelle's dress, I grab the dagger concealed in her flamboyant bow and chuck it in the smile's direction. Huge orbs of pale blue trickle into existence, eyeing the knife sailing through its transparent body, before fading from view completely.

"I'll get it one day," I grumble, tugging the blade free from the trunk it became lodged in. Arabelle just laughs, swaying her head side to side.

"The thrill is in the chase. The death is the emptiest part." Handing her back the knife, I follow her lithe frame to the tree-formed cave at the far end of the path. A brook babbles near the entrance, curving around the rocky mound and spiraling upwards to the waterfall beating off the back. My bare feet step on the mossy stepping stones leading through the stream. Vines hang between the thick trunks that curve overhead, creating the cave's circular ceiling. Mushrooms nestling in the grassy bases at the trunk bases glow gold, illuminating our path. Arabelle hops from one stone to the next with the grace of a ballerina, her giggle echoing all around.

"Incy wincy mushroom, leading to the water's spout. If Tweed doesn't take a wife, I'm sure to give him a clout," she bursts into further laughter and I roll my eyes. For just one day, I yearn for a break from being me.

Rivets of pure blue water creep through the trunks, dancing down the sides of the cave like flowing curtains. At the end of the stream, the ground opens out into a cavern. A meadow that thrives amongst the trunk roots that rut through the land. And in the center, a giant cocoon hangs from a long branch, stretching out from the rest. The casing is powdered blue, with tendrils of white and gold lacing around its gnarled shape. At certain angles and if the sun hits just right, a pair of mosaic wings can be seen reflecting through the center, the silhouette of a man curled up inside.

"Once we do this, there's no going back," I warn, even though it's fruitless. I'm already defying another prophecy by refusing to pick a mate, but that's a tale for another time.

Not answering in words, Arabelle takes her dagger and uses a heightened root to throw herself into the air. Gripping the top of the chrysalis, she abseils down the outside, stabbing her knife into the fleshy pulp. The ripping reverberates through the cave, joined by the rumbling of trees shifting to close *us inside. I wonder how Arabelle knows if she's struck a wing with her blade but with keen accuracy, she drops down just in time for the cocoon to peel open and drop its contents onto the hard ground.*

Unfurling her wings, a woman with bronzed skin and tribal tattoos stretches out her naked body. Aided by nature, the roots below retract and lift into the air to open a hidden cabinet in one of the thick trunks. A hookah awaits there, entrapped in the elm's hollow body for the exact moment the butterfly emerges. Embellished with golden swirls, the center of the pipe bubbles while the base bowl has been designed as a skull carved from ice. Curling around the hookah, the branches navigate the air to gift the Butterfly her prized possession before digging through the moss to retrieve her some clothes. A robe is all they manage to produce, silk like a kimono with a panel missing in the back for her wings. It barely touches her thighs but the thin cord at the middle means her tits are just about covered when she stands at full height.

"Who. Are. You?" she puffs through the smoke billowing from her mouth on each deep drag. High cheekbones hollow, full lips purse. Dropping into a cross-legged sit, the branches whip out just in time to catch her and her nipples slip free of the robe, looking me right in the eye.

"You know who we fucking are. Get on with the prophecy," I growl and Arabelle places a steady hand on my chest.

"We've waited long enough and done all you asked. Tell us how to revive our world to what it once was." Arabelle stands tall, the image of a Queen who will make a fine ruler one day. If there's anything left worth ruling. Blood coats her skin, weapons concealed all over her body that has the posture of a true warrior. I'd almost be honored to be her knave, if I could let go of the horrors that brought me to this point. The decisions of her family that ultimately became their downfall.

Sighing around the tobacco smoke, the butterfly reclines against the ever-shifting branches that accommodate her movements and she peers into a break of sunlight spearing through overhead. Her already large eyes widen further, bleeding through with milky white as they crystalize into actual crystal balls. No one can see what goes on inside of her mind, and for that matter, can be sure she relays the truth, but she's the last of her kind. The last caterpillar, the last prophecy teller.

"Mirror, mirror in the eyes, show us what evil will suffice," she relays, stealing the air from the cavern. It whips around her in a tornado, colored by the yellow smoke seeping from the hookah affixed to the corner of her mouth. The mushrooms that permitted us a comforting glow shrivel back into the earth, hiding in the soil as an ethereal voice booms around us.

To fix the curse and reverse the clock
Retrieve the key to our future's lock,
Return the Alice from an unworthy land,
To remove her mind, accept a helping hand.
One twin will thrive, the other will fall,
But only one queen can claim her of mind, spirit and all.

"No fucking way, I'm not teaming up with that asshole. No way, no how. Let Wonderlust perish." A sharp slap cracks across my cheek, enough force behind it to wheel my head aside. Despite her size, Arabelle's strength is only second to my own – evident by the years of warrior training I gave her. But it doesn't matter if the swell of pride only a master can feel blossoms in my chest or that she's my Queen, I grab her throat and slam her back against the nearest trunk. Her blade enters my abdomen with ease, inches above my groin, her amber eyes never wavering from the steady anger she has burning inside.

Releasing her black boots to the ground once more, Arabelle snaps her fingers, commanding the branches to lock around my wrists and heave me down to my knees. I bellow, straining against their solid hold, refusing to kneel to the Queen – even now. The butterfly watches on, a blank expression on her lips as she puffs on the hookah like a lifeline. Crouching down, Arabelle meets me eye to eye as she snatches the blade free from my abdomen.

"You heard what she said and we've come too far to turn back. Everything we've done up to this point, the lives and transformations we've taken," her eyes glide down to the stab wound that's already scarred over. "The prophecy stands, whatever it takes. Find your brother and return Alice to us, tonight. Regardless of how she's retrieved, only one queen can lay claim to her fate. That queen must be me."

CHAPTER 6

MAL

"You guys own a strip club?" I ask, my senses dulled to the fact I've just been through a portal to get here. I've dreamt of returning to Wonderland so many times, I stopped letting myself sleep for days on end. I didn't want to be taunted, nor did I want to build up a false sense of belonging. Neither here nor in the real world was I ever accepted by those around me. But now I'm back, just like I wanted. I'm just wondering if this version of Wonderlust will want me.

"Not us, just me," Cash smirks, holding out his arm for mine. I accept it, letting him lead me closer to the circus-style music rolling from the club's exterior speakers. There's nothing else for miles, just flat land coated in debris and I wonder why people would come so far out for a lap dance. But then I suppose the man on my arm is evidence enough.

"Tweed decided to announce his arrival by blowing the fucking doors off last night, and I see his handy men have been hard at work rebuilding it." Cash's eyes narrow on the heart-shaped doorway before tossing an angered look over his shoulder at Tweed. A walking lizard strolls around the corner, hammer and nails clutched in his hands.

"There you are!" he shouts, storming our way. "I can't switch out the sign without my ladder. Where is it?!"

"You touch my sign, you'll be banned from watching me dance for the rest of your miserable life," Cash growls and for the first time, I see the underlying of a savage beast rise to the surface. "This is *my* club."

Releasing my arm, keeping the tension trapped in his posture, Cash approaches the red plastic heart bordering the main glass doors and rips it straight out of the wall. Screws fly in all directions and I'm so stunned by the display of strength, I don't even move as the heart topples over me, the spoke of the inner dip just catching the back of my blonde mane. The lizard goes crazy, running in circles, screaming about all his hard work until Tweed's arm lashes out and grabs his throat.

"Bill, put the heart back on," he demands, a dare in his eyes as his eyes penetrate Cash's.

"No, Bill, put the original spade back and I'll see you well compensated," Cash snaps back, the lizard and me stuck in between their stare-off. It doesn't seem of concern to anyone else how Bill takes the opportunity to grind against Tweed's leg, his tail dipping between his legs to stroke the twin's crotch. Tightening his grip on Bill's neck, Tweed merely growls and in a flash of movement, Cash has shot forward to rescue the lizard from imminent death.

"Pussy," Tweed chuckles, strolling inside without looking back. I follow as Cash barks orders at Bill, my curiosity getting the better of me. If there was any confusion on where Cash's loyalty lies, one look around the inside of the club would clear that up really quick. Spades everywhere. From the shape of the stage, with a single silver pole at the tip that reaches the heightened ceiling, to the photo frames, whiskey glasses, mirror behind the bar and every inch in between. The color scheme is classic, black and white with splashes of silver in the extravagant chandeliers. The diamonds hanging from the various tiers are, you guessed it, cut into spades.

"So, just to give me a fair chance at catching up here," I say, dropping onto a spade-shaped stool at the bar, "Wonderland is now called Wonderlust because...everyone is sex-crazed, possibly into blood play and you boys don't get on anymore. Did I leave anything out?" Tweed hops over the bar, grabbing two bottles of vodka and places them in between us.

"Only everything of importance," Tweed drawls back. Placing the neck of the bottle between his teeth, he bites down, crushing the glass in his mouth. Spitting the glass onto the floor, blood pours from his mouth as he drinks from the jagged edge of the bottle, contaminating the clear liquid with blood rivets. A darkness stirs inside me, the strange urge for him to tear chunks from my flesh and bathe in my blood bubbling from the center of my thighs. "Stop that," Tweed growls, catching me out.

"Stop what?" I ask innocently. Tweed's hand reaches out to grab the back of my hair, tugging my face upwards for my lips to part on a gasp. Leaning over the bar, Tweed waits for the blood swelling around his mouth to drip into mine.

"Thinking about what's making your pussy smell so damn sweet. You might just get what you want and will quickly live to regret it."

"You fucking bastard!" Cash roars, his body flying over the bar to slam Tweed back into the glass shelves. There's an almighty crash and I look over to Bill who's gaping at the destruction from the doorway. Poor dude must have to work here full time. While the twins continue to throw punches and yell weird obscenities at each other, I decide to go for a wander.

"Come on Stan," I muse, breaking into a skip with the two books in either side of my cargo pockets weighing me down.

Venturing deeper into the club, I enter a hallway labeled 'Fantasy Walk' by a neon sign over the archway. The wallpaper is black and rough to the touch, like crocodile skin, between closed doors in all shapes and sizes. One as small as a thimble, another as huge as an elephant's ass. Statues of the four card suits stand in a square at the end of the hall, facing each other on opposite sides and paired by either their red or black coloring.

Testing out the handle of a door shaped as a tree trunk, I find an enchanted forest beyond. Like an actual forest, no walls or limitations. The roar of a beast I vaguely recognize pierces my ear drums and I slam the door shut. Trying another in the shape of a curved wave, salty water rushes out and knocks me off my feet. I float the length of the hallway, swishing all the way back into the main club. The Tweddle's are still in full fight mode, although they've managed to make their way across the room and flattened several tables in the process.

A staircase in the back corner peeks out from behind a black netted curtain, spiraling up to a second level with silver railings. Heading up, I marvel at the height of the pole across the club, imagining Cash in tiny pants climbing all the way to the top. The way his muscles would ripple, or how the pants would barely contain the monster leashed behind his tight waistband. Yum.

The top of the steps presents a pair of drapes, speckled with diamonds, and a concealed apartment tucked behind. Unlike the club downstairs, filled with sensual textures and opulent furnishings, the décor up here is like that of a boy who never grew up. Primary colors burst from every direction, the cupboards, cabinets and window sills all rounded as if bubbling out of the structure themselves. A ceiling fan above appears to be a larger version of the tweedle hat I knew the boys to wear. Hanging upside down, its yellow propeller spinning a cool breeze across the living area. Playing cards have been flicked into the wall opposite a rounded sofa facing nothing but an empty fireplace.

Despite all the bright colors and whimsy, there's a coldness here. A loneliness I resonate with. Removing Stan from his perch embedded in my scalp, I place him in the fruit bowl on the kitchen side and sigh. We really made it buddy, just like I said we would. The drapes shift and Cash appears, a softness to his vibrant green eyes. His cashmere jumper is thick with blood, glistening in the low-level lighting.

"Where's Tweed?" I ask, having no real concern that he can hold his own.

"Gone, for now. But he won't stay away while you're here," Cash replies gravely. Something in his voice says I should be worried about that, but the coppery taste of his brother's blood still lingers in the back of my throat and the low drumming of arousal knocks at my g-spot when I think on it for long enough.

"What happened between you two?" I wonder, running my finger over an empty shelf. The dust patterns suggest there were frames here that have been removed, and all that remains is a single, blue bowtie.

"That's a story for another time," Cash catches my hand and brushes off the dust. Walking backwards, he leads me into a room away from the main living area and adjoining kitchen. His bedroom. "Tonight, I'm more interested in your tale. When tasked with your retrieval, I'd expected to drag you away from a husband who didn't deserve you. Not a mental asylum."

"Correctional facility for convicts," I correct him. Smiling and kissing the back of my hand, Cash peels off his blood-drenched clothes and strides into a bathroom. Scars litter his back, both fresh and healed, like that of a whip's lash. Turns out this particular Tweedle has quite the fetish nature. The shower is on and I'm left searching through his drawers for something comfortable to sleep in. It's been a really long night and as if conjured by my very mind, when I turn back to Cash's bed, there's a steaming cup of tea on the side table.

Cash showers quickly, returning in a matching set of boxers and t-shirt to the ones I picked out and changed into. White with black spades, naturally. His eyes ignite to glowing orbs of green, the heat of his gaze searing my skin. I breathe too heavily, a violent twitch jerking at my neck and I swiftly slap myself out of it. Literally. Cash steps forward, cupping my reddened cheek with a curious furrow to his brow.

"Ignore me. My meds are wearing off," I try to shift out of his hold. He doesn't let me.

"No," Cash's voice drops an octave and my being sparks as if touching the end of a live wire. "It's you remembering exactly who you were always supposed to be." Goosebumps prickle my skin, my head too easily leaning into his hold. Nope, nah ah, I shake my head and push myself a step back using his chest. Taking the cup of tea in hand, I slide beneath his cover and rest against the leather headboard.

"So, you want to hear a bedtime story?" I swiftly change subject, dousing my own sexuality with a wash of ice cold, unwanted memories. Shifting my pile of discarded clothes at the base of the bed aside, Cash's biceps shift as he crawls over me, sucking the air from my very lungs until dropping down to roll his head across my thighs. I part my legs, allowing his nape to rest on my crotch. "It's filled with death and betrayal," I warn, more because I'd rather not indulge my memories on wasted breath.

"As the best stories are," Cash replies, wriggling to get comfortable. Hooking an ankle over the other and his fingers over his stomach, I sip my tea, feeling the drowsiness of a long-awaited return hitting me hard.

"Very well then. There once was a girl with a curious nature and naive intentions. She witnessed a world no one believed existed and told tales no one wanted to listen to." I sip my tea, settling back into the plump cushions as another wave of sleep washes over me. "You know what, it's easier in rhyme if you don't mind." Cash's dark chuckle tells me he doesn't mind. In fact, he'll probably prefer it.

They laughed at her you see
when she spoke her fictions,
The headlines raged; the mockery plagued
And doctors made false predictions.

She tried to escape the ridicule
Tried to flee the strife
And when that failed, her sanity bailed
In attempts to take her life.

Since the real world lacked adventure
And beings that proved kind
The girl turned to her father
Praying the truth he'd find.

Yet in his bid to leave a legacy
He came to a conclusion
To grab the nearest typewriter
And take note of her delusions.

A yawn stretches my mouth wide as Cash lifts the empty cup from my hand. I snuggle down further until his head is nestled on my breast, the sweet lull of dreams calling to me as I rush to finish my narrative.

The girl was outraged,
utterly betrayed
As he took note of her story.
So she stole a knife,
stabbed him twice
And in doing so,
took back her glory.

CHAPTER 7

MAL

Waking, it takes me a full minute to realize I'm jostling. My whole body being thrown up and down like a bouncy castle, except the landing beneath me isn't soft and welcoming. It's hard as shit and no doubt going to need spinal correction. Pushing myself upright, the next bump beneath me sends my head crashing into the roof of whatever I'm concealed inside. Other than one circle of light bleeding through a hole before me, darkness claws at my wild hair. I can feel the shear height of it from each bump and subconsciously, I reach up to check Stan is okay. The empty gap behind my ear draws a sharp breath from my lungs.

"Stan? STAN?!" I cry out, peering directly into the light. My retinas burn but I hold strong, spying the length of the tunnel that curves upwards. I try to wriggle through but it's too thin so I continue to shout inside.

"Your rat's fine," the booming voice sends me flying back onto my ass from the earth-shattering rumble. I'd recognize it anywhere, but why it's so damn loud is beyond me. Enough's enough! Feeling out the crevice of a lid, I brace my hands on the roof and shoot upright on my legs. *Pop*. Blinded by sunlight that beats on my skin in a rush of heat, I lift a hand to spot the intricately patterned teapot holding me.

"Why is this fucking tea pot so big?" I ask, spotting the firm hand gripped around its handle. Tracking said hand with my eyes, up the attached arm to the heart tattoo flourishing from a giant chest, I frown. Wait... "Why the fuck am I so small?"

"You're easier to manage when two inches tall," Tweed's voice booms again, harming my fragile, tiny ear drums. He gives the teapot a rough shake and I drop back down onto my ass.

"I resent that!" I scream through the spout to amplify the sound. "I'm never easy!" Crossing my arms like an insolent child, I recite my ABCs in an effort to stay calm. I can't hurt Tweed at this stupid height, but I can let my irritation fester. I'll find a way to grow four times his size and step on his puny head.

A is for assbadger, B is for bumblefuck, C is for cuntpuddle, D is for-

"Fucking Christ, you're more annoying small than average size," Tweed grumbles and I snort. I despise the adjective 'average' when it comes to describing me, in any aspect. "Next time, I'll make sure to use a higher dose and shrink you to the size of an ant." I frown, rewinding back to the last thing I remember. Cash's head becoming heavy on my chest, the tale of my past that usually sparks nightmares drifting me into an abyss of tranquility. Unless something else did that...

"You spiked me! That's an abomination against tea!" I scream, bucking out my legs against the great wall of China. It's then I realize air drifting between my legs, the ruffles scratching at my thighs, the boned corset correcting my usual hunch. That offensive dress I was presented with back in the cabin. Not only is the satin making an unpleasant return, but now it's on *me*. Tweed must have changed me while I was asleep and that's *not* okay. If I'm going to be dressed up like someone's forgotten fantasy, I could at least be awake to feel the contact of his fingers on my skin and direct them down to my clit.

This time when I shoot upwards, I don't stop at just popping out of the teapot. I throw myself over the edge of it. The edge of the skirt becomes hooked on a chip in the rim, tearing as I spiral towards the ground like a corkscrew. Severing from the bodice, I drop to the ground and eye the pair of hot pants banded around my waist. Shimmering red with white hearts stitched over my moo-moo and into each cheek of the butt. White stockings stretch up the length of my legs, spanning over my thighs with delicate lace. Yuck.

A ma-hoosive hand rushes towards the ground, the fingers forming a cage around me as they pierce the earth. Slipping out before they snap inwards to crush me, I roll across the ground and take off in the black pumps clinging to my tiny feet. Each blade of grass smacks against me like bollards, slowing my get away. A pebble hiding beneath a fallen leaf I try to volley over catches my shin and I tumble forward, the rush of heat searing my leg proving I've really fucking hurt myself.

Another pound crashes against the ground. A flash of mocha and black rushes at me. Dipping a pink nose beneath my belly, Stan tosses me up onto his back and shoots forward. Clinging onto his fur for dear life, the roaring bellow of Tweed the Colossal shakes the ground beneath us. I peer back through the rush of movement, squinting to see him holding his eye and bent over in pain. Dragging myself up Stan and peering over his face, orange junk leaks from his mouth.

"Did you bite him in the eye?!" I gasp, a smile spreading across my face as I pat the black diamond on his forehead. "You utter legend. Such a good boy." Adjusting my stance, I straddle Stan properly with my hands wrapped around his large ears. The forest whips past, or perhaps it's just a garden. From his vantage point, it could be a freaking jungle but the red rose bushes make me think otherwise. If I am where I think I am, I need an exit strategy pronto. Vaulting over the bone of what appears to be a humongous dodo skull, Stan clearly has a destination in mind.

Stomp, stomp, stomp.

The ground quakes as Tweed takes chase, my body juddering all over the sugar glider's back. He nears us in no time, his long strides eating up the distance like a scrummy plate of lasagna on toast. My stomach rumbles but there's no time to think of anything but an escape plan. The meaty hand crashes into the dirt again, just as Stan dives aside and saves us from capture. I can't keep avoiding Tweed from this puny height. I need to be tall to stand a fighting chance and something around here *has* to make me grow.

Dropping aside with one hand gripping Stan's ear, I scoop up a handful of dirt and shove it into my mouth. Nope, that's just mud. Next, I catch the tip of a leaf and snatch it off, chewing on it like tobacco. Ugh, nah that didn't work either. Where are all the fucking mushrooms when I need one?

One long jump sends a scream tearing from my lungs and Stan's body flying into the trunk of an oak. Scurrying upwards in a spiral that makes me feel nauseous, we slip out of Tweed's view as a stream of glistening tree sap enters mine. I'm quickly running out of options so here goes nothing. Yanking back on Stan's ears, he slows enough for me to lean aside and stick out my tongue. Dragging it up the length of the sap, my insides curl up and die. Have I found a new low point? Quite possibly.

Regaining his speed, Stan leaps onto a branch hidden with lush greenery and I dive from his back. If I'm about to grow, I don't want to kill him in the process. But hey, guess what? My life fucking sucks and nothing happens. Tweed rushes past the tree, swiping a large hand in the air to shove the branch from his face and in the process, knocks us aside. Stan's winged arms snap out above me as he descends over my falling frame. I reach for him, refusing to scream and give away our position this time. There you have it folks, this is the way I die.

Softness envelopes me, the kiss of tender petals wrapping around my body and drawing me back into their clutches. Retracting its stem back into a natural position, I freeze as Tweed turns with a curious expression. I'm literally lying here, open and exposed on a rose like a pretty present waiting to be claimed. Bucking, the rose's petals snap shut like a straitjacket.

"Shh!" it whispers. I double my efforts and the petals tighten. "SHHH!" the sound comes again. "The oak's sap has camouflaging abilities. He can't see you." Lying still and true to the roses' words, Tweed twists back the way he was walking and leaves me behind. My body sags and for the first time since I woke, I relax.

"Gee, thanks buddy," I sigh. The petals don't feel as tight now and I am embraced like a floral cuddle. The flower wobbles and I peer over to see Stan at the bottom, gnawing on the stem. "Stan! Take it easy, flowers are friends – not food." He continues nibbling, intent on bringing down the rose that saved me. I twist, realizing the petals are white just as a sharp stinger pierces my side. I hiss, trying to break free as the splinter deepens - that of a rose's thorn.

"Stop wriggling, little prey. How do you think we make our petals red?" The whisper echoes around the curved petals. Well, that took a turn, but luckily for me, this isn't my first time in a straight-jacket situation. Lying as flat and still as I can, I wait for the flower to believe I've resigned to my fate. Another stab penetrates my body, my teeth biting into my tongue not to react. Rolling my head to the side, I see the field of roses standing tall and proud, most of them with a defenseless creature in their grasp. From door mice to robins, all flustering and fighting to escape.

The petals relax, losing their tension so I hastily throw my arms upwards above my head. Breaking the hold, the flower yells in protest as I wriggle from its clutches, standing tall on the very edge. The thorn protruding from my side like a humongous dildo sticking where it's not wanted, a trickle of blood oozing from it. Hearing the crack of Stan's successful chewing, I preempt us going timber and scoop up a droplet of blood.

"Here, my leaving present." Scraping it against the snow-white softness of the petal, the flower twitches and shrieks loud enough for me to cover my ears.

"She's infected!" it screams and all around, the roses snap shut, shooting back into the earth. This particular rose doesn't have the chance to shrivel up as Stan breaks through the thickened stem and once again, I'm free falling towards the approaching ground. Stan does his best to catch me but without a real saddle – which we are so getting, by the way – I just roll off his back and land chest-first on a cushion.

Leaving my face squashed against the fleshy feel, I inhale the scent of earth and blink my vision clear. One lone orange mushroom with white spots sits amongst an otherwise barren wood, all the flowers having disappeared from view except the one Stan chewed down. The petals have retracted like an acid burn, the spot where I smeared my blood turned black and bubbling. *Weird*.

Stan hops up to lick my face with a long scratch of his tongue, protecting me with the length of his furry body. Such a good guard-joey. Gasping, I shoot upright and knock him aside. A fucking mushroom! The only one for miles and it definitely wasn't here before. Without hesitation, I start grabbing handfuls of its flesh from each side, remembering only one will make me grow and the other will cause me to shrink into a blip of non-existence. How cheery.

Stuffing each lump into the butt of my shorts, giving myself a stunning Kim-K backside, I stand on the mushroom to peer around. A chess-piece castle looms about a mile away in one direction, a wall of green in the other. In between, the jungle I need to navigate.

Hopping down, I pull up a trampled vine laying across the ground and start manufacturing a rein for Stan. Finding a hollow acorn, I thread it through for a bridle, tying a series of sailor knots to hold it in place. Stan's giant nose sniffs at my ear, probably wishing he could crawl into the nest of my hair while I measure him up. Preparing to loop the harness around his middle, the ground shakes violently.

A boot slams down on top of the mushroom, the blow back from it tossing me aside. I land on my hip, nudging the thorn further into my side. Agony curdles in my gut, the taste of blood and bile rising to gurgle in the back of my throat. Rolling onto my back, I peer up at the giant leering above, his tweed jacket swaying in an invisible breeze. Ahh man, the return of Tweedle Dick.

Slamming my arms down like a starfish, my arms distort from view. With the tree mucus still in my stomach, color trickles from my fingertips to shoulders, blending me into my surroundings perfectly. Camouflage sap, my new bestie. Sparked by my inner admission, Stan darts away, half the harness hanging from his fur and in doing so, attracts Tweed's attention with the movement.

"Get back in the teapot, Stan! Back in the teapot!" I call out, hoping it's his best chance of hiding his mocha fur and pink nose amongst the greenery. Tweed's boot lifts in slow motion, passing over my body with a delayed shadow. His shoulders are taunt, the veins in his arms protruding like rivets of lava coursing beneath his skin. Once passed, I hop up and begin limp running as fast as my side will allow. Somehow, I'll have to hope Stan can hide long enough for me to emerge from the canopy of the trees and guess which piece of mushroom flesh rammed against my ass I should eat. There's a sentence I've never thought of before.

"Over here!" a small shout stops me in my tracks. Skidding out, my white stocks becoming thoroughly fucked beyond fixing, I hunt for the voice's owner and see a hand waving through the grass. A tiny hand the same size and shape as mine. The thorn is unbelievably deep now, deep enough to prove standing upright to be a challenge.

Without much other choice and the confidence Stan can take care of himself, I stumble forward with the support of stones along the way. A girl stands in a doorway etched into the tree trunk, her height matching mine. Her brown eyes dart around the woods, panic etched into their chocolate depths as she refuses to take a step over the threshold.

"Malice!" Tweed roars. My head whips around, seeing his glowing green eyes focused on me. Oh shit, camouflage has worn off. He's running in the next second, the ground bouncing beneath me as I hobble against the ripples. Stretching her hand out, my fingers just thread through the girl's and she whips me through the door, slamming it closed behind me. Crumbling against the wood, the pain at my side sears too hot, my heart thumping too quickly and before I can find out what smells so damn awful, the girl's concerned gaze is the last thing I see.

CHAPTER 8

MAL

P epper burns my nostrils. The more I scrunch my nose, the harsher it hurts. The familiar tingle of an impending sneeze lingers, despite the fact my eyes won't open or my body feels numb. It's coming, it's happening.

"Haaa-" the high-pitched sound escapes my lips. My heart rears back in my chest, anticipating the fall out. As if my body is being sucked forward by an invisible force, I shoot upright. "Choooo!" The sting of release in my side is dulled by the satisfaction of pepper flying free of my mouth and nose.

"That's one way to do it," the girl marvels, rushing to wrap a dressing around the side of my torso. A woman opposite, with a witch's wart on her nose and gnarled fingers, rips off a length of tape and begins strapping me up like a fed-ex parcel. The blood seeps through almost immediately, although the pain is non-existent, and the obvious answer is – stick another dressing and strip of tape on top. By the time they're done, my back is ram-road straight and I'm rendered immobile in the middle.

Crossing the room in her mucky white apron, the girl braces her feet either side of the thorn my sneeze shot out and uses all of her strength to heave it from the wall. Black hair flicks around her slender neck, stopping short of her shoulders. Her limbs are equally tiny, like splinters of pale flesh on bone as she relieves the thorn and struggles with the weight of it. Frowning, the size of the thorn seems at odds with the room we're in, but I've learnt not to question these things.

"Useless lass," the woman to the left of the table I'm sitting on mutters. "Hurry it up Mary Ann!" Picking up the pot of pepper she must have used to revive me, she shuffles across to a cupboard and swaps it for a slice of lemon cake. I watch her walk away with interest, my eyes spazzing out briefly when she steps out of a door and shoots to full size.

"Hey, wait! Gimmie some!" I shove myself off the table, as the Cook's massive shoes stomp away. Finding another slice of cake in the cupboard, I wait to give my rescuer a piece and lean all my weight on her to leave the tiny room behind.

"Mini treehouse in the tree trunk? I like it," I smirk. Mary·Ann doesn't return my smile, just keeps her gentle hold around my waist as she nibbles on the cake. I do too and fuck me if multiplying your size by a thousand whilst mortally wounded doesn't hurt like a bitch. A scream escapes me, sending birds flocking from the tree overhead. Knocking the tiny door closed with my foot, I spot a wheelbarrow and lower myself into it.

"So, maybe I'm being too logical here, but shouldn't I be getting some stitches or some shit? You know, before I bleed out," I loll my head back, watching Mary Ann struggle to heave the wheelbarrow up the incline to a farmhouse ahead. The ground is rather rocky and if it weren't for the slickness seeping through the double dressing, I'd be happy to walk.

"It's necessary," she grunts, sweat lining her brow.

"Mmhmm, bleeding out is necessary," I nod along, not sure why I didn't think of that myself. Reaching the back door of the farmhouse, she tips me out and I have to use the wall to stay upright. Blood has pooled in the wheelbarrow, which she artfully whizzes around to tip onto a patch of weeds between the flowers. They sizzle away on impact. "And, just to clarify, what are we doing with my corpse after all the blood has gone?"

"Regeneration bath," Mary Ann states matter-of-factly.

"Got it. Cool, cool, cool." She hands me a broom to use as a crutch and opens the door to a dated kitchen. Cook is bent over huge pans bubbling on a lit hob, the stench as worrying as the random objects she's chucking in. An old boot, some screws, a cable. The only area not currently in use amongst worktops of molding peelings, a lone metal tea pot sitting collecting dust. "Well, I'm going to make tea while I wait to die. You want one?" I ask. The girl freezes one foot inside the door and I don't miss Cook's quizzical look over her shoulder.

"You're offering me tea?" Mary Ann asks in a tiny voice.

"Sure, why not?" I shrug one shoulder, a rush of dizziness almost causing me to lose my balance. "I've only ever had one friend before and being made of plastic, she never appreciated my teas."

"Friend?" she echoes back. Geez, don't hurt yourself.

"You know what, you start running that bath. I'll fix us a cup." Venturing into the kitchen, I get as far as pouring some water into the kettle before changing my mind. Either because the water is vomit yellow or the energy quickly zapping from my limbs forces me to take a wooden seat.

"What's- "I wave my hand around, "all this for?" My voice sounds breathy but if the Cook is expecting company, I'd rather know before they get the chance of free rein over my dead body.

"Dinner for the Queen of Spades," the woman grumbles. I can't tell if the hump in her back is growing or if my vision is just swimming. Her feet shuffle around in open-toed sandals that immediately prove why they're a terrible choice, given her various missing toes. It defies gravity she's standing at all. Over a shit-brown dress, a matching white apron to Mary Ann's covers her front with a maid's fabric hat over her greasy brown hair.

"Spades?" I mumble, my head sinking towards the table. "What happened to the Queen of Hearts?"

"Silly girl," she tsks, not looking my way. "You think because she's the only queen you met during your *brief* visit, that she is the only one we have?" If I had full consciousness, I'd have bristled at the way she spat 'brief' belittling the time I spent here. Wonderland is where I needed to be all those years I struggled to come back, convincing myself I'd found it the first time for a reason. If it was nothing but a *silly girl's* mistake, then where does that leave me? Desperate to fit in when all I do is fit out?

Now she's said it, I begin to notice spades hidden within the decor. Used as cupboard door handles, spanning the floor tiles, etched into the wallpaper and the shape of photo frames visible in the hallway. If I squint, I can just about make out the white rabbit in each image, Mary Ann a constant in the background.

Hands slip under my arms, dragging me limply across the lower level. As Mary Ann comes to the stairs, she braces herself each time, heaving me up with a heavy clonk, thud, thump. Step by step. My chin seeps further into my chest, the trail of red following like a brush stroke of red showing my journey. At least my senses have dulled enough to escape the wretched stench of the kitchen wafting through the house in billows of smoke the others seem accustomed to.

Reaching a bathroom on the upper level, my head is dropped heavily as slender fingers rush to undress me. Chunks of mushroom topple out of my hot pants and Mary Ann mutters words like poisonous and lethal. Ripping off the dressings which had no real use, she proceeds to roll my body up a wooden plank she's strategically placed and shoves me off the end, in the tub with an almighty splash.

The water is fucking. Freezing. I'm practically dead, and even I can feel the frost clawing at my bones. Maybe it's a preservation thing. Huge chunks of ice knock against my jaw and scrape over my nipples. Bottles in all shapes, sizes and colors line the other side of the tub, and as Mary Ann yanks a crumpled scrap of paper from her apron pocket, her elbow knocks one into the tub. Lime green liquid snakes through the water like eels with their own lifeform.

"Oops!" she cries, fishing it out. Oops? What does she mean 'Oops'?! My mind splutters in and out from then on, each time I come to presenting with a different scenario. Mary Ann trying to fish out the green liquid with a sieve. Her scrubbing my skin raw with a piece of coral. At one point, she pulls a welder's helmet over her face and powers up an angle grinder. I wonder if I'll emerge as a cyborg...

CHAPTER 9

MAL

Gasping awake from my third induced nap in the last twenty-four hours, water splashes over the side of the tub and Mary Ann screams in shock. Placing a frail hand over her chest, her chocolate eyes widen and I know instantly something is wrong.

"What" I choke on my own voice. Swallowing a lump of bile, I brace myself and try again. "What is it?" Not answering, she fetches a thick robe and holds it out with her face turned away. Guess I'm doing this shit on my own now. Surprisingly, my legs only wobble a fraction when dragging myself upright, the gaping hole in my side absent. There's a circular scar but who doesn't love a badass scar? Stepping into the robe, I pull my hair free of the neckline.

"Fuck, I need to introduce you to the benefits of conditioner," I babble to fill the stale silence. My hair feels even worse than usual, scratchy and heavy upon my he-

"Whaaaaaaaat the fuck did you do?!" I catch sight of myself in a mirror. It has elongated rabbit ears so I need to duck to see my full reflection. "My hair!" My hands hover over the lengths, not wanting to touch it. Protruding from my scalp, the brambles of a holly bush in ripe season fall to my lower back. Tiny spikes shine amongst the red berries flourishing from my damn head, giving me the appeal of a forest nymph.

"It's okay, don't panic," Mary Ann reassures me, heaving the large window open. Whistling weakly, it takes a few seconds before the hum of wings can be heard. A sea of blackbirds blocks out the otherwise grey sky as they swarm into the room and attack me. Beaks peak at my head, spearing my scalp as I scream and bat them away. My hands become victims next so I resort to covering my face. Not my beautiful face.

As quickly as they appeared, the blackbirds flock from the room while I marvel at my blonde lengths in the mirror. Thank fuck for that. Holly leaves surround my feet, plucked free and leaving my hair rather glossy in fact. The blackbirds don't make it any further though, venturing just beyond the windowsill before exploding in a mass of feathers and guts. Cook screams about her veg patch from the lower level and Mary Ann's eyes slide to mine sheepishly.

"Forgot they're allergic to red berries," she confesses. Fetching a broom to sweep up the leaves, Mary Ann comes to stand behind me, teasing my waves in her fingers.

"Good as new now, Alice." A bolt of fury zaps through me and I clench my fists, pushing my nails into the flesh of my palms. It's not her fault, she wasn't to know about my trigger word. Exhaling deeply, I grit through my teeth.

"It's Malice now. Mal for short." My tone makes her flinch back a step, bowing her head in submission.

"Oh, I'm so sorry," she starts to cry. Focusing on my breathing, I briefly close my eyes.

"It's good, I'm cool," I tell both her and me. Flexing my fingers wide, I try to ease the quakes of my body. Nope, can't do it. My eyebrows snap together and I grab a storage unit of duck egg wood and wicker baskets to launch into the mirror. It shatters into the pile of holly leaves, a shudder of release shifting down my spine. Okay, now I'm cool.

"Time for tea?" I ask, perking up with a full smile. A gust of wind blasts through the window, the heavy flap of wings sparking my curiosity. The purple hint of a cashmere jumper catches my attention and my heart judders. Never have I been so happy to be rescued by a man.

Skipping down the freshly cleaned stairs, I enter the kitchen just as Cash does through the other side. His emerald eyes seek me out immediately, a relaxed tilt of his lop-sided lips expelling any trace of trigger-word meltdown that may or may not have just been. I've spent years conditioning myself to the insanity of Wonderland, eager to fit in if I were to ever make it back. Now I'm here and I need to make sure there's no reason for me to leave again.

Slinking his way over to Cook, he places a slow kiss on her cheek, his eyes never leaving mine. "Thank you for your service," he mutters just beneath the hissing of the pans. Her hands continue to stir bubbling mixtures but Cook's body angles itself towards Cash, her hips rolling as if they have a mind of their own. And they definitely want him. What did Cash say about sex being a currency in Wonderlust?

Passing her an oversized turnip, she shrieks in glee and hastily begins to chop it up. Cash crosses the kitchen, sweeping his arm around the back of my thick robe and brings those full, sinful lips close to mine. I'm *not* complaining.

"You ready to go?" he breathes, expelling lust and longing. Or maybe that's just me.

"Fuck yes," I agree, my eyes backtracking over my shoulder to see Mary Ann's sad face. She hangs back by the stairs, her chocolate eyes pleading with my last heart string. Ahh shit. "Should we, you know, take her with us? She could wait tables at your club," I shrug. Even with the thought of her dropping trays of drinks or tripping over her shoelaces, it seems better than leaving her here. Cash merely chuckles, his eyes darkening.

"Oh Malice. You've been gone so long; your tale has fallen to legend. And in none of these tales are you betrayed with a bleeding heart." I stand there after he's strode away, clearly expecting me to follow. Crossing my arms over my chest, I wait for Cash to turn back and look over my raised eyebrow-twisted lips combo. "You can pout those pretty lips all you like. I can't remove that girl from here anymore than you can remove your face from my wet dreams. Don't they have slaves where you come from?"

My head snaps aside, watching Mary Ann retract into the shadows. There's something about a frail girl being held against her will that resonates with me and I silently vow when I've got my bearings, I'm coming back to free her. Right now, however, I barely know how I'm alive and where to begin hunting for the real reason I needed to return. Striding after Cash, chunks of turnip fly over my head as he leads me outside to...

"What the fuck am I actually looking at?" I tilt my head to the side. Two giant wings of glimmering aqua and green flutter around a creature that looks conflicted. An elongated snout stretches in front of beady black eyes, a ruffle of silvery hair shifting around its face. The body of a powerful horse, yet a lengthy curved tail that, like the rest of it, is coated in shimmering scales.

"Sea-horse fly," Cash frowns. "You haven't got those in your world either?" Without waiting for a reply, he shoves me up on the horse backwards. My robe parts but I don't have the chance to arrange myself as Cash hops up a moment later. His thighs run the length of mine, the denim rubbing me just the right way. Topless, other than purple braces, his chest rises and falls steadily beside my cheek. Kicking his foot against the horse's rump, we shoot into the sky like a firework, soaring high just to explode into a million pieces. Gravity throws me into the solid wall of his body, my hands gripping his hips as a gurgled neigh ripples beneath us.

And you know what, it's been a rough fucking day. I've been shrunk, kidnapped, chased, stabbed, regenerated and now I'm flying, so I put any reservations aside and slam my lips onto Cash's. Not even a beat passes before he's leaning into me, grabbing the robe like a lifeline. His lips move with impressive accuracy, curving across mine from corner to corner. Peppermint and licorice cascade over my tongue, his mouth opening to invite me in. The sharp scrape of his teeth only heightens my awareness of the danger lurking beneath his alluring green eyes, and although he's careful not to dig them too deep, I want more.

A flex of the horse's muscles shuffles me that last inch forward, grinding my bare pussy over Cash's zipper. So close yet too far. Breaching the gloomy clouds, sunlight awaits on the other side, blessing us in rays of warmth. Ripping his braces from his broad shoulders, my fingers return to investigate the dip between his traps and biceps. It's silky soft, his creamy skin practically glowing over the sinew of his muscle.

The robe tie loosens before opening altogether, releasing my body from its confines. The towel-like material flaps open and billows in the wind. Yet Cash doesn't break our kiss. He lets his hands roam, starting with a yearning squeeze of my neck before trailing down to my breasts. Massaging them with deft fingers, his tongue sweeps away my senses as I reach for his jean's button. This is happening, we're fucking on the back of a flying sea horse.

"I can't take you yet," Cash growls, his voice a restrained grunt. *Yet,* sounds promising. "I can't mark you with my scent." Okay, that's a little weirder.

Despite myself, I push a hand into his pants and palm his solid monster cock. He gently takes my wrist, groaning as he pulls me free of his jeans and I sulk. But now Cash has a full, unobstructed view of me, which is causing his eyes to ignite neon green in his head.

Soaring higher on the sea horse's powerful wings, every ripple of his defined muscle is on display for me to drool over. A jawline made from granite, abs chiseled from ice and the smoothest, most lick-able skin I ever did see. The closer we venture towards the direct sunlight in fact, the last of my doubts burn into dust. This is exactly where I wanted to be, riding the high of an alternate life and as a bonus, the Tweddles got *buff*. Why deny myself who I've always dreamt of being with?

"Are you happy staring or are you going to show me what you've learnt in the past twenty years?" Triggered by my words, Cash grabs my calf and draws it up to rest on his shoulder. His hand trickles down to my thigh, where he grips the fleshiest part like a vice. Then, *finally*, his fingers enter me in one slick motion and I melt against the sea-horse's rigid spine. Curling his digits, Cash finds my g-spot like a missile locked on a target and destruction is his only aim. The complete obliteration of my soul. The release of any inhibitions. The welcome home present I've been damn well waiting for.

Pumping his fingers steadily, his green eyes continue to glow, unwavering from mine. Drinking in my moans that are drowned out by the neighs reverberating beneath us. Absorbing every detail of my face as I writhe, desperate for more friction. When I don't get it, I smooth my own hand towards my clit and Cash promptly withdraws.

"Did I tell you to stop?" I growl.

"I want to watch you," Cash replies without a flicker of emotion. If it weren't for his eyes, I could mistake his relaxed posture as completely unaffected by my nakedness sprawled out before him, a glint of mirth sneaking into his smirk.

"What do I look like? A self-service machine? A monkey that clashes symbols together on demand?! You started this, you damn well fini- "

A roar splits the sky in half, my ear drums shriveling up to die. Jerking upright, I grip the sides of my head while a neutral Cash swiftly ties the robe back in place. His hands on my hips is the only indication before I'm tossed up into the air and spun to straddle the seahorse in the correct direction. Following Cash's command, our aircraft dips below the cloud line where bleakness thrives and guess what? It's fucking raining.

Spears of water pierce my eyes, blinding me as the rumbling roar comes again, closer this time. I grip the sea horse's silvery mane, unable to find the source through the haze. It finds us though. A shadow collides with the side of the seahorse and only Cash's grip on my damn hair keeps me from falling off completely. Coiling it around his hand like a whip, my feet use his boots as stirrups and I'm confused as to who's riding who here.

"Fancy telling me what the fuck's going on?!" I scream, yet my words are lost to the wind. Ducking back and forth, the sea horse picks a course to follow, spiraling onwards like a corkscrew rollercoaster. Fuck theme parks, this is beyond the most epic ride I've ever been on. It's only when a flash of lightning ahead presents the beast that my gut really drops and I push back into Cash's chest of my own accord. "Is that..."

"A Jabber-cocky," Cash finishes in my ear, proving he could hear me the entire time. The silhouette shows as much. Thick horns protrude from its gangly head, elongated by a snake-like neck. The size of a winged dinosaur, its jaws open on a roar that I now realize is acting as thunder. Talons flare in the piercing white light, sending a shiver down my back as if it's already on me. I've never actually seen one before, not believing it to be real. After my father made his fortune turning my tales into a storybook, he continued to write of the fictitious creatures and characters I would see in my dreams.

"Wait. *A* Jabbercocky. What do you mean, *A*?! Surely, it's *the* only one?" I half-turn back as far as the tight grip on my hair will allow. Cash's eyebrows crinkle, a strange smile lighting the side of his mouth.

"Seems unrealistic to have a creature without predecessors or a way to continue the species. Did you think there was only one and that no more existed? Doesn't make much sense."

"It's Wonderland! It's not supposed to make sense!" I scream back, gripping the mane tight as the seahorse suddenly dives forward. Why am I the only one who seems to remember what a loon-filled place this once was?! Cash chuckles, his voice smooth and calm as ever.

"Wonder-*lust*," he prompts and I roll my eyes. As if I need any more of a reminder than the solid erection sticking into my lower back. A woodland below is approaching way too quickly, my stomach lodged in my chest. A fork of lightning cuts through the sky, the Jabbercocky nowhere to be seen. Just then, a huge yellow eye appears at my side, the size of the thing stretching from my head to hip with a slitted red pupil centered on me. Spreading its huge jaws to reveal two rows of razor-sharp teeth, I pull my leg over the sea horse, out of biting range when heavily rasped words puncture my eardrums.

"Bring him back!" the Jabbercocky bellows before releasing a bolt of ice from its throat. Tiny shards cascade over my body where the robe is failing to cling on, freezing me to the bone. Just beneath my feet, the canopy of trees becomes coated in a thick layer of ice that the seahorse uses to its advantage. Tucking up his legs, the creature slides the length of the icy path on his scaly body and just as the shimmering blue runs out, he tosses us aside onto the forest floor.

Cash is forced to release my hair as we slam into a heap of limbs, the eruption of pain rocketing through my shoulder making me writhe and groan. The white robe is now a lovely shade of mud and you guessed it, my damn hair is full of dead leaves again. Today is enough to make me consider shaving it all off and being done with it.

A blonde-haired shadow hangs over me, dragging me up by the robe's lapels. I hiss in pain, frowning further at the hardness contained in his simmering green eyes.

"I can smell him on you," he growls, dipping his head to inhale along the length of my neck. I see what's happening here – I've switched twins. Cash's outline is slumped on the ground, yet to rise from our fall. "Humor me. What does my brother have that I don't?"

"A dazzling personality, cheery smile and an understanding that girls don't like possessive, broody assholes? Take your pick." That was a total lie – I love a broody asshole on the best of days, but when faced with a challenge, I'll say whatever it takes to win.

"Hmmmm." Tweed tilts his head in genuine curiosity, raising a hand to smooth back my hair. With his other hand, he reaches into his tweed jacket pocket, reveals Stan and eases him into his hidey hole behind my ear. Tiny claws scrape at my scalp, but it's the squeeze of my heart at

Tweed's gentleness that makes me gasp. Keeping one palm against my jaw, his thumb reaches out to trace my bottom lip.

"I didn't realize you were so fickle." In a movement too swift for me to track, a capsule is shoved between my lips and his hand on my closed jaw knocks upwards *hard*. The capsule bursts between my teeth, copper liquid with a harsh tang sliding along my tongue and down my throat.

"Fuck's sake Tweed," I choke, trying to scratch my tongue free of the disgusting taste threatening to make me gag. "Stop forcing me to drink your blood!"

"You fucking bastard!" Cash yells and I have a wash of déjà vu. Shooting upright from the forest floor, he tackles his twin. And here we go again with the brawling. The pain in my shoulder ebbs away all at once and I roll it in all directions, hunting for the discomfort I so recently felt. There's no evidence it was ever there. Drawing the robe around me, I settle on a boulder, watching the pair roll around on the ground. Punches fly, feet kicking out and words shouted in fits of growls.

"You can't...have her!"

"She's already...mine!"

"As long as...marked...not...yours."

I tune out with an exasperated sigh at that point. I can't decipher who's saying what but it's obvious both these twat-knuckles think I'm a possession up for grabs. The glint of a curved smile catches my eye, drawing my attention to a town beyond the trees. A rogue signpost labels it as 'this way' as opposed to the other side which is obviously 'that way.' The smile has led me right before so as the boys continue their pissing match, I hop up and follow the swaying teeth in the direction of some clean clothes. Bye boys. I have some shopping to do.

CHAPTER 10

CASH - THE NIGHT BEFORE MALICE'S RETURN

G ripping the pole with one hand, my leg bent around the cool chrome, I spin slowly, relishing the stretch of my torso. The soft breeze stroking my face empties my mind, as it does every time I climb the length of the pole high above the varnished floorboards, artistically painted as a checkerboard.

Leaning into the stretch, I take time to limber up to the gentle melody easing from the speakers whilst waiting for tonight's sole client. I only dance for the flocks of women pounding on the other side of the door on weekends, keeping my weekdays free for pleasure of a different nature.

Placing both hands on the rod, my legs gracefully draw in a semicircle, tilting to give the illusion I'm floating. Clasping the pole above my head, the sound of heels clicking across the floor resonates as I freely hang upside down by my ankles. Even from this angle, the raven-haired beauty doesn't fail to appease. Not a strand out of place, she takes a seat, peering up with large golden eyes to watch her personal show. And I give it to her.

A sensual sway of muscle in black leather slacks. Tight enough to hint at what's lurking underneath yet leaving enough to the imagination to entice a keen stare. Righting myself and hanging on with one hand, I slowly descend like the angel of promised pleasure until my feet ease back onto the stage. Circling the pole with lazily, dragged movements, our eyes remain joined and a small smile pulls at her black-painted lips.

"Do you always toy with your clients?" she asks, acting coy as if she isn't my most regular.

"No, only with my food," I flash a dazzling smile of pointed canines that never fails to send the crowd wild with need. Leaning all my weight aside, I make a flourish of splitting my legs high in the air and twizzling around the pole before making my way to the steps stage right. She joins me there, standing tall on gorgeously long legs with her hand held out before her.

"Your majesty," I bow, kissing the back of her hand with a knowing smirk. Lillianna dips as low as her intricate black corset will allow, the silver clasps trailing her breast to abdomen catching the light of the chandelier. Floral lace curves around her tight cleavage, mirrored in the short puffy skirt bursts in frills around her upper thighs. Boots stretch past her knees, tied by silver cords crisscrossing back and forth. Righting myself, I lift the onyx embellished tiara from her head and place it on the stage. A move no one else would dare *try, but this is no place for a Queen. Women are all equal in Dirty Dee's, no exceptions. Even if she did gift it to me.*

"Shall we?" I ask rhetorically, already placing her hand in the crook of my freshly inked arm. The Mocking Turtle may be Wonderlust's most notorious gangster, but he's also one hell of a tattooist. Slow and steady, a true master of his craft. He's still packing his kit away in my suite, moving at a snail's pace but his emergency trip had been necessary. Whatever work he completes on my brother, he's rewarded double to replicate on me.

Lillianna's eyes trail the newest addition of a snake amongst the shaded roses, a metaphor I'm certain. Her pink tongue pokes out to wet her lips as we walk through the club, her anticipation palpable.

From Jubjub-birdseye view, the layout of this building is creatively a giant spade. The entrance creates a box stem, the laid-back bar and lounge splayed before the stage filling the center while the matching hallways either side round the edge of the structure, curving towards its point. Turning down the corridor opposite 'Fantasy Walk' Lillianna and I walk to her favorite addition to the club. The one she insisted was installed first. 'Evasion.'

Suede wallpaper lines either side, aiding the backdrop for the same leather armchair and tarnished coffee table to be repeated every few feet. Upon the mahogany surfaces, vials of luminescent liquids and bitesize cakes which never spoil sit at the ready, waiting patiently to take the consumer on a trip they won't remember or forget. There's only one doorway at the end of this hallway, a nondescript dungeon door complete with peekaboo grate. Makes me feel right at home each time I press my palm against the metal.

"Ladies first," I taunt, opening the door for Lillianna. She nods her head before returning to her full five foot nine and enters with her back ramrod straight. Good girl.

Closing us in the darkness, my trained ears pick up on her shuffling out of her lengthy boots and the clasps popping free of her corset. I can hear the shift of her movements so acutely; I can practically see her through the swarming nothingness. Her cinched, slender waist below full breasts, the flare of her hips and smoothness of her cream legs. Maybe I'm relying on memory for the most part but as my eyes begin to glow in my head, she's drawn to me. Like a moth to the flame, mesmerized swirling in my irises.

"Free your mind," I beckon her, cupping the sides of her face. Together, we lower onto our knees, drowning in a forgotten part of Wonderlust where no one dares come looking for uninvited. Drifting into the emerald sea of my eyes, Lillianna's shoulders sag as her inhibitions float away on a long sigh.

"My spies have returned from the Red Castle. The butterfly has awoken, the prophecy...has begun," Lillianna sighs again. Her golden eyes never waver, resisting the urge to blink as I draw all of her truths from her blackened lips.

"Continue," I summon, ensnaring her in the trap of my hypnosis. Not that this isn't exactly where Lillianna wants to be. To relieve herself of all trauma and woes that have brought us to sitting on the floor of a self-made dungeon. Evasion doesn't need an elaborate backdrop or to tap into one's deepest desires like Fantasy Walk, for this room isn't about sexual release. It's a mental one.

"Alice must return, aided by both Tweddles, to finish what was begun all those years ago. Arabelle intends for her champion to capture the girl, to break her will, but we can't let that happen. For the good of Wonderlust, you must recover her first. Bring her to the Black Castle, help me salvage our future. Alas, he is already on his way to retrieve you."

"Hush now," I breathe, tethering her onto the hook of my swirling irises and dragging her into their glowing, seaweed depths. "Feel your qualms floating away on the feathered wings of a raven. Permit me to carry your burdens, my Queen."

The moment I sense her completely relax in my hold, I twist her head aside and drive my fangs into the base of her neck. She doesn't startle, doesn't even whimper as the hypnosis takes hold and the sweetened taste of her blood skates across my senses. I feel her everywhere, my hyperawareness igniting with the living entity pouring into my veins.

Retracting my teeth, I hang my head there, inhaling the coopery scent radiating from her smooth skin. It glistens in the reflection of my eyes, dripping in a thick trail towards the valley of her cleavage before my tongue halts its slick path. Free from tainted thoughts, empty of her human affliction to carry unnecessary weight, the purity of her blood sings to me. Beckons me to consume every drop the puncture is willing to offer. There's nothing sweeter than the taste of complete submission.

Time fades into the background, my host remaining frozen for as long as I suck on and mark her. My own desire is as intoxicating as hers, the addictive pull dragging on our session until I know I can't take anymore. Not if I want her to continue living. Salivating for one last taste, on a strangled mutter I make it my own. Biting into the flesh of my wrist is the quickest way to bring me back to my senses, the congealed bitter taste washing away all haze of euphoria. Smearing the orange liquid over her lips, I will Lillianna to come back to the present by withdrawing the glow of my eyes.

An earthquake rocks through the room, causing the limp chain hanging over the dungeon door for aesthetic to rattle. Lillianna clings onto me, her hands around my biceps uninvited and drawing a growl from my throat. Catching myself, I pass it off as a cough and pat her on the shoulder. It's never a good idea to grip me in the visceral aftermath of an Evasion session, when the blood pumping around my system is not my own and I'm craving to put her back under my trance and tear the carotid from her throat.

"Was that us?" Lillianna breaths and I raise her to her feet.

"No, your majesty." I scent the air drifting under the doorway. Burning wood and thickened ash. "I dare say, my dear brother has arrived."

CHAPTER 11

MAL

What was it Cash said? Lust is currency in this version of Wonderland? Well, if that's the case, I shrug one shoulder out of my robe and put on my best catwalk strut all the way down the graveled hill towards the rows of buildings below. Stan clings onto the side of my scalp, his claws slotting into the gashes he left previously.

Reaching the edge of the odd town, the curved smile guiding my way fades from view and I step over the threshold. The air is stale here, still overshadowed by thick gray clouds that don't seem to shift. At least there's no sign of the Jabbercocky anymore. For that matter - there's no sign of anyone. Guess my sexy strut was for nothing.

Lined in a grid of cobbled streets, each brightly colored building is leaning on the next like dominos. Those on the ends are defying gravity, threatening to topple as I pass underneath. Windows tilt inwards at angles as if the tiny shops are crumpling in on themselves, the doors in a range of sizes.

A clothing rail catches my eye and I rush over. Grabbing a dress from the hanger, I strip from the robe and drag it straight on. I get stuck halfway, leaving my ass on full display to the empty town until I manage to wiggle the satin down my body.

Black covers my breasts with a sweetheart neckline, above an orange corset wrapped with black strings that I pull super tight. The skirt is full, like that of a ball gown in black and orange stripes. Matching with the buttons alongside the corset, a gold octopus brooch adorns where the puffy short sleeves meet the bust. The hanger also provides netted black gloves, a small top hat and pair of chunky ankle boots to complete the look.

Spinning in the window's reflection, I curtsey to myself, surprised how much I love the garment. Especially when it was *my* choice and not being forced upon me by a stranger. Smiling to myself, my eyes focus beyond the glass to the front display and my stomach rolls. 'The Alice Special' stands tall on a mannequin with blonde hair and blue eyes, a replica of the outfit Cash provided me with secured to its fabric torso. Oh hell no.

Fully intent on stomping inside and ripping it free of the doppelgänger, I halt in the doorway after spying the entire store is filled with similar dresses in all sizes and curse under my breath. Burning the establishment to the ground it is then. Looking for a source of kindling, I'm drawn further into the empty street. The 'Sugar Candy' store stands out in bright pink, a slogan hanging above the entrance boasting that every item of clothing is edible and all other thoughts are forgotten.

"Hello?" I call out, stepping inside. No one answers so I shrug, donning a thong made of strawberry laces with conversational hearts on either hip. Yanking it on beneath the heavy skirts I've chosen, I then opt for a candy necklace to finish the look and provide a snack for later. Wrapping the necklace around my throat, I ruffle out my blonde hair and give Stan a little stroke. Beyond a table of Haribo pajamas and sherbet handbags, I pose in a full-length mirror by the dressing rooms. Yeah, I'd do me.

Nothing like a bit of retail therapy to reset my mood, I think and return to moseying around. Back in the high street, crooked windows of the 'Space Café' show furniture floating around inside. Chairs, tables, tea pots and even the cash register. Suppose there is a real type of currency after all. The toot of a horn catches my ear and in the next alley, the weirdest pet shop I've ever seen presents itself.

A full-sized otter in an apron strolls around, dusting empty cages while humming between her twitchy whiskers. Her tail sweeps the floor behind her as she goes, not noticing me entering until that same horn with eyes over the door blares to life again.

"Look, I've already told you. We're all out of humans until-" the otter begins, turning her large brown eyes on me. Dropping her duster on the wood planks, she takes a webbed foot step towards me and then halts. "Wait. It's you. You're..."

"Malice," I supply for her, flicking my hair over my shoulder with a wink. Never was there a better time for a reinvention. Instead of approaching me with grabby claws that make me think she was preparing to shove me into the nearest cage, she retreats to the countertop and disappears behind it. Tracing her steps, I peer at the wooden slats, tapping them with my foot in search of where she went. Just then, an alarm rockets through the town, almost as loud as the Jabbercocky's scream. Something tells me that's not good, and probably about me. Tearing into the streets, I twist each way, spying the forest up on the hill.

"Tweedles!" I scream through the alarm, taking off running. "I fucked up! I don't think I'm sexy enough!" Pink floods from the alley up ahead, a wall of flamingos barring my exit. The klaxon shuts off, swapping for their deranged squawks and crazy stares from their blood red eyes. What the fuck did I do to piss off the flamingos? Thundering footsteps trample behind, closing me in as I spin, both arms raised to hold off any advances. Animals of all types draw to a halt behind me, all standing upright around my height with feather dusters, rolling pins or spatulas in their paws and claws.

"It's about damn time you showed your face!" a wolf in granny's nightdress and bed cap shouts. The sea lion at her side barks in agreement, slapping her fins against her pot belly beneath a frilly floral dress.

"We've been waiting for years," a red panda growls. Her fur is the same shade as the dots on her white cami, yet there's no pants in sight. I respect that. Lowering my hands, I hold the range of beady eyes, ignoring how the flamingos take a menacing step forward.

"Look, I don't know what you want but I've been trying to get back here since I left. Trust me when I say, it's not as accessible as it may seem."

"Enough small talk," an army of hamsters, guinea pigs and meerkats shout in unison, breaking free from the wall of furry feet in dresses and heels.

Wow.

"Get on with it already!" another squeals and I push my lips together in an effort to not burst out laughing. The barred teeth between clumps of lipstick tells me they don't mean to be entertaining, but damn do I wish I had a phone to record the crowd and die of fits of hysteria about it later.

Soothing myself with even breaths, I pop my hip with a hand on it for extra sass.

"I'm going to need some context here, chubby cheeks." The whole crowd gasps, paws-to-chest in offense. For a bunch of predators, they sure seem touchy. Taking a final step forward, a flamingo stabs its beak into my spine and I bat it away.

"Don't touch unless you're willing to finish the job," I smile at the narrowed beady eyes glaring back at me. A curved beak like that could open me right up to new pleasures and give me a pap smear at the same time.

Sheesh.

"Bring our men back!" an owl hoots, flapping into view and landing on the antlers of a domesticated moose. Pearl earrings dangle from her oversized ears while the brown fur off her huge chest is trying to break free of a frilly blouse. My eyes slide to the wooded hill beyond the town, figuring they mean the Tweedles.

"I mean...I'm really not that attached. They're hot, sure, but you're welcome to them. I've never really been one of those do-it-yourself or bully-me-into-submission types," I shrug and apparently that's the wrong answer. The animal housewives launch forward, rolling pins bashing me from the front while beaks peck at me from behind. Shrieking, I twist and grab a flamingo's neck in my gloved hands, swinging it around wildly. Batting the crowd back, the bird continues to hammer at where the lace stops at my wrist until the skin breaks and a splatter of my blood coats its beak.

"Squawk!" the pink bird cries out. "She's infected!" Everyone stops dead still, me included as the black-tipped beak begins to sizzle and steam. Eroding before my very eyes, the acidic blood splatter destroys everything it touches, a rogue splash burning through the flamingo's forehead until its neck falls limply in my hands. I toss it aside, not wanting any part of the blame for this daylight murder, even though everyone saw it.

"You-you've already drank from them," a lemur stutters, her skirt swaying as she slinks back into the crowd until only her black and white ringed tail can be seen. "The vampires."

"Vampires," I snort, spotting a balloon floating overhead. It's heavy, struggling to float more than an inch above our heads and on instinct, I remove Stan from behind my ear and throw him into it. *Save yourself little buddy, bitches be crazy down here.*

One touch of his claws and the balloon pops, pouring an unbelievable amount of water from its latex confinement. The street floods in an instant, waves gush between the buildings and sweep me up in its flow. Somehow, the animals were prepared for such an instance, pulling toggles from their clothes to activate buoyancy jackets.

"Don't trust the queen! Bring back our men!" is all I hear, the weight of the water dragging me under. Bubbles escape my mouth, my arms flailing to find the surface. Thanks to the dark ominous clouds, it's impossible to tell which way is upright as another wave crashes me further through the street. Something sharp bites down on my toe and I lash out with my other foot, kicking the furry guinea pig beast off as my face breaches the water.

Gasping in a lungful of air, I catch sight of a shop set back from the rest. There's no lights on within the hat-shaped windows. The water helps to wash away thick cobwebs spanning the doorway. Pinned onto a sign above, a green top-hat with 10/6 printed on the label and an extravagant peacock feather bowing out next to the calligraphy claims the shop as the Hattery. I gasp, fighting against the waves to swim in that direction but it's useless.

Forced into the inky depths once more, I tumble in a heap of limbs and hair all the way to the edge of town where I'm suddenly spat onto the hard ground. I lie panting, staring upside down at the wall of water looming over me but not one drop crosses the threshold as if it's tied to the town as much as the Step-heard Wives back there. Pulling myself upright, a tiny shadow inside the wave draws closer until Stan is also ejected, directly into the center of my chest.

"Oh buddy, you're shivering," I stroke him, brushing droplets of water from his mocha-fur coat. Never mind the fact I'm also trembling; Stan is my main concern. Boots scuffle up behind me and before I can even guess who it might be, a claggy throat clears.

"'Cuse me? Do you need a ride?" Deciding my eyes are deceiving me, I lean up on my elbows. A stumpy little woman stands before me, with miniature legs holding up her dwarfed frame, only to wobble side to side under the weight of her giant egg head. A wig of straw-like hair rests precariously upon her head, a yellow braid hanging limply either side. Her large brown eyes blink genuinely, her white gloved hand gesturing to the military of horses trailing down the path as far as the eye can see.

Upon each horse sits a soldier in matching attire to the equestrian clothing mounted on their steeds. Checked with a club symbol in every white square. Plumes of black and white feathers flourish from their steel helmets, thousands of long eyelashes fluttering through the eye holes in wait for my response.

"You're all human and...female," I breathe, tucking Stan safely into my damp hair.

"All the King's horses and all the King's men, at your service," Little Humpty Dainty bows. I catch her as she threatens to topple over, standing to lift her onto my shoulders. "After all, the best type of men are wo-men."

I laugh, the whimsical sounds drifting around us, piercing the darkness of the approaching night as I gesture for the lead horse to show me the way. I can just tell we're going to be great friends.

CHAPTER 12

MAL

D ry leaves crunch beneath the heavy sole of my boots, only my grasp on the horse's rein guiding me onwards. He sure must love his carrots, being able to see in the dark and all - because I can't see shit. The darkness of night settled before we entered the forest, trudging forward without a particular destination in mind. My neck cramped long ago from Humpty Dainty's weight on my shoulders. Since when have eggs been so damn heavy?!

"Here's good," she finally announces and the horse comes to a swift halt. His rider disembarks and sets about rummaging around while I place Humpty Dainty on the ground, visions of a horse's hoof smashing through her head plaguing my mind. At least it's too dark to see the smirk that thought brought me. Not even I'm stupid enough to anger my savior. Not when my stomach is rumbling louder than the distant thunder.

A glow ignites before me, directing me to a clearing which the soldiers rush to provide seating for. Huge, heavy trunks slam on the ground, creating a hexagon, yet none of them sit. I do, though, with Humpty Dainty opposite.

"Set up camp," she barks the order with a voice much harsher than the one that's been singing nursery rhymes the whole way here. "Make sure our guest has a tent of her own." My eyebrow rises and I nod to myself. Look who's making healthy friendships for once. The fire grows, brightening the woodland around us.

Trees loom high, each of their trunks winding upwards in a different pattern. Some wavy, some zigzag. One loops around and has grown through itself, like a giant knot. The canopy shifts in the slight wind, completely blocking us from the sky. A thud of a hammer draws my attention behind me, to where a soldier begins nailing a tent to one of the overhanging thick branches. Each time she strikes, a teeny voice leaks from the tree's bark.

Ooh. Eee, ahh, crap balls, ouch.

Once that side is cemented in place, she moves to fix the other to an adjacent branch, and in doing so pitches the tent completely upside down and several feet from the ground. More soldiers begin to pitch their tents in the same way, until an orchestra of pained cries bleed through the forest. Humpty doesn't seem to notice, too invested in a backpack which has been produced for her.

"Tea?" she asks, pulling out a long flask. Almost two liters in full length, and my heart just about combusts.

"Oh, you smooth-faced angel, yes please," I nod like a bobble head. Any pretense of being nonchalant vanished when she twisted open the cap. Perfectly sweet, just the right shade of sepia in the fire's wavering light. Accepting a China cup, little finger poised, I sip slowly and melt down onto the dirt-covered ground. That's the fucking stuff right there. The things I would and have done for a cup of tea. My own moans fill my ears, drowning out the fleeting screams of the trees.

Ooch, fah, gee, ugh, hoochie mama.

"Can I ask you something?" Humpty Dainty shuffles closer and I shrug.

"You just did." Lost in a world with my tea, I only notice her stumpy little leg bump against my shoulder because the liquid splashes over the cup.

"Do you know which Tweedle you intend to accompany back to their queen?" she continues anyway. I sip my tea, carefully thinking through where to begin with that. So, the Tweedles have their own separate queens, that I supposedly should be accompanying them back to, and I can only choose one...Interesting, yet I've learnt my lesson about asking too many questions. The answers only lead to more trouble.

"I intend," I begin, noting how all the soldiers halt and twist their helmet-clad heads in my direction, "to find a little patch of Wonderlust for myself and live out my days in peace. A house made of feathers in the eye of a storm perhaps, or I could bundle myself into a time capsule and give the unlucky fucker who uncovers me one hell of a fright. Would need an endless supply of cheeseburgers though. They might start to smell after a while...or mold, and then maybe I'd turn to mold."

My thoughts carry me on a tangent, adrift in the flames dancing before me. The fire is tainted in a purple hue, silvery tendrils swaying back and forth while I wonder how long it'd take for mold to set into the pores of my skin. Would I become a living fungus? Transform into a mushroom? Then I can feast on myself...

"I could show you the right choice, if you like?" Humpty Dainty nudges me again. Placing the empty teacup down on the woodland floor, I ease myself back up onto the log to peer into her large brown eyes. "The only seers we had were the caterpillars, and the Queen of Hearts has the last one in existence, but I have some psychic powers myself. I can give you a glimpse at your future, and it'll help to show you which path to take."

I remain quiet, noting how she trembles slightly on the trunk. Beneath her words and level tone, there's something in the way Humpty Dainty spears her soldiers with a quick glance that tells me there's more to her offer than a friend helping a friend on her time capsule journey. Either way, I've never had a clue as to where I'm going. It could be fun to find out, and if I don't like what I see - what to avoid like the plague.

"Sure," I half shrug, holding out my hands. Humpty looks at them curiously, then releases a sharp whistle that cracks the darkness in two. A soldier rushes forward, the metal of her armor clinking loudly. Saluting, she stands straight, easily several inches taller than me as a horse also charges forward. The creature stops just short of crashing into her, bowing its head low in submission.

A heavy weight settles over my shoulders, invisible other than the glint of a faint smile that catches my eye. I roll my neck, trying to dislodge it without much luck. The soldier reaches into a sheath on the horse's flank and pulls out a large instrument. Shiny enough to be a gun, until the rounded end breaks free. It's a giant fucking teaspoon.

Humpty pulls the blonde wig free of her egg head, the shine to the tip gleaming in the fire's purple glow. The soldier kicks off her clunky boot and plants her foot between us on the log. Raising the spoon high, she slams it down on her ankle, a sickening crack ricocheting around the tree trunks. I gag, trying to turn away but the horse's head is there to keep me in place. A snarl rumbles from his carrot-loving teeth, the silver of yellow in his gaze telling me I should probably not piss him off.

Another crack sounds, then a third and despite myself, I brave a look. Just have to see what the sweet loving hell is happening before I find a way out of this damn wood. The soldier rights herself with a wobble, leaning down to retrieve her severed foot. There's a distinct lack of blood but that doesn't concern me as Humpty Dainty starts to pick at the shell on her temple.

Finding the spot she was looking for, the circumference of her head splinters in a smooth line. The soldier shuffles forward, helping to yank the tip back, revealing the yolk. It bubbles like a pit of lava and fuck me, do I salivate. Lick my lips and lean in. I love a perfectly dippy egg. Until the soldier dips her manky foot into the yolk and puts me off eggs for life. Humpty groans, taking me to a whole new level of weird when the heavy weight curled around my neck whispers in my ear.

Run.

Yeah, no shit, but I'm currently cornered by a crazed horse and a vitellus-based orgy. All three pairs of eyes swivel on me, an expectation thickening in the air as the breath locks in my lungs. Well, Malice, you've been in some strange situations, but one really takes the biscuit. I don't know who moves first, but somehow I jerk back into the horse's face and find the foot shoved into my face.

"Suck the big toe and your future will be revealed," Humpty Dainty says, her tone natural and soft as ever. I cringe at the jagged toenails, smothered in yellow. The smell of egg and athlete's foot burns the hairs out of my nose, so I suppose that saved a trip to the salon, but still. I'm not sucking that damn toe.

"You know what, I've decided the future is overrated. I'll just see what comes my way," The horse's nose at my back nudges me forward and the tippiest of toe tip grazes my lip. I choke on the vomit that spurts up the inside of my throat. Not even the gormless hulk-wannabe I went down on awaiting my trial was this bad.

"Suck it!" Humpty says again, becoming more angered.

"I could just lickety lick your brain juice directly from the source." I swallow hard and the foot is jerked towards me once more.

"The visions won't work that way. You can't have a dippy egg without soldiers," she rolls her huge eyes. In my peripheral, I notice the top of her shell head is back in place as she adjusts the wig into place to cover the crack. "Now start sucking."

I've heard that before, multiple times. Yet as I open my mouth with another protest, the girthy toe is shoved into my gob. I jerk back, utterly trapped and as the offensive digit knocks against my tongue, I relent. Fuck it, it's in there now. Clenching my eyes shut hard enough to blind myself, I suck that big toe like my life depends on it. The yolky lubrication is a blessing as the sounds around me drown out and images appear behind my eyes.

Two women stand on a hill, high above a sea of carnage below. Dismembered beings, human and animals alike. Thick rivets of blood carving a stream back towards the town I fled from. More specifically, right up to the front door of the abandoned hattery.

Movement on the hill draws my attention, a shadow stepping out from either side of the women. I notice their crowns now, tall against the sunset. Regal dresses burst from their tiny waists, dwarfing their similar heights. The shadow's outlines betray who they are, but not once do their features come into

the light. The Queens lean into the side of their designated Tweedle, staking
their claim as a voice booms from the sky.
One is your destiny,
the other your demise.
Revive the world that once was
Before twin blood moons rise.

A pop brings me back to the present, the soldier deciding she didn't like me sucking her toe like a pacifier. Placing it back into her boot, she then shoves in her stumped leg and hobbles off with the aid of her horse.

"Well," Humpty Dainty breathes and I suddenly realize she's so close. As in, straddling me. "What did you see?"

Lie. The voice at my neck sounds, the invisible furry body shifting across my shoulders. I mean...I wasn't exactly going to blurt out the truth. What it sounds like is some egotistical asshole in the sky just told me I'm doomed to belong to a man and the future of Wonderlust is on my shoulders. No thank you.

"Tell me! I need to know; will the King be resurrected? Will he return for his army and take me as his bride for keeping the zombie army in check?" With each word she desperately grabs onto, Humpty drags herself further up my dress. Her pleading tone tastes more bitter on my tongue than the toe ever did.

"Mmhmm, that's literally what I saw. It's like you're in my head or something," I nod, peeling her away from me. Without the horse blocking me in, I'm able to slip off the trunk and brush off my satin skirt. "Well, this has been awesome, but I have a destiny to fulfill. Thank you for your...yolk." Taking another step backward, I bump into a torso coated in metal armor.

"Wait. You didn't say which Tweedle you'll follow. If the outcome is to return my King, I need to know who to put my faith in. The rascal or the reject?" My poker face almost breaks at that. Almost. I wouldn't answer even if I could because this egg is giving me major creepy vibes, but which Tweedle was meant to be which? Either way, the air is growing thinner in the kind of way when I'm about to have a psychotic break and I need to get out of here.

Duck left. The zombies are invincible, but they're slow.

Peering at the faint smile to my side, the brush of a tail skates over my chest. Don't query it, Malice. If snitches get stitches, questions get sanctions. I grab the furball at my neck, stopping it from dropping off as I duck left. Dodge right. Skid on my knees beneath a horse and dart around the upside-down tents being used as glorified hammocks.

Humpty wails for the soldiers to grab me, but the voice on my shoulder was right. They're slow as fuck. Arms stretch out of the tent openings, uselessly trying to grab for my knotted hair trailing in the wind I'm creating. Stan clings on for his poor damn life and I vow to treat him to a spa day after this. I'll massage his fragile little heart myself if I have to. Dude deserves a break from running for his life.

With the dimming flame behind me, I'm sprinting blind until a figure steps out from behind a trunk. Slamming into the solid chest, I vaguely register this one isn't covered in a steel plate. A hand wraps around my mouth, my body curled inwards until the rough press of bark scratches at my front. The smile on my shoulder brightens, its furry weight finally lifting.

'I'll leave you in good hands. Well...if that's the path you choose.' I watch that taunting smile spin like a Catherine wheel, spiraling away and leaving me at my captive's mercy. Yeah, cheers bitch-tits. The chest at my back leans in, caging me as lips graze the curve of my ear. At the same time, fingers

trail the front of my thigh, smoothing the satin in small circles towards my pussy. I blanch, more at my body's reaction to a possible rapist until his voice caresses my senses.

"Who prefers the possessive, broody asshole now?" I hate the smirk that brushes my ear as much as the heat pooling in my core. A stifled groan sounds beyond the tree trunk, the drag of a detached foot shuffling through the leaves on the ground. One hand still clamped around my mouth, Tweed snakes his free arm around my waist and the next second, I'm airborne.

Air whooshes past my ears. Branches claw at my skin. Leaves pound onto my scalp, giving me a foliage headache until we breach the canopy. Tweed lands with the agility of a panther, flipping me around in one smooth motion and holding me against him as he skates over the treetops. My head buries into his neck, my legs around his waist. Each jostled movement rubs me against his waistband in such a way, I struggle to control myself. This is the art of not knowing my future. I end up in situations like this, forgetting my own damn name or why I decided I didn't like this twin in the first place.

Muscles flex. Veins pop. The coolness of his skin spears my heated flesh, my mind traveling to all sorts of naughty places. Would riding Tweed be akin to fucking a popsicle? I wonder what flavor he'd taste like. A rumble sounds in his chest, vibrating through my jaw and directly to my clit, as if he knows what I'm thinking.

Dropping from the height, a scream lodges in my throat. My thighs bind around his waist and nails dig into his back until the thud of us landing judders through me. It was gentler than I expected, all things considered. The tree line of the forest looms over me and Tweed begins to stride away, not saying a word or attempting to put me down.

"Um...I could probably walk from here," I mutter, my arms still as tight around his neck.

"Yeah, you could," he agrees in a low voice filled with lust. "But I got the impression you were enjoying yourself." With the jolt of his crotch, I reckon I'm not the only one who doesn't want to break away just yet, but sure, I'll take the blame. I'll cling to this slice of muscle and put my thoughts on hold. After all, how often is it you get to test a supposed-vampire's restraint?

CHAPTER 13

MAL

Waking on a snort, I sip back the drool spilling from my lips. My arms are limp, hooked over a pair of hefty traps. My ass supported by unmoving palms. The evidence of my sleep has pooled in Tweed's collar bone and soaked into his purple and black pinstripe t-shirt. We're no longer moving, and if it wasn't for the husk of a moan ratting in his chest when I lick at the rest of my dribble, I'd have thought he was a statue. It's only polite to clean up my own mess.

Emerald green eyes lower, desire swirling in their depths. I feel that; my morning-after hair is my best look, but usually I have the satisfied ache between my legs to go along with it. Unfurling from his hold, Tweed's large hands remain on my back until I'm standing, but still in his embrace. The unmoving chest at my cheek oddly comforting.

Morning rays breaking free of post-storm clouds span across a derelict play area. A set of swings sway slightly beside a rusted seesaw. A curled yellow slide attached to a climbing frame takes up half the fenced confines. Abandoned, but fairly normal in retrospect.

"You just stood in here while I slept," I comment. Tweed's head inclines, his stuck-up bravado sorely missing.

"It's hard enough to control myself when you're awake. An unconscious victim," he grumbles and forces his eyes away. "Too tempting."

There's something wholly sexy in being referred to as a victim. All these years, I've been the perpetrator. Caged and feared. Tweed's right - I also want to be awake for whenever he's ready to 'lose control' with me. Fuck destinies and downfalls, I live for the moment. The *feels*. Although that reminds me, and the little bell starts tring-a-linging in my head.

"You have some explaining to do." Breaking free of his cool hold, I move towards the swings. The metal clinks and squeaks as I sit on the eroded rubber seat, gesturing for Tweed to take the other. He complies.

"What do you want to know?" his graveled tone rings out, fitting into the barren setting perfectly. Counting out three fingers, I twist to straddle the seat and face him.

"Number one, the vampire thing." Tweed's shoulder's lower as if he wasn't expecting to explain something so trivial.

"Easy. We were bitten by Norris, the vampire bat," he half-shrugs. Fair enough, but now I want to know where to find this bat. Immortality sounds like fun, the blood-thirsty hunger is an added bonus. "It was the last of his poison venom before he died," Tweed grunts and I huff. Fucking typical. Moving on, I point to my second finger.

"The last time I was unconscious, you tried to kidnap me. Is there a reason I'm not locked in a teapot or strapped to a bed this time?" I ask, trying to hide the disappointment in my tone. Tension erects Tweed's spine, probably from sharing the same mental image as me. Handcuffs on my wrists, bent over a mattress, possibly gagged. Focused on the horizon, a hauntedness returns to Tweed's green stare as he rises to stand, the pinstripe t-shirt stretching over his back.

"I thought your retrieval would be easy. I should have known you'd be anything but easy," he huffs. I make a satisfied sound in the back of my throat. As if Tweed ever thought he could drag me off and I'd obey like a cute little sub. He sighs, running a hand over his nape.

"You should know, Cash and I serve different queens, both with their own ideas on how to save our world from ruin. It's impossible to know whose method will succeed, so it's been left up to you to choose." Turning, Tweed sets those emeralds on me and crosses his arms. "The fate of Wonderlust rests in your decision, Gopher help us all." Chewing on the inside of my cheek, I rise too. That's the second time I've been told to make a choice, whereas I sit firmly in the 'why choose' category.

Passing his puffed-out chest, I skip over to the climbing frame. Grabbing the side railing of a rickety, wooden bridge I wouldn't let Stan cross alone, I pull up the length of my bodyweight until the metal rests beneath my sternum. Flipping myself around, I settle myself upside down, suspended by the backs of my knees hooked over the bar. Then, I close my eyes and let my arms fall past my head.

"What are you doing?" Tweed's boots crunch closer, but I don't look for him. I'm too busy drawing the cold morning air into my lungs whilst stretching my abdomen. The black and orange skirts flutter towards my head, revealing my strawberry lace thong while the tight, corset bodice holds everything else in place.

"I'm thinking. Women need to hang upside down to relieve pressure on the vestibular system. Eases stress and helps to center the mind." And boy, do I have a lot of thoughts racing around this noggin. When I get too muddled, I lose control. Past experiences indicate an impending lash-out at the nearest person, or my limbs will turn to jelly, and I'll collapse into a puddle on the floor. Neither I'm particularly in the mood for currently, so I create a list inside my head.

The facts I have:

1. I've made it back to Wonderlust in one piece.

2. I've yet to encounter another human.

3. There's a severe lack of males in *all* species.

4. My real reason for returning is seeping into the background.

5. I have some seriously disgusting morning breath coated in eggy athlete's foot going on.

"What was the third?" Tweed's voice slips through my thought process. Blinking my eyes open, his chest is right in front of me. Those tattooed arms hang by his sides, his eyes level with my chest.

"Hmm?" I reply, suddenly too aware of my breath now to open my mouth. Stupid brain remembering things. Not moving to put any space between us, he holds up three long digits an inch from my nose.

"You held up three fingers when I asked what you wanted to know. What was the third?" My vision gets a little hazy as I stare at those fingers, imagining exactly what he could do with them to get me out of this conversation.

Pushing his rock-hard abs to force him back a few steps, I sit up to grab the bar. Hoisting myself up and over it, I land on the rickety bridge and quickly make my way to the main platform. A series of monkey bars and a rope swing later, I'm ascending a ladder to the curly slide. I think this is far enough away for Tweed to smell my breath, but who knows with these damn vampire senses. Leaning over the top of the slide, I rest my chin in my hands.

"When's the last time you laughed?" There was no way out of that question. The need for the answer is too great. Tweed doesn't move, like a robot who needs a heavy dose of oil. He's seized up, and it's not him who answers me.

"Laughed?" Cash stands on the other side of the fence, amusement lighting his face to be a stark contrast to his brother's. "Why, Tweed here hasn't so much as smiled since you left us twenty years ago. Mind you, he hasn't had much reason to."

I watch Tweed carefully, hunting for a hint of emotion. There is none. No wonder he's been classed as the reject in the eyes of simpletons. Although, I did always like a challenge. Tossing myself into the slide's mouth, it wobbles, helping me to wind around and around until spitting me out at the bottom with a rumbling belch.

"Okay, I've made my decision," I nod. Tweed turns then, joining the hard stare Cash is giving me from beyond the fence. Tension ripples between them. I stroke my hand over the yellow plastic of the slide. It purrs in response. "I'm not big on making life-affirming decisions before breakfast, but I also have business to attend to. You're both going to help me, and at some point I may or may not consider this prophecy bullshit."

"What business?" Cash queries. He's yet to enter the playground for some unknown reason. I pat the slide goodbye and make my way towards the gate. Placing my hand on the peeling yellow paint, I spot a line burnt into grass just beyond. It stretches into the lush green fields on this side for as far as I can see. On Cash's side of the line, the grass is dead and patchy. The sun peaks free of cloud, only seeming to shine over here while the path beyond the gate is speckled with rain and I roll my eyes.

I don't need the sign posted on the fence to tell me I'm currently in the Red Queen's territory. Presumably a line that Cash can't cross and as I throw a glare back at Tweed, he merely shrugs. Possessive fuckwit.

"First, I need my dictionary. Then, you boys are going to get me into that Hattery undetected," I spin to put them both in my eyeline and point. "No more fighting or biting unless I'm begging for it. Sentence first, verdict afterward," I nod.

Exiting the playground and pulling Stan from behind my ear, I walk along the winding park and brush my fingers across his back. He blinks those huge, brown eyes up at me and I have to agree. Two vampire strippers don't make the best accomplices, but I'm clearly in need of some help. They can aid me, whilst under the guise that I'll fulfill their ridiculous prophecy and choose between them.

Too bad they won't know I've already made my decision to choose myself and build a bus-stop to live out of. Cushioned seat, metal can for newspaper bonfires, open plan lounge with mother nature and an oasis for the drunks who want to stop by for some company. Only the best if I do say so myself.

CHAPTER 14

MAL - SIX MONTHS AGO

*T*he echo of a heavy metal door slamming closed works its way through my thumping skull. I blink, clearing the fog claiming my vision since my head connected with the wall. There's no padding in this room. Only cold, hard floors and no escape.

The figure in front of the door steps closer, his baton swinging from his wrist. A naked, singular bulb casts the box room intended for solitary confinement in a bleak, orange glow. But I've never once been thrown in here to be alone. They know I like my own company too much, which defeats the punishment, so they got creative.

"Let's try this again," the Terminator thumps his heavy boots around the small space. "Did you break into the kitchen last night to make jam tarts?" Dragging myself up onto shaky legs, my head swings and I wobble sideways. A meaty hand grabs my paper-thin gown, holding me in place.

"Did the illicit baker not leave evidence behind?" I smirk, knowing for a fact I left an obvious trail of crumbs leading to Crazy Joanna's room. "Curiouser and curiouser." The Terminator growls, lowering his face to mine.

"When are you going to drop this stupid fantasy? You're not some special girl destined for another land. You're a pathetic," he slams my back against the wall, "delusional," and again, "psychopath." I manage to withhold my groans of pain and incline my head.

"Thank you," I smirk. The electric end of his baton sparks and it's jammed into my lower abdomen. Releasing a shriek this time, I'm allowed to topple to the floor. Curling in on myself, I struggle to find that confidence I've come to rely on. Through it all, knowing I'm not the crazy one here.

I'm Malice, and that bitch is completely sound of mind – despite what everyone else believes. I don't know why I was chosen for Wonderland as a child, nor why they haven't seemed to want me back, but I won't fall into the trap of losing the memories I know are real. My faith has never faltered, although times like this, my loyalty does.

The terminator drops over me, hitching up my dress. His hand shoves my face into the floor, not able to help himself from hastily unbuckling his slacks. That's the way it goes. Those who deem themselves of power take from the weak. The deranged, who's word wouldn't be believed otherwise. Too bad for this horny fuckwit, being easy prey just isn't me.

In this world, I need to be my own hero.

Dropping the back of my canvas shoe from my heel, I leave my ass in the air in favor of snaking an arm down and grab the knife stashed in the sole. While the attendants were so concerned with the mess in the kitchen and stolen ingredients, no one thought to take stock of the cutlery drawer. To their credit, it was a fucking bomb site in there. Flour and jam everywhere.

The Terminator doesn't see it coming, too preoccupied with whipping out his tiny dick. Swinging my arm wide, the glint of metal jerks him backwards. It's impossible to know if I made any contact, but it did the job. The pressure on my face is relieved. Twisting, I don't hesitate to swipe the knife in an upwards curve towards his shocked face. Blood splatters across the length of the dress scrunched at my waist. An unholy scream batters around the cell as the Terminator stumbles backwards, holding the side of his face.

"You bitch! You fucking, crazy bitch!" he roars, regaining a hint of composure through the blood pissing out of his fingers. Slamming his fist against the alarm button on the inner wall, his good eye falls on the baton discarded between us at the same time as I see it. A moment passes, a high-pitched shrill splitting through the hallway beyond the door. Then, we move.

Diving across the floor on my front, the Terminator swoops down, his hand closing around the baton before I can knock it out of his reach. Electric sparks at the tip in slow motion, crackling just before the baton is jammed into my neck. Shaking violently, I roll aside as a boot connects with my face and the lights go out.

Time passes behind my sealed eyelids. My body crying out in pain, yet my mind isn't ready to return. It's happier in here. Filled with color and fantasy. Soaked in desire and yearning. Fields of mushrooms, tea parties every day. Flowers to talk to, pathways to stray. Oh Hatter and Hare, Cheshire's and Pillars of Cat. How I long to be where you are, how I wish to come back.

"Pssssst," a voice hisses through my subconscious. I try to ignore it, but after some solid persistence, I groan and crack an eyelid. A smile hovers in front of my face. Curved, gleaming white in the dimmed room. Circling, it floats out of view and a moment later, a heavy weight settles across my back. The lick of a heavy tail drifts over my exposed thighs, the dress still bunched up too high.

Pushing myself upright, the weight remains as I ease onto all fours and take stock of my body. Aside from the thumping agony awaking in the side of my face, possibly a fractured jaw and concussion, I'm otherwise intact. Shrugging off the furball curled into the dip of my spine, I move to sit and in the next moment, the smile is back. Nestled into my lap, I absent-mindedly stroke the invisible body.

"Why is a raven like a writing desk?" I mutter aloud. The smile tips upwards, the two lines of straight teeth not parting, although a female voice rings clear in my head.

"Because they both- "

"Hush," I bark, placing an index finger over the smile. My brows cross angrily. "Those too logical to seek an answer prove themselves to be just that. Rational, sensible. Too sound of reason. All attributes deemed offensive by those in Wonderland. I must remember who I am, must avoid the dilution of my mind. If I am to return. If..."

My voice becomes too small. My feisty spirit taking a lunch break. At least I'm alone, locked in the concrete cell with no one to witness this. Staring at the wall opposite, my eyes become unfocused, my hand continuing to stroke the unseen cloud in my lap. The wall ripples. I tell myself it's a trick. I gave up allowing my hopes to rise each time something fantastical happens. There is no telling what drugs they pumped into me whilst unconscious. But sure enough, the wall moves again.

Flickering in mini waves, warping the gray stone as fluidly as water. Scooting closer, keeping my legs crossed, I cock my mane of blonde hair. Before my eyes, a crack appears, splintering downwards. A slither of silver gleams through from the other side, wherever that may be. Spitting out an object, the crack closes as quickly as it appeared. I lift a hand, pressing my palm against cool concrete that freezes in place with no indication it ever moved at all. Except...

Lifting the object from the ground, I peer closer in the dimmed light. A small fabric hat sits in the center of my hand. What was once artfully stitched from lime green felt, is now singed around the edges. Three mini feathers are stuck into a purple ribbon circling the hat, tickling me as I stroke them. One white, one orange, one yellow.

"Something tells me your appearance alongside this hat isn't a coincidence," I tell the curved smile still seated in my lap. It twists to face me, all pearly whites with the slightest hint at a large pair of blue eyes.

"You've stayed and lost your way, Malice, as have I." Drawing in a deep breath, I briefly close my eyes. I'm accustomed to voices, to navigating a path between daydreaming and reality. But this would be the first time I've received a sign. A physical piece of evidence to the world I once walked.

Still stroking those feathers, the white one sets alight, burning my fingertips before I can move away fast enough. The flickers of flame drift into the air before me, swirling with the faintest trail of orange following behind as letters are formed.

Find me.

As soon as they appear, they disappear without a trace. Dread curdles in my chest. My teeth sink into my bottom lip. No, this isn't a sign. It's a message. A cry for help. Blowing away the white feather's remains; I tuck the hat into the base of my shoe. A shudder runs the length of my spine as the door to isolation is wrenched open and two guards rush in to seize my arms. I've played this game many times, I know what to do.

Hanging limply, I allow the guards to drag me back to my room and toss me inside. As per the rehabilitation system, there will be a tribunal with the board of governors to discuss my misdeeds and an 'open discussion' about my punishment. The worst part is my family will be present and that in itself is reason enough not to act out more than usual. When it comes to rapey assholes, however, I'll do whatever it takes to protect myself. No one else is going to do it for me.

"The shadows should be here soon. Are you prepared for the worst? If not, too bad." The smile ebbs back, disappearing just beneath my bed. I drop down, an idea sparking to mind and reach into the dust-covered darkness. Taking the thickly bound dictionary in hand, I conceal the felt hat into the dust cover. The attendants thought they were hilarious gifting me the only book I didn't want to read upon arrival, but who's laughing now.

Making sure the book is tucked into the back corner, I scoot back on the cold tile. Looking at my shoe, the remains of the orange feather is left in the base. Disintegrating before my eyes. Crumbling into tarnished ash. If I hadn't already come to a similar conclusion, this would have sealed my decision.

I need to keep that felt hat safe until I'm able to return it to its rightful owner.

I need to return to Wonderland.

CHAPTER 15

MAL

R emoving my precious concealment from the dust cover, I toss the dictionary over my shoulder. The green felt has curled into itself, the outline of the hat no longer recognizable. No more feathers remain on the purple band, the last having withered and died around the same time my efforts to escape Charmsfield did. But it's clear to me now, I never would have found my own way back to Wonderlust without help. I needed to be *retrieved*.

Tucking it into my cleavage and leaving Cash's bedroom, I find both Tweedles sitting on the rounded armchairs. The cushions are so plump, neither can touch the floor and as much as they're trying to maintain an angry façade towards each other, their legs swing in unison. There are so many questions to be asked there, but at some point, I realize it's wholly none of my business. Curiosity killed the cat and all that jazz.

"Hey!" the smile twisting in the background deepens into a frown. "I resent that!" Ignoring it, I move to the coffee table and take a seat on top of it. Each table leg is a different height, the wood bending and dipping to accommodate. Lifting a teacup, I wriggle my ass into a groove and narrow my eyes at Tweed.

"This isn't going to knock me unconscious, is it?" Tweed holds my gaze, the hint of a smile behind his full lips but it's Cash who answers.

"That's my tea and no, it's not," he grumbles. I point my pinkie high and take a sip. The burn of whiskey slams into the back of my throat, using my tonsils as a punching bag. "Will put hairs on your chest though."

Spluttering, I toss the cup aside to cover my cleavage. He'd better be joking or the red queen won't be the only one who sets head's rolling today. Luckily, my skin remains smooth beneath my palms and I suck in an even breath.

The hem of the black vest follows the curve of my breasts, the soft cotton hugging my frame down to the army green cargos it's tucked into. I found the baggy items left on Cash's bed with a tag that instructed me to pull it once dressed. Always one to follow instructions, I yanked on that tag like a bell ringer and the material conveniently sucked inwards until it fit as if made for me alone. The same with a pair of Cash's high-top sneakers after I gave the laces a tug.

"So – the Hattery, if you please," I gesture a hand at the fireplace. Surely one of them has some of that portalling glitter stashed somewhere nearby.

Both of the Tweedles eyes intensify on me, although I get the distinct feeling for different reasons. Cash leans his forearms on his knees, threading his fingers together.

"You won't find what you're looking for," he breathes, a moment of seriousness falling over his features. I straighten.

"And what do you think that would be?"

"The Hatter, for a start," he inclines his head towards the miniature hat nestled between my cleavage. My cheeks flush, the thought of being so transparent not sitting well with me.

"Answers, for another," Tweed interjects. His stare has yet to leave the curve of my neck and my pulse kicks up a beat at the primal hunger in his eyes. I grit my teeth, knowing I'm not going to get answers unless I push for it. Standing, I push my hands into the cargo's pockets, my hip popped to the side.

"Well, you two sure as shit aren't going to give them to me, so I'm going back to the Hattery. With or without you. Although, if I step out of this room – you can both kiss goodbye to your prophecies," I shrug. Emotional blackmail at its finest. Neither twin moves, calling my bluff.

Fuck. I have no bluff.

I don't have the faintest clue where I am, since Cash glitter portalled me back to his club, or how to navigate this world. How many more zombie toes must I suck before I put my bravado aside and admit I need help? Sixty-nine million I reckon, so I'd better get to it. Striding for the door, Tweed stands to block my way.

"Ask me where he is, and I'll give you the honest answer," Tweed dares me. Everything in his tone says I don't want to know, and he's right. Since the moment that hat dropped into my lap, I've had a niggling worry about what I'll find at the end of this fragmented rainbow. There's only so much thread I can pull before the sweater runs out and all that's left is the undeniable truth.

But I refuse to contemplate it. The Hatter can't be dead. There's no way that's a reality, fantastical or otherwise, I will be a part of. So instead of humoring Tweed's request, I grab a handful of his hair and drag his head aside.

"Backing me into a corner is never a good idea. You don't want to see me desperate," I warn. Nudging the rest of him aside, I stride for the door when another hand grabs for my wrist. A gentler touch from the twin I didn't see move.

"This way, Malice," Cash smiles, leading me away from his apartment. My mind was fully made up for a dramatic solo exit, but his hand shifts south to interlink with mine and I'm a goner. After all, I'm still a warm-blooded woman beneath all of this hair and bravado. For one moment, it might just be nice to hang up my survival instincts and be taken care of.

Leading me down the winding staircase into his strip club, footsteps ring out of the steps behind. At no point does Tweed allow more than a few feet to separate us, remaining close as I'm directed towards the hallways labeled 'Fantasy Walk.' The motion-sensored lights blink on as we pass underneath, illuminating the crocodile skin wallpaper. Nothing has moved since the last time I was here, not even the delectable cakes on delicate plates upon each table.

Cash stops abruptly, facing the wall where there is no door and I frown until my eyes lower. Of course. It's a miniature door in the shape of a hat, practically a mirror image of the one inside my cleavage. Winding an arm of cashmere around my shoulders, Cash produces a tiny bottle of yellow liquid from his pocket, a 'drink me' tag hanging from the neck. I go to take it and he jerks it back from my reach.

"Favors require payment. What are you going to give me for safe passage?"

"I don't have any money on me," I shrug under the weight of his arm. A melodic, husky laugh sounds beside my ear.

"So forgetful," Cash muses. Tugging the cork out of the bottle with his fangs, he nudges my head back and holds the bottle just above my mouth. "Lust is the currency in Wonderlust. Especially in my club." The liquid is tipped between my lips, the smoothness of a banana milkshake swirling around my tongue as those same fangs pierce my neck. I gasp, a spike of desire shooting through me.

I vaguely registered a grumble shout in the background before another pair of fangs sink into the other side of my neck and I'm gone. Stars dance behind my vision with each suck, pulling on an invisible chord to my pussy. My panties soak in an instant. Pins and needles race across the inside of my thighs, my core twisting. The button of my cargo pants is popped, two hands nudging inside my panties. A fight for control happens but I don't care for it, lashing my hands out to grab both of their erections through their jeans.

"Someone better enter me or I'll rip both of your dicks off," I growl through the powerful sucks on my throat. Between them, they'd better leave twin hickeys or we're doing this shit again. Who am I kidding – this is going to be an hourly occurrence. Fingers thrust into my wet cunt and fuck me; I think it's from both of them. I'm stretched wide, four fingers stroking me in unison. A palm pushes against my clit, giving me the exact pressure I need.

Without breaking their connections with my neck, my blood is drawn out in long, even pulls. Each one edges me closer to the most explosive climax I've ever experienced, my head dropping back on Cash's arm with a wash of dizziness. Whoever is pressed against my clit curled their digits inside of me, holding onto my g-spot while the other fucks me with his fingers. Thrusting hard enough for the sound of my slickness to be heard over my heavy pants, I detonate.

Screaming, my pussy clamps down just as my entire body begins to tingle. The air rushes past my ears, forcing Stan to abandon ship. Shooting towards the floor, I ride out my orgasm on the Tweedles hands, panting for more. They've awakened a fetish I didn't know I had, and it's only when their teeth withdraw from my bruised skin, I blink my eyes open to see the hat-shaped door before us.

"Holy shit," I groan at the hands retracting from my panties. Cash keeps his arm around me, which I'm grateful for. Leaning against him, Tweed pushes his fingers into his mouth and cleans them with slow, languid licks. Just like that, I'm ready to go again but a gigantic sugar glider sniffs at my chaotic hair.

Turning in Cash's hold, I spot the dropped bottle of yellow liquid. Lifting a hand to stroke Stan's pink nose, I lead my best bud over to it and encourage him to drink from the spill I could probably swim in. Without need of blood being drained or a climax, I hope, Stan shrinks to the size of a crumb and scurries up my body to dive back into the safety of my blonde hair.

"Let's get this over with," Tweed grumbles, opening the hat door and waltzing in as if we didn't just have a little freak feast in the hallway. Cash hangs back to answer the question in my brows with his cheeky grin.

"Shrinking potions don't work on us." Holding out his arm for mine, we enter the room that's a combination of a library and a castle. "Our metabolisms are too lethal, so I needed to take it directly from the source. Didn't count on a hitchhiker though," he glares at Tweed's back.

"I go where she goes," Tweed barks harshly, firing a hate-filled gaze at his brother.

"And the orgasm?" I interject. "Was that part of the process too?" No answer comes so I'll take that as a Tweedle special. Pulling a cupcake from the deep pocket of his tweed jacket, Tweed hands it to me. I lick the frosting suggestively and the tension in his shoulders lessens just a fraction. Trying to fight a smile, he whips the cake back to signal that's enough and I wiggle my fingers, shooting back to full size.

I presume the Tweedles don't need my blood to re-grow, but just then, a pair of tiny piranhas attack my ankles. Rejoining my sides, I swipe a small amount of frosting from the cupcake in Tweed's hand and push it behind my ear for Stan.

"At least my clothes stayed on this time," I chuckle when both Tweedles groan regretfully. Tweed strides away while Cash steps into my body, his hand snaking up my vest.

"We've made a few advancements since you were last here," Cash tugs on the tag at my side and the material tightens snugly around my middle. I gasp in delight. When I get the chance, I'm installing a resizing label into every piece of clothing I own. Or will own when I manage to get my hands on some.

Cash strides away, leaving me to face the inside of the Hattery. Observation one, it's a shithole and two, where are all the hats?

Beyond the crooked windows, water still puddles in the crevices of the cobbled street from the tsunami Stan created. Thick clouds coat the sky, casting the interior in shadow but I dare not power up the lanterns dotted around the room.

"Hatter!" I whisper shout, walking directly into a spider web. Stumbling back, I trip over a stack of boxes and land hard on my ass. The shop is a mess, even by the Hatter's standards. Ribbon and reams of fabric thrown everywhere, hanging from the railing of a second level. The stairs are lost amongst towering boxes, Damp tingles my nose, drawing a sneeze from me and Stan in unison. The Tweedles have abandoned me amongst the shelves stretching high so I drag myself up and navigate the material maze alone.

Ducking beneath a length of lace, I shuffle forward, reaching around for stability. Dust coats my fingers from the shelves, the boxes wrinkled from lack of use. Wrapping my hand around the base of a railing, I trip up the first step of the staircase and then continue onward. No noise sounds beyond the low whistle of wind through a cracked window above, yet the distinctive tingle of being observed raises the hair on the back of my neck.

The twins are somewhere, watching my every move to see what I do. Curious to see what I uncover. Breaching the top level, I decide I'm safe to twist the nozzle of a lantern and light the rest of my way. It's tidier up here, as in I can actually step forward without falling onto my shins. Bookcases line the walls, a desk of papers and scribbled notes displayed before me. The chair has been tossed over the railing, shattered on the floor below.

Skating my fingers over the notes, Stan's nose wriggles against my ear. Dropping onto my shoulder, he clambers down my arm to glide across the desk and land in an ink well. His little feet scurry over the pages, marking the words with splotches of ink. I bat him away, grabbing the sheets that appear to be diary entries torn free from a notepad. Dates mark each page that I roll into a wad and stuff into my pocket for later. Grabbing Stan, I shove him back behind my ear before he can mark any of the photographs concealed underneath.

Large blue eyes glare out from the image, a mass of blonde hair filling the frame. A sheet of plastic clutched in the girl's hands displays my birth name, prison number and the date of my initial arrest. I lift it, trying not to shake at the sight of my hollow eyes and chewed bottom lip. Blood is splattered across my porcelain cheeks, an orange jumpsuit clinging to my shoulders when the pajamas I entered the station in were taken as evidence. Certain memories I was happy to suppress, so why is this here?

Beyond that, my eyes skim the desk and cork backboard in more detail this time. Newspaper articles litter the surfaces, screaming the headlines my sister wrote.

Crazy Carroll's Kid Spins Another Story.

'Wonderland' woes for Author's Delusional Daughter.

Locals call for Alice to enter Asylum.

Breaking News: Crazed Kid turned Killer. Lewis Carroll Stabbed by Psycho Offspring.

That last one is my favorite. A brown envelope holds my police statement, the words of a nineteen-year-old murderer staring back at me. From the court's findings, jury's verdict and all corresponding paperwork, my entire life is summed up in this wad of paper. More curiously, it seems the Hatter has been trying to make sense of it all in a mixture of scribbles, post-it notes and highlighters. Tucking the file into my pants, I pull my vest over the top and move to leave when a flash of red catches my eye. Lifting a newspaper on the backboard, a message has been written in what I hope isn't blood, for the Hatter's sake. The small flies feeding from it though, prove it is.

Believe and you'll receive.

Frowning, a shuffle catches my ear to the left. I twist my head, hunting for movement in the shadows. A figure ducks aside just as the bookcase shifts, slotting back into the wall. Running towards it, I try to pry it back out of the wall with no avail. Pulling out books in quick succession, I throw them over my shoulder. I know what I saw. There must be a secret hatch somewhere.

A brass statue of a rabbit stands beside the shelves, a pocket watch clutched in his paw. Rolling my eyes, I tug on the floppy, brass ear, which turns out to be a lever. The bookcase pops free of the wall behind. Peeling it open, I duck into the hidden room without thinking twice. The bookcase closes behind me, locking me inside a circular space. Like that of a turret, lit by a large chandelier a few meters above my head.

"Malice!" a Tweedle shouts from the other side of the bookcase. I hear him tugging the shelves in an effort to free the lock, but I pay it no mind. Before me, a series of paintings hang from the round wall at uneven angles. The scenes are all baron, devoid of life and displaying a different scene. A farmyard around Cook's and Mary Ann's cottage, the forest upon the hill, a large nest made of feathers, a lengthy table set for tea and more I don't recognize yet.

The frame holding a painting of a maze entrance judders, knocking against the wall. Lifting the edge, I peer at the wall behind. Except there's no wall there at all. A spiral swirls, just big enough for a large rodent to wriggle through. Or a slender woman who's passed on puddings for the past twenty years for this exact reason. Couldn't be too big to fit down the rabbit hole when the opportunity arose.

With the image of the maze entrance on the other side, I spy a hare in a blue waistcoat and glasses. His brown fur is tufty, evident by the way he scratches his arm with indecision. Peering back through the portal at me, he flinches and hops into the maze, with me right on his tail.

"Malice, wait!" a shout sounds behind me as I launch myself into the portal. Fingers skim my ankle but they're not quick enough. Hurtling onto the hard ground, I barely wait long enough for the pain to shoot from my knees to hips.

Scrambling upright, I dart past two sentinel statues of playing cards holding their spears in an X above the entrance, diamonds decorating their fronts. The tip of a white tail disappears from view so I race inside, intent on catching that hare. No thought process on what I'm doing or why, only that it feels right. The Hatter is missing, after apparently stalking me, and Hare is my best shot at finding him. Damn all other consequences.

CHAPTER 16

TWEED - TWO YEARS AFTER ALICE'S DISAPPEARANCE

"*A*gain!" *the Red Queen's whip slices across my back. This time, the strangled cry doesn't escape my mouth and she praises me, flicking the propeller atop my hat with the crop in her other hand. Quite the sadist, and that's without mentioning what she does with the heads she cuts off. Things a ten-year-old shouldn't know, but my innocence is far behind me now.*

Rocks cut into the knees of my sweatpants; the uneven path cold beneath my overheated palms. Blood trails through my torn t-shirt and down my shoulders, webbing my shaky arms like veins. Blinking sweat from my eyes; I peer up at the entrance to Diamond Maze. A brass statue stands either side, the face of a playing card staring down at me. When I don't immediately follow the Queen's order, they shift, pointing their sharpened spears in my face.

"You heard her, Dumb-ass," the King of Diamonds kicks my ribs. "Go again." My body falls to the side and this time, I can't hold back my whimper. A brass spear jerks my head upwards, a trail of blood spilling from the fresh cut beneath my chin. Between the dirt, sweat and blood, I doubt I'm recognizable from my twin, but the King knows. He continues to mock me with my name and laugh when I peer up at him with tear-filled eyes.

"Looks like you picked the wrong champion," he chuckles, turning to the Red Queen. She glowers at me, her forearm resting over her baby bump. I know that look. I see it in my nightmares, whenever sleep eventually comes for me.

Dragging myself up on wobbly legs, ignoring the burn of exhaustion, I push myself into a jog. Past the card statues who have resumed their posts, into the depths of the maze that chews you up and spits you out if you don't find the center in time. A buzzer rings out, although mostly lost to the rumbles of thunder overhead. Rain patters onto my flaming skin. Chewing the inside of my cheek to focus my pain away from my legs, I turn a corner and disappear from the view of those watching on.

At first, it started as a joke. See the fat boys run. Watch them waddle, tumble and struggle to get back up. Then came the royal wager, and that changed everything. The sneakers on my feet skid on the tiny rocks in my path, the laces so frayed, they won't hold their knot. Grabbing a tall hedge of leaves to get my balance, it shrugs me off and groans. I shrink back, not wanting to be expelled already. Not wanting the Queen to lash me all the way back to the dungeon cell I now call home.

The maze may be ruthless, but at least there's light. The air is fresh enough to burn my lungs. It's unknown how long I'll be locked away before my next trial, and my new motto is I'll rest when I'm dead. These days, that final breath can't come fast enough, but I'm not living for me.

"Dee!" I shout, hoping to sweet hell my brother's lack of appearance means he's made it to the center. Slipping through a gap in the hedges, I sneak my way onwards, retracing my steps. This time, I know not to take the next left and find myself at a dead end. Dead ends mean game over here, and as the maze's difficulty level increases, eventually game over won't be an ejection. It'll be an execution.

Turning right, walls of green block me in. I blink, shrinking back but the maze shifts, closing me inside a leafy cage. I gasp, my heart beating in my throat. This isn't...this wasn't... A hand the shape and size of mine shoots through the branches, fingers outstretched. I grab the clammy palm, feeling the soft tug of Dee's weak pull. Diving through the hedge, I collapse to the ground as the sound of walls snapping shut echoes behind me.

"Dee," I clamber up his body. My limbs are shaking, not just from exertion now. The maze tricked me. Tried to kill me. I'm not surprised but I am scared. We've entered a new phase of test, most likely upped by the King of Diamonds in his rush to prove himself right. He doesn't believe my brother and I can be trained into soldiers, and he's probably right.

Green eyes stare back at me, Dee's crimsoned cheeks puffing in and out. Helicopter hat upon his head, his slender body movements mimic mine, our hands still clasped. Two years of starving and regular beatings makes for a fantastic weight loss routine, though not one we would have opted for.

"That was a close one," he mumbles. I shake my head.

"Contrariwise. If it were close, I'd be scrambled egg." Movement shoots from the side, a vine shooting between our faces. Near enough to nick me with thorns when retracting, Dee's face falls to horror. Without warning, I tug him to fall into step, running at my side. There's no use being cautious if the maze is set on torturing us. We can only delay the fact.

Turning one way and another, round and back, we race as speedily as our legs will carry us. Branches lash out, trying to knock us down. We duck and jump in unison, a pair of synced spirits seeking an unreachable final line. Over my shoulder, the vines have taken chase, thundering along the ground like snakes. Dee releases my hand to grab the back of my neck and heaves me aside. I lose my footing, slamming onto my side.

"Dum," Dee groans, on his back, still holding me down. I spy with my weary eye, three thick branches, studded with diamond thorns, have whipped out. There was no way over or through them, the glint of stone promising a swift death. Swallowing thickly, I follow Dee shuffling beneath the hedge's limbs. He prefers to remain on his back while I army crawl to freedom, hopping up on the other side. The chasing vines halt, not continuing beyond the barricade. I exhale loudly.

"Shall we?" I hold my arm out for my twin's. Dee winds his inside, jutting his chin upwards when I do. Mirroring each other, step for step, we continue on. Two unsensible boys in a battle we can't win.

So much has happened since Alice left, not that we think about her. Tweedle pact. She was here, until she wasn't. Those are the facts. Dee and I thought we'd unknowingly entered a game of hide and seek, looking for her for weeks. We lost. The Red Queen scooped us up in Tulgey Wood, declaring us her prisoners. Great fun, as you'd imagine, telling stories and playing charades in a cell. Dee and I were best at entertaining ourselves. Until the torture started.

A sharp slap cracks across my cheek, one I couldn't anticipate. "You're thinking of her again," Dee frowns at me. Rubbing my face, I nod and we continue on in silence. No use lying. We share the same thoughts, and then it's my turn to frown.

"As were you!" Twisting to bat hands with Dee, keeping our closest ones interlinked, a growl sounds on the other side of the wall before us. We freeze. An exit sits to our left, but from stupidity and curiosity, we stand and wait for the danger to present itself. A worm the size of a dragon shoots through the hedge, mouth wide and missing me by inches.

Despite the large glasses over his lack of eyes and fancy necktie, he swiftly turns and snaps his toothless mouth. His lips slap together, catching the back of Dee's t-shirt. I yank him free, dragging him behind me as I run. Dee isn't as fast as me, but through sheer will, I force him to keep up. The worm slams from wall to wall, blindly rushing close behind. Contrary to his lack of senses, his blood-instinct is on point.

Fumbling from one alley to the next, the pathways beneath our sneakers shift and change. From reddish and rocky to white and slippery, we stumble into unfamiliar territory and my heart hammers for another reason. I've not entered this part of the maze before. The blunt head of the worm skims my back, its body crashing aside as we twist around a sharp corner. Dee rushes to run past and I grab the back of his t-shirt.

"Hold up," I grit, tugging him back a step. Damp asphalt assaults my nose, the grainy texture before our feet bubbling. Quicksand. Trying to retrace our steps, the worm is there, hanging tall over us. For a creature without lungs, his body heaves as if he is breathing, inhaling our scent without use of a nose. Gripping the material at Dee's chest, I hold him still. He tries to jerk against me, making a run for it but I keep us steady. Silence weighs heavily on my weak shoulders, a tremble working through my limbs.

The worm thrusts forward. Shoving my twin aside, I jump into the closest hedge, parting like a banana peel. My stomach growls, intensifying the ache that lives there as I tumble to the ground. The worm dives through the center, *his diamond print tie flapping in the wind as he lands in the quicksand. It takes hold almost instantly, clawing around the slimy body fighting to be free. Staring on, a judder rolls through the worm and too quickly to track, a mouth appears at its butt end and clamps down on Dee's leg.*

He screams. I scramble. Grabbing his arms, I tug him backwards, filling the air with more shouts of pain. Toothless or not, the worm has a vice-like grip. It jerks, twisting Dee's leg at an unnatural angle. The color drains from his face. I panic and my grip slips. Dee is torn from me, tossed aside into the quicksand and the worm shudders again. White asphalt has clawed around his body, dragging him under. Spitting, the wobbling surface settles where the worm so recently was, bubbling occasionally. I stutter, crawling backwards.

"Dum, go," Dee cries desperately, tears spilling from his eyes. He's a few feet away, my fingers just short of reaching him if I stretch. The rush of blood fills my ears. Shaking my head, I push myself to stand. "Go already! You must win."

Win? There is no winning without him by my side. But the sand is moving quickly, Dee's frail body sinking. Biting my bottom lip, I drag off the stupid helicopter hat they force us to wear and toss it aside. Then, I turn on my heel and run.

"Really?!" Dee yells. "You're actually going to leave me here?!" Retracing my steps on swift feet, I only make one wrong turn to the wall of diamond studs. Vines wind through the gaps, slithering and snapping as I near. Not wasting time, I grab the longest and wrap it around my wrist. Then I tug. It tries to pull me forward, to impale myself on the sharpened stones. Bracing my feet on the wall of branches in between them, I yank with all the might I have left until it snaps. I hit the ground hard but there's no time for pain.

Returning to Dee with the cut vine still flailing wildly, I gasp to see his body almost completely sunk. His nose and mouth, one hand and two feet are all that remain. Whipping the vine towards him, it rears back and punches me in the face. I try again, kicking it straight with my shoe and toss it in Dee's direction. Detecting the foot on his broken leg, the vine settles long enough to wind around his ankle. I heave, a scream drawn from Dee's exposed mouth. Guilt slices through me, but it's dragging his broken leg to safety or say goodbye forever. It's a no brainer.

Dragging the vine over my shoulder, I force my legs to move. Each bellow is another blow to my ears, my eyes burning with tears I won't let fall. Finally, the feel of his body meeting solid land has me dragging the vine free of his ankle and I toss it into the quicksand. Dee rushes to scrape the sand from his eyes, curling on his side. My hands hover uselessly over his leg, twisted at the knee.

A caw comes from above, the shadow of a giant raven dropping onto the maze's hedge. I steel myself for another challenge. Not having time for pleasantries, I grab Dee's thigh and shin, I snap the joint back into the position they should sit in, really hoping I haven't done more damage. No bones broke free of his skin, so there's that. The sounds that come from Dee, however, drown out the raven's croaks. Taking Dee's arms, I link them around my neck and pull him onto my back. My own legs threaten to buckle, my body quivering. Skidding a foot forward, I continue on.

He'd have done the same for me.

The raven hangs close but makes no move to attack. Unless it's peaking at Dee's back without my knowledge. His screams are continuous and at one point, I've resigned to becoming deaf.

It doesn't matter anyway. These trials are continuous. What we don't lose, break or suffer in one, the next will be sure to catch up. The nobility of this realm lost their plaything when Alice disappeared, and they soon found a new hobby. Placing bets on the suffering of those they captured, creating games we weren't meant to survive. But Dee and I survived, and then came the arguments.

It was decided at a high council meeting, where Dee and I were chained by the neck and forced to watch, only one suit could own each of us. Claim us as their property. Declare us as their Champion to train up and force us to prove our worth. Royal boredom at its finest.

For some unknown reason, the Red Queen wanted me. Without reservation, she made her declaration quickly and loudly. I was to belong to the Hearts or die by them. Dee's fate is yet to be decided, but if I'm strong enough, or if I'm just enough in general, maybe it won't matter. The other suits will decide there's no use pitching us against each other, and she'll let him stay at red castle. It's a frivolous idea, but currently, it's all I have. A silly dream and my twin.

My legs grow shakier, Dee becoming heavier. At some point, my knees bent and I'm now crouched, navigating the maze on deadened feet. I can't do it anymore. I can't save him. Wetness touches my cheek and I violently wipe it away on my shoulder. There was a time when tears didn't exist. The notion of sadness, despair, and guilt – none of it existed. And best of all, no matter where we went on our endless journeys through Wonderland, the danger never occurred to us. We weren't phased by death, only seeking the next joke and riding from one babbled laughter to the next. Now...I can't even remember what laughing feels like.

Turning one last corner, I fall. My shins hit the ground; Dee's arms locked around my neck taking me with him as we topple sideways. The rain falls harder, dousing us in misery as we lay, exhausted and in pain. Defeat eases into my limbs and once it's settled, I don't think I could move if I wanted to.

"Bravo!" The rain stops instantly, or rather a large umbrella has covered my face, acting like a shield. Blinking upwards, the Red Queen stands proud, her chest puffed out further than her baby bump. At her back, the center of the maze presents itself. I did it. I made it. "It'll be a warm bath and hot dinner for you tonight," the Queen beams down, an evil glint to her dark eyes. With

each challenge I pass, I sense her interest in me growing. She's preparing me for something and I'm not going to like it.

Dee groans, barely conscious now. I twist to see the umbrella doesn't cover him, the rain soaking his hair into a dark shade of blonde. Scooping my brother into my arms, I hold him close.

"Save your bath and food, Dee needs medical attention." My brother whimpers in my hold, his head on my chest. I squeeze tighter, a new sense of dread raising within. He's too pale, flittering in and out of consciousness. I'm not wise but even I know his symptoms are concerning.

"You'd trade your prizes for him?" she sneers. I don't understand where the belief came from that Dee's life is any more or less valuable than mine. We're the same person in spirit and mind. I peer up into the Queen's eyes and nod without hesitation. She tuts and whips away the umbrella.

"Had you shown a hint of ruthlessness, I would have granted your wish. However, your feeble mind will cost you both." She strides towards a swirling portal with a chamber of hearts on the other side, sparing me one last look. "You will learn. There isn't room in this world for weakness."

Disappearing into the portal, the image shifts to that of a dungeon. The only home I've known for two years, and as the portal begins to grow smaller, I force my legs to move. Dee lays limply, jostling in my bony arms. The more his head bounces around, the more worried I become.

Diving through the portal just as it's about to close, I crash to a stone floor, never once losing my hold. We may reside in our own corner of hell, but I refuse to stop fighting for my brother. The one who I'd thought could charm his way through life before his confidence broke. Before the nobility shattered it to pieces and for some strange reason, decided I was worth their attention.

"B-bitch," Dee curses and I smile. A stupid boyish smile at hearing his brother curse for the first time.

"*Total fucking bitch,*" *I nod in agreement. A laugh bubbles from his lips, his eyes still closed and body too still. I join, our chuckles drifting through the darkness as our bond warms with the love we share. It's clear no one wants Dee, but I sure do.*

CHAPTER 17

MAL

My lungs burn, my feet sore inside the high-top sneakers. Years of yoga in my own leisure time at Charmsfield has not prepared me for exercise like this. My poor, subtle feet protest with each step until I drop down beside a wall of leaves. Just like all the others closing in around me, just like the ones I've been staring at until night fell. I could be running in a square for all I know, no sign of the blasted Hare who dragged me in here.

Okay, maybe he didn't force me into a maze I might not be able to escape, but he sure as shit didn't hang around to say "hey, don't come in here. You're not built for hours without food and no one to annoy."

Removing the file stuffed into the front of my cargos, I slump back. What the hell have you been up to Hatter? A firefly flitters past and I gasp, whipping my hand out to catch it. Bopping him on the nose, a stream of light blares from his ass like a torch. Opening the file, Stan reappears, sniffling at the shell of my ear. I hold the file away from him since he seems intent on destroying any evidence I have, but it's not the papers that hold his attention this time. It's the fly in my hand. Trying to read through the Hatter's notes, Stan shoots out of the confines of my hair.

"Piss off Stan! I'm trying to read here!" I jerk the firefly away from his tiny jaws. Landing on my thigh, the sugar glider I've befriended digs his claws into my leg, launching himself at my hand again. I twist the fly's light towards his face, hoping to blind his retinas but it's useless. Stan nearly takes my finger off whilst ripping the fly from my grip and gobbles it down. Plunged back into darkness, I throw the file into the air.

"What's the fucking point anymore?!" I scream and then slap two hands over my mouth. Oh god no. That question was far too logical. My stomach growls, cutting through my thoughts. That's it – I'm just hungry. Stan's stomach glows with the fly safely inside, faintly shining a path to nothingness. There are exactly zero options of dinner down either side of the endless alleyways. Taking the scrunched newspapers from my pocket, I stack them together.

"It's a cheeseburger. Just a scrummy cheeseburger dripping in burger and cheese," I tell myself. Squeezing my eyes shut and stretching my mouth wide, the newspaper stack graces my tongue and...fucking hell. It's actually a cheeseburger.

Grabbing Stan, I run his glowing belly over the wad in my hand, squinting through the fading glow. Sesame seeds splatter a golden bun, onions and lettuce poking out the sides of a greasy, cheese topped burger. Not questioning it, I stuff the whole lot in my mouth before it turns back to paper. Groaning, I swallow hard and a moment later, a hiccup of indigestion bubbles from me. Pushing a palm into the center of my chest, I whistle for Stan to resume his position behind my ear – I need to hunt down a cup of tea if it kills me.

Two mirrored half moons hang above the maze's leafy walls, orange in color. The prophecy about twin blood moon's trickles back into my scope of memory lane. All nonsense and poppycock, I presume. Nothing in Wonderlust has presented any danger to me before, I doubt it'll start now.

"How about a song Stan?" I ask my accomplice; certain I need his tiny nod. Hiccupping again as the heart burn twists in my chest, I clear my throat.

There once was a man called Michael Finnegan,
Who likes to stroke his sister's shinnegan
He went to jail and she snuck in again,
Naughty, incestual Finnegans, let's sing again!

"Come on Buddy," I shake my head side to side, "it's better as a duet! Therrrrrrrrrrre once was a man-"

"Oh, do shut up!" a voice shouts and I halt. The glow of the moons illuminates the shadow that steps out from the grass wall. Half my height, scruffy in a blue waistcoat. It's the March Hare himself, from a fidgety button nose to jittery, floppy ears. His brown eyes hold a hint of nervousness, his whole get up giving me serious anxiety vibes. I smile in relief, then realize he just insulted my singing.

"Rude," I hiccup. "I may be a tad off tune but - oooh tea!" I spot a cup in his hand. Snatching it, I take a gulp and then spit it out in an even spray, all over his twitchy face. "Yuck! What the fuck is that?!"

"Iced tea,"

"I...iced tea?" I blink several times, severely offended he let me drink that shit. Okay, it's decided. Screw setting up a bus stop retreat; I'm going to have to open a café and show Wonderlust what a decent tea is supposed to taste like. Being plied with caffeine and only accepting lust as currency, I'm going to be one stimulated, satisfied slut-butt.

"Hey!" Hare clicks his tiny, hairy fingers in my face. "There's no time for inner monologues." Pulling out a cracked pocket watch with a gleam of crimson splatter beneath the glass, he taps it with an overgrown nail. "Reality is coming."

"Then there's only one thing to do," I nod seriously, wrapping a hand around his ear. Turning, I run for my fucking life. Hare's feet drag along the ground, his body bobbing up and down in the wind I create. "We can't let reality take us alive!" Twisting down alleyway after alleyway, the moons follow my trail.

"No, you nitwit! I didn't mean-" Hare shouts until I pull to a swift stop. A post stands tall before us, the signs pointing in all directions displaying 'This Way' - 'That Way' - 'Underway' - 'You're Doomed' and all the usual. Hanging from the lowest sign, labeled 'Certain Death' a turned wooden handle hangs from a cord like an old-fashioned toilet. Yay, I do like an antique flush. Yanking on it, Hare tries to tug himself free of my tight grip on his ear without success.

"Wait, no, don't!" he cries out as the ground begins to shift. The dirt swirls into a whirlpool, covering my sneakers and pulling me along with it. Twirling in circles, the bottom gives out and we freefall into the earth. Landing on my back, I begin to slide south inside a tilted tunnel. Rings of rainbow lights flash when we skid underneath, the addition of a water jet fastening our descent. Planting Hare on my lap, I throw my arms above my head and enjoy the ride.

"Weeeeee!" Swishing through the tunnel, it curves and winds a path all the way down until we're spat out of the end into a dank cave. Flame torches light the walls, the rumble of a roar echoing from somewhere in the distance. Chains rattle, the walls vibrate. Worse than that, Hare hops up and slaps his paw around my face. People have died for less.

"What the hell were you thinking?! I intended to lead you to the maze's center but now we're trapped in the Bandersnatch's lair with no way out," he rants and raves. Tossing the broken pocket watch into the ground, he taps his elongated foot irritably on the ground.

"Perhaps next time, you really should say something before we start running for our lives," I shrug, moving out of the mini waterfall spewing out of the tunnel and onto my back. Brushing myself off, I start walking. "Come on, no use sitting around for death to find us. We must find it first." I shove an index finger high in the air, counting left and right with each stomp of my corresponding foot. The distinctive hop of Hare bounces behind and I smile. I knew he'd see it my way.

"The Hatter was wrong about you."

"Is that so?" I cock my head, intrigued by Hare's flustered ranting.

"He believed you got what you liked, but I see the truth now. You just like what you get, which means all hope is lost. All lost, no hope. You couldn't save a blind man from a piss-up in a brewery, never mind saving

Wonderlust from itself," he continues to grunt, his nose all twitchy and claws scratching out large tufts of fur.

However, I tuned him out after the word 'believed'. What was it Hatter wrote on the backboard of his desk? *Believe and you'll receive.* A crazy idea comes to mind and I tend to agree, they are quite the best kind.

Walking with long purposeful strides, the roar of the Bandersnatch grows louder. I imagine the walls of the extended cave turning to foliage, the brightening light ahead emanating from the sun. Warmth prickles my skin as my theory begins to work so I slow to allow the March Hare to hop by my side.

"I get the feeling you don't care for me so much," I muse aloud. Don't ask me what it is about his furrowed, thick brows and snarl to his two protruding teeth that gives me the impression, but I pride myself on my intuition. Usually.

"You're damn straight," Hare grunts. He tugs the waistcoat down, more blood splatter trickling around the collar.

"Hmmmm." I flop my head side to side, sifting the strands of my thoughts together into a web so they might start to make sense. "Yet you knew I'd follow you into the maze. By your own admission, to lead me to the center, but not to the Hatter after all. So...this was to be a trap," my eyes widen in excitement.

Partly because I've activated my inner Sherlock Holmes and deduced what's-on my mind. I burst into a laugh that ends in an ugly snort, cracking myself up. What's-on, Watson, you get it. But returning to the moment, my anticipation is palpable. I do love a good trap. Hare freezes, falling behind my strides. "Well, it's a good thing we're in the center of the maze then, isn't it?"

The next step I take is on a dirt path, the cave disappearing in favor of a floral archway. At the top, a metallic flourishing holds a diamond in the middle. Just like the main entrance, two playing card statues reaching over ten feet stand either side, their spears lowered to create an X over the entrance. I duck underneath, stepping into the morning sun. We weren't underground for more than ten minutes, yet the night has broken and passed without a trace, both moons missing from the sky. Hare follows.

As it so happens, the center of the maze is also home to Diamond Castle. A vast creation of marble and metal. Columns holding up the main entrance are carved into chess pieces, a King and a Queen. Other pieces can be seen amongst the design, turrets that replica rooks, windows in the shapes of knights. The main section of the building is one giant bishop, its rounded point stretching high towards the gray clouds seeping in. Statues of pawns line the walkway towards the front door, but I don't need to go that far. To my right, on the manicured lawn and in plain sight of the morning sun, a guillotine stands tall and proud. The sharpness of its blade winks at me and I can't suppress my laughter.

"What were you going to do? Follow me with the hopes I tripped and fell headfirst into the shackles," I point at the wooden stocks before me, another fit of laughter rumbling through me.

"No," Hare grunts. "I was going to do this." I twist my head back in time to see him launch high in the air, slamming his furry feet into my back. I stumble forward, just catching the edge of the stocks and shove myself away. Diving across the ground, Hare comes for me again. I roll onto my back, my arms raised to catch Hare's chubby cheeks around his vicious pointed teeth. Gnashing wildly, froth foams at his mouth.

"Ew, Hare. You really should look at the mouthwash you're using," I grunt out, shoving him aside. Rolling over him, my hands close around his neck just as a thin rod slides beneath mine. I'm torn away, gripping the metal that starts to choke me. Tugged against a hard body, the other playing card statue waltzes into view, rearing back his spear to stab me with it. I scrunch my eyes closed.

"The spears are made of liquorice," I croak out. Sucking in a breath, I brace myself. "It's just liquorish." The rod at my throat falls limp, the other lashing me with the effectiveness of a wet noodle. Grinning, I drop to a squat and use my fists to side-hop like a chimpanzee. My head twists to the side, my eyes widen while that Cheshire grin pulls so hard, it hurts my cheek. Half of winning the battle is psyching out your opponent.

"How-how did you do that?" Hare shuffles back on his tail. Crossing the mini courtyard and scooping up the golden lace, I stand slow, flicking it back into a solid rod. The diamond spear at the end gleams in the sunlight, practically winking at me as I raise it over my shoulder.

"What, this?" I bat my eyelids, not bothering to hide my smugness as I mentally tell myself the playing cards are made of paper. The brass of their body's ripples, fizzling away to reveal the flimsy sheets underneath. Panicking, they run into the center of the confined space, trying to hide behind each other's backs while I close one eye to aim. Picking my moment carefully, I throw the spear like a javelin, impaling them both to the wooden beam of the guillotine in one hit.

Hare tries to make a run for it, diving into the grass wall. I lunge forward, snatching him by the tail. Carrying him at an arm's length when he tries to gnash his jaws my way, I drop the oversized rodent into the stocks and knock the top half closed over his neck and paws. Perfect fit.

"N-n-n-no, d-don't do this! I-I can help you!"

"You sealed your own fate by attacking me, my furry friend." Rounding the side of the guillotine, I note the thick rope coiled around a brass diamond holder on the opposite side to where I speared the playing cards.

"It's not what you think! The queen, she is out for your head!" he babbles. I roll my eyes, untying the rope holding up the blade until Hare's fate rests solely in my hand. Feels lighter than I anticipated. "When you left Wonderland, you took the crazy. It's been seeping from the land. Only your death can secure our future," he rabbits on. I yawn.

This heavy, foretelling shit is growing old real fast. If all that's required of me is to die, why would the Tweedles have been sent to 'retrieve' me? And why would the Hatter deliver a message to find him. Surely his tiny felt hat would have provided a razor blade and his mystical feathers could have instructed me to slit my wrists. Job done. Not all this hoopla.

"If it's crazy you need," I lower to Hare's eye level, holding the rope taut around my hand. "All you had to do is say so." Opening my fingers, the rope unravels, unleashing the blade in quick succession. It slices through Hare's neck as smoothly as butter, blood spraying me from hair to chest. I quickly grab his ears before his head makes it to the ground, holding it up in front of me.

"I do have to thank you, March Hare. It becomes so easy to forget who one is in light of who others prefer them to be. I'd almost forgotten what gave me my name." Pushing two fingers through the crimson dripping down my cheeks, I draw in a set of military lines on either side. I'm Malice. Daughter of asshole and owner of vengeance.

Tossing the head away, I stand to look over my handy work. Not bad, if I do say so myself. Pacing around the stocks and kicking the remaining body, I notice a slip of paper poking out of Hare's waistcoat. Fishing it out, along with the pocket watch, the sheet unfolds, revealing a letter that was intended from the White Rabbit. Makes sense, since I deduced in the tunnel that Hare was wearing my tardy friend's clothing.

Hatter,

It won't be long now.

Rumors are spreading the caterpillar has called for Alice's return.

You can't trust those aligned to you when destiny comes to call. If you need a place to hide, come to the Enchanted Wood.

You know where to find me. Be careful out there.

W. Rabbit.

Turns out this trip wasn't for nothing after all. I got to get my murder on and found a clue. That's the equivalent of winning in my book. Now I just need to get back on the right track. Bracing myself on a wide stance, I flex my fingers out and wriggle them.

"There is definitely a Tweedle Dick in my hand," I say aloud as my fist clamps shut around a meaty sausage. A resulting Tweed cries out as I give him a tight squeeze and yank hard for good measure.

"What the hell?!" Tweed roars, not making a move to withdraw his hardening cock from my grip. "Where the fuck are my clothes?!" His abs flex, his thighs tight with muscles and I lick my lips. Fuck, how have I been around him for three days and have only just seen him naked? New record.

Black ink trails his right arm, fingers to shoulder and down his right side. Every inch of skin is covered with roses, but the closer I look, the more I notice skulls webbed through the design with a rogue snake in the grass, slithering across his bicep. On the adjacent hip, a stopwatch on a thin chain hangs, the second hand ticking backwards. And that just leaves the only pop of color – a red heart directly over his heart.

I have no reason for the jealousy that tingles within, so I pay it no mind. I'll let it fester under the surface until I meet the queen Tweed has pledged his loyalty to, and then unleash the envy in whichever way I see fit. Tweed's dick jolts in my hand, reminding me of my manners.

"Want some?" I scoop two fingers through the blood coating my chest and offer it out to Tweed. His nose wrinkles and he fights a gag.

"Ugh fuck no. I can only consume human blood. Care to explain how I came to be...here?" Tweed looks around for the first time, noting the guillotine, dead playing cards held up by a spear, pool of blood and headless Hare's body by his feet. "Oh no, Malice. What have you done?"

"Defended myself via decapitation as any self-respecting woman would," I wink, tugging on his dick for good measure. Or hell, just because I felt like it. "Enough small talk Big Balls - take me to the Enchanted Wood."

CHAPTER 18

MAL

"Fascinating," Cash lowers onto his hunches to stare quizzically at me. I pay him no attention, my back against a tree trunk whilst chewing on my fingers. I told myself they were southern-fried chicken sticks and have found myself a new hobby. No matter how many I eat, they just reappear. Brings a whole new meaning to finger-licking good, but I had to do something to preoccupy my time.

Without cell phones, it took ages for the pigeon-carrier to reach the Hattery and tell Cash to get his ass over here. I wrote the note myself, specifying 'Change of plan, heading to the Enchanted Wood. Hurry the fuck up or I'm fucking Tweed,' and damn if I was joking.

Since he forced me to believe some clothes onto his fine, muscular frame, I haven't been able to get the image out of my head. Double that by two Tweedles and I'm ready to get me some action. I need the twirling smile to return and ask me at what cost, so I can smack that bitch down and tell her I don't care for her wisdom. I'm aroused, adventurous and ready to take what I want.

But what you want is an answer to the Hatter's location, the smile appears right on cue, over Cash's left shoulder. He doesn't seem to notice, raising my hand to inspect the steamy chicken closer. I narrow my eyes into slits at the smile and re-imagine my fingers back to their natural state. Fine, I'll find *one clue* – then I'm getting my sexy on.

Pulling myself upright, I turn to face the wood. Trees curve in an arch over the entrance, a canopy of leaves hindering the light from here on out. Not that there seems to be a reprieve from the storm clouds lingering overhead. Shooting out my hands, I beckon for a Tweedle to take either side with the full intent of skipping down the checkerboard path splayed out before us.

Tweed has the shoes for it, a sturdy pair of unlaced biker boots that his leather trousers easily slip into. On his upper half, a jacket covers a white vest that hangs loosely, the thin straps reaching low to grace his nipples. He told me to dress him, but he didn't say how – and I'm not done tracing the linework of his tattoos with my eyes, fingers or tongue yet.

Cash is still in his usual pinstripe, transparent purple vest, braces and electric blue jeans that I enjoy seeing how much of an erection he can get before cutting off all blood supply, so I'll leave him be for now. Speaking of which, do Vampires even have a blood supply?

Bracing myself to break into said skip, movement zips from between the trunks and rushes forward. A little book on feet skids to a halt, barring our entrance. Bursting open his pages, a map of the wood is helpfully displayed, a red dot marking 'you are here.' Bending low, I admire the crisp whiteness to his page, as if this is the first time one has needed to gaze upon his illustrations.

The wood is in the shape of a cat's head and labeled with the fluid cursive I used to have my knuckles lashed for not being able to do. Apparently, we are about to enter the jewel forest on the cat's left cheek. In the ear to the west, a waterfall trickles into fairy hollow, connected by the lazy river to a mysterious plume of blue smoke in the opposite, bottom corner.

A darkened area seeps from the cat's chin, marked as Death Valley and I make a mental note to absolutely pass through there. The best way to live life is to start at the end and work backwards. The rest of the map is hard to read as the letters keep rearranging, a cloud of gray smoke shifting back and forth through the center.

"Why thank you," I give his pages a stroke. He shudders, groans, then tears himself into a million tiny pieces and floats away in a rapid gust of wind. Typical. No one tends to stay around me for long, except good old Stan and let's face it, I've glider-napped him. This time when I step forward, my foot lands on the uneven ground and I power onwards.

Cash keeps up with my side, Tweed straggles along behind. He really didn't need to come, but then his words ring in my mind to go where I go. His loss. I hum a tune to myself, swaying one foot in front of the other. No destination in mind, I'll just go where the wind takes me.

"Why don't you just believe the Hatter is here and be done with it?" Cash queries at my side and I snort a laugh.

"I don't tend to elect for the easy option. Quick fixes make for a boring narrative." Jerking forward the curtain of my hair, I don't let him see the frustration in my features. Of course, believing Hatter is here with me would be ideal, and that's exactly what I've been trying to do this entire time. Trust me, chicken fingers wasn't my first thought, although it was a close second.

The checkered path winds towards a wall of trees and disappears into the ground. I slow, allowing both twins to catch up before delving deeper between the trunks. Given my last experience in a forest, I'm not in a rush to be sucking any appendages that aren't vein-covered and throbbing. Branches hang low, twisting and turning like a timber laser field.

"You can go first Tweed," I nod my head in the branch's direction. He obeys, hopping onto the first with ease while I smirk at the sight of his ass. He suits leather. Following close behind, the three of us navigate the wood without a destination in sight.

I clamber over and shimmy under until my calves burn. The incline deepens, presenting a hill that we never seem to peak. Who knows how much time passes and at this point, I'm wondering if we've covered any ground at all or remained in the same spot. Nothing but branches as far as the eye can see in all directions.

Neither Tweedle is yet to speak, though that's not to say their expressions don't have plenty to say. Tweed has closed down, the impassive calm of a trained soldier slammed over his features. Cash is pissed, his careful smirk a distant memory. The further we go, the more agitated he seems, his gaze continuingly looking over his shoulder to see exactly where Tweed is at all times. His brother's presence vexes him, that much is clear. We need to do something about that.

"Let's play a game," I announce. "It's called Selfish. If you say 'I' you have to take a forfeit."

"What kind of game is that?" Tweed grumbles, though he nears with the pique of interest.

"The best kind," I shrug, "just made it up." Dodging a patch of toadstools, the unsupportive sneaker rolls aside and I crash into Cash's chest. His fingers linger on my arms, prickling my skin with coolness as he stands me upright, his grin beginning to regrow.

"Tweed used to have night terrors and call out your name."

"I did not!" Tweed shouts and I see the spark of green twinkle in Cash's eye.

"Forfeit!" I shout, pointing my finger gun his way. A hint of color pinches Tweed's hollow cheeks, his mask of indifference slipping for the unadulterated rage at his twin to filter through. Now we're getting somewhere. "You have to tell Cash you love him."

"Fuck no," Tweed growls, turning his back on me. Ducking behind the branches in a flash of movement, I have to run to catch up.

"Then you will have to take a double forfeit. You have to give your dear brother a kiss – you may choose where but if it's below the waistline, give me warning to be seated."

"I wouldn't touch that asshole if my life depended on it," he mutters back, not realizing his mistake. Intent on pushing back a branch of hanging fruits and slapping Cash in the face with it, I round Tweed's front and cross my arms.

"Triple forfeit!" Cash and I both say while Tweed tells us to go fuck ourselves. He doesn't move this time though, remaining still to stare at my tits in the black vest. Running a tongue over his fangs, I smirk and tingle in all the right places. He's hungry. "Very well, Cash wins the game and gets to take me to his Queen then," I challenge him, ignoring the niggling voice that hated referring to any queen as 'his.' I do not wish to have a claim over these vampires when I struggle to dress myself in the mornings, but my chest doesn't get the memo.

"Fine! Fine. Fuck!" Tweed twists and throws his fist into the nearest trunk. A rounded piece of fruit falls from above and I catch it. The size of a mango, teal in color and my stomach rumbles. Tweed eases it from my hands with surprising gentleness, holding the fruit in one, large palm. "I...luff you Cash," he grinds out without parting his lips.

"Come again, I didn't quite hear that," I hold a hand around the shell of my ear and Tweed's eyes lighten on mine.

"Forfeit," he says, his tone low and my heart drops. Fuck, I lost at my own game. The rules were so simple too.

"Well played," I slap my hands against my thighs in the cargos. "Choose what you want me to do." Indecision tears across his beautiful face, stretching parts I don't think have been used in a long time. Tendrils of luminescent green trickle into his irises, his index finger raising to be pushed into his elongated fang. Orange blood puddles at the point of impact, which he then orders out in my direction.

"Trust me," he rasps, a hidden message behind those two simple words. Cash tries to butt in, saying something about needing to move, but I hold up a hand. I lost the game; I have to take the forfeit. End of.

Extending my tongue, I hold it there and let Tweed come the rest of the way. Sliding the tip of his finger over my tongue, I act quick, snapping my lips closed and sucking him in further. I've never been one to pass up an opportunity. His eyes ignite now, glowing emerald orbs that captivate me and cause the rest of the forest to fall away.

Pulling his finger back with a small pop, his body moves automatically, stepping into my space. I'm forced to tilt my head upwards to hold his gaze. My tongue darts out to lick my bottom lip, every movement carefully tracked. I shiver, ready for him to take what he so clearly wants.

"Do it," I dare him on a bated whisper. Not one to be seen chasing a man, or vampire in this case, I flutter my eyelids closed and wait. Leaving myself vulnerable to his lips, his fangs, his...everything. I shiver again, his cool fingers interlinking with mine. A breath tickles my ear, the only heated part of him glazing over my neck. The softness of his lips brushes my ear, my nipples hardening. Every part of me is alive, thrumming with anticipation and preparing to be feasted on.

"No." One word. That's all I get. Flashing my eyes open, he moves back with a trace of a smirk at the corner of his full lips. He's toying with me. Teasing me, and I don't care for it. Flashing out a hand, I wrap Tweed's loose vest in my fist and tug him back towards me. Cash clears his throat when I'm about to angrily tongue-fuck his twin, refusing to be denied.

"If you're quite finished, I was trying to tell you, we need to move," Cash growls. Sparing him an aggravated look, I stutter. An eye, larger than Cash's six foot, blinks behind him. Slitted down the center and yellow from corner to corner, I barely make out the rest of its face before it begins to move. The ground beneath our feet shifts, lifting high into the air. I grab onto Tweed for stability, the rush of air flying through my hair almost dismantling Stan.

The interlinking branches crack, breaking into dust as the creature shakes his gigantic body. Turquoise scales shimmer underneath, reflected through the rounded fruits wobbling on the remaining trees. These ones have thicker trunks and create a straight line down the back of its arched body. Either side, a wing unfurls and my stomach drops.

It's a fucking dragon.

A puff of smoke curls around us, a pair of nostrils flaring an inch from my feet. Dropping down on the snout, I spy the two rows of razor-sharp, pointed teeth.

"What the hell happened? Does it want a piece of me too?!" I start plastering kisses along the scales still partly coated in dirt, and that just seems to piss it off more.

"That jackass knocked down her baby," Cash shouts between a rumbling roar stemming from the dragon's throat, pointing at his twin. The teal fruit is still clutched in Tweed's hand, a crack forming around the outside. Placing it down in the curve between the huge yellow eyes, I just about make out the small head of a baby dragon breaking free of the fruit-egg before Tweed tackles me off the edge.

Cash dives just after, his hands outstretched for me. I reach back for some unknown reason, not wholly comfortable with Tweed's shoulder rammed into my gut and hurtling me to my death. Our fingers brush as Tweed lands on his feet, his arms wrapped around my middle to set me down on uneven ground. Diamonds and jewels glimmer in a ditch the size of a football field. Evidently, the same one the dragon was laying on. Cash lands a second later, the power of the thud mimicking Tweed's.

Crack.

Every jewel in a fifty-yard radius shatters, sinking us further into the ditch of swallowed screams. This angers the dragon more. A roar pierces the air just before a stream of fire blasts between where the twins and I have fallen. It's no accident we've been divided, I just hope Tweed and Cash resist from killing each other before I manage to save my own ass.

Scrambling on my hands and knees, gems slip out from beneath me, making my ascent to the edge of the ditch slow. Fireballs rain down, the heat blasting into me from all directions. Sweat drips down my cleavage, my cheeks puff out. Closing my hand around a protruding branch embedded into the dirt's edge, I drag myself up onto solid land.

Devoid of trees, I spot the entrance to the wood beyond the webbed, turquoise feet in the way and it somehow all makes sense. We haven't traveled far, but rather, trekked over. A shadow hops on the edge of my vision, but when I look, it's gone. Cash plows into me, sweeping me away on swift feet.

"Wait! I need to go back," I start but my words are lost to the wind. Tweed is at our side, giving me a nod to trust him. And damn myself, I do. The dragon groans, filling the sky with a rumble just before it begins to sway. Tilting this way, then that, we're covered in shadow and this time, I don't hold back my scream. Dipping my head into Cash's shoulder, I hold onto his shoulders until a thud rockets through the earth and we're thrown aside into a layer of grass.

Flat on my back and panting, the clouded sky above sparks with a glint of lightning. Now devoid of trees to act as cover, I'm left laying like a starfish wondering what'll come next. A lightning bolt to the chest or just a simple heart attack. Neither apparently, but a blasted snore at my side that has us barreling over several times into a Tweedle sandwich.

"Dragons are quick to waste their energy," Cash tells me, stroking the hair back from my face. "They can only remain awake for short periods of time." The beast shuffles back into the ditch now a short distance away from the black grass we're nestled in. With a giant flap of its wings, the dragon kicks up enough dirt to fill the air and settle over its scales, effectively camouflaging it from view.

"Good to know," I mutter to myself, already taking in my new surroundings. Some might call my lack of attention span ADHD. I call it being a nosey bitch.

Pushing up on my hands, the black blades tickle my fingers, a trail of blood red roses leading towards a portal in the distance. A rectangle, framed by intricate iron gates I can't make out in clear detail, which opens into another universe. A sea of stars rests against swirling crimson and merlot, coaxing me closer. Black smoke plumes from the doorway and I'm already running when an arm snatches around my waist.

"Nope, not yet," Tweed growls, dragging me away. I fight and claw at his forearm, trying to throw my head back to connect with his nose.

"I wanna see! What is it?!" I beg of Cash who takes Tweed's side.

"The entrance to Hell," he eyes me seriously and I still my struggling. Tweed relaxes his hold, making the mistake of setting me down. Elbowing him in the balls and kneeing Cash in his, I'm running alongside the roses with a string of cackling trailing behind me. Sorry boys, but now I *have* to see.

CHAPTER 19

MAL

B ound by the twisted twigs locking my wrists behind my back, I jostle on Tweed's shoulder. My throat is raw from screaming every obscenity I could think of, then a few made-up ones. Tweedle McCunty Twat Tickler, and the likes. When that didn't work, I turned to singing a made-up song to the tune of 'It's a small world.'

It's a world of douchebags, it's a world of dicks,

It's a world of assholes so just take your pick,
It's more than looks that they share that it's time we're aware
They're the same cunt after all.
They're the same cu-

Tossed to the hard ground, pain trickles through my shoulder. Not as bad as it should have been, and I can only think of Tweed's blood being responsible. It's about time he did something that worked in my favor, and yes – I'm still pissed about that rejected kiss. Cursing, I roll across the concrete until my back meets a pillar. Scraping the twigs against the stone, I free my damn self and glare at the twins. They ignore me, tearing down sticks and clawing at the moss clinging to a small building.

The windows have been bordered with wooden planks; the doorway covered in a network of vines. With the sunlight peering through, I can make out a single desk and random assortment of seats, from dining chairs to beanbags.

Outside the building, I sit beneath a rickety canopy preparing to collapse on me. A sign postered beside a broken bench signals the left as the 'Right Way' and other as the 'Un-Right Way.' A wonky yellow stripe painted along the edge of the concrete beneath my butt lines the platform, leading my gaze to an abandoned train further down a set of overgrown tracks.

"Where are we?" I breathe, pushing myself upright. Thick foliage coats the steel exterior, spots of bubblegum welding the metal sheets together. That train isn't holding anyone, despite the row of seats visible through the open windscreen and is barely the size of a van. I don't get an answer, but rather Tweed drops off the platform and onto the tracks.

"I'll get her some dinner, before she takes a chunk out of me," he grumbles. My eyes narrow dangerously.

"You know, I'm starting to think you really don't want to fuck me." His eyes burst into a glow, spearing me with a heat that is at odds with the rigidness to his stance.

"Oh, trust me, I want to. I just can't," Tweed replies and strides away into the tree line. His leather attire glints in the spears of sunlight through the leaves, reminding me I gave him those clothes. I could just as easily take them away.

"Well why the hell not?!" I shout into the wood instead. Cash chuckles, tearing a branch of poppies from the hut's entrance and tosses it inside.

"His queen won't allow it." Holding out his hand for mine, he guides me inside. The second my feet cross the threshold, a downfall of rain drops so suddenly, I flinch into Cash's arm. His chest rumbles with a chuckle, and I peel myself away. Damn me for being so eager to have their touch. Water pounds against the tin roof, leaking in various places.

"And why is some overprotective queen pussy-blocking me?" I shout over the deafening noise, dropping into a beanbag. It's damp but I'm comfortable now. The walls have been left as brick, except for one that has had every color of paint splashed on in a haphazard fashion. Cash drops between my knees, pushing my thighs wide and my breathing hitches.

"Why worry about him? I have no such reservations," he smiles devilishly. Everything inside of me clenches and suddenly, it's not just the beanbag that's damp. Shuffling closer, his body leans along the length of mine, Cash's hands teasing a cold path along my arms. I shiver, my nipples puckering behind the cotton vest

Fuck it.

Grabbing Cash's braces, I drag him the rest of the way to slam his lips onto mine. Cash doesn't deny me simple pleasures or force me to question my appeal. He embraces my crazy, sinking his hands into my wild hair and causes Stan to abandon ship. Scraping my scalp, my moans are lost to the ringing of downpour on metal. His lips claim mine in fiery, short bursts, unable to get enough yet he doesn't go any further. Not even when my legs wrap around his waist, his erection pressing into my center.

Don't do it, a voice sounds in the back of my head and I swallow thickly. A heavy invisible weight sprawls across my shoulders, the glint of teeth catching my eye. I don't know if I can stop myself now, my hips grinding on their own accord. And since when did I let my subconscious control me?

A bang sounds through the symphony of sound. The weight on my shoulders disappears and a millisecond later, Cash's slumps into me. I spy Tweed with my little eye, striding across the shack with a gun in one hand and a dead rat in the other. Shoving his boot into his twin, he dislodges Cash and sends him rolling across the ground. Only then do I see the hole in his neck, gunky orange liquid spewing slowing from the wound. I check myself for remnants, then furrow my brows.

"Hey!" I stand, shoving a finger into Tweed's hard chest. "I'm not eating rat meat. Isn't there any chicken around here?!"

"There are only two chickens in Wonderlust. Sam and Ella. They own the tadpole farm in the Club district. Do you have a taste for reptile eggs, or just my brother?" His eyes alight with a challenge, jealousy painted all over his sharp features. All the while, I'm shuddering just at the thought of eating egg ever again. Chicken, frog or otherwise.

"You can't have it both ways, Tweed. Loosen the fuck up or stand aside. I won't be told who I can and can't fuck." My own brows hitch at that rapey statement, but I've said it now. I can't be considered a liar so if he wakes to me jumping on his morning wood, so be it. He doesn't seem to catch onto my meaning, or he's silently giving me consent when he looks back to the open doorway.

"The rain will stop in twenty-three minutes, exactly one hour and four seconds before another storm hits. Our next safe stop is the tumtum tree and I'm not prepared to listen to your stomach rumble the entire way."

Right on cue, my tummy groans and I cross my arms over it. Damn, I never thought I'd miss Charmsfield, but regimented meals were a huge plus. Tweed snaps off the legs of a dining chair to start making a fire anyway, leaving me to stomp around to his front.

"Fine. I'll eat, if you hand feed it to me." I high-five myself. Well done at taking back control of the situation Malice. Tweed attends to skinning the rat, while Cash groans across the hut. Forcing himself onto his back, he clamps a hand over the hole in his neck and gasps in deep breaths.

"Bastard," he snarls, pulling himself into a seated position. I wave, welcoming him back to the present and a riddle, then sink cross-legged. Cash shimmies over, the mention of a riddle piquing his interest too. Tweed sets the rat, now skinned and skewered over the fire, turning his gaze on me and I straighten my spine. Two pairs of hungry green eyes I'd rather see between my thighs.

"I'll sweeten the deal and throw in some DP," I nod, sealing the deal.

"Dr Pepper?" Cash cocks his head. Oh, that does sound good. I'll believe some up in the aftermath of my seventh orgasm.

"No, you square. Double penetration, on my end – not yours. But there's a catch."

"Naturally," Tweed grumbles, twisting the skewer.

"If you want to make me wetter than an oyster, you need to solve my riddle. First one to get it right goes down on me first. Ready?" Both nod, fully invested now. Clearing my throat, the rain dims to a dribble in anticipation of my next words. "How much wood could a good fuck chug, if a good fuck could chug wood?"

Silence follows.

"Um, I don't know – nine inches?" Tweed guesses. I believe a baguette into my hand and bop him on the head with it.

"Wrong."

"Two feet?" Cash tries.

"Wrong." *Bop.*

"An oak tree? An entire cabin? A carpenter's workshop full?" they try in turns, *Bop, bop, bop.*

"There is no solution," a feminine voice trails down from above. "Riddles don't have answers, only logic does."

"Ding, ding, ding. We have a winner," I point my baguette in the direction of the curved smile, twirling around the sky to settle on my shoulder. Tweed's face immediately darkens, a growl torn from his lips. The flick of a fluffy tail curls around my neck, brown and cream stripes of a feline seeping into existence. Large teal eyes fade into the hollowed head last, winking up at me as I gaze upon my sporadic companion for the first time. "Hmmm, maybe it could be considered cannibalism for a pussy to eat out another, but you won and them's the rules."

"Considering the company you keep, I'll pass," she purrs, rolling onto her back. "His queen is responsible for the loss of my kind," she lazily waves her paw towards the twins without specifying which one. Tweed snatches the baguette, ripping it down the center with his bare hands to dump the barbequed rat inside. Bon appetit.

"Come Malice, we have much to reminisce about," the cat whispers, floating into the sky. I shrug, more intrigued by Tweed trying to still me with a warning hand. Yeah right, as if I've ever been one to do as I'm told. Following the pretty pussy, I figure it has been twenty-three minutes as the rain suddenly stops and we're permitted entry outside. Pools of water drain from the shabby train carriage, pouring down the sloped tracks we turn away from. Fresh earth perfumes the air, the rain churning fresh soil and varnishing the wood in a layer of gloss.

Eating as I walk; I track the cat drifting into the tree line. Every so often, she looks back to check I'm still here, along with the two shadows looming over each of my shoulders. Two rows of sharply pointed teeth slot together, her smile wide and permanent. Whereas her head and tail are thick with fur, I now note that the body in between is hairless. Like a sphinx in pale brown with cream lines – not stripes as I first thought – but twisted markings that avoid each other like tribal tattoos. The paws, though, are huge. Triple the size I'd expect with deadly extended claws.

"I hate that fucking cat," Tweed snarls so close, I can't hide my flinch. His breath skates over my neck, my pulse thrumming in excitement. Surely, it's almost their dinner time too. Leading us past a field of mushrooms, ranging from the heights of the tree trunks to the piddly tiny excuses for fungi, we venture towards the sound of trickling water. The sky rumbles, pre-empting that storm Tweed warned me about. A black cloud sails overhead, below the canopy and zipping around with unusual speed. Just like the cloud on the map, which was shaped like a cat's head...

"Are these your woods by any chance?" I muse, tossing the rest of my baguette aside when I feel a carb stitch coming on. A daisy shoots out of the ground, blooming in size to snap its petals like a Venus flytrap and gobble it up, before retracting to miniature again. The cat circles its tail a few times, floating backwards to reply.

"Once home to all felines. Alas, I'm the only one left." Slinking over a stream that flows in slow-motion, Cash scoops me up and leaps across, setting me down at the mouth of a cave.

"So, you're a Cheshire, I suppose." I had only met the one, and foolishly presume just like that Jabbercocky – that's all there was. Slipping into the cave, purring echoes around the walls, drawing me further inside.

"My provided name is Chelsey Cat, but you once called me by another," she says. The words bounce around, her body faded from view so I can't tell where they are coming from. Fingers slip into both of my hands simultaneously, the Tweedles preferring to keep me close.

"I'm fairly certain I'd remember meeting you," I call back. My sneakers tilt on the rocky ground, my vision going blind. The vampires can see though, bringing me to a swift halt as the smile reappears in front of my face.

"Meet, not so much. Abandon would prove more accurate," she grins. The lock is unbolted, a doorway in the darkness swinging open for a burst of light to bleed out. Feathers. White feathers, everywhere. A disco ball of artificial light glimmers across the poultry graveyard, giving me insight as to why there are no chickens left either.

Chelsey Cat dips, sprawling across the features and stretching out her back. She twists bell-up, scratching her furry head against the softness. Peering up at me from this angle, a memory filters through my empty skull and I gasp.

"Dinah?! I thought...I thought you ran away," I breathe, releasing the twins to skid into the feathers on my knees. A heap of bones and blood splatter hides in the corner of the cavern, a giant litter tray in the other. Free of shit and piled high with sand, the roll patterns suggest she's had a jolly old time playing in there above anything else. Chelsey grins, a malicious twinkle in her teal eyes.

"Not ran away – ran after. I followed you down the rabbit hole," she purrs as I scratch her tummy. "Lost my way, found my kind," she shrugs her boney shoulders like she isn't affected by being trapped here all this time. But I can see the truth. I mean...look at her. Her deranged smile, her ever-glinting eyes. A body that's more bone than meat.

Shifting against my knees, the fur of her large head and fluffy tail leaves brown hairs on my cargos, whilst the skin of her torso is smooth and soft to touch. My heart slows as realization settles in. She's not my Dinah anymore, not by a long shot, and the housemaid I stabbed with a steak knife for losing my beloved cat was, in fact, innocent.

"What happened to you?" I whisper, tracing the tribal lines with my finger and pointedly ignoring those who lurk by the doorway. Especially when Tweed tries to order me into leaving - 'or else.' Chelsey shuffles upward, dropping into my lap on her back.

"I'm on my ninth life you see, a stripe for every time. But this loyal pet will set you free, with her last life on the line." I smirk, her lyrical sense appealing to my better nature. She slots into my lap the same way she slots straight back into my life. As if she never left, and I'm starting to wonder if she really did.

"Was it all doom and gloom last time, or was I just too naïve to notice?" I mutter, half to Chelsey and mostly to myself. Stroking the soft patch of her belly back and forth, I become lost to the movements. Falling under my own trance as misery knocks at the fringes of my mind. Sorry pal, no one's home. "I don't suppose you know where the Hatter is?" I sigh, already knowing her answer will be another dead end.

"I've spent the best part of twenty years in this cavern, curled up to focus my energy on astral projecting to you. Anytime I leave, I'm reminded of exactly why I shouldn't." I knew it. Chelsey wasn't a voice in my mind. A figment of my imagination I created to not feel alone. She was always there.

"You never left me," I stroke the length of her fluffy ear. The black slits in her teal eyes regard me like twin lasers and that's when I nod sharply. "And I won't leave you either. You're coming with us." Scooping her up, her huge front paws push at my collar bone and just when I think I'm about to be ripped to shreds, Chelsey leans into me. The rumble of her purr resonates inside my chest, her face nuzzling my neck as I return to an amused Cash and pissed off Tweed.

"No fucking way," Tweed tries and I barge past him. Cash extends an arm, trying to stroke the kitty as I go. Chelsey hisses at him over my shoulder, the fur of her tail standing on end like an electric shock has zipped through her body.

"No need to be like that, Chels," Cash chuckles. I slow to let him catch up, intrigued by his admission. "You were fond of me once." Her hissing increases, her obvious hatred hindering the use of her jaw.

"I was on my first life and stupid. I've learnt," she grits through closed teeth. I chuckle, stroking her back into submission. Chelsey snuggles into me, lulled into a soft sleep despite one of her eyes remaining open, watching the Tweedles every move through her dreamy state.

Breaching the cave, the darkness of night is falling incredibly fast. A rumble of thunder overhead fails to mask the crackled roar of a beast amongst the gray cloud that batters around between the trees like a ping pong ball. My footsteps still. You know what, on second thoughts, perhaps waiting in the cavern of feathery fluff is best.

CHAPTER 20

CASH - TEN YEARS AFTER ALICE'S DISAPPEARANCE

"*H*urry, *brother!" I shout, running barefoot through the manicured gardens. Wiping the jam tart crumbs from the corner of my mouth, I whoop loudly, uncaring of the fish-faced chef cursing me from the back door. Diving behind a hedge shaped as a heart, I grab Dum's ankle as he races by. He trips, kicks out at my hand and then ducks into my hidey-hole too.*

"*She'll be looking for us," he grumbles and I nudge his shoulder.*

"Find your sense of fun, for fuck's sake, Dum. Or else we might completely lose sense of who we are." Producing the last of the tarts from my pocket, I blow off the fluff and offer it to him. His green eyes narrow and he pushes it back in my direction. Such a prude for the rules. I have no such qualms myself, shoving the tart into my face and grinning around the mouthful. My twin continually looks behind the hedge, checking for the pompous queen who no doubt won't be far behind. She never is where he is concerned. Fascination turned obsession; I've decided.

Movement glides across the lawn, a beige and brown feline losing its fur with each leisured step. Yawning wide, she strolls on, a trail of mice following like the pied piper leading them to their certain deaths. Upon seeing our hidden, hunched figures, her back rises and she hisses violently. Tweed juts out his foot, ordering the Cheshire to 'move the fuck on'.

I don't know what he has against the cat we found once in the Enchanted Wood. Maybe she reminds him too much of the Alice, considering that's all she would mewl for at first. I brought her home, gave her some milk, and she attacked me in my sleep as a thank you. Swings and roundabouts.

A rustle sounds from above, the faintest moment of the leaves before a shadow descends. Quicker than my eyes can track, Dum has shifted. Shooting to his feet, a tiny lithe figure falls into the trap of his arms. He throws her to the ground, whipping a blade from his boot and presses it to her neck.

"Sloppy, to say the least. Do better," he growls, shoving the small girl aside. Arabelle rolls to her front, pushing up to her knees with a fitting scowl for an eight-year-old spoiled brat. Personally, I'd been rather impressed with her stealthy attack, but for Dum, she's never good enough. There's a deep psychological issue there I won't bother delving into.

"Give the girl a day off," I use his shoulder to push myself upright. "It is her birthday, after all."

"Soldiers don't get birthdays, and they certainly don't have days off."
Raising to stand beside me, Dum stares down at the expectant eyes peering
up at him with such desperation. The day Dum compliments her, I reckon
she might just explode. I hope I get to see it.

"Well then," I bow low. "Happy un-birthday, Princess." Offering out my
hand, she accepts and returns to her full four and a half feet height. Aside
from the ponytail of vibrant red curls bursting free of a ski mask, she's donned
in full black. Leggings cling to her lower half, a tight long sleeve top in the
same spandex material covering her wrist to her chin. Much like a gymnast
would wear if performing a ninja routine. Because that's all this is – a
choreographed routine for her to gain attention. "Now go change before your
mother beheads you."

"She's too distracted to care for my outfit," Arabelle smirks, her attention
oddly on me for a touch too long. "You should report to the ballroom. There's
quite the display being erected in your honor." I frown, the expression not
sitting right on my face. Releasing Arabelle's hand, I wipe my palms down
the length of my sweatpants to be rid of her cooties. Can never be too careful
and I'm positive becoming royalty is a fatal condition I don't want to catch.

"Hmmm, so the queen is using her sprog as a messenger now," I grunt to
cover my piqued curiosity. I'm accustomed to Dum being summoned, or plain
abducted from his bed in the cupboard-sized room we share, but me? I've
become part of the furniture. Forgotten, ignored, and that's just how I like
it.

Retracing my steps, I enter through the rear of the main lobby. Dum is
right behind, his swift steps catching the back of my sneakers. Still threadbare
and torn, I haven't earned the right to tailored combat training like my
brother. I slow right down, forcing him to bump me along with his chest before
stepping around me altogether. I link my arm to him, putting us in step with
each other the way we used to be.

"Hey now, no need to be jealous. Whatever they want me for will be fleeting, and then it's back to you being the star prodigy," I bob my eyebrows. Dum bristles.

"I'm nothing to no one," he grumbles and I let the lie slide. The entire Kingdom of Hearts knows of Dum, whether they praise or hate him for taking up so much of the Queen's time. She didn't even show up to her own jubilee celebration, preferring to follow Dum through the Enchanted Wood with a whip – not in the kinky way either. I've taken my fair share of lashes, and the more I receive, the more insolent I become. Foreplay doesn't tickle my fancy. I prefer to get straight to the fuckery. In this sense, which involves screwing with the Queen's plans before screwing her maids in waiting.

Coming to a halt outside the ballroom, we can hear voices through the closed doorway. There's plenty of them, all bubbling with excitement. I pick out the King of Diamonds, the stuck-up asshole ranting about not having enough ice in his drink before a glass shatters. So quick to shout, yet the one time I snuck up behind and held a rolling pin to his neck, he could only squeak. Dum squares his shoulders, huffs and pushes the door open. Silence falls, a sea of eyes swinging to the two men standing arm-in-arm at the doorway.

"Ahh there you are!" The Queen puts on a smile for the crowd, but her dark eyes are simmering with barely contained rage. Ushering us inside, a pack of lizards rush by with a ladder braced across their shoulders and tool kits in hand. A stage has been built in the center of the ballroom dance floor, giving a 360 view from the armchairs placed around the outside. Butts fill them all, from Royals to the high council and any other who holds a pointless title. The Duke of Baked Goods twists to grin at me, his full-bodied mustache twitching with full-on creep vibes.

Gripping my wrist, the Queen of Hearts tugs me into the room and my sixth sense prickles. The one that tells me to run. Drawn to the stage, shining like a spill of ink against the marble of the dancefloor, a glint of metal catches the dual chandeliers. A pole of solid chrome, from the stage to the ceiling. I halt, pulling back against the hold on my wrist. Nope, I don't like this.

"Come now," the Queen grits out, desperate to keep her smile in place. "We've finally found a use for you. Every Queen needs a Jester, does she not?" I swallow, shaking my head. Dum steps between us as she plucks a riding crop from her belt and lifts it high, sensing his Queen's unstable mood better than I can.

"We've barely just become men," Dum tries to reason with her. The heart-shaped crop comes down with a sharp snap. Dum doesn't even flinch.

"Eighteen is plenty of years to grow up, and I've waited long enough. Time to earn his keep or I'll consider selling him to the King of Diamonds." My eyes slide to the stout man, more gray hair than sense, sneering at me. Jerking forward with my fists curled, a high-pitched scream penetrates the air and he shrinks back into his seat. I chuckle to myself. Being twin to the Champion of Hearts sure has its perks. Taking the crop from the Queen's hand before she has a chance to stop him, Dum turns long enough to slap me across the face with a warning to 'behave.' Gently placing the leather instrument back into his Queen's hand, his back flexes on a deep exhale.

"You have no need for the money. You are, however, indebted to me for my service." Dum tilts his chin upwards, despite having a fair few inches on the woman before him. The silent room stills further, those watching not daring to breathe.

"Is that so?" the Queen asks mockingly. She'll be of the disposition that we are indebted to her for molding us into men we wouldn't have been otherwise – and for good reason. But Dum doesn't back down.

"More than so," he holds her stare. I slink back a step, towards the shadows where I'm comfortable. Unseen, unnoticed. All heads are turned towards the power play happening by the stage, except for one. Golden eyes hunt me through the darkness, a spill of jet-black hair falling over delicate shoulders.

A dress of gold hugs her frame in the furthest armchair, buckled tight in the waist. Netting along the low bust gives me enough hint at her full breasts, her fingers sitting delicately against her cheek. 'Who is that?' I think to myself.

She watches me, a spark of interest I'm unused to pulling me a step towards her. Scorns have become second nature, even by the maids in waiting I gag and fuck from behind as to not see their disgust. It doesn't matter that I have Dum's face, I'm not him, and no one will let me forget it. But maybe...

"Very well," the Red Queen inclines her head. My attention is redirected with the gasps echoing around the room. Dum held his ground, and the Queen before him has relented. A momentous feat, yet a small smirk plays about her painted lips. "Dee stays. But I won't have him running about this castle, stealing snacks and bringing havoc. There's enough of that around as it is," she drops her voice to mutter. "What with the death of my dear husband causing the realm to question my sole leadership skills, I don't need Dee causing trouble beneath my nose as well."

"But it is such a fanciful nose," I raise my finger to pitch in. Dum tosses a glare over his shoulder and I can hear his thoughts telling me to shut the fuck up.

"Is it time, your majesty?" a viscountess stands, a bundle of material wrapped in her hands. The Queen nods.

"You've proved yourself a fine warrior, Dum. Against all odds," she glowers across the crowd of nobles, "you've become a citizen worth keeping alive. The lessons you are providing Arabelle will prove our Kingdom is the strongest for at least another generation. My legacy is only as strong as my kin, and I'm entrusting you to make her the best. Do you accept this challenge? It is possibly the toughest yet?"

"I have no other reason to live," Dum kneels before his Queen. My heart sinks. Where she heard acceptance, I heard the words of a young boy that never stood a chance. It was kill or be killed, and Dum saved my life more

times than I can count. All at a cost to his soul. He's a soldier alright, a mindless drone for the Queen to toy with. Clicking her fingers for the viscountess to bring forward the bundle, the Queen flicks it open to reveal a jacket. Draping it across his shoulders, she orders Dum to stand.

"You've outgrown your name and the mockery it has brought you. From this day forth, you shall be known as Tweed, my prized Tweedle and Knave of Hearts to Arabelle upon her coronation."

Slipping his arms into the tweed jacket, I saw the image of my brother melt away. Charcoal gray dons his muscled frame, fitting from the high collar to the cuffs at his wrists. A red heart stamped into the back brands him as property to the Red Kingdom, for better or for worse. The material hugs his thighs, chunky heart buttons gleaming as he swishes it back to push his hands into his pockets. Too comfortable in his position, too at ease with the stench of bullshit in this room. I imagine he's numb to it by now.

Holding out her hand, the Queen waits for 'Tweed' to accept and leads him towards a pair of empty armchairs facing the pole in the center of the room. Becoming distracted by the knighting of a damn jacket, I'd forgotten why I was summoned here. My heart clenches as my brother turns to face me, his expression hidden behind a stoic mask. The blood in my veins runs cold.

No. I'm not doing anything for these shitheads. Especially feeding their insatiable appetites with the death of my soul. Sensing my hesitation, Tweed crosses the ballroom to where I'd almost made it out of the door.

"You have to give something, Dee. After everything I've done to keep us together, this is your weight to bear." He grips the back of my neck and forces my face into his. Green eyes glare through my own, the itchy fabric of his jacket cuff scratching my skin. There's a plea in his frown, but that's not what tumbles from his lips. "It's your fucking turn."

I scoff. Shoving him back a step, I throw a flattened head to my forehead. "Sir, yes Sir!" I mock, clicking my heels together. Pushing past him, a whirlwind of thoughts race around my mind, filling my ears with the noise this room is sorely lacking.

"Better hit me with a beat," I snap my fingers in the viscountess's face. She seems to be the provider of knighthoods – she can damn well provide a decent backing track to witness me baring my dignity for mine. Isn't that how it works? Do as we're told, color in the lines and receive a noble title?

Kicking off my sneakers, those golden eyes captivate me again. Hopping onto the stage, I have a better vantage point. The gold of her dress sparkles against a heavy necklace I hadn't been able to see before. Black diamonds claim her slender throat, the obnoxiously large gem shaped as a spade claiming her suit. The male to her right, a beast of a man with a bull's head and ring piercing in his nostrils reaching across, placing a hoofed hand on her lap. It would seem the King of Spades, who happens to be the non-human member of the royals, has a new wife. One who has taken a keen interest in me.

The lights dim, throwing a spotlight over the pole, but I sense her. I feel her smirk drifting to me on a windless breeze. In my vicinity, Tweed settles in his given armchair, knotting his fingers over his stomach. The thought slips into my mind as the music starts playing, if the Queen wants my brother here to further torture him or to keep me in check. Probably both.

Swallowing hard, I take a steady inhale. Never have I been the center of attention. Even before I proved myself of no use at the royal trials, I was one of a pair. Now I'm thoroughly on my own, needing to earn my keep at the castle. I knew this day would come eventually, that I couldn't ride my brother's new tweed coat tails forever. I'd been wholly prepared to pack my minimalistic bag and walk, but it's true I need to pull my weight. Carry the burden of our imprisonment for a change. So, peeling my stained t-shirt over my head, I place a hand on the pole and slowly pad around it. Testing its sturdiness, feeling the coolness beneath my palm.

I work slowly, allowing the music to delve into my being and direct my actions. All the while, I keep those golden eyes at the forefront of my attention. Fuck the rest who fade into the background. They want to be entertained; I want to be free. Yet as I spin myself in a circle, head dropped back, a gush of excitement ripples through the crowd. It patters into my psyche on nimble tiptoes, arousing my awareness. Slipping a thumb into the dirty sweatpants at my hips, I roll my body and a small applause breaks out.

Woah.

From ignored to praised, a rush of adrenaline floods my system. The louder the music grows, the harder the beat hits, the more natural my movements become. In my peripheral vision, Tweed tenses, the veins in his hands popping from the tightness of his gripped fingers. He's uncomfortable, bless his cotton socks. I, however, let the grin split across my face as I hang back, dry fucking this pole like it's the temptress across the way. Her eyes never divert, a hint of a tongue poking out to wet her lips and I harden against the tent of my cotton pants.

Oh, it's a jester the Queen wants, and that's what she'll damn well get. Watch me cause a scandal like this realm has never seen. How's that for entertainment?

CHAPTER 21

MAL

We emerge in the bleak hours of morning. The storm took hours to pass, and once I'd decided hiding away was the best option, Tweed made sure I stuck to it. He wouldn't let me peek out of the cavern door once, despite the amount of whining or singing I hit him with. I suppose he's right, *again*, even if I hate giving him the satisfaction of knowing it. I'm not in a rush to be shot at with a Jabbercocky's ice blast today. Not when I haven't had a single night to enjoy Wonderlust since arriving.

I'm no closer to finding the Hatter, or any closer to finding a clue to find him. To be honest, the whole thing is weighing on my playful mood, and that's not good for my un-mental health. If I forget who I am, I might as well roll back into the boring world I was spawned from.

Chels stretches across the length of my shoulders, hissing at any Tweedle that gets too close. Her eyes double blink, igniting a pair of teal lights that spear the night like a torch. Thankful for her assistance and warmth, I venture towards the lazy river first. Cool water seeps through my fingers, somehow slipperier than usual. Hardly any of it makes the journey to my face, and the little that does, I have to scrub in for a pathetic attempt at a wash.

A trickle of bubbles float down the center of the stream, slow enough for me to scoop up and scrub beneath my pits and into my cleavage. Inhaling deeply, a minty scent draws me to pick a few leaves from a nearby shrub. Shoving them in my mouth, I start chewing the leaves into a lather and continue my journey down the river bank, already feeling much more Malice than I did a moment ago.

Footfalls tread behind, keeping as close as my new bodyguard will allow. My body thrums with restlessness. Having the twins so close, with the image of Tweed's naked psyche at the forefront of my mind is akin to torture. The river winds this way and that in a true lazy fashion, diverting sharply to cut a route through the mushroom field ahead. Despite Chels' warning growl, a hand wraps around my wrist.

"Do you have an idea of where you want to go?" Cash's grip loosens to hold my hand, his green eyes glowing softly, set on mine. "I know these woods. If you tell me your plan, I can help."

The letter and pocket watch I stole from Hare's waistcoat are burning a hole in my pocket, hidden from sight and mind. I have no doubt Cash could rush me through my quest, dumping me at the end with a dazzling smile and lustful promise. Sounds promising, but something holds me back.

"Ninety percent of the journey is the travelling," I retract my hand and cross the boundary into the mushroom field. An invisible force passes through my body, the hairs on my arms rising to stand at attention. Chels face nuzzles mine, a soft stroke of her whiskered cheek smothering my apprehension. Onwards and upwards it is.

"This was the home of the caterpillars," she purrs. I nod, not needing to ask questions. It only makes sense if the cats are almost extinct, so are the caterpillars. Add to that the lack of male species almost everywhere and Wonderlust is shaping up to be a rather empty place. Does that have something to do with the Hatter beckoning me to join his game of hide and seek, or should I give up all hope now?

"Never," I snort to myself. I've tried drowning in self-pity several times in the institution. Seemed like a fitting way to commit suicide, but alas – I couldn't even do that right. I'm just too fucking awesome at surviving.

Mushrooms span across my horizon, as far as I can see. All colors, all sizes. The air is thick with earthy scents and the undertone of sweetness. Stalks as thick as trunks stretch high. Those too tiny to be seen are stepped on, squashed screams sound from beneath my sneakers. Tweed says something about looking for firewood before we venture too far and strides off, leaving me in the care of Cash watching my every move with keen interest.

I wander aimlessly, no destination in mind. But there has to be something in this world worth discovering, and I won't leave until I've scoured every part of it.

The shadows of the stalks around us shift, closing inwards while their fleshy canopies lean back. Two half-moons on opposite sides of the

CHAPTER 21   187

sky appear to have once been united but are now split and amidst an argument.

In the heart of the lit area they've provided, a single blue mushroom stands just above my eye height. Yellow spots prove to be too symmetrical, their repeated pattern around the flesh too perfect. Skimming my hand over the surface, I round the mushroom, my curiosity alarm blaring. Returning to where Cash hung back to watch, my fingers fall into a slight dip at the edge of the last circle. Invisible to the eye, I trace the crease and then push my weight into the center. The circle pops open, attached by a teeny brass hinge that glints in the moonlight.

"What do we have here, Chels?" I muse, lifting out a weighty object. Smooth metal slips into my hand, around twelve inches in length with a clear chamber in the base and ribbed pipe attached to the side. It won't prove any use to my investigation, but it sure will provide a fun reprieve from the stress clawing at my insides.

"Blue Caterpillar, you sly dog," I chuckle and then abruptly frown. These weren't just characters in my dreams, these were real creatures who both aided and vexed me no end. And now they're gone. In all the years I've dreamed about my grand return, I never once imagined the Blue Caterpillar wouldn't be here to ignore and aggravate me. A moment passes where I'm utterly still, then shake off those bad vibes and break into a grin. "Well, waste not, want not."

"Nope," Tweed storms through the field like a vamp on a mission, trying to swipe the hookah from my hands. "Not a chance. We need you at least semi-aware to survive the Enchanted woods."

"And I need you at least semi-erect to hold my attention," I smirk back, already scrambling up onto the top of the mushroom. Oh yes, I'm doing this in full style.

"Will you listen for once?" Tweed dumps the firewood to the ground to ball his fists. I shake my head, checking the crushed shisha tobacco in the base on the hookah. "These woods are no joke."

"Life's a joke, Tweedle-Dick. The goal is not to be the punch line." Locating a match attached to the side of the mouthpiece, I strike a flame against the mushroom and light the hookah coals. Sprawling out on my back, I inhale the first blissful puff and exhale the accumulating stress from my lungs. "If you guys need me, I'll be up here – living my best life."

"Leave her be, brother," Cash chuckles. I'd know his lighter tone with my eyes closed, which they are. "It's been quite the day." Chels shifts to curl up on my stomach, taking a hit of the hookah when I pass the reed to her.

"Don't fucking touch me you piece of shit," Tweed snarls, preceded by the tearing of his leather jacket.

"Can't we all just get along?" I sigh, dancing my fingers through the air. Tweed ignores me, continuing to growl at his brother.

"Isn't it about time you checked in with your Queen?" Interest piqued, I roll my head aside to watch the exchange. Tweed shoves a hand into Cash's chest, shoving him away when he tries to take the firewood.

"I'm not bound as tightly to mine as you are to yours. You made your choice," Cash chuckles again, giving no hint of the leg sweep he whacks out on his twin. Tweed preempts it though, jumping high to land back on his feet and grab Cash by the scruff of his pinstripe vest.

"We both know that for the lie it is," Tweed spits, swinging his fist back. Oh, for fuck's sake.

"You know what - I'm sick to death of hearing about these queens you both serve. From now on, until we leave this wood, you both serve me. I'm your queen, now dance for me." I click my fingers, believing a pair of stripper poles has sprouted from the nearest and tallest mushroom. Cash's chest visibly puffs out and he cracks his fingers. This is his element, where he's comfortable. Tweed, however, glares at me with a thousand emerald shards splintering in his gaze.

"There's no way a mushroom's head would support anyone," he grits out. I burst into laughter, so many innuendos about his head supporting me but I keep them to myself. Teasing someone who falls so easily into my traps isn't half as fun.

"Sure, it will – that particular mushroom is made of steel." At my words, chrome begins to grow up the stalk, coating the stem and flesh high above in a shiny, steel coating. Cash kicks off his shoes and leaps, grabbing the right pole and swings around it freely to prove a point. I spare Tweed a half-satisfied smile, daring him to provide me with any other reasons he's not shaking his ass on that pole for me tonight. Some call it spoilt, I call it getting whatever the fuck I want and screw the labels.

"What's it going to be, T-Dick? Are you going to dance for me, or let Cash take the spotlight?" Chels slinks off my stomach, stretching her back before hopping down from the mushroom.

"I'm going to take myself for a stroll, let you get...this...out of your system," she grins. "Care to join me?" I look around, confused for a millisecond until Stan glides out from his hiding spot and lands on my shoulder. Jumping, his furry wings spread far enough to glide onto Chels' back as she begins to float away.

On her way past the firewood, her fluffy tail flicks out and zaps a spark into the pile. A fire roars to life, her body fading into just a smile that twirls beyond the flames and floats away. Well, that's new. Tweed has yet to move, a war happening between his eyebrows. I sigh, sitting upright and pat the spot beside me on the mushroom.

"Come on, I won't bite – unless you do," I wink. For a moment, I think he's frozen in indecision, but he suddenly moves and appears at my side in a flash. "Relax for once. You might enjoy it," I pass him the hookah. He pushes it away.

"My metabolism-"

"Is taking a break," I urge, believing it into existence. He eyes me wearily but doesn't fight this time as I push the reed between his lips. Taking a long, intense suck, his eyes dilate and I smile. "Now doesn't that feel better?" Taking turns, Tweed and I toke on the hookah, filled with a particularly strong tobacco that tastes suspiciously like weed, until our heads are slumped together and Cash announces he's warmed up.

Without the assistance of my apparent superpower, a tune leaks through the wood of stalks. Soft at first, a trickled sound from a collection of mome raths growing from the ground. Tufty grass for hair, their eyes bulge wide on slender, vertical bodies. Much like a worm, reaching for the morning sun, offering themselves up to the early bird. Wiggling from side to side, small rounded mouths open wider to increase the volume of a pleasant tone with some decent bass. The baritones sweep in on wings of purple cabbage, a flock of lettuce butterflies aiding Cash's slow and rehearsed movements.

He commands my attention. Starting on the ground, Cash's large hand wraps around the pole. His muscles flex in the moonlight, preparing to sweep his legs wide and slowly spin in lazy circles. Through his purple striped vest, the deep ridges of his abdomen flex and I push the hookah into Tweed's hands. For this, I want to be mostly lucid.

Coming to a stop, his hand drips to his waistband, those slinky hips rolling in time with the music. Drool puddles in my mouth, salivating at the glimpse of an engraved V leading into his jeans. Then he's airborne. Pulling his entire weight up with one arm, Cash lifts his legs in one, smooth movement, landing a perfect upside-down roly poly to lock his ankles on the pole.

Stomach splayed against the metal, he uses his hands to peel off his vest and drop it beneath his hand. The muscles flexing between his shoulder blades cause my mouth to go dry, and when Tweed shoves the hookah in my mouth to distant me, I almost choke. Popping the button of his jeans before righting himself, Cash twists upright and shoots me a sly grin. His groin grinds against the pole in mid-air, held in place by just one hand and his ankles.

"I don't like this," Tweed grumbles to himself. I spare him a quick glance, as much as it is a struggle to take my eyes off Cash. Tweed's limbs are languid from the hookah, his shoulder slumped into mine and face downcast. I'm not sure which part of this he is referring to not liking – the one-man show people would spend thousands for or the lack of feeling of the stick up his ass. Gripping his chin, I turn his face upwards, a breath away from mine.

"Look at me instead." Cash has climbed the pole now, making me curse under my breath that I missed watching his biceps pulse. Veins travel the length of his arms, from shoulder to wrist on his inkless side. A thin layer of sweat prickles his skin, glistening like a thousand diamonds activated by the moon. Working his legs as if walking on air, Cash works me into a frenzy with his displays of grace and strength. My thighs clench, my heart hammering. I need him, on me, under me, everywhere. Sliding down the length of the pole, those green eyes settle on mine, unwavering as he begins to slide down his jeans.

"Did I ever tell you…" Tweed slurs, sinking his weight into me more and more with each toke. Cash's jeans make it to his knees before he tears them clean off, standing in nothing but a skimpy pair of black boxers and moonlight.

"Tell me what," I whisper back angrily, not breaking my eye contact with Cash. I won't miss a single movement, won't waste a second to salivate over his glorious form.

"How fucking beautiful you are." Trance broken. I swing my head to Tweed's. He jerks forward, catching my lips in a forbidden kiss. For whatever reason, the logical part of his brain refused to give it to me. But now, his consciousness is locked up tight with a do not disturb sign on the door. He wants me on a primeval, base level.

With Cash's protests swirling in the background, I drop back onto the mushroom, taking Tweed with me. His cold hand slides across my waist just beneath the vest, his hot lips at contrast with everything else about him. He pushes his tongue into my mouth, using a grip on my chin to open me up to him. And I do, without hesitation. This is what I've wanted since the moment I watched him stubbornly break his face on the Perspex mirror in my cell.

To see his ego snap. To witness his soul submit to me.

Another form joins us, too large for Chels to have returned and question my life choices. Additional hands slip around my front and into my cargos, ice cold and causing me to gasp into Tweed's mouth. He pulls back, a hint of awareness returning at Cash's presence. Those icy fingers sink lower, finding the hem of my thong and tearing it in one smooth move. Not necessary, but the show of power was certainly appreciated by my lady parts.

Through half-lidded eyes, I see Tweed glaring over my shoulder, preparing to move away from me. I grip his leather jacket, forcing him to stay in place.

"I didn't peg you for one to run in the face of a challenge, Tweed." Cash chuckles, goading his twin. "But I'm sure pegging is an option, if that's more your speed."

"Stay," I softly urge, keeping his eyes in my direction. He looks through me, lacking the raw emotion I just felt radiating from his chest and into mine. "Crack for me. Break for me. Return the boy that always had a smile at the ready."

"I'm all man now, and I won't give *him* the satisfaction of watching me fuck you."

"Then don't make eye contact with him." Let's be honest, that would be weird in any aspect. "Keep your focus centered on me." Slipping from the mushroom, both twins sit up to watch me slink towards the pole. What? They thought Cash was the only one to get all the fun?

Pushing the cargos over my hips as I stride, I walk straight out of them, my ruined thong falling away too. Stripping from my vest, I stand amongst the mushroom forest in my birthday suit. The pole is cool to the touch, but I don't even manage to complete one full spin as a body blurs forward and slams my back into the metal. Tightness ticks at the silhouette's jaw, tension riding his shoulders. A taste of danger crackles in the air, while Cash watches on from the overgrown toadstool.

"There isn't a test I've yet to fail," Tweed growls, the vibrations from his chest making a beeline for my clit, "and I'm always ready for a challenge." Pushing myself into him, my brow lifts and a dare escapes from my lips.

"Prove it."

CHAPTER 22

MAL

Without closing my eyes, I press my lips against Tweed's. He doesn't move, the hookah in his system enough to forget his no kissing rule. But he doesn't push me away, so that's a green light in my book. Nibbling lightly, my mouth travels to his jawline and down his neck. I take a moment to breathe over his pulse, enjoying the role reversal of his breath hitching.

Like the wood around us, a fresh earth smell clings to his skin. Like recently churned soil mixed with a hint of smoke. Homely, with an undercurrent of danger and a heavy helping of mystery. My mouth travels to the collar of his leather jacket before his hand wraps around my throat, halting my descent.

"We-" Tweed grunts and stops himself. "I've waited too long to let you take control." I open my mouth to respond and Tweed's other arm shoots upwards, catching an apple that was hurtling towards my head. I spear Cash with a narrowed gaze as he slips off the mushroom and strolls over, as if he didn't just try to kill me by Granny Smith. Tweed shoves the apple into my mouth like a prized pig in time for Cash to hand him the hookah.

"Take the edge off, brother," Cash drawls and Tweed shoulder barges him.

"Fuck off," his twin growls back, taking a long drag. His eyes not leaving mine for a millisecond. "Either of you talk, I'm gone." Careful to not let either step into their eye line, both sets of glowing green eyes feast on me. From my gigantic blonde hair to my blue eyes and slender neck. Down to my tits, where my nipples harden beneath the sheer heat of their gazes against the chill of night.

Cash moves first, bending low. I widen my stance, but nothing apart from his breath fans my pussy. Retrieving a vine, he slinks it around an ankle and ties a knot there. Tight enough to cut off my circulation, before doing the same on the next. Another piece scrapes my calf, dragging the rough length upwards. With deft fingers, theatrical knots are fastened around my thighs, more for decoration than purpose.

All the while, Tweed stares on. The hand cemented around my neck is at odds with the soft pad of a thumb stroking my erratic pulse.

I struggle against the desire to move, my hammering heart ready to dive into this twin freak fest. But with the hookah in Tweed's hand practically empty, I know I need to savor this. The fantasy I almost didn't dare dream, because not having it hurt more than admitting I might never find Wonderland again. Yet here we are.

Cash stands now, drawing me a step forward by my wrist, putting me directly in Tweed's personal space. Winding that same wrist behind my back, he takes the other and I'm sure he's about to secure me to the pole. Wrong again.

Placing my hands on my own elbows, the vine is threaded around my forearms, fastening them tight. Tugging tightly, he uses that same vine around my stomach and beneath my breasts. They grow heavy, aching to be touched as Cash slides the root up my cleavage, framing them in an outfit of his own creation.

Tweed only shifts his hand for my throat to don a vine collar, complete with leash. My teeth sink further into the apple at that last addition, not wholly happy in the role as sub. But fuck if I'm not ready to see where it'll get me. Then, we're walking.

Cash tugs me through the mushroom field, the vine wrapped around his large hand. Loose strands flap from my individually tied ankles, dragging across the dead leaves littering the ground. The mome raths duck back into their holes, barring their eyes from my bare display. Their loss. Turns out I'm quite the exhibitionist.

Jutting out my chest, my head held high, I walk with confident strides. Tweed follows close behind, the occasional brush of his knuckles on my ass giving me goosebumps. It's as if he can't help himself, and I know the feeling well.

Cash's naked butt wanders aimlessly, seeming to enjoy parading me through the forest, even if there is no one around to see it. The twin moons glint through the canopy, lighting my path to a huge mushroom head in the ground. Free of a stalk, soft beneath my toes. Like a giant pillow of purple and yellow spots, the size of a super-king size mattress.

Unraveling the vine on his hand, Cash's movements are slow and precise. The indents of his smirk are deep as he turns and hands the leash over my shoulder to Tweed. The twins circle me like predators, smoothly switching places without the need to look at each other. Tweed's leather trousers do nothing to hide his erection and take barely a thought to rid from his body. His clothes fly into a pile a few feet away, and his expression dips dangerously.

Gripping my cheeks, his fangs extend in the moonlight and my breathing stills. A monster, lethal and alluring, standing before me. A true hunter of the night. Nudging his head forward, his fangs tear through the apple and rip it from my mouth.

"You're not in control here," Tweed rasps, his voice thick with lust. "You will only do as we say. Otherwise, remain still, quiet, and take your fucking like a good girl." He pats my head and yanks on my leash when I begin to growl. Cash's chuckle sounds behind me, his fingers moving through my hair. Pulling the strands high, he fastens my mane into a ponytail.

Once finished, his hands smooth down the length of my back, ass and legs, making me clench everywhere. Tweed enters into another stare stand-off with me, drinking in every emotion I refuse to give him. I break our trance when something hard is placed over my feet. A stick, solid and long enough to be a wizard's staff, that Cash proceeds to tie the loose ends of my ankle restraints to. Dude just whipped up an ankle bar in the middle of the forest.

Testing its sturdiness, Cash holds my attention until Tweed wrenches me forward. I topple, landing on my knees in the mushroom flesh. Somehow, Tweed beats me there, his body sprawled out before me like a buffet for the eyes. From this angle, the grooves of his abs appear deeper and the veins surrounding his girthy cock make me salivate.

The ink along his right arm, shoulder and side seem to glow, highlighting the snake slithering amongst the roses. Across his left hip, the stopwatch ticks backwards while the red heart over his pulses. I ignore that particular one, not enjoying the bitter taste of jealousy clawing at the back of my throat.

A hand splays across my upper back, pushing me down over Tweed's cock. I don't object. The veins ripple between my lips, his sheer size stretching my mouth wide. Taking him as deep as I can, I marvel at the sweet and salty bead of cum already waiting there. Like a chocolate on a hotel room pillow, heightening the experience.

My knees are pushed further beneath me, the bar keeping my ankles spread and jutting my ass up in the air. Cash draws his hands all over me, not-so-subtly brushing over my pussy but completely avoids my clit. I groan around Tweed's dick, wriggling for more contact.

Whack.

I yelp at the sharp sting across the back of my thighs, jerking back until Tweed's hand grabs my ponytail. Shoving me onto his cock, I hold my breath, remembering his orders. Keep quiet, still, and take my fucking. So, for once, I do as I'm told. Cash resumes his playful stroking, from my ass to pussy and back again. Slowly, Tweed releases the chokehold of his dick halfway down my throat so I can breathe through my nose again.

The rough pad of a tongue is drawn up my cunt, catching me off guard. I only jolt a little bit, allowing Cash to continue burying his face in my ass. His tongue flicks at my swollen lips, heady with an anticipation that's never fully met.

Impaling me with a cold, blunt object, he slides it in and out of my pussy lazily whilst spitting on my ass. Satisfied at how wet I am, he removes the metal object and slides it back to my asshole. I push myself back in eagerness and this time, he doesn't punish me for it. With small thrusts, the object I presume is a butt plug eases inside of me the same time his finger spears my pussy.

One finger. Two fingers. Three fingers. Four.
Play my body right if you come in the back door.

I'm lost to the sensation, barely present when Tweed starts to bob my head up and down on his cock. Cash fills me, stretches me. Works me into a frenzy where the binds don't bite as sharply and my body tingles with ecstasy. With the plug jostling and I don't know how many fingers inside of me, I bring my focus back to Tweed. I will not be seen to crumble alone.

His green eyes hold mine, one arm casually behind his head. Lowering as far as I can go, Tweed nudges the back of my head down that bit more and I gag. He smirks, for the first time ever, and I can't bring myself to hate him for it. Pushing my tongue flat to open up that tiny bit more, I slide up and down, tracing the veins and committing them to memory.

"Such a pretty pussy," Cash murmurs to himself. Spanking me with his hand, the other pushes inside of me. "Have you ever been fisted before, Malice?" he chuckles, knowing I can't respond. His hand slips in, twists a full turn and pulls back out, leaving me whimpering.

"Come, beautiful girl," he coaxes me and I scrunch my eyes closed, preparing to show these vampires I'm all woman. One more twist of his wrist is my undoing, my scream lost to a muffle around Tweed's dick. He doesn't let me up for a reprieve, not as my pussy clenches and convulses. My poor clit, yet to be acknowledged, pulses. I've barely finished jerking beneath the weight of my orgasm when Cash grips me by the veins binding my arms behind my back.

Heaving me upwards, I'm forced to release Tweed with a loud pop. The hand from my hair goes to his shaft, bracing his dick vertically for Cash to lift and sit me directly on top of it. Not a second to adjust. Not a moment to adapt. A wash of dizziness rushes through my mind, my toes curled to the point of breaking.

Tweed doesn't shift, his head still resting on his hand and watching me. I tilt my hips, just to take the pressure off my g-spot and he flicks my clit in punishment. At my back, the ankle spreader resting across Tweed's thighs is lifted and Cash wiggles into the gap before letting it drop behind him. If the echoing thwack hurts Tweed, I wouldn't know it, but my attention is elsewhere.

The butt plug is removed from my back passage, replaced by the blunt head of Cash's cock. He pushes my nape to lean forward, easing his way into me. My teeth sink into my bottom lip. It's not going to fit. It'll never fit, but Cash is adamant. One hand curled into the binds on my forearm, he nudges me up and down ever so slightly. I hang there, a slave to the unknown pleasures that are twin vampire-induced cocks.

"You don't come until we do, understood?" Tweed growls. I manage a half nod, not in a position to argue. I should have been prepared for their sudden movements in unison, given my predicament, but I wasn't. With the release of one dick smoothing out of me, the other slides in. Never empty, never left wanting. Tears I refuse to let fall prick at my eyes, my head dropping forward. But Tweed won't let me tap out now. I asked for this. I knew what I wanted.

Gripping my chin, he holds my head up. All that can be heard through the fungi field are the strangled noises torn from my throat and the sound of skin slapping on skin. Their groins hitting my ass and pelvis, the dull knock of ballbags following soon after. Embedding my nails into the fleshy part of my inner elbow, I feel another climax building, vaguely aware I could castrate at least one of them in doing so.

Cash's hands smooth over the knots lining my stomach, rising to knead my full breasts. I groan at the long-awaited contact, tilting myself backwards. My head lolls on his shoulder, resigned to being their plaything. An object for their desire. My nipples are plucked, my cunt thoroughly fucked. Sweat slickens my skin and I slump further into Cash's chest, thankful for the coolness of his body. Teeth nibble my ear; kisses grace my cheek. Despite his authority, Cash is quick to remind me of his softer side.

Their thrusts quicken. Their own pleasure escaping in muffled rumbles. I smirk, thankful I'm affecting them just as much. Working with each other, the fullness of my passages aches for release. Their cocks glide against one another, a rhythm as natural as their need to remain close to each other – despite what they might believe. They need to be united, and I need them to destroy me until I see stars. Cash's fingers dip to my clit, barely completing one small circle and I'm a goner.

"Don't you dare," Tweed grinds through clenched teeth. Too late. My pussy clamps so hard, I'm certain without Cash catching the binds, I'd have passed out. Tied too tight to move, I'm forced to ride out my climax with the twin's pound into me relentlessly. Harder, faster. I try to force Tweed out but he smashes against my walls, forcing me to take every steely inch of him. Wave after wave of bliss beats through me, from the flush at my neck to the ripples of my cunt.

Suddenly, two roars worthy of lions break out around me, the force of a battering ram slamming home in both my passages. Hot cum spurts into me, erupting with such power, it's impossible to tell where my orgasm ends and theirs begins. Intensity wins over, and I believe myself free of the restraints. They vanish and I collapse onto Tweed, his chest firm and barely panting. Still hard and rocking inside of me, this time I don't even wait for him to ask for the lasting need building between us.

Driving my blunt teeth into the fleshy part of his shoulder, I bite as hard as I can. His blood fills my mouth, sweeter than before. Or I'm growing accustomed to his taste. Licking his wound clean, I visibly feel him relax beneath me. I may not have all the facts, but I know Tweed is a tidbit calmer when his blood is in my system. Like a failsafe I won't flee him again, and I don't intend to. I've spent too long alone, wishing for them back in my life. A vow cements in my mind to do whatever it takes to make that dream my reality.

Cash's throaty rumble turns to a jealous growl with the longer I lie on Tweed. Both of their cocks are still rock hard, not showing any sign of slowing. I, however, know my limits.

"My turn," I find the energy to dive aside. Rolling on my newly released shoulder, I flex my back muscles and shuffle up to my knees. Not a hint of pain is shown, despite the itchy tingle across my stomach and thighs from where the vines were tied too tight, as I click my fingers and order them to stand. Restoring their factory settings, they comply, albeit slowly.

Tweed's expression darkens, Cash's smirk deepens. Standing side by side in their naked glory, my eyes devour them as greedily as my body just did. Both Adonis' in their own right, yet together – they're the epitome of my fantasies. Primeval predators I should fear. A pair of brothers who shouldn't be at each other's throats all the time. My mind starts to wander, until Tweed grips my ponytail too tight and tilts my head upwards.

"You think you have what it takes to handle us?" he barks an unfamiliar laugh that has my eyeline lowering.

Perhaps my previous sexual exploits have been too intimidated by my crazy to talk to me in such a way, preferring I take control. But in the face of being dominated myself, I can't say I hate it. I don't feel weakness as expected, but empowerment. They test me because they know I can withstand any test thrown my way, and for the briefest moment, take my control. The voices in my head are unusually quiet. In fact, everything is. My stubbornness, my fierce nature, my soul. It's all...calm in the face of relenting to Tweed and Cash's desires. For tonight at least.

Together, they step forward. Their cocks, coated in my cream, glisten in the moonlight, jutting right in front of my face.

"Open," Cash nods to me, his brow raised in a challenge. Pushing through every barrier I've put in place to prohibit such a thing, I do as I'm told. My mouth stretches wide and Tweed thrusts inside. His twin's hand locks onto the other side of my hair, holding me in place as Tweed shoves his bulbous head all the way down my throat. Whipping back out, Cash repeats the action. Again and again. One by one. I gag on their cocks, forcing myself to remain in place. How did the tables turn so quickly?

Eyes glow green, brighter than emeralds and a thousand times more beautiful. In turns, they lay claim to my mouth until my eyes and nose are streaming. I try to shy away from the mess I must appear as, but the hands in my hair jerk my eyes back open. They want me to pay attention and in turn, they want to see it all.

Somewhere along the way, impatience wins over. Cash tries to shove himself into my mouth before Tweed has pulled back, and a competition ensues. Jerking, thrusting, grunting. I merely sit on my knees and stretch my mouth wide, watching the fight break out between the brothers. Safe to say, Tweed's hookah high has worn off.

Twin dicks jut into my throat, the gagging subsiding as my throat accepts its fate to never swallow again. Pulling back and releasing my hair in unison, Tweed and Cash have the same idea – to pump their cocks as quickly as possible to lay claim to me first. Hot spurts of cum shoot over my face in no time, covering me in their seed. Tilting my head back, I let their arousal drip down my neck, my senses filled with the salty scent.

One must have succeeded by a millisecond because I hear a round of gloating and the pads of feet stomping away on the mushroom. I can't tell who, as my eyes are currently out of action, but whoever remains kneels before me, sharply twisting my nipples.

"Don't forget who you belong to," the voice says and I shudder. I just wish I knew which one it was.

CHAPTER 23

MAL

"Psst." Furrowing my brow, I shift my head. "Pssssst." Darkness surrounds my vision, my body heavy and sated. Damp hair tickles the length of my back, having washed myself in the lazy stream before session number two started up. Limbs hold me down, the twin's even breaths beating against my face. Pushing myself up, I hunt for the noise through the night. A faint light glows between the trees, a teeny figure hopping back and forth like a jumping bean. I wriggle out of the Tweedle's hold, intrigue settling in.

Grabbing a bundle of clothes on the way, I dress in the dark while tiptoeing through the crushed leaves coating the forest floor. The closer I get, the more defined the silhouette becomes. A pair of tall, floppy ears. A flat, rectangular body. Hopping backwards, he pulls me forward of an invisible thread before disappearing altogether. Peering over a grassy mound, I find the golden glow emanating from a rabbit hole and being me, dive straight in.

Tumbling a short distance and landing on my face, my body flops into a tunnel without room to move. A knee in my cheek, my arm trapped around the back of my neck, ass in the air. The figure hops around in front of my face, a fraction of my size.

"Monster!" a rabbit screams in my face. Not the rabbit I once knew, but a mutated version. The rectangular body of a playing card sits upon white, furry feet. No suit in particular, just a blank slate as if his future is yet to be decided. Tiny hands poke out either side and on top, the entire head of a white rabbit. "Monster! In my house. Dodo, where's Dodo? He knows what to do. He would...burn the monster out!" Upside down, I watch his pair of white floppy ears pounce away while I call after him.

"I'm not a monster, Rabbit! You pssst me, practically invited me in!" Hopping back my way with a single match in his stubby hand, the White Rabbit leans in and I puff, blowing the flame clean out. "Stop this nonsense and shrink me at once!" I put on my big girl's voice and the rabbit falls still. His large eyes shoot to the side. A table behind him holds a glass bottle of brown liquid I really hope wasn't produced by his, or any, butt. Twisting my head and sticking out my tongue, I lick at the straw until it enters my mouth and automatically begin to suck. No questions asked.

Chocolate milkshake washes over my tongue and I moan. The perfect after-threesome treat.

My bones shrink and thankfully, my skin shrivels to match. As soon as my fingers are free, I hunt for the magical tag inside the vest and tug hard. It grazes my thighs, hugging my body in a reformed dress. I realize too late, however, the vest I've thrown on is Cash's striped, purple one – which is fairly transparent. My nipples show through the fabric, the cotton cinched tight at my waist. Oh well, does the job.

The tiny home splayed out before me is meticulously clean. Completely at odds with the character hopping about inside, pinging around like a bee in a jar. His head twists this way and that, his whiskers twitching so hard he might take flight. Grabbing his cheeks, I hold his attention while long ears flop over my arms.

"Hello Mr. Rabbit," I smirk. His blue eyes spiral in his head so I give him a little shake to come back to me. I know crazy. I'm comfortable around crazy.

"I'm late. Late. My watch, I've misplaced my watch and oh. Waistcoat. Must look smart for her majesty. The queen is so mad. Mad, I tell you. We're all mad, but Hatter. Wait, where is Hatter?"

"That's what I was hoping you'd tell me," I sigh, releasing him. He starts hopping again, looking beneath the coffee and side tables. Scratching at the coal alight in the fireplace in an effort to peer underneath, I whistle sharply. Taking the watch from my pocket and swaying it in the air, Rabbit rushes over.

"Oh, such a good girl. A good girl, like Hatter said. Nutty on the out, good on the in." Following him through his burrow, I watch the white puff of a tail sticking out the back of the card's body twitch. I drop into a sofa, rolling my neck. The tension pressing on my spine doesn't budge.

"Sit, Mr. Rabbit," I bark, clicking my fingers to the nearby armchair. He halts, sliding over to obey. Lowering as much as he can, his feet shake back and forth. It unnerves me to see what they've done to him, beyond the obvious. Shimmying forward, I warm up my hands and hold them in front of me. "Focus on my hands," I tell him. Clapping, I begin to play pattycake with his stumped hands, forcing his attention elsewhere than my questions.

"Why are you a playing card?"

"Queen," he nods along with my patting and I move on. Clap, pat, clap, crisscross, repeat.

"Why are you hiding?" I settle on next, recalling his photographs around the Cook's farmhouse. Rabbit either lived or frequented there often.

"Don't trust the champion. Too alluring. Alluring, must resist." His eye twitches and I tap his palms harder. Clap, pat, clap, crisscross, repeat.

"Which champion?"

"Traitor of kin. Patriarch of armies. Don't drink the blood you must repay." His head trembles violently, his whiskered nose starting to shake. I'm losing him but I have to push my luck. He's all I have to go on.

"Where is the Hatter?" I press and suddenly, he freezes. Two large eyes stare through me, a scene playing out within his irises. Leaning in, I watch a figure sharpen into existence. The Hatter, sitting at his desk in the Hattery, hunched over a crystal ball. From the rabbit's point of view, presumably on a stool beside him, I watch the Hatter's fingerless gloves rub the ball and mutter inaudibly. I almost smile at his image, forgetting where I am. His frantic orange hair, the gap in his teeth.

I spent many a night wishing he were my father instead, pretending it to be so. The Hatter understands me, cares for me.

That much is evident as he reaches for the newspapers he's been scouring, tracing the words with his heterochromia eyes. One blue, one green. Both more focused than I've even seen of him. Returning his focus to the crystal ball, I squint upon seeing a yellow-haired figure reflected in the iridescent sphere.

Me.

A younger version of me, from my college years. Sitting on a stone wall, book in one hand, travel mug in the other. The days were peaceful, the nights were promiscuous. I discovered many things about myself during that brief period away from my family home and the fateful Christmas that saw me committed to Charmsfield. My fleeting smile slips as I realize he was watching me, possibly this entire time. Whilst I was convinced I was utterly alone.

The image shifts, blurring to a scene practically the same. This time, the Hatter sits at his workstation, all fabric shoved aside. At first, I thought the memory was clouded, but I soon deduce it's the Hatter's coloring that has dulled. His hair is paler, his skin ashy and irises turning white. Hugging the crystal ball to his tattered chest, the Rabbit is more jittery this time, trembling and frantically looking at his pocket watch. Except when he does, the hour hand twists to point towards the Hatter. Like a compass seeking north, whichever way the rabbit turns, the hour hand remains on the man I'm seeking.

Elation burns in my chest, the answer I've been looking for nearing. Breathing a sigh of relief, I go to sit back when a shadow in the vision steps forward. No, not a shadow. A soldier in steel armor. His face is covered by a full-fronted helmet but there's no hiding the body I've come to know well.

Thick traps protrude from the high collar of a steel chest plate, his arms brazenly bare. His right arm coated in ink, one rose blending into the next. As if that wasn't damming enough, the red heart stamped onto the left peck of the chest plate is. Twisting his head sharply, a glowing green glare shines through the horizontal eye slit as if he is staring right at me.

Storming forward in heavy boots, I edge back in my seat before remembering this isn't happening. It's a vision, a memory. Snatching Rabbit by the ears, he's torn from his hiding spot and the setting blurs. A castle looms in shadow, red and black smoke curling from an unknown source. Then, it stutters and fades away.

Reaching out in an attempt to grab the vision and bring it back, or possibly find a rewind button, I accidentally poke the White Rabbit in the eye and he bounces from his seat. There's no chance of calming him down now, a foreign incantation bubbling from his mouth.

It doesn't matter anymore. I know what I saw.

Fumbling around the small burrow, I find a kitchen and start raiding the cupboards. Above a metal bowl that acts as a basin, I find a medicine cabinet and stock up on lotions and potions I might need. Anger churns in my gut. Not at the Tweedle in question, but myself. Blinded by desire, swept up with eagerness to seize every opportunity. I wanted to be a different version of myself this time, one that was strong enough to handle herself and shrug off what she couldn't.

But in one single moment, I've shown myself to be that naïve girl that's easily taken advantage of. My tastes have grown darker, my preferences more profound, but I've still been manipulated. When will those around here realize I'm no one's pawn. I'm a badass queen in my own right, and this is *my* game we're playing.

Filling a tote bag I find on a railing empty of waistcoats; I throw in the bottles of milkshakes and an entire plate of dainty cakes sitting on a random table in the center of the hallway. Rabbit's bedroom is visible via a cracked door, the OCD-level cleanliness reflected throughout. Whoever's been attending to this burrow, it's not the jittery loon currently knocking into every surface possible.

Not quite the wooden stake I'd have opted for, but it'll do if I should need an out. What I currently have is a much more valuable tool, one I intend to hold close until I know what to do with it. Knowledge. Heading back to the burrow's entrance, I bid the White Rabbit goodbye. He doesn't turn my way, a bloodied gash dried and crusted from ear to ear across the back of his head. That damn March Hare. If he weren't dead, I'd kill him again.

Using the ladder this time, I emerge into the woodland. Nothing has stirred, the air eerily quiet. Nudging the bag's strap up my shoulder, I turn away from the campfire and slam into a hard surface. It shifts to place two hands on my waist, an entertained smile glinting in the dim lighting. My shoulders sag.

"Where are you going, Crazy One?"

"Mind your fucking business Cash," I return his smirk. Checking over my shoulder, I spot Tweed's outline still slumped across the ground. "I'm just going to get some air. It's stifling back there," I huff.

That sense of rage returns, mixed with a heavy dose of embarrassment. Obviously having a threesome with those dubbed the 'rascal and reject' was never going to pan out well, but once I've discovered the extent of Tweed's part in the Hatter's disappearance, he's dead meat.

"I'll come with you," Cash shifts to wrap an arm around my shoulders. "You never know who you might meet in these parts." Too tired to argue, we stroll into the darkness together, a million thoughts racing around my mind. It's almost enough to run back in the opposite direction and smoke a shit load more hookah, but that'll solve nothing. Only finding the Hatter will.

CHAPTER 24

MAL

"We're leaving," I kick Tweed's ribs hard. So much for vampires never sleeping. If I didn't know any better, I'd say this lazy shit had been dead the entire time. Maybe I'd be more sympathetic, if I hadn't discovered he knew more than he's been letting on this entire time. He saw the Hatter at his workshop, he knew about the newspapers ridiculing me. But you know what they say, keep your enemies close, and there's nothing closer than the ache of my enemy's solid cock pounding still evident between my legs.

Morning broke hours ago and if Cash tries to pander to my feelings one more time, I'm going to scream. No, I don't want a hug while I cry. No, I'm not hungry. No, a morning fuck-sesh won't help. Betrayal cuts deeply and all that will help is following the damn watch clutched in my hand.

Groaning, Tweed rolls onto his back, grabbing his side with a hiss. I throw his white vest and leathers at him, putting everyone back in their own clothing. The vest and cargos feel much better on my body, Cash's see-through vest appearing much more suited to his.

"Chels!" I scream and a smile bursts to life in front of my face. Her face follows, twirling around in circles with Stan clinging to her back. "Time to go." Stepping forward, the kitty throws herself into my arms and snuggles against my neck. Stan hops and leaps into my hair, nuzzling back into his spot behind my ear. I stroke Chels, finding a modicum of solace in her smooth skin. Eight stripes for eight lives dance across her back, and I have to wonder if it's been worth it. To live on repeat, to feel the sharp lash of life without reprieve. Wow, the events of last night sure have set me on a dark path today.

Pocket watch held out in front of me, I follow the arrow precisely.

"What's that?" Tweed asks, jogging to catch up to my side. Chels hisses at him and I join her. I'm not in the mood to be mocked, and after what I saw in the vision, he knows very well what this object is.

"None of your fucking business, that's what," I snap anyway. I don't know if it bugs me less or more that Tweed doesn't react, his impassive mask firmly back in place. Deciding it bugs me more, I slam my spare fist in a downward arc and punch him straight in the dick. He falls to the ground, moaning and I nod to myself. That feels marginally better.

The hour hand on the watch judders, spinning slowly to settle on the number eleven. I track it, leaving the mushroom field far behind until my calves burn. I relish the pain. It reminds me I'm doing something productive, that I'm finally on the right track. Twins in tow, I track through further dense woodland until the sound of beating water hums ahead. If I'm not mistaken, the map mentioned a waterfall just beyond fairy hollow.

I slow to take stock of the trees, spying rows upon rows of tiny doors in the trunks. Glitter rains down from the leaves, pooling into a stream that glides upwards towards the waterfall hinted at further ahead.

"There's a hidden exit through the cavern behind the waterfall," Tweed fills the silence. Hopefully, he's feeling my cold shoulder and seriously regretting his life choices.

"Who died and named you King of the Wood?" I reply with a bite to my tone. Like a 'hear how I'm not talking to you, by the way I'm talking to you' kinda thing. Cash finds this highly amusing.

"Tweed was thrown out here for a survival training camp with Red Queen's daughter. He was her *personal* coach. They formed quite the bond," Cash nudges Tweed's shoulder. His twin twists back and punches him in the face. Cash didn't even try to dodge it.

"Since you're so forthcoming, why don't you tell Malice why I was chosen for the Knave position instead of you?" Tweed snarls and a distinctive silence follows. There's a conversation happening in the air, passed via narrowed eyes and pulled back top-lips. I continue on, not even trying to decipher what I'll never understand. What happened to their bond will remain number one on that list.

Suddenly, the hour hand on the pocket watch jerks aside and I halt. Tweed slams into my back. The little pointer is adamant my treasure is now firmly at the number eight, and the only explanation I can come up with is the Hatter. He's here and moving.

Twisting, I run, following the trail that I can sense quickly going cold. High-top sneakers aren't recommended for trekking across the woodland, evident by the number of times I nearly roll my ankles leaping over fallen logs.

Tossing a look over my shoulder, the twins haven't bothered to follow this time, strolling a fair distance behind. On my lonesome, I struggle against the damaging effects left behind after yesterday's storm. Mud slows me down; trees shake their droplets over my head. Both Stan and Chels curl into me, not a fan of the rain that's been reserved for us.

The hand turns again, settling on an arch created by two crisscrossing trunks at my three o'clock. I slow, nearing it with an unusual level of caution. No beings make themselves known, especially not a six-foot man in a top hat and fanciful giggle.

Unlike others that seem to have cracked as a result of a lightning strike, the two trunks before me appear to be chopped at the base. An ax lies amongst the shrubs, not even an attempt at concealing the weapon being made. Chels perks up when I stop, a tuft of orange hair sticking out of a crevice where the trunks overlap. Taking the hair between my fingers, I test it in front of the watch, and sure enough the hour hand tracks it back and forth. But I'm not convinced.

"Smells synthetic," Chels sniffs at the tuft in my hand.

"Feels it too," I agree. Sprinkling the orange hairs over the ground, I eye the ax once more. "Someone went through a lot of trouble to set me on the wrong track."

"Who?" Chels' gaze jerks up to my face. I shrug, huddling her close.

"And why?" I chew on the inside of my cheek. I only realized I had the Hatter's tracker in my possession last night, but someone else must have been watching. Stalking from the shadows. Spinning around, I search the trees for movement but it's a tiny creature sitting just before my feet that ends up capturing my attention.

"Oh, hello there," I kneel down. Chels doesn't pay the creature any mind, busy licking the length of my neck with her scratchy tongue.

"The vampire blood is quickly leaving your system," she says between licks. "Soon, you'll be free to go where you please."

"Hush Chels, look. We have a visitor." Offering out my hand, I allow the creature to sniff before going in for a stroke. Huge eyes like saucers blink vertically, white fur extending to a pair of mis-proportioned floppy ears from its small head. The body is much like Stan's, but he doesn't seem interested in coming out to say hello. His claws are currently embedded in my scalp, a spike of warning there that I completely ignore.

"Hey little one, it's okay. I'm not going to hurt you." Easing two fingers across the patch between its ears, it shudders and closes its large eyes. "Aren't you a cutie? I think I'll name you Snowy, the flying bush baby."

"Not Toothy, the flying squirrel piranha cross?" Chels asks, just as the creature's eyes re-open, now a worrying shade of blood red. Its mouth extends in a flash, several rows of jagged teeth as sharp as razors gnashing at my wrist.

"Nope!" I jerk upright. "Not cute!" Snapping at my ankle, I quickly swing my sneaker into the freakish piranha squirrel's face. It flies aside, preceded by a disappearing Chels who manages to land on the hilt of the ax and spin it upwards. The creature slots straight onto the blade, sliced clean in half with a fountain spray of crimson. The tree trunks around me audibly gasp and that, ladies and gentlemen, is when I know I've fucked up.

"Run," Chels laughs, as if she's commencing a new game. The pounding on the ground that beats in time with my erratic heart tells me this isn't a game I want to sit around and learn the rules of. Something is coming. Something big. A roar splits the trees as they pick up their roots and move aside, leaving me in the direct eyeline of Momma Piranha Squirrel. Oh. Fuck.

My feet can't move quickly enough. Darting through the trees with the tactic of disguising my route, the trunks continue to shift as I pass. A clear path is never far behind. Chels floats by my side and I quickly remove Stan from my ear to place him on her back.

"Protect him with your life. He's got so much left to live for," I tell Chels. Her smile drops, some lost sentiment about her life being lost waiting around for me going unsaid. But I have my own issues right now. The stomping of four heavy feet closes the distance, hindering my sprint for freedom. Wobbly legs, uneven footing, I yell for Cash, leaving all pretense of not needing a man to save me firmly behind.

A blur of speed rushes at me from either side, one pair of arms reaching me that millisecond faster to toss me in the air like a salad. A scream is torn from my lips as I tumble, landing upright on a broad back. Hands round to cup my ass and I grin against Cash's ear until I spot the leather jacket. Wait, this isn't...

"How many times am I going to have to save your ass?" Tweed shoots a look back but I turn his face forwards.

"At least four more before teatime," I grumble. Cash runs alongside us, keeping pace zipping through the forest. The same one that took me two days to navigate, and within minutes we're ascending the jewel dragon's dirty back. It doesn't escape me how Tweed keeps a line of trunks between Cash and I, but at the first sign of a clearing, I make a leap for it. Tweed's fingers dig into my thighs, holding me in place and when the piranha squirrel roars, I decide I'll stick it out right here.

Clearing the hump of the dragon's spine, I brave a look behind. The creature has nothing on vampire speed, but as a flash of white paws appear on the mound, I realize it doesn't need to be. Pouncing, the beast leaps high into the air and spreads the furry flaps beneath its arms.

"Tweed!" I shout, the looming shadow akin to a flying Bandersnatch blocking out the sun.

"I'm on it," he yells back, taking a sharp right. Leading us down a roundabout path to the entrance, we skid to a sharp halt. Only Tweed's hands on my ass holding me in place. Shoving at him to put me down, I peer into the wood, unnerved by the eerie silence of the Enchanted Wood.

"Where's Cash?" I whisper, not wanting to spook the wood. The trees across the clearing are stacked side by side, almost as if they don't want me to peep into its secrets. Tweed steps in beside my shoulder, his arms crossed and blonde hair perfectly quaffed.

"Who cares?" he shrugs. I stomp on his foot, doing myself more damage than anyone. Anger bubbles within, this troubled waters bullshit rubbing on my last nerve.

"Go fucking get him!" I point, jutting my chin out. If they want to act childish, then I will spank them. Wait...I'm getting off track. Tweed's eyes slide to mine with the roll of his head across his shoulder.

"For what? We're better off without him, trust me."

"Well, I don't trust you. You give me half-truths and – and...trick me with your dick," I huff. Stomping away, I do a U-turn and stalk straight back. In all my years of shouting at Polly, I've never been at a loss of what to say. Yet one hookah-induced night and a glimpse of teamwork, their rivalry just doesn't seem as sexy in the light of a new day. Rather it's pissing me off no end and I refuse to be the sanest one here.

Tweed drops his hands on his leather-clad thighs, sighing loudly.

"For the record, you never wanted the entire truth. You said so yourself. And there was no trickery on my behalf. You wanted my cock; you found a way to get it." I narrow my eyes into dangerous slits, refuting his insinuation. Yeah bitches, guess who went to finishing school.

"I swear to fuckery," I grab him by the vest and hurl myself forward when he doesn't budge, "if you don't go in there and retrieve your twin, you will never see my pussy again." I put on my best stern face, hoping he can't see through the cracks. I said he can't see it, not that he can't have it in the dark. When I'm high. And drunk, horny and desperate – in that order. Tweed looks to the sky for a slither of patience.

"Don't blame me when it all goes to shit."

"Oh, I will!" I shout after he's begun to walk away. Fury laces my tongue, his retreating back as offensive to me as the accusation he didn't want any part of what took place on the mushroom head last night. Dude just left me here, on my own?! Pacing back and forth, I'm seething. Unable to decide who I'm really mad at. Myself? Tweed? Hatter for this wild goose chase he's set me on. Shoving my hands into my pockets, I hold onto the pocket watch and small felt hat like my lifelines. Everything has been screwed up. The stress-free girl that found her way home fleeting on swift wings.

"I must say, that was rather touching," a graveled voice sounds from inside the trunks. I spin, spotting Cash leaning against a trunk near the entrance. Apple in hand, he pretends to be cool, biting large chunks that he spits onto the forest floor. My eyes track the way Tweed went, putting together the pieces.

"You've been there the entire time?" Cocky expression in place, Cash walks his long legs over to me, tilting my chin upwards with a single finger. Dipping his head, he inhales alongside the pulse thrumming at my neck. A move I now know as him checking for Tweed's blood in my system.

The same blood that's preventing me from entering certain territories, according to Chels. Where is she, by the way?

"You were in a rush to ditch his ass this morning. I was doing you a favor." Cash grins and I shift back, putting enough distance between us to pinch the bridge of my nose. I might as well be talking to myself. Something I'm well apt in, but when others are within ear shot, it's damn frustrating.

"Let me simplify this for you, Tweedle-*Dumb*," I emphasize that last word and Cash's smile slips. Tightening his shoulders, a snarl curling at his lip, the mirror image of Tweed shows through before he can catch himself. "This," I make a wide circle with my hand, "is an all or nothing situation. Guess you've made the decision loud and clear on everyone's behalf."

"Come on babe, we don't need that asshole. There's so much of Wonderlust I've yet to show you," Cash tries to reach for my hand and I jerk back. The list of my trigger words just gained a new addition. I'm no one's 'babe.'

"Your queen's castle, you mean?" I purse my lips at him. He can't even deny it and I laugh to myself. Well done Malice, you fool. You took these fuckers at face value, hoping you could reconcile them with your magical pussy. But everyone here has an ulterior motive, even me. "Fucking typical. You know what, Cash? Enjoy reacquainting with your right hand. I'm no one's pawn."

Swiveling, I make it all of two steps before Cash appears in front of me with a flash of movement. He has the audacity to look sheepish, his thumbs hooked in the loopholes of his jeans. I refuse to look beneath his neck, not going to have my libido pulled into the trap of his well-defined muscles through the see-through vest. Leaning into my space, Cash's lips scrape my jawline as he shifts to speak into my ear.

"Do I really look like the kind of guy that needs to rely on masturbating?" Pulling back to lick the length of his fang, I snort in his face.

"Oh of course, silly me," I shake my head. "I forgot everyone around here was desperate enough to take the only cock for miles as their last resort." We're not going to discuss how I did that exact same thing last night, times two. Without waiting for Cash's next douchebag response, I close my eyes. A strangled cry sounds from inside the wood, the roar of that beast shaking the very foundations, but my shits have run out. Tweed is un-killable and at this point, he and Cash deserve each other.

Opening my eyes, I find the setting I believed myself into. Alone at last, I wrap my arms around myself and let the first tear fall.

CHAPTER 25

TWEED - SIXTEEN YEARS AFTER ALICE'S DISAPPEARANCE

*T*he carriage pulls to a swift halt, the dragonflies hovering in front, just above the bark-covered ground, dropping their reins. Pushing the door open, I peer into the still forest, listening intently.

"Our first mission!" The bubbly redhead bounces on the suede bench behind me and I slam a hand onto her cargo-covered knee.

"Be still," I bark harshly. We've test-run this exact job time and again in the castle gardens. Forcing playing cards to act the role of any foe we may

encounter, Arabelle is as ready as she can be. If she keeps her damn head.
"The Enchanted Wood is no joke. Keep your focus, or next time I'll leave you
behind."

"Yeah, yeah. I can't 'learn from the master' from in here now, can I?"
Nudging passed me, her boots hit the ground and I follow after. We're
dressed the same, in combat fatigues and military grade boots. Still inside the
carriage, the Dodo shuffles around, puffing on a pipe as he grabs Arabelle's
backpack. Halting him in the doorway, I snatch the backpack and toss it over
my shoulder with mine.

"I don't think so," I growl. He stutters, fumbling his pipe between his
feathers.

"But the Queen said-"

"I don't give a shit what the Queen said. Arabelle is training to handle the
weight of the realm; she doesn't need you to carry her damn bag. Besides, when
the night gets dark and we grow hungry, you'd be the first item on the menu."
Shoving him backwards, I slam the door shut and call to the dragonflies.
"Return in three days. We will be waiting!" At least they have the good sense
to obey me.

Skidding away, the Dodo screams instructions for Arabelle to be careful,
wash behind her ears and not to fall for my charm. Fucking charm, there's a
joke if I ever heard one. The Queen assigned her fourteen-year-old daughter's
future to me, but doesn't trust me to set up camp with her for a couple of days?
Give me a break. I didn't realize the title of Knave of Hearts actually meant
glorified babysitter.

Throwing her backpack, Arabelle catches it with a smirk. She knew I'd
ditch the entourage, just as she knows she won't receive special favors from me.
I didn't become what I am today, whatever the fuck that is, by having others
carry my shit. Striding for the wood, a small book on legs rushes forward to
greet us and I kick it back into the darkened hole it crawled out of. I don't need

a map to know these woods. The parts Dee, I mean 'Cash' and I didn't create ourselves, are made up of the creatures left over from the royal trials once I'd defeated them. Marvelous concoctions made up in a lab with nowhere to belong. I resonate with that, but still doesn't mean I'll roll over and let them kill me.

"So...this mission," Arabelle slinks into my side on silent feet. I smirk internally at the stealthy ability she's mastered but withhold the praise. She doesn't need an overinflated ego getting in her way. "Are you going to tell me what it is, now we're finally here?"

Pulling a piece of paper from my back pocket, I present the princess with the sketch of a jeweled heart. Not the clipart type with a bowed arch and point, but an actual heart – aortas, valves and all. The drawing is in black and white, artistically shaded to form an exact replica from the memory of the vulture who saw it. How the Red Queen managed to force him to focus long enough from the starved-maddened state I found him in, discarded on the castle's doorstep, I don't need to know. Whatever brought him there was worth risking his life, the information slurring from his beak sparking her majesty's interest, and hence, I have a new quest to complete.

Satisfied Arabelle has committed the sketch to memory, I fold the paper and push it back into my cargo pocket. A storm is brewing and it's time to move. Cutting right, I lead Arabelle away from Jewel Forest. Too obvious, I decided the instant our destination was disclosed. Another fool can presume the Jewel Dragon holds this rare and sought-after heart, because they don't know what it contains.

A checkered path winds through the trees, bushes shrinking away from my presence. Arabelle remains a step behind at all times, my back acting as her shield. For weapons, we rely on our fists and the dual daggers concealed on our bodies.

A cry of a Jabbercocky filters in from the south and I pick up our pace. It won't take long for word to be mumbled between the mome raths, filtering through the land that the Princess of Hearts is wandering the Enchanted Forest. No one would dare make an attempt on her life in Red Kingdom, but out here, she's fair game. The fact she represents the last of a royal bloodline is a huge bonus.

"I'm...proud of you," I grunt beneath my breath. If it were anyone else, I'd presume they wouldn't hear me, but not Arabelle's refined hearing. Knowing not to leave the safety of my back, she places a hand between my shoulder blades, knowing exactly what I'm referring to. The events of yesterday.

The Queen entrusted her daughter's safety to me, but she never could have known I'd take my job so seriously. Strength is not only in the body, but of the mind. So, when suitors came calling, offering to wed the fourteen-year-old and impregnate her as soon as she is able, she shocked the kingdom by slitting each one of their throats. In cold blood, our trophy room of mounted heads just doubled. What can I say, she's her mother's daughter.

The path fades into the dirt, no longer inviting tourists to follow its track into the darkening depths. The deeper one journeys into the wood, the worse the weather becomes. Repetitive storms, like the one promised in the gray clouds overhead. I smell the air, not scenting acid rain. Only sulfur, the hint of electricity burning my nostrils.

"This way," I tell my companion, ducking into the thickened canopy. Bushes scratch our legs, vine snakes slithering across the forest floor. An X marks the trunks I am to follow, forming a shortcut between the foliage to Lazy River. Water spiders float on the surface, the leisurely flow refusing to be sped up by the gale blowing my hair back. We need to follow the river, but now isn't the time.

Jumping between boulders, I clear the water and land heavily on the other side. Another set of feet drop behind just as a rumbling bolt of lightning ignites the forest in a flash of spite. The forks split, hitting the ground. Explosions of dirt fly in all directions, like that of a minefield. Avoiding the newly blasted holes in the earth, I run. My backpack jostles, my awareness acutely on the shelter I seek. None of my instincts, however, are on Arabelle. She can fend for herself. A sheet of rain falls, thundering on us as sharply as hail.

The ground becomes slippery within an instant, squelching beneath my boots. Forcing the water from my eyes, I race practically blind, relying on memory to steer me right. A hill slope dips, my feet skidding to the base where rain is pooling rapidly. Wading through the murky depths, my toes hit the metal railway lines. Arabelle runs past, her tiny frame working in her favor as she throws her hands onto the brick platform and heaves herself up. I'm right behind her, bundling us into the hut and slamming the door as another spark of lightning hits, swiftly followed by a crack of thunder.

"Fire," I snap my fingers at the ashy pit in the center of the hut. Arabelle skids to her knees, snapping the legs of a dining chair into splinters. Sparking a rock against the metal patch on her gloves, the flames take instantly. I cross the space, yanking at a forgotten curtain crumpled in the corner. Dust flies free as I shake it out, fixing the edges over a discarded clothing rail.

"Change," I direct her to enter behind the curtain. Arabelle follows my instructions, no argument needed. When fight or flight sets in, the Princess is narrow minded. She can complete a test, no problem, but always to the cost of herself. She forgets to check her wounds, shed her wet clothing, hunt for food before she's racked with hunger.

I've vowed to protect her, but I won't be seen holding her hand to do it. Part of her training, which I crafted, is learning to trust her gut. Fundamental lessons which aren't teachable but are wholly necessary. She has to feel how to act on instinct, how to make split decisions within a second from losing her life and know not to regret them. No matter the cost.

While Arabelle changes into dry clothes from her waterproof backpack, I do the same on the other side of the curtain. She knows better than to look, not that she would. For 'Cash' as he's been renamed, maybe, but not me. A bond has formed over the years, one too much like siblingship to deny. Whereas Cash drifts further from me every day, the business of a Queen's Jester keeping him thoroughly entertained, Arabelle and I spend most days together. Morning jogs around the Kingdom, combat training before lunch, followed by a tutor session which I provide in the afternoons. The mind is as sharp a tool as any weapon.

"What is this place?" the Princess asks, wiping the curtain down to rest her damp clothes on the rail. I place mine there too, aiding her to carry it closer to the fire.

"It was supposed to be a train station," I sigh, peering around the walls. Shadows cling to the random splodges of paint on the brick wall. Rain pelts on the metal roof, only saved from the lightning by handmade pylons postered on all four corners outside.

"Supposed to be?" Arabelle asks, lowering into a cross legged sit on a beanbag. "Is it not?"

"What it should be, it isn't. And what it isn't, it is. If it were so, it would be, but it's not so it ain't."

"That's logic," Arabelle nods, a beaming big smile on her face. I pat her red curly head, retrieving some snack bars from our separate bags. We've packed individually, in case of a separation. "I like when you talk like that," she muses, biting into her bar. I huff. I do not. It reminds me of a time I don't bother dwelling on. When I had no care in the world and the only thing I knew how to do was talk nonsense.

"Cash and I spent a considerable amount of time in these woods in our teenage years. More so me, as he decided early on, he'd hide by the entrance and wait for me to complete whatever task your mother had set us. But on

the few occasions he joined me, we would stay here. Work on building the train outside. It was supposed to take us to another world," I bitterly chuckle to myself and hang my head.

"To the world where Alice is?" Arabelle breathes. I knew indulging her curiosity would lead here, to the one topic I refuse to speak about. But maybe it's time I opened the pandora's box I keep locked tight in my mind and delve into why exactly I struggle with this subject. The mere mention of Alice. Arabelle shuffles her bean bag closer, blinking up at me with large questioning eyes. "What was so special about her?"

"It's not so much her, per se," I shrug, using a stick to shift the fire's kindling. "But the chaos she brought. Whereas we were all bumbling along, playing the only roles we knew, she made us question everything. She rewrote the world we knew, turning the whimsical on its head. Everything was great before her, but when she left, the realm grew cold."

I shudder, uneasy with the ink spill of tainted memories filtering through my mind. My chest grows tight, the bitter taste of regret lingering on the back of my tongue. Not just from Alice's sudden disappearance, but the unknown of what happened to her, where she is, if she's even alive and the knowledge of what took place after. A dungeon filled with misfits, comforting one another in the dark while the royal trials killed us off one by one. I lost more than I knew I had, but I would always have Cash. No matter how distant he forces himself to be.

"Alice is an idea, that's all. A fantasy to cling onto when the world seems bleak, because not to have a dream is to resign altogether."

"So, she's your dream then? Your perfect fantasy?" Arabelle leans closer. I push to my feet, strolling to squint through a crack in the wall. The rain slams fiercely against the platform, creating a flood in the dip below. Lifting a stone from the ground, I mark off the tally on the inside of the brick, studying the rise of blizzards with each visit.

"We should be safe to leave in fifty-two minutes. Eat, rest up and make sure not to leave anything behind." Particularly your scent, I finish in my mind. The creatures of this wood may have been lab-created, but they're evolving. Adapting to their environment, reproducing with other species.

Arabelle obeys, shuffling her fresh fatigues into a tiny ball in the bean bag and closes her eyes for a brief, power nap. Turning my back on the wall, I lean back, assessing her. So small, yet wise and as tough as steel. It's times like this, I remember just how young the Princess really is. In a culture where we have been forced to age faster, the lines between our development and mentality merge into a mess of hormones and emotion. The overriding one for me was anger, yet Arabelle has yet to display any. She takes her training in her stride, compartmentalizing better than I ever could. For now, at least.

***

Trudging through the lengthy grass along the riverbank, we trail the water's edge as a rare blink of sunshine shines down. Not warm in any sense, but the mere yellow hue does much to boost Arabelle's mood. She's too used to the glorious weather that covers her home every day of the year. A mystery to us all, myself included. While the rest of the realm has fallen into gloomy darkness, the Red Kingdom thrives. With a skip in her step, she tries to venture ahead and I hold out my arm to prevent it. Tapping my temple, I warn her to keep her wits.

The river veers into a cave, gleaming against the illuminated cracks amongst the rock. Splashing my boots into its shallow depths, I steady myself for the vision I stumbled onto a few years ago. Not even Cash knows about this place. A solitary secret I've kept, until now. A soft blue glow awaits at the other side of the cave, which is more like a tunnel. Despite myself, I slip my hand into Arabelle's small one, steeling us both. Her eyes shoot to mine, a crinkle in her brows at the unusual affection, until we breach the opening and her confusion is forgotten.

"Woah," she breathes, and I nod. A cavern opens up before us, taller than the palace and possibly as wide. The river dips beneath a cover of crystallized cloud across the ground, swirling in tiers towards the ceiling. Shifting from the purest of icy blues to the depths of sea green, the clouds shift slowly, every spark of crystal embedded within catching the light from above. Across the other side, an archway of similar color awaits.

"This way," I tell Arabelle, not releasing her hand. Slowly carving a path through the cloud, her hold tightens on mine just before I ease us through the archway. Cloud consumes our vision, shifting over our skin with a trace of water droplets. Breaching the other side, my face tingles, my body alive with awareness. A gasp is torn from my side, Arabelle's mouth dropped open as our final destination trickles into view.

"Where...what...?"

"I call it the magician's library, as I've yet to hear of another name for it." Bookshelves line the edges of our vision, this space and time not appearing to have defined walls. Floating above the ground, the bookcases stretch for as far as I can see and as long as I've dared walk. Across the expanse, the cloud drifts along the ground to a portal. Sparkling blue, inviting and alluring. To where, who knows. Tilting Arabelle's chin upwards, I raise her eyes to the swirling, endless moon hovering above.

"Tweed," she whispers, not wanting to disturb the serenity. "It's stunning." I have to agree. The cloud, floating around the portal and up to the lunar sphere, feeds it with a million crystals, all churning in a never-ending spiral of beauty. "Y-you think the heart jewel is here?" Arabelle clocks on to the reason for our venture, eyeing the bookshelves with a trace of panic in her eyes. I release her hand now, shoving mine into my pocket to retrieve the sketch.

"Not quite," I lift the sketch into the air, tugging her closer to peer through my eye level. Beyond the page, on top of the arched portal, sits a particularly similar stone. One I'd committed to memory as the most cherished piece of treasure I'll ever set eyes on. Now I have to steal it.

"Oh Tweed, we can't. I don't care what my mother wants it for. This place...it's too sacred," my companion fumbles, yet my feet are already moving.

"We're all slaves, Princess. Slaves who are given pockets of freedom to hold the revolts at bay, but slaves none the less. We abide by the will of our captor or lose our heads." The cloud concealing the trickle of the stream beneath my feet wafts against my swift movements, my haste to get this over with riding me hard. Unlike any of my previous visits, I don't want to lose myself in the splendors of this alternate world. To wonder and ponder until I curl up and fall asleep on a shelf amongst the hardbacks.

I have a job to do, that's all. A command to fulfill in order to maintain my position as Knave. Nothing is too valuable. No gem too precious. If the Queen demands it, it is to be hers, whether retrieved by me or the army she has at her beck and call. At least I have the good sense to not destroy the rest of this heavenly place, as they would. Arabelle is at my back in a second, tugging on my arm and asking me to think. Clearly our lessons haven't been successful.

"There's no point questioning our orders," I whip my arm from her hold. "And you can't fail your first real test. This is where you prove yourself Arabelle. The Kingdom is watching for your success and our enemies are waiting for you to fail." Spurred by my words, the Princess stills her arguing. Sighing, she falls into step at my side, resigned to her fate. Not that she had a choice. Not if she wants to take charge of her future.

Nearing the portal, the pull latches onto our bodies. An invisible tie, trying to drag us inside. I steady my boots, forcing one foot in front of the other to near the edge of the void. A golden frame arches around the edge, adjoining *in the top center where the jewel heart pulses from the inside. Bursts of red and blue, brightening and dimming, igniting the network of veins inside. The exterior appears tough, like tinted crystals melded into one another, but it's the grid of golden webbing attaching it to the frame I'm worried about. Too thick for our blade to cut, too many to yank free.*

Testing the sturdiness of the frame, I climb, using the grip of my boots for traction. Halfway up, the cloud from the ground swirls higher, barring my view. Wafting it aside, the heart jewel gleams from above and I continue to climb. The cloud thickens, clogging my throat. I cough, the condensation droplets causing my hands to slip. Shaking the mist from around my face, I spy Arabelle on the ground, her gaze also fixed on the gem.

"You've always taught me to trust my instincts," she says hollowly. I don't have time for a lesson recap right now, leaping upwards to grab the top of the archway. My legs hang loose, the pull of the portal trying to drag me inside. Gritting my teeth, I stretch aside the heart, grazing my fingertips as a dagger spears through the center. I gasp, inhaling too much of the crystalized cloud. Razors slice at the inside of my throat, my boot just touching the frame long enough to kick myself backwards. Freefalling, I land hard on the ground and scramble away from the portal before I'm sucked inside.

"What the bloody hell was that?!" I shout, using Arabelle's body to pull myself upright. She hasn't moved, her head tilted and the hand that threw the dagger hovering in the air. Smoke spews from the cracks in the jewel, crimson intertwining with cyan. Floating down towards us, I try to pull Arabelle away but she's transfixed. Not a single goosebump on her skin or tremor rocking through her body. I swallow hard, tightening my grip around her upper arm. She's right – I did teach her about listening to our instincts, so with a weighted exhale, I close my eyes and trust hers.

The smoke drifts around my head, filling my senses. My eyelids fuse together, unable to open as an image takes root in my mind. The castle I reside in filters into view, from the tall white towers, rose-covered trellises and hearts carved into the arched entrance. But even as the sun continues to beam down, something doesn't seem quite right.

Upon grayed twig bushes, devoid of leaves, red roses hang, death clinging to their limp, discolored petals. At the base of the bushes, yellow dandelions have sprouted, poisoning the land with weeds. The gardens are overgrown, trampled and derelict.

The Queen storms from the main entrance, her cheeks stark red, puffing in and out violently. The heart-topped crop clutched in one hand is weathered, a small hand clutched in her other. Red hair curls between her fingers, the face that appears too much like her own frozen on a silent scream. Arabelle. Movement shifts in the doorway and I see myself, walking on numb feet before falling to my knees, the body of my twin laying dead in my arms.

"You are my Champion!" the Queen screams down at me. "Defy me again and it will be your head!" The vision shifts, blurring and resetting.

The castle stands tall on a crisp summer's day, the gardens luscious and green. Red roses thrive, not a weed in sight. Crowds gather on the steps of the large entrance, cheering as Arabelle strolls free from the doorway. Her body has grown, evident by the dress's corset cinched to her waist, her breasts threatening to fall free amongst the waves of her vibrant red curls.

On a painted smile, she waits for Cash and me to step in behind her as stoic bodyguards, before raising the head of her mother high in the air. The crowd goes wild, praising her like a rockstar and what strikes me as the most damming evidence, is the smile rooted on my face. The vision clears, leaving my mind in total blackness as a voice speaks gently into my ear.

This world hangs on a precipice,
the outcome still unknown.
The Knave is the deciding factor,

on what happens to your home.

Should he choose correctly,
No more blood needs to be shed.
A soul intended to be a pair
Will fuse to the one he weds.

Heed this final warning,
Should you remain to stand.
For one queen to thrive, the other must fall,
by her descendant's hand.

Find the final Caterpillar's cocoon,
keep it hidden until the day,
That marks the twentieth anniversary,
of when Alice went away.

Blinking free of the smoke, finding it too has dissipated, my eyes lock on the jewel heart. Bleak, colorless. Dead. The exterior has shattered, tumbling to the ground and rolling into the portal's depths. I stand, numb, confused, but the truth is as simple as it is horrifying. It wasn't simply a jewel at all, but a prophecy holder. What would the current Queen have done with such knowledge? Would Arabelle be dead by morning? Turning to the young girl, she peers up at me with tears streaming from her eyes.

"Did you...see that?" I ask, only to fill the silence. I can see the truth in her dread-filled expression. She did. Shuddering, Arabelle falls into my body and wraps her arms around my middle. I pat her back slowly, trying to regulate my heartbeat so she can't hear it pounding inside my chest.

"Talk to me, we can work this out. What do we know?"

"The heart said-"

"No, facts, Arabelle. What are the facts?" I give her a slight shake, bringing her attention back up to my face. Wiping away her tears on the back of her hand, she sniffs and nods. Her eyes fly wildly, catching the strands of her thoughts.

"We have two more days before the carriage arrives," she says, almost to herself. I nod, urging her to continue. "And no jewel heart to present my mother. So..."

"So?"

"We have time to formulate a plan," Arabelle nods. Resolution eases her shoulders back to a natural position, the hint of a smile pulling at her lips. That's the girl I know. Catching myself about to smile back, I clear my throat and step away, biting the inside of my cheek.

"I know this escalates things, but you are meant to rule. There's no doubt in my mind about it. Yet, I'm simply a Knave. Your Knave. I will follow whatever instruction you give, but I can't order you to give it. If you want to plot against the Queen, it has to be your idea. Your plan," I state and Arabelle finishes the rest.

"And my head on the line, should I fail." She nods to herself. It's a harsh reality, but I won't be caught undoing all the work I've put in over the years. Whichever Queen is on the throne holds my life in their hands. I'm a pawn in their royal games. A slave to their command and an accessory on their arm.

Arabelle understands this better than anyone, and although I thought this would be a trial of an entirely different nature, this is the chance to prove herself. Will she have what it takes to be a true warrior or fall at the last hurdle. Will she let her loving bond override her sense of duty? Bringing her hardened stare back to mine, her jaw is set and shoulders are squared.

"I'll take any head I need to secure the safety of the realm."

"I know," I cup her small, tear-stained cheek, "and I can't wait to watch you do it."

CHAPTER 26

MAL

E very time I straighten one of the crooked frames on the wall, another jerks out of place. I sigh, resigning myself that they are just supposed to be lopsided and step back. Chels raises her head from the fluffy bed in the corner of the cupboard, not a stranger to the hattery it would seem.

"Are you actually going to go anywhere, or are you happy staring?" she asks, tucking her head back into her feet. Stan is curled up on her back, sleeping soundlessly.

"Nope. This is exactly where I'm meant to be," I mutter, glancing over the paintings for the millionth time. I now recognize the nest of feathers as Chels' cavern, although the long table set for tea still has no visitors. I reach out to straighten the farmyard, picturing the black-haired girl who's probably mixing all the whole ingredients into Cook's soup.

"Don't even think about it," Chels says without batting those huge eyes in my direction. "Mary Ann must stay where she is. Enough of Wonderlust is out of balance already." I pout, folding my arms. I'm sure there's plenty of institute guards and attorneys who said the same about me, but here I am. Our surroundings don't define us. Then again, a life in hiding isn't much more glamorous than one in isolation.

Slinking out of the cupboard behind the bookcase, leaving the portals for another time, I drop into the Hatter's chair and drop my head onto the wood surface of his desk. Chels follows, pushing the cupboard closed with her tail and stretches out her back.

"You're annoyed they haven't come looking for you," she grins, floating to sit on my head like a Russian hat with alopecia.

"No, I'm not!" I shout against the wood, the lie falling flat. Okay fine, yes I am. I'm beyond annoyed. I'm fricking agitated as hell. And worse, starting to doubt myself. It's easy to inflate my ego when there's no one around to disprove my awesomeness. But in the cold face of rejection, this time seems to be taking forever. Two days in fact since I appeared at the Hattery to continue my investigation alone. And so far, I've found a whole stack of nothing.

Dislodging Chels to lift my head, a newspaper sticks to my cheek and I peel it away. 'Crazy Carroll Kid Causes College Chaos' spans the header in chunky ink block letters. I chuckle to myself, taking a rare trip down memory lane whilst Chels blinks impatiently for an explanation.

"Every college has that head bitch and her bunch of minions. Mine happened to be the planning committee for the summer ball and decided, due to my attendance, a Wonderland fancy dress theme would be fitting. Thought they could humiliate me, maybe force me to drop out. But I sure showed them – for no Wonderland party is complete without a heavy dose of magic mushrooms in the punch. Funnily enough, I wasn't the only lunatic then – those virgins went ape-shit, high as kites and made even *me* look sane."

I shake my head, the smile rooted on my face. The dynamics of high school cliques sure changed that night, and I was on hand to photograph every second of it. Head bitch with her tongue down a math geek's throat, the vomit he spewed over her just after. Three guesses as to who really dropped out of school and spoiler alert, it wasn't me.

A siren sounds in the street outside and laughter forgotten, I duck beneath the desk. Not again. I've been so careful to creep low, stay out of sight from the Step-Herd Wives when they pass the warped windows. Drawing my knees up to my chest, my trousers I tried to sew for myself stretch, more than a couple of the seams snapping. Chels wafts into the small space, giving me a 'told-you-so' look. The pattern was already cut, the sewing machine was collecting dust and I tried my best. What else does she want from me?

Curling into a ball over my bare feet, she purrs and I rest back against the wood. At some point in the near future, I need to assess what I'm doing with my life. Today is not that day. The sirens outside continue to blare, so loud I'm convinced there's a speaker on every building. Communication sounds just beneath the noise and I'm certain this time – I've been rumbled. Say goodbye to stalking around the Hattery in hopes its long-lost owner will pop out of one of the painted portals.

Stan hops from Chels' back to the ground, his tiny claws scratching at a wooden panel. I try to shoo him aside from making a right mess of the flooring, my fingers stroking the slight bump to an otherwise smooth surface. Picking him up when he tries to claw my hand, I shove him in my hair and pry the panel back.

A beautifully crafted wooden box provides an assortment of random objects anyone else would throw out. But not Hatter. He saw treasure amongst the trash, keepsakes within the crap. That's probably why he liked me so much. I pick at a thimble, some paperclips and the torn-away ends of his fingerless gloves. All ten are right here, stashed for safe keeping. Lifting a red ribbon, it unravels to reveal a tooth. A tiny spec of a canine, definitely human and I'm fairly certain it's mine. The rubble that rains down from the rest of the ribbon confirms it – fyi, the damn rock cakes in this realm are actually made with rocks.

As quickly as it began, the siren cuts off, leaving another noise to frown at. Cheering! I crawl out of my hiding spot, climbing the desk to peer through a circular window. Being on the second story, I'm provided a clear view of the street outside and no one would spot me, unless they were specifically looking for a peeping Tom.

A crowd of animals has assembled, all in their best dressed attire. Frilly frocks, high heels. Huge fascinators fixed between their furry ears and purses clutched in claws and hooves. Straining to see who or what they're cheering for, I smush my cheek against the glass.

At the far end of the street, where I was washed up and spat out, a row of playing cards with spears waddle forward. Their bodies sway in time, stubby feet stepping in line. Working their way closer, I watch all of the Hearts leading the parade. A whole deck of them, from aces to tens, preceded by a float.

Smothered with roses, it rolls smoothly up the cobbled street. A stage on off-roading wheels, draped in red and white sashes. Amongst the flowers, painted illustrations fill the gaps, much too dainty to make out from up here. They wind and twist as a comic strip would, taking the eye of the beholder on a journey to the tip of the podium. And there she is. Amidst a tall, vertical heart, stands the Queen.

Younger than I remember, her beauty radiates. Flawless creamy skin, vibrant red curls. I'd put her around my age, with a body to die for. Tall and athletic, cinched at the waist by a corseted dress in black and red, split thigh up one side of the skirt. Killer black boots are visible on her dainty feet, her appearance that of a rockstar as opposed to a Queen. But fuck that bitch, for it's the male at her side that has my undivided attention. The very same one with his arm around the Queen's waist, his cold green eyes observing the gathered crowd.

Tweed.

My breathing stalls. My chest tightens. I drop low when his face tilts upwards, not missing the keen interest he has in the Hattery. Balling my fists, I slam them down on the wooden desk at my feet. So that's where he's been. Probably where they both were the past couple of days. They took my hissy fit at face value and ran back to their precious queens. So much for liking a challenge.

"Chels, I'm free of vamp blood right?" I double check, already jumping down to the floor. The curved smile follows me racing down the stairs, swinging in front of my face as I hit the bottom step.

"All clear. However-"

"So, I can go wherever I like undetected?" She gives the slightest incline to her head and I bat her out of my way. Rushing over to the Hatter's workstation, I gather up all of the material offcuts and bundle them into my arms.

"The twins will still be able to scent you-" Chels says in the background but it's too late; I've already stopped listening. Ducking behind a tall stack of boxes, out of sight from the thin netted curtains over the main windows, I throw the materials high into the air and snap my eyes shut.

Show me the beast.

My limbs contort, shrinking and spasming as I lose two feet in height. Material rains over me, clinging to my body and pulling tight around the gray fur that spawns there. My nose lengths and twitches, a pair of ears popping through the blonde hair I retain. Although, to my credit, I make sure to smooth it down and twist into perfectly set curls that Stan can use as a slip and slide when he gets bored. Chels watches on keenly, until the material has settled and I give her a spin of my dress.

"Well, what do you think?" I ask. In the reflection of her huge eyes, I can see the black patches smeared across my beady eyes, the white whiskers fanning from my cream nose. Ringed stripes circle my petite face and when I smile, it's all sharp, tiny teeth.

"A raccoon was your go-to?" Chels drawls, as if she's not massively impressed. I nod, stepping out of the discarded rags and threads in my chunky wedges.

"Raccoons are my spirit animal. Cute but feral," I shrug my little shoulders. Drawing the slender claws I now have for fingers over my arms, I shudder at how good it feels. I'm definitely scheduling in a decent back scratch for later. Through the netted curtains, I see the float has just passed, followed by the rest of the playing cards. Two rows of a Jack, Queen and King to finish the parade and permit the crowd to bundle along after them. It's showtime.

"I think I'll hang back from this particular mission, for when you get yourself killed. Someone will need to make sure your affairs are in order," Chels twirls over to an open notepad on the floor. Her tail swoops up a pen.

"What would you like them to be?" I stop halfway to the door, tapping an elongated nail on my chin.

"Ensure the porn site I set up in college continues to run - Chicks on Dicks. Chipping away at my family's money and providing the world with jerk material is my legacy." Bopping the rest of the way to the door, a sharp scratch behind my left ear makes me pause. Stan hops onto my shoulder, and then to my paw. His large eyes stare up at me, the twitch of his whiskers mirroring my own. I sigh, pulling him close for a nose bump. He's right – this isn't his fight. Placing him on the floor, he runs into Chels' body and snuggles into her hind leg. Two lonely souls finding solace in each other – I admire that.

Straightening and puffing out my furry chest in a lace sweetheart neckline, I slip through the main door and join the parade. Huddled with the rest of the foxes and badgers, we jog to keep up with the float, twisting through the streets until a raised stage becomes visible.

"Did you hear what the grapevine said?" a red panda growls to my left, her voice thick with anger.

"I spoke to it this morning whilst at the wishing well. I can't believe he's dead!" a stalk replies, keeping her beak low. I lean into their small group to listen closer.

"It was his own stupid fault," another scoffs. Intrigued, I slow my pace to keep in step with them. A squawking voice joins to ask what's happening and the rest rush to shush her.

"The King of Diamonds has been murdered." A round of gasps follows. "Apparently he was trying to avoid the men's curse by disguising himself as the March Hare and hid inside his own maze."

"He didn't hide well enough! Someone decapitated him with his own guillotine."

"He always was a paranoid man, but it's still treason. Someone must pay with their own head!" They fall into hushed aggravation and I balk. Swallowing thickly, I push on by. Remaining hunched, I worm through the crowd towards a concrete fountain in the center of the clearing, only stepping on one hedgehog along the way.

What kind of stupid asshole would disguise themselves as an animal in the first place? Looking down at my clawed hands, I roll my beady eyes. Well really, the King ruled a kingdom – he, at least, should have known better. And he did try to behead me first. What was I supposed do? Lay down and die when I'm a woman on a mission? What's done is done and I'll just add this indiscretion to the lengthy list of why everyone around here wants to kill me.

Stretching high and featuring a statue of a salmon jumping upstream, I stand on the fountain's edge to see the Queen ascending her podium, a golden crown posed on her delicate head. Tweed holds her hand to aid her on the steps, joining her side at the top. His stance is wide, hands clasped before him like a guard. Yet her lingering touches around his steel chest plate suggest otherwise. I growl a raccoon-worthy snarl.

"Ladies and Fur-Folk!" she smiles her heart painted lips behind a microphone stand and the crowd erupts in applause. "Thank you for hosting me on the second anniversary of the Frabjous Day! We shall all party like royalty today, rejoicing in our recent history.

"With your support and faith, I was able to fulfill my destiny, ridding this land of one traitorous queen and banishing another in the same, joyous day! It was you, the people, who chose to put me in sole power of Wonderlust. And for that, I thank you. May you enjoy a day of festivities and laughter with your loved ones!"

The next round of cheering is so forceful, I wobble on my wedges by the fountain's edge. Flats would have been much more suitable but I'd wanted to fit in, for once. Brushing down the monotone dress, incredibly similar to the Queen's, I brace myself against the fountain's second tier. The pool in which the salmon is trying to flee, helpfully giving me the perfect cover from Tweed's shrewd gaze. I don't know what I expected, but he's just as tense and broody as usual, scanning the crowd. For me? That's probably wishful thinking.

The Queen clears her throat and the cheers lessen, every creature around me hanging on bated breath for her next words.

"Before the celebrations begin, I must share some worrying news. As you are all aware, the Alice has returned," she lowers her head and I twitch. Gripping the edge of the fountain tighter, I summon all of my strength to not freak out here. Trigger word or not, I must. Stay. Calm. Yet the raccoon's savage nature thrums within me. My eye starts to tick, quickly followed by my cheek.

Not here, Mal. Not now.

Shuddering, eyes closed tight, I hop to the ground and push my way back through the crowd blind. One hand outstretched to shove creatures aside, the other clamped over my head to hold in whatever sound is about to burst free of my jaws. Something between a screech and a howl, I reckon. Through the speakers, the Queen's voice continues on, oblivious of the rat in their midst. Ahh dammit, I should have transformed into a rat.

"A new prophecy has awakened with the rise of the last Caterpillar. It is imperative, if you should run into this individual, to call for the champion. He will deliver her to the Red Castle, where we can begin returning Wonderlust to what it once was." I peer back through the heads to see her patting Tweed's chest plate, and this time, there's no cheer. Silence echoes through the clearing, somehow seeming louder. Either these women don't like or trust Tweed, but I don't have time to stand around wondering how to board the hatred bus. If the Queen is bothered by the frosty response to her 'Champion' her smile doesn't show it.

"After Alice's sacrifice, your men shall be returned!" This time, there's no stopping the eruption of praise, or my outburst. Diving free of the throng and into the nearest alleyway, the roars behind cover my own, a full flip-out taking hold of my tiny limbs. Two trash cans become my victims, my heels bashing them into the brick wall behind. Grabbing the lids, I smash them either side of my head, like a defective mechanical monkey.

Bang, bang, bang.

Agony explodes at my temples, a scattered scream rattling from my snout. With each bash, my tiny teeth chatter together and a further cringe is drawn out of me. Still, the instant headache is welcome over the urge to scratch my own flesh from my bones. I hate that word. That name and every blonde cliché that follows it like a bad smell. I'm not that girl. I'm a badass bitch who carves her own future, creates her own destiny.

Stopping short of giving myself brain damage, I hurl the lids aside as the applause dies down. My chest is heavy, and when I catch the eye of a concerned four-foot owl in a snazzy jumpsuit, I snarl for her to move the fuck on. I've got business to take care of, and a plan to formulate.

Between the chaos battering around my head and doubling over to vomit a furball full of raccoon hair onto the ground, something filters through.

"Your men shall be returned."

So, the red queen is hiding all of the men I'm being accused for...I don't know what – scaring them away? Who the fuck knows, but what I do know is where there are men, there must be the Hatter. In the one place I've been avoiding, he's probably caged and waiting for my valiant rescue. And after knocking some non-sense into myself, I'm ready to go get him back. With a long exhale, I close my eyes, tap my heels together and pay no notice to the grip closing on the back of my head as I whisper, 'there's no place like home.'

CHAPTER 27

MAL

Appearing in a suite fit for a king, movement shifts on the huge, heart-shaped bed. Interlinking limbs, bruised bodies. Heads of all hair colors rise, gasping in excitement for the male holding me in place.

"Tweed!" their voices all mutter together. "You've returned so soon."

"He's back for more and he brought a snack," a woman with a mermaid tail, gills and pointed teeth smiles. My eyebrows touch my hairline. I notice a hint of feathers and scales amongst the mix before Tweed rushes me from the room with a burst of vampire speed. The scenery blurs, my stomach churning as we spin down a spiral of gray I'd guess is a staircase. Next thing I know, my cheek is being slammed into the hard metal of a locker.

"What the fuck was that?!" I grit out, my elongated mouth smushed. Tweed's grip on my hair tightens, a spike of discomfort beside my pointed ear becoming apparent.

"You're bleeding," he groans as if feeling the pain himself. "Turn back to yourself so I can heal you." My tiny nostrils flare, my stubbornness screaming to refuse. But then again, the migraine that's becoming one with my skull isn't going to do me any favors when I start kicking his ass for being a slutty vampire asshole. Shuddering back into my human body, my legs stretch the two feet I was missing to put me directly beneath Tweed's heavy breathing that fans my neck. His chest pushes against my back, sandwiching me between the cold metal of his chest plate and the lockers.

"Drink," he orders, tearing a chunk into his own wrist and pushing it in front of my face. Orange liquid pools there, dripping onto the floor with each second I refuse to obey. Tweed growls, pushing it against my lips and I push them together. Nope, not today. His hand in my hair shifts to wrap around my neck, his fangs brushing my ear.

"Do you want to know your problem, Malice?" I shake my head. "You don't want to ask the questions burning in your mind, scared of the answers. Scared that your body will still react to me this way." I snort, but when his knee shifts between my legs, I can feel how wet I am. I didn't bother trying to fit human underwear around the raccoon's tail, so now I'm bare and seeping into Tweed's slacks. Dammit. "I'm the monster of your nightmares, remember? But you can't hate me. Everything that annoys you about me, turns you on that much more."

My mouth parts and he pushes his wrist inside. Droplets skate over my tongue, sugary sweet now and my headache eases instantly. Pulling back from him, I lick my lips, savoring his taste. Unlike the bitterness I tasted before, his blood calls to me now. Like the perfect builder's tea, a mix of sweet and strength that could power me for the rest of the day. But, with the relief of pain, comes another realization.

"My access to Wonderlust is restricted now," I whisper, cementing the fact to myself. Tweed doesn't step away, cheek scraping my temple as if he can't help himself.

"Only to the mainland. You can't pass into the Shadow Planes with my blood in your system." I manage a nod, piecing together the queen's speech I only caught parts of.

"Where Cash's queen has been banished," I finish the rest. It makes so much sense he would want to keep me from finding the Queen of Spades. At this point, I have no reservations that she is the one who could help me in my quest the most. The Red Queen is evil, ruthless. She kills whoever she deems a threat and banishes those she can't. Tweed's mouth quirks, the hint of a smile touching my cheek when he drops his head.

"You have been listening. Good girl," his free hand pats the side of my ass. I struggle beneath his dominance, wanting to regain the upper hand. He refuses to budge. "Do you want your reward?"

He's mocking me, making me ache for him so hard. I want to refuse, but the words never come. So, I do the only thing I can think of to take back a modicum of control. Throwing my head back, Tweed's nose crunches and his hand on my throat tightens throughout the duration of his roar. "Have it your way."

I hear the clink of his buckle before a strap of leather whips against my calf. I yelp, trying to reach down to stroke my leg. The strap catches my wrist, then the other in front of me as Tweed deftly loops the buckle through his belt with one hand. Pulling tight, he releases my neck in favor of wrenching my arms upwards, slamming the end of his belt in a locker high above my head. Then I'm left waiting. Trembling for contact, but nothing except for cool air graces the tops of my thighs where the dress has risen.

"Tell me you want me," he groans. I try to look over my shoulder but Tweed pushes a hand against my cheek to hold my face against the cold metal. Never one to be seen begging, I settle with enough of the truth that my voice doesn't quiver with anticipation.

"I want you...to kiss me," I whimper. He chuckles, a raw and unused sound that seems unnaturally cruel. Then why does my pussy clench even tighter? Why do I want to draw that rumble from him a thousand times more?

"A predator doesn't *kiss* his prey. He destroys it." Removing his hand, I see his silhouette in my peripheral vision. A loud clang from his chest plate hitting the floor makes me jump and without time to recover, the back of my dress is flipped up and his cock slams into me. I gasp, pushing myself into the lockers in an attempt to escape his invasion. Tweed rocks himself within me, allowing my pussy to stretch to his manly size.

"Doesn't that feel better, Malice?" His forearms come to rest either side of my head, not an inch of space between us. I rise onto my tiptoes in the wedges, sinking my teeth into my bottom lip. Sliding back, Tweed thrusts into me with the same force as before. "Don't you love being fucked by your enemy?"

"Yes," I answer honestly. His fingers trickle up my thighs, his palms spreading my ass.

"Yes, what?" Thumbs toy with the edge of my pussy, Tweed feeling himself sliding in and out of me.

"Yes...cuntface." The top half of my dress is whipped down, my breasts suddenly exposed and nipples pinched hard.

"Keep goading. You'll learn to regret it." I seriously doubt that. Irritating Tweed is the last scrap of control I have left. My body is his, my mind is surrendering. My words are all I can still lay claim to. Tugging on my wrists, I work with Tweed's increasing rhythm, meeting his thrusts with the same vigor. His groin slaps against my ass, drowning out the muffled cries I try to hold back. My G-spot takes a beating, and when Tweed's hand rounds to rub my clit, his lips meet my ear.

"Oh, by the way, you're not allowed to cum."

"Well, you're not allowed to be a twat, but you still manage-" Tweed's dick is torn away, my body spun harshly and thrown into the lockers with my hands twisted.

"You will do as I say, or I will leave you high and dry, wishing for once in your life, you'd let yourself submit to someone." Tweed's green eyes begin to glow and I shudder at the wave of power he tries to wash over me. I'm sure such a display had the entire flock in his bed cowering. I'm not so easily persuaded, but I want to be.

When I'm with Tweed, I'm not the little girl who never grew up. Or the crazy bitch people would prefer to be locked away than leave unleashed. But old habits die hard and I hold his stare with a bit too much focus to concede.

"You've been waiting so long to be dominated. Why deny it now?" Without waiting for an answer, Tweed grabs my thighs and hoists me up, sliding me onto the length of his glistening cock. It fills me entirely, the open angle giving him full access. Free from the chest plate, his torso is exposed. Abs flex, his chest rising and falling evenly. I would trace his tattoos with my tongue if I could reach, the snake slithering amongst the roses threatening to take a bite out of me. The stopwatch inked on Tweed's hip has stopped ticking, both hands on number six.

He doesn't care for my exploration. Tweed is intent to screw me into submission, and that's exactly what he tries to do. Locking my ankles behind his back, I try to slow his harsh movements, but it doesn't work. I can't control Tweed as much as I can't understand him. Holding my stare, his eyes bore through mine, a snarl pulling at his top lip.

"Do! Not! Cum!" Each word is punctuated with a hard thrust. My core tightens, his words having the opposite effect. Stretching my head to the side, gripping the belt to hold myself up, my eyes scrunch closed.

Teeth sink into my areola and I gasp, Tweed's mouth closing around my nipple. He sucks hard, sending jolts of pleasure encased in pain directly to my clit. I push my chest into him, wishing my hands could claw through his blonde hair and down his broad back. I'd scar him so deeply, not even his vampire blood could heal the marks. Moving onto the other side, I roll my hips in time with his increasing pace.

Not even Tweed can hide the effects my pussy is having on him, a strained expression overtaking his face when his head rises to my lips. I push my mouth forward on instinct and he diverts last minute, the shadow of a smirk denting his cheek.

I'm going to slap him. The instant I am free.

The blunt head of his cock slams into me. Faster, deeper. His nails dig into my ass, fingers drawing closer to my puckered hole. I push into him, wanting it all. Willing to take everything he gives. Ripples flutter against the inside of my pussy, my toes curl. Tweed's realization dawns.

"Malice," he growls, warning me to obey. Unfortunately for Tweed, all I hear is a dare to do the exact opposite.

"Fuck you," I grind out, convulsing all over his cock. Throwing my head back on a scream, his teeth sink into my throat. My climax intensifies.

Pleasure rips me in half, throes of ecstasy blinding me. Preparing to break my fingers through the death-like grip on the leather, I hold myself still while Tweed powers on. Fucking my body, claiming my blood. He sucks in time with his thrusts, drawing untold noises from me. The sea of my rapture doesn't cease, and soon enough Tweed has fallen over the precipice with me.

Hurtling into the unknown, his body falls into mine. Spurts of cum fill me with nowhere to go, dripping onto the floor at his feet. Eventually, finally, Tweed stills, his head on my shoulder. The warm trickle of blood pools along my collar bone and travels down my cleavage.

"I'm starting to get the feeling you're punishing me for something," I breathe through my ragged pants. Sweat coats my skin, my wrists growing as sore as the ache between my legs. Tweed grunts, raising his dulled gaze to mine.

"Perhaps for sending me back into the Enchanted Wood for the dickhead I share DNA with." Ahh, there it is. "That beast tore me to pieces, took days to knit my limbs back together." I cock my brow, fighting with myself to ignore the hard-rock cock still buried inside of me.

"All those women in your bed don't seem to mind stroking you better." This time, Tweed does smile and I almost forget I'm trying to be mad at him. A smooth curve from one hidden dimple to the next, his jaw appearing squarer. It changes his entire face from handsome brooding asshole to stunning brooding asshole. The prominent Adam's apple in his throat bobs.

"Green really isn't your color," he muses, taking a strand of my wild hair in his fingers. "Try orange, it's much more becoming."

"Ex-excuse m-me, Sir?" a quivering voice sounds from the doorway. Tweed shifts to the side, blocking my view and I'm not sure who's benefit that is for. "You're required back in the m-market place. There's been a...development in finding Al-"

"I'm on my way," Tweed quickly interjects. His green eyes hold mine steadily and I exhale. That was a close one. The door closes and Tweed unhooks my hands before setting me down. Pulling out of me, he doesn't care that the evidence of what he just did to me is running down the inside of my legs. In fact, I think he prefers it. "There's a hot tub and sauna through that door. Relax out of sight until I return. Then we'll...talk."

"Talk?" I lift a brow, popping a hand on my hip. Tweed nods slowly, unsure but agreeing anyway.

"Whatever you wish to know, I will tell you." Whipping his belt from the locker and not bothering with his chest plate, Tweed tucks himself into his pants as he walks, shoving the locker room door open with every ounce of tension back between his shoulders. I sigh, picking up the pieces of my spirit and slink towards the room he pointed out, peeling off my dress as I go. Pushing through the door, a cloud of steam envelopes me.

"You took your time," a voice seeps through and I flinch. The steam clears and a mirror image of the man that just ruined me is sprawled inside the hot tub on a mounted, stone base. Cash tilts his head, his eyes drinking me in. Particularly the puddle of blood at my neck, dripping down the center of my body that has his nostrils flaring. Easy smirk in place, his tattooed arm thrown over the back of the tub. From his fingers, the Hatter's stopwatch swings back and forth. I gasp, rushing forward and Cash drops it as my hands lunge forward to catch it.

"Did you pickpocket this from me in the woods?" I frown. The hour hand is pointing to the number six and I look to the ground. Instead of answering, Cash chuckles.

"Come here. I have something else you want," Cash tells me. Those same fingers that held the watch reach out. Placing it down safely on the pile of his clothes, I take his hand and climb the two stone steps. The water is gloriously hot, bubbling and hiding Cash's body from his chest downwards. His hand doesn't release mine, pulling me effortlessly into his lap. His dick juts between us and I roll my eyes.

"Is it your dick, the thing I'm supposed to want?" I quirk a brow. His smile deepens.

"Usually, but not this time." Sliding a wet hand around my nape, Cash's mouth crashes onto mine. He catches me off guard, my lips opening on a gasp that he takes full advantage of and spearing his tongue inside. Gliding over mine, Cash does indeed give me what I want.

A band-aid for the open scar on my soul. A crevice of closure I haven't been able to fill. Anyone can be fucked and cast aside, but to be kissed. To feel wanted. That's the side of myself I struggle with the most. Someone so independent shouldn't crave comfort like I do. Shouldn't yearn for intimacy. But here Cash is, giving it to me anyway.

Melting into his body, my hands travel the span of his steady shoulders. His thick traps dip into bulging biceps. The Tweedles had the glow up of the century, and I'm glad I'm here to see it. Damn. I'm just glad I'm here. Amidst the chaos and mystery, I'm home.

Succumbing to the freedom Cash provides, I dive further into his kiss. My tongue dances with his, skating back and forth where no one is more in control than the other. We're one body, one being, falling into tune of the song our spirts create. His hands shift into my hair, massaging my scalp and I break away on a sigh. Heavy-lidded eyes, relaxed limbs. I sink into Cash's body, languid in the water raging around us.

"Let me show you the way your body should be worshiped, Crazy One," he mutters beside my ear, and without reservation, glides my channel, slickened by his brother's cum, onto his solid shaft.

CHAPTER 28

MAL

Turns out, the locker room doesn't hold many clothing options for humans. Luckily, the red basketball jersey I chose is long enough to cover the rear hole in my leggings for a tail of some sort. Another plus side is Cash groans when I bend over to finish tying the heart-printed sneakers on my feet. White otherwise with red laces, I'd have easily worn these in the human world. I stand, turning to find him by the door with Tweed's chest plate secured in place.

"Hey, watch this," he smirks, pushing a hand through his hair. Hunching his shoulders, a scowl falls over his face and he stares upon me with the same reserved hunger Tweed does. It's freaky really, but I hold back my laughter. Slinking from the locker room, Cash leads me down a hallway of checked flooring and heart shaped wallpaper. The open archways are framed with gold, flourishes of roses in each corner.

Pocket watch clutched in my hand; the hour hand is yet to move. Cash remains close to the wall, blocking my view as we enter a main lobby. A few playing cards reaching up to ten-feet tall shuffle by, paying us no mind. Their expressions are sunken, their movements so sluggish, I imagine they don't care either way.

Passing through the entrance, I peer around the varnished double doors on one side, an open exit to the gardens on the opposite and grand staircase against the right wall. Cash grabs my wrist, hurrying me along the next hallway to a door unlike any others. Steel and bolted, secured with a thick chain around the handle. Cash lifts a petite glass bottle on a nearby table, exposing the key underneath and pushes it into the lock.

"S-sir?" the same voice I heard address Tweed drifts down the hallway. A clip-clop of hooves trot closer, the tall piglet on hind legs blushing at the sight of me. Yeah, I'm sure he saw my naked body shoved between Tweed's and the lockers. Ducking his head into the butler suit he's wearing; a series of small snorts and a sneeze tickles his snout. "I th-thought"

"Can it PB, or I'll can you, in pieces with gravy," Cash snarls. PB flinches, falling back on his curled tail with a squeal. I cringe at the pitch, thankful when Cash pops the door and I enter into the darkness. The hand at my wrist travels down to interlink with my fingers once we're concealed from view, Cash leading me in the dark.

"Watch your step," he warns. I slowly feel my way down a stone staircase until Cash grows bored of my hesitation. Whipping me into the cradle of his arms, he jumps the rest of the way. Wind sails through my hair, my lips clamping together to conceal my scream. Landing on the ground gracefully, Cash lowers me and strikes a match against the wall. Lighting a flame torch, a dungeon is displayed before me. Thick bars glint in the flames, the captors not bothering to look our way. I frown, stepping closer to peer into the six cells creating a U around me.

"They're..." I whisper, unsure if they're asleep or have just given up on living. Slipping his hand into mine, Cash rescues the pocket watch from my tightened grip before I smash it.

"Playing cards," Cash answers for me. "Every suit except hearts. Only the hearts are allowed topside." Piled high, the cards lay on top of one another in stacks to the ceiling high above. Their heads, hands and feet hang floppy, but it's the last cell I'm drawn to. I approach the mini playing cards. These are vertical, slotting together like vinyl records in a box.

"I don't understand. Why are the other suits being kept prisoner?"

"They're not playing cards, not really," Cash lowers a hand onto my shoulder. "These are all the men missing from the realm." I gasp, covering my mouth when a few of the mini card's heads turn my way. Their eyes are bleak, a spark of life returning when they spot me. I crouch low, reaching through the bars to the nearest one. A white gloved hand reaches out, brushing my hand with a silent plea on his lips.

Help me.

"They're children," a shudder rolls through me. "I still don't get why they are here. Just spell it out for me, Cash. No riddles."

"As you wish," his hand draws me up and over to a wooden bench facing the cell in the center. This one houses the animals, hints of tails and pointed ears poking out of the stacks. The bottom card is the biggest, almost the size of the entire cell floor with a thick, scaled tail and head of the missing Jabbercocky.

"I'm sure you've wondered why you were ejected from Wonderland all those years ago," Cash starts, his hand trailing over the thigh of my leggings. My heart thunders in my chest.

"To some, magic is power. To others, it causes jealousy. While you were running free in our land, a war was breaking out for which suit should claim you to join their ranks. But someone was smarter. They knew hiding you in the human world would remove you from the clutches of those who would be unstoppable with the magic you demonstrated."

"But...I don't have magic," I shake my head. Sure, I can conjure a cheeseburger or dick in my hand at will, but magic? Give me a break. Cash continues as if my world isn't tilting on its already precarious axis.

"When you left, the magic of Wonderland began to seep away. Color drained, happiness was a distant memory. And then, something unexpected happened. The men began to grow restless, obsessive. They all sought to find and return you as theirs. They left their wives, abandoned their children. Many fled to the human world to find you, none returned. Hence, Wonderland became Wonderlust." Cash shifts to brush my hair behind my ear where Stan should be.

"Riddled with those seeking pleasure they couldn't find. I believe where you come from, it's called sex addiction. We call it 'every male on the realm forcing women and creatures to dress as you, wear blonde wigs and fuck them to death. Literally. It was a massacre." My eyes widen and I look upon the cards in horror. Sadistic assholes with their brains in their ball bags. Yeah, that sounds just like my world too.

"So, the Queen of Hearts placed a curse on all males left, turning them into playing cards and locked them down here to be forgotten. In a bid to have her elected as the single ruler of Wonderlust, she has promised the realm, once she has your head, to return them back to their families. But it's a lie. She seeks to turn them into her personal army instead, and Tweed will be by her side every step of the way."

"But the hearts are roaming freely upstairs. They aren't subjected to...this," I wave my hand at the cells. Cash nods his blonde hair in the light of the flames.

"The curse worked to declare the suits of those who supported each kingdom. The queen of hearts saw her opportunity to capture those who would refuse to bow to her and contain them indefinitely. Even if your death happens to break the curse, the men will still be trapped and forced to follow her. If not, she already has the people on her side and appears to be the loving queen her mother was not."

That's my next question in a long string of curiosity answered. This Red Queen doesn't appear to be the one I once knew, because she isn't. She's the devil's spawn instead. A long exhale seeps through my parted lips. My brain is scrambled, like eggs in a pan and I shake it in search for some sense. There is none. I don't have magic, and the one place I was seeking to fit in has just proven that I will never be able to settle down, like the homeless bus-stop bum I am. Those out for my head outweigh the ones that want me. Which right now are Cash, Tweed on a good day and the Hatter I can't find.

"You said in the hot tub you might know where I can find my next clue. Is it here - is Hatter amongst the cards?"

"I'm afraid not, Crazy one. Follow me, I'll show you the way." Cash stands and this time, I don't need to wait for his hand to be offered. Taking it, we climb the stairs with heavier steps. I peer over my shoulder at the small seven of clubs that held my hand, his eyes seeking mine.

It feels wrong to leave them behind, but what use is freeing them? They would just be re-captured, or worse. Another issue I have to contend with -

how to free the cards, return them to men without becoming sex-trafficked along the way and keep my head while doing so. Simple, right?

When we reappear in the hallway, there's no one around as Cash locks the door and replaces the key beneath the bottle. We slip around the corner of the lobby and jog up the grand staircase, turning right twice and becoming lost to the maze of hallways. Cash's strides are confident, his steps never faltering as I rush to keep up. The wallpaper bleeds from striped prints to bland, dulled crimson. Cobwebs grow thicker, dust coating the surfaces and I reckon, even without the residents at the festival, this part of the castle is mostly forgotten.

"How do you know the way so well?" I whisper-shout but Cash doesn't respond. Halting, I crash into his back, peering around at the wooden door he opens with ease. Sunshine streams in from a large, semi-circular window, casting light over the workshop before me.

Much like the Hattery, it's a mess of disorganized materials. A desk and sewing machine are hidden beneath streams of ribbon, a row of mannequins standing off to the side. Matching jackets have donned the fabric bodies to the hats upon their non-existent heads. Glitter catches the light like disco balls, batting back and forth against the sequins scattered across the floor.

Cash enters first, pushing the fabrics aside with his foot until a metallic sound joins. Closing the door behind me, I investigate. A shackle on a length of chain snakes across the ground and beneath the material Cash has shifted, blood smears the ground. My lungs constrict. *No.*

"He was here," I say mostly to myself. Crouching to lift the shackle, I hold it to my chest. It's pointless to have hoped he escaped any form of torture all this time, but the evidence is still hard to accept. Never has there been a kinder man, so open to offering a little lost soul to join him for tea. The Hatter found me during my first travels to Wonderland, he took me in and made me feel safe. Now Cash has told me of the war, my memories start to make sense and I take that journey, I so often hate, back down memory lane.

"Oh, hello dear. You must be the one causing such a stir," a man approaches me through the trees. *His eyes are different colors, the blue one prone to wander. His hat is green, like his jacket with split tails around the back. My mother would say such a person appeared to have dressed in the dark. I take a step back. Halting, he smiles and removes his hat to bow. A cup on a saucer balances on his head of orange hair.* *"Hatter, at your service. Do tell me, how does one take her tea?"*

"More sugar than milk and half a cup of cream," *I reply without blinking.*

His smile widens. Removing the cup, Hatter tilts his hat and a long pour of steaming liquid pours out, filling the cup perfectly. Plucking a spoon out from behind his ear, he hands both to me. Raising my pinkie, just as my etiquette tutor showed me, I whisk a small whirlpool into the tea without the spoon even touching the sides.

"Quite the stir indeed," *he praises.* *"Careful, it's hot,"* *Hatter urges with raised hands. Slips of frayed material cover his knuckles to fingertips, catching my eye as I sip the best tea. Not even Thelma, my etiquette teacher, can make it equally as sweet and strong as this.*

"It's perfect," *I nod, replacing the cup on his head and giggling.* *"I like your fingerless gloves."*

"I prefer gloveless fingers but I've misplaced the palms. Come, my dear, my home is nearby and there's an awful storm brewing our way."

"Where is your house?"

"Wherever you need it to be, it shall appear. Do you need a place to go, young Malice?"

"It's Alice," I giggle, falling into the man that feels like home to me. I suppose I would like to rest a while. I've been walking since I fell down the rabbit hole and lost my way.

"Malice suits you. I expect you're going to bring a great deal of change around here one day. But no need to worry about that now, it's time for tea. Reach out and let yourself inside, I'll gather the wood for a fire."

Following the funny man's instruction, I outstretch my hand and close it around an invisible nob. Feeling the cold weight, I turn it and jump when it screams in pain. Hatter's laugh can be heard through the trees so I presume it doesn't mind, and I push the door open.

Invisible on the outside, a cozy living area opens up, the fire already lit and a kettle steaming above. The dining table is spread with all of my favorite desserts, from chocolate trifle to that delicious gray stuff no one knows the name to. My instincts warn against entering a stranger's house, enticed by desserts - but my father did always say I read too many fairy tales. I just never expected to live in one.

A tear escapes, curving a path down my cheek and pats onto the blood-stained floor. Sure, looking back now, a full-grown man coaxing a child into his home seems pretty shady, but anyone who wants to think that can meet the business end of my fist. Hatter and I were like two lost souls meeting in the abyss. One needing a child to love, the other needing a father who cared. I've spent my whole life waiting for another one of his warm hugs that fuses all the dismembered thoughts in my mind into place. I won't stop hunting now.

Cash has left me to my devices, having moved across the room to keep watch out of the window. Lost to his thoughts, his easy-going façade has slipped. The sun beats on his pale skin, highlighting the ridge of his jawline. How long has it been since he's felt the sunshine? Since he's gazed upon the gloriously green garden below, punctuated with red roses throughout.

"Do you miss it?" I ask, coming up behind him. I'm starting to get the feeling this mission wasn't solely for my benefit. His green gaze slips over his shoulder and he gives me a fake smirk.

"The red castle? No fucking way," he chuckles but that's not what I meant.

"Being with Tweed." His laughter dies. Whatever happened between them, I've seen enough today to deduce enough. Cash knows this castle too well; he's heard too much not to have been a resident once. The fact Tweed remained and he didn't, means Cash either ran away or was exiled, and that's the cold face of rejection I understand all too well. My whole family may have turned their backs on me long before I was committed to Charmsfield, but I've never had someone as close as a twin cast me aside. Cash can joke and smile if that's what helps, but I want him to know he doesn't have to. Not around me.

Unbuckling the chest plate, I let it fall and wind my arms around his front. My cheek rests on his back, an exhale echoed through both of us. The room falls still, not even a breeze rattling at the window. Outside, croquet holes are visible amongst the lawn, trees artfully positioned to create a pattern of hearts, the next starting within the dip of the last. Sculpted hedges create the border, featuring playing cards, white rabbits and teacups in various colors of flowers. Stunning really, and totally at odds with the evil that owns it.

"I don't like it when you're quiet," Cash says, leaning back into me. Threatening to topple over, he whips around and holds me low, like the ending of a dance number. Smiling, Cash's eyes roam my face, wholly satisfied with what he finds. What a way to make a girl feel special. Dipping lower, his mouth claims mine in a long, unhurried press of our lips. "Can I tell you something? I held off coming for you. I was sure you'd have forgotten and moved on. If I'd known you were sitting there, so ready and waiting..."

"Regret is for the wasteful. I don't live in the past for that very reason." Nuzzling my neck, Cash inhales and then groans.

"Looks like we have to wait a few more days before I can take you to the Shadow Planes. Tell me, Crazy One, why do you keep drinking from him?"

"I mean, I was kinda suffering from a head injury," I start. Cash whips me upright, all mirth vanishing. I wave away his concern. "I'm fine. Anyways, what more is a few days? We haven't found anything of use here." Easing out of his hold, I spin on a sigh. I'd really hoped I would have walked out of something more than a dredged-up memory I'd been suppressing. Cash heads for the exit, a shelving unit behind the door catching my eye. I smile sadly.

Displaying a range of fantastical hats in every color of the rainbow and all sizes, I pause to appreciate the hard work left behind to gather dust. Many follow the same style - a top hat laid with velvet and lace, a thick sash around the center. My fingers trail one in navy blue, a steampunk pocket-watch fixed within a netted fascinator. Peacock feathers plume from miniature to large, all with the distinctive shimmering green eye detail. A hat deserves a head, as Hatter would say. But I can't bring myself to put it on.

Moving on to admire the stitch work on a tiny trio of head wear, small enough to fit a dormouse, Cash clears his throat from the doorway. Yeah, yeah, I'm coming. Walking away, a hat on the bottom corner shelf catches my eye. Mostly because it wobbles, but on closer inspection, it appears familiar. Green with three features in white, orange and yellow protruding from the purple ribbon. An exact replica of the hat which was sent to me in the institution. Kneeling, it bops again and I lift the hat.

Sitting on a tiny wooden perch, a budgie blinks back at me. Grey pollutes his green and yellow features with a spot of blue over its beak. A monocle sits over one eye, a walking stick under his fragile wing. It's a wonder he's still on the perch at all. Opening his beak, a small cough comes out in place of what he was trying to say.

"Malice, we have to go," Cash urges me. Just then, I hear the slam of the main doors below bursting open.

"Where is she?!" a female voice cries out. Sharing a look like Cash, I apologize to Mr. Budgerigar and grab him from his stand. Stuffing him in my cleavage, I straighten the basketball jersey and run from the room. We navigate the hallways, appearing at the railing by the side of the grand staircase. Cash shoves me down to kneel, his hand on my back as we peer around the corner. The Red Queen has strolled inside, a playing card peeling off her long gloves and removing her crown.

"Well, someone speak! Where is the Al-" Tweed steps in behind her, whispering in her eye. The Red Queen nods, plastering a shrewd smile over her painted lips.

"Oh, I see. I'll try again. Malice, my darling Malice! I've been so looking forward to meeting you. Do come out to play." I bristle, hating Tweed's sway over her. He remains postured at her side, his eyes scanning the lobby, knowing I never would have stayed in the hot tub like a sitting duck. Cash's hand is removed from my back and he drags me up by the jersey, swinging the same arm around my shoulder to step into view.

"Cash!" the Queen gasps, snapping her fingers. "How did he get past the defenses?!" Playing cards rush in, vexed with spears in their hands. Tweed attempts to join, until the queen's hand on his bare chest makes me growl. "Do not hurt Malice! She is our top priority!" Cards storm the stairs, yet Cash makes no attempt to move.

"Forgive me Arabelle," he mock bows. "I figured I would see what you've done with the place in the past few years. Turns out, it's still a shithole of lies and deceit. Congratulations."

"You have the audacity-" Arabelle begins until Cash pulls a handful of glitter from his pocket. Throwing it high in the air, the cards lunge at us with spear points and the Queen's haunting scream is all I hear before the landscape dissolves. Dirty Dee's trickles into view, a pair of female foxes behind the bar setting up.

"Expecting company?" I ask, pulling Mr. Budgerigar from my cleavage. Probably the most fun he's had in years.

"I perform on weekends. Stick around, enjoy the show. We'll conquer kingdoms once my dear brother's blood has left your system." Cash winks at me, his fingers gliding over the pulse at my neck.

I look to the fox bartenders, now understanding their snarl of hatred. From the girl in the human world no one would touch with a ten-foot pole, to being the most desired woman in Wonderlust is a big leap. Luckily, I don't give a fuck for bitch's jealously so I flick my hair and follow Cash to his suite, all qualms washing away with each confident step.

Quite the stir indeed.

CHAPTER 29

CASH - SEVENTEEN YEARS AFTER ALICE'S DISAPPEARANCE

Screams, drowned out by the music seeping into my soul, send a shiver down my spine. I've only just stepped onto the stage, a permanent fixture in the ballroom now. An elongated catwalk was quickly installed when word got out the useless Tweedle had a knack for dry humping the air.

Females flock from all corners of the realm, unknowingly pledging their allegiance when crossing the borders to the Red Kingdom. Rumors have been circling, the lack of males present at my shows backing up the maid's overly loud gossiping. Men are becoming a rare commodity, which is all the better for my shows.

Lifting my hands to my nape, I drag off the cashmere sweater that has given me my name, sexy boy style. The soft material strokes my blonde hair, peeling away from the washboard abs and solid chest I now possess. Whenever I'm not dancing or fucking, I'm in the gym, owning the newly acquired state-of-the-art equipment. 'Only the best' for her majesty's jester apparently, and I've been sure to milk the shit out of those generous titties.

Hands claw at my feet, desperate for a touch before the butch female ox's hired for security are able to bat the women back into their chairs. Slowly gliding to the pole at the end of the catwalk, I roll my hips side to side. Pausing to roll my abdomen, flexing each ab so it pops, I make it to the metal rod. My fingers close around its length, stroking slowly as if it were my own shaft.

All the while, females scream and I peer through the strobes lights to pick out who I'll be taking back to my suite tonight. That's right – suite! Turns out I don't need to risk my life to be a Royal Champion, just a cupboard full of condoms and the occasional tetanus shot when a fox or similar gets too comfortable with her teeth. Easy peasy.

Gripping the pole in both hands, I walk my feet through the air, twisting my hips and gliding back down to the stage. Hearts line the edge, a constant reminder of who I've sold my soul to. As the rhythm of the music picks up, I fall into the routine I repeat every night. An hour of traveling up the pole, just to slide back down. Enjoying the movements of my own body and blocking out the audience. All the while, edging my slacks down my legs, just to whip them off in the last fifteen minutes. That's when the crowd goes crazy, screaming and putting the security guards to the test. Roses are thrown, littering the stage amongst the various thongs catapulted my way.

This is the life. Or at least, this is enough to fill the void of my twin ghosting me to train his protégé. I don't have to beg for his attention anymore or hang around hoping he's not too tired to play.

Skidding across the stage on my knees, I take my cock in hand, pumping it hard at the lights and then they cut out. Now all I need is someone to finish the job. Across the room, beyond those who scramble over one another to get closer, a torch flashes twice. My chest expands, a very real smile spreading across my face.

Bingo.

Tugging my slacks on in the dark, I slink off the stage and disappear around the back of the armchairs. By the time the lights come back on, I'm ducking out the back door while hollers and cries explode behind me.

"Where is he?! Where's he gone?!" they all cry. I smirk, linking my hand in the dainty one awaiting me. Tugging her through the castle, avoiding the main passageways, we slip into a stone staircase and make our way to my suite. Only once inside the master suite, the door clicking closed softly, do I release her, bouncing around like a puppy on catnip.

"Did you bring it?!" Lillianna reaches into a deep, concealed pocket of her silk gown and eases out a creature no bigger than her hand. A bat with flopped ears and heavy eyes. His fur is graying, the gentle rise to his wing showing how she was able to catch him so easily.

"The last of his kind, I'm sure," Lillianna gently places him into my hand. Below his pink button nose, two fangs protrude from its top lip. A vampire bat.

"I'm more certain than ever that my husband is responsible for the men disappearing from the realm, Cash. He's offered them refuge and..." she looks away. Her hair, smooth as ever, slides over her exposed shoulders as fluidly as water. Tilting my head, I cup Norris in one hand to slip my other into her inky black hair.

"And what?" I ask, urging her to tell me. Since our first meeting after my forced strip show for the Royals, I've known Lillianna would need someone on her side. Betrothed to a man with a bull's head, and no one wants to wake up to that, Lillianna is young, merely a few years older than myself. The weight of Spade Kingdom rests on her shoulders since her husband took to being a hermit. She attends ceremonies alone, handles political affairs herself and reports back. Not to mention, the longer she goes without baring the King's child, the more endangered to his mood swings she becomes.

"And...he's promising them access to," Lillianna looks around the empty suite and lowers her voice, "the Alice." I jerk back, as if smacked with a battering ram to the chest. My heart constricts, the memory of a girl that has an unexplainable hold on me slamming back to the forefront of my mind. No matter how hard I try to suppress her, convincing myself she was a foolish figment of my imagination, I can't escape. Lillianna's hand strokes my arm, an apology on her lips.

"Forgive me, I know how she continues to affect you." I sigh, shaking my head free of unwanted thoughts.

"No, it's fine. She doesn't," I lie, returning my attention to Norris. "I need to find Tweed, to show him this. He will help to free you of your husband, I know he will."

"What if he doesn't?" Lillianna turns away, her voice incredibly small. I frown, stepping in behind where the low cut of her dress reveals an intricate swirling tattoo with the spade's suit in the center. I must ask her who does her ink when the atmosphere isn't so tense. "Don't you see? He's too ingrained with the hearts. His loyalty lies with them – there's no way Tweed would aid me. Besides," she spins into my chest, "there wouldn't be enough to go around."

"What do you mean?" I lightly shake my head, not liking the thought of lying to my twin. Lillianna strokes my hand with the bat nestled inside, seemingly gone to sleep.

"Norris is old, he probably only has enough venom left in each of his fangs for one person. That's two shots. Me and you, Cash. We can take down the Spade King ourselves and then," her finger skates along my arm, up my bicep and to my shoulder. I know what she's doing. I've done it a thousand times myself, but for some deep-rooted fucked-up reason, seduction doesn't work on me.

"There will be an opening for a king. Can you imagine, after everything they've done to you, after all the ridicule you've experienced, to sit across the High Council and put your own laws in effect. To screw with all of the Red Queen's plans," Lillianna smirks.

I can in fact picture her words, my ankles crossed on the meeting table while I make the Duke of Baked Goods hand feed me pastries. But in the same image, Tweed is there, on the red side of the table. Lillianna has a point. My brother has been brainwashed for almost two decades, forced to obey if we were to survive, but still...

"Eternal life without Tweed," I whisper, staring at Norris. Suddenly, his weight doesn't feel like so much of a blessing. The legendary vampire bats are just that – thought to be extinct. When Lillianna told me she was able to procure one, I couldn't sleep for weeks. It no longer mattered that this life was stolen from us; we could carve another for ourselves. Live a thousand times until we got it right. But if Lillianna is only offering me that fate, it's not something I could even contemplate. "We'll find another way," I promise but she jerks away from me.

"There is no other way! I can't keep up the charade of my marriage anymore. I can't lie with the King one more night, pretending I'm not dead inside." I hate to see her in such anguish, but she should have known better than to expect me to leave Tweed behind. A bond like ours is cemented before birth. There is no me without him.

"Look, Tweed and I may have taken different paths, but we're the same person. Identical in mind, body and soul."

"No, Cash, you're not," Lillianna huffs, dropping into a high-backed chair before a coffee table and pre-lit fireplace. Like the enormous bed, all furniture in this room is overly large and plunged in red suede. Hearts are repeated through the décor in every aspect possible, from the curtains and bed linen to a hand-crafted rug and the upholstered chair Lillianna is dwarfed in.

"Maybe once, but you aren't the same as him anymore. You're better. You're more." Hanging my head, I block out her words. Still, after a year of praise, I'm unable to accept it. I'm not better than the scumbag everyone dubbed me as for a majority of my life. Riding my brother's high when he proved of use to the kingdom. When he proved he was strong enough to carry us both.

"I'm sorry Lillianna, but you've lost my part in this." I place Norris on the bed and walk towards the door. No idea how I'll explain her presence after she's done what she feels is necessary, but between Tweedles, loyalty means something. I won't betray my brother, nor will I choose between him and the chance of a happier future.

"Okay, okay, fine!" Lillianna shoots to her feet. I pause, my hand on the door handle as she tries to coax me back. "I hear you, and I trust you," she sighs, walking directly into my arms. "Saving the realm is what's important. Take the bat, use it for you and Tweed. Once you're superior, immortal men, you'll come back for me, right?" Her golden eyes peer up at me, so full of hope. A grin splits my face in two, the giddiness of a life I'm finally going to get to live swelling inside tenfold.

"I'll save you too. I promise," I press a kiss to her forehead, ignoring the fact I just signed Tweed and I up to kill the King of Spades.

CHAPTER 30

MAL

M r. Budgerigar isn't a fan of talking. I've tried everything. Crushed up a cough sweet, gave him a steam bath in a saucepan, massaged his tiny chest with my pinkie finger. Either he no longer possesses the gift of speech, or he just has nothing to say. But then why was he left under the hat that appeared to be an exact replica of the one I was gifted. Even by my standards, this makes no fucking sense.

Placing him in the fruit bowl, I leave Cash's kitchen with my self-esteem dragging along the floor behind and drop onto the window ledge. The Vamp in question left an hour ago to prepare for his weekend show, the queue of females impatiently waiting to enter stretching for miles. They must know they're not all going to fit inside the club, but they wait anyway.

Lightning flickers through the thick, black cloud, casting an ominous shadow over all who dare venture here. The layer of grass spread across this derelict land appears charred and trampled. Yet, like the beacon of a lighthouse, Dirty Dee's shines against the night, enticing the moths to the flame. Music filters from the floor below, a soft beat that has the females bouncing with excitement.

Deciding I should probably get ready, I go to move when the main doors beneath the window open. No one moves, aside from bobbing on the spot. I hover, curious as to why a stampede hasn't ensued, and then I see it. Or rather, see him.

Cash strides into the night, a pair of black trousers encasing his strong legs. No shoes, no shirt, but a ski mask on his head and a whip trailing in his hand. He assesses each female with keen, green eyes, gently pulling a slender woman with a duck beak and webbed feet from the crowd. Kissing her hand, he permits her to waddle her upturned tail in a mini skirt to the front of the line and enter the club. Then he moves on. Selecting specific women, ignoring the rest.

If there's a criteria to Cash's decision making, I can't tell what it is from up here. Human, panda, giraffe, hunchback. A real mix of predator and prey, but no one is focused on anything except Cash. The otter from the pet shop is chosen, her apron swapped out for a glittery two-piece and thigh-high boots. Kinky. I wonder what else she does with those empty cages laying around her shop.

A French hen - or at least, a hen in a French maid's outfit - tries to accompany her friend inside, creeping past Cash when he's turned away. His shoulders tense. A fork of lightning ignites the sky, reflecting off the corded muscles rippling through his back. Barely moving his wrist, the whip lifts of its own accord and cracks sharply, catching the Hen's feathery butt. She squawks, flapping around and runs into the night, leaving everyone else staring wide eyed at Cash's display. If anything, they appear more turned on and I don't blame them. But I've also seen enough.

Jumping up, I pad to the bedroom and pace around Cash's bed, suddenly unsure of myself. One week ago, an invite to watch a Tweedle Boy dance and strip would have been the epitome of my wet dreams. But after spending time with Cash, with his cocky smirk and easy-going attitude, I'm skeptical of the male outside. The persona he's demonstrating. I don't know that Cash, and I'm not wholly sure I like him. Shoving my hands into my hair, I tear my head back to the ceiling and scream.

"You rang?" Chels' heavy weight drapes over my shoulders, Stan pushing up on his hind legs to give my cheek a twitchy kiss. I smile, dropping onto the edge of the bed.

"Hey guys," I sigh, calmness washing through me instantly. My constant companion from the institution, Chels understands the war raging in my mind.

"Not everything you expected, huh?" Her fluffy tail curls around my neck, stroking the patch where Tweed's markings are still visible. Considering his blood is in my system, he must have drove his fangs extra deep. My core flutters at the thought, and I instantly know where I'm going wrong.

"Fuck, I'm so cliché," I push the heels of my palms into my eyes and drop back. Chels slithers out the way just in time. "Falling for the bad guy despite keeping Hatter from me, and ignoring the playful, equally as handsome, cheeky one right in front of me who is my usual type. Why am I such a dick?!"

"There's not enough hours in the day to delve into that question," Chels grins, winding around in the air above my head. She's right. If the intensive therapy at Charmsfield couldn't shed any light on my dickishness, we definitely don't have time now. Not when the music from below is growing louder, a voice through the speakers announcing the show will commence in ten minutes. A scuffle sounds at the door and I turn my face away from Stan's continual kisses to see Cash there, chest falling heavily and worry in his green eyes.

"Aren't you coming? I've reserved you a front row seat." I pull myself upright.

"You did?" I frown.

"Of course," Cash closes the distance between us, ignoring Chels' presence. Winding a hand around my nape, he holds me close enough for only his face to fill my vision. From his chiseled jaw to straight nose, stunning emerald eyes and blonde hair falling forward, there isn't a part of Cash that isn't flawlessly beautiful. When his full lips part, they relay the words I needed to hear. "I may have to work, putting on a show for the crowd, but everything I do tonight is for you. I want you there, front and center."

His mouth covers mine, a fierce, possessive press that has me rising on my tiptoes to seek more. More of the male who's accepted me from the second he swung those incredible eyes my way. He *wants* me, amongst all those outside falling at his feet, and who am I to deny him? Smiling against his mouth, I nod and blink myself back to reality. Sort of.

"I'll be right down. I just couldn't decide on an outfit," I lie. Cash smirks, seeing straight through me.

"It doesn't matter what you wear. It'll be torn and crumpled on the floor later anyway." Stepping away, his hand rests on the top of the door jam in an effort to hold himself back from taking me right now.

"Perfect," I wink. "I'll wear something of yours then." Cash's chuckle follows me into the bathroom and I close the door between us. Leaning on the counter, my reflection grins back at me. Puffy lips, flushed cheeks. A vitality of life radiating from my sky-blue eyes. Never in my life have I looked so alive. Previous irrational thoughts forgotten, I set about taking my sweet time showering. After all, Cash looks better beneath a layer of sweat.

***

Every vein in Cash's body ripples. Power thrums from his hands, gripping the pole with ease, to his well-defined calves. The point to his toes is worthy of a ballet dancer, but there's nothing dainty about his commanding movements. From the very top of the pole, Cash walks his legs through the air, body extended horizontally. A singular spotlight remains on him at all times, the rest of the club falling into darkness.

From my seat, front and center as promised, I have a full uninterrupted view. Those behind me whoop, roar and quack as Cash spirals downwards, now in nothing but a tight pair of pants. White with spades littered across, the fullness of the spotlight shining straight through. His feet touch the floor, toes first and the rest follow slowly. His green eyes find mine instantly. While one hand stays on the pole, his fine body rolls, highlighting each muscle in his crafted body.

I'm drooling into the skirt of my dress. No judgements needed – I went for the corseted powdered blue dress Cash picked out for me. Helpfully dry cleaned and hanging in his wardrobe, it seemed rude not to. Black under-netting fans out the satin skirt, the boning cinched tight either side of the white panel up the front. The black sash at my middle is tied into a splendidly large bow at the back, matching the one fixed into my hair. Oh yes, I went for the whole shebang. Elbow-length gloves on my arms, white stockings to my crossed thighs, and blue heels upon my tippy tappy feet.

Bending low, Cash slinks across the stage on his hands and knees. Lifting one of the black roses that were thrown at him, he leans across the gap of the stage and hands it to me. Various hisses of jealousy sound and I smile, accepting his offering. The audience are appeased when Cash crawls away, his back dipped and butt popped out. I sneak out of my seat, going in search of a drink while he's distracted. A stiff one to douse the heat Cash has pooling in my core.

The fox-tenders make a point of avoiding me, even though there's no one else at the bar to serve. Fair enough, I'll help myself. Reaching over the polished surface, I grab the first bottle that my hand touches and pull it free of the shelf it was hidden on. Ooh, champagne with a gold cork – I'll take that. Untwisting the wire cage, one of the fox-tender's now wants my attention but I hold up a hand.

"Don't panic, I've got this. I grew up in a country manor house that hosted parties for royalty. If there's one thing I know, it's the art of sabering." Pulling out the butcher's knife from Cash's kitchen that I stashed in the back of my bow, because you know...bitches be crazy, especially around hot men, I push my thumb into the indentation at the base and strike the knife upwards. The entire neck of the bottle shatters on impact, spraying glass shards over the foxes instead of bubbles. All that's left in my hand is the jagged base around the size of a large mug. Perfect.

"Hmmm, maybe I'm out of practice," I shrug, sipping around the cracked shards. Liquid fizzles over my tongue, as crisp and fruity as I remember when going on a bender from my dad's drinks cabinet. Those parties I mentioned - I was not actually invited, but I sure had a blast. The fox-tenders pick glass from each other's fur and the rest of the crowd are facing the stage, so no one but me notices the main door peeling open. A slender girl with black hair slithers inside, a bag of turnips clutched to her dirty dress.

Mary Ann.

She yelps when I rush at her, broken champagne bottle in hand. Dropping her turnips, she tries to flee and I wrap my arms around her.

"I've missed you," I hug her tight. She stills but doesn't reciprocate, reminding me of the many nights I would praise my doll, Polly. She never cared for my soppy moments either. Jeez, what was in that champagne? Or is it just becoming easier to let my true nature rise to the surface? Either way, I release the poor maid and tell her to drink the champagne while I collect up her turnips.

"For the Queen, I'm guessing?" I ask, handing the bag to one of the foxes. Mary Ann nods, her brown eyes wide like a frightened mouse. Placing the smashed bottle on the edge of the bar, she tries to leave but I grab her slender arm. "Hey, stay with me a little while."

"I-I'm not allowed to be here. I have to get back," Mary Ann whimpers, her voice small. Sadness befalls her delicate features and I set my jaw. Nope, not today.

Keeping my grip on her arm, I tug her behind the bar and spot the outline of a hatch in the wooden floor. Prying it open, I shove Mary Ann down the steps underneath and she has no choice – descend or die. Might seem like an exaggeration, but a girl as frail as her would never survive the fall. The foxes snarl at me and I give them both a middle finger, hopping down onto the steps and disappearing into the cellar.

Mary Ann has found the light switch, a single bulb swaying above our heads. Barrels to the right, wine racks to the left, the ground and walls in between are pewter stone. Mary Ann's quivering has intensified, probably from the chill sweeping through the basement. Unraveling my bow, I wrap the thick ribbon around her shoulders and rub her arms. It's not much, but it's all I have.

"I want to help you, Mary Ann, truly. But you have to let me know what I'm up against. What did you do that was so bad - that they're forcing you to be a slave as punishment?" For a long while, I don't think she's going to respond and my arms drop.

"I-I was sold, to the King of Clubs," she whispers, practically inaudible beneath the pounding of music overhead. But I heard enough to roll over a barrel and sit her on it. I prefer to pace, my hands clenched behind me as I tell her to continue.

"He was horrible. An old, fat man that forced me to...well, he-he wanted an heir, you see. It was all he talked about, all he desired. I was locked in his bedchamber, tied to the bed. When I wasn't ovulating, he...used me for whatever he liked. Mostly as a release for his anger."

I pinch the bridge of my nose, not needing the details but she surrendered them. I have no doubt this is the first time someone has listened to Mary Ann's story, and I'll be damned if I ask her to stop now. Owning her truth is the first step in her recovery. I continue to pace as Mary Ann tells me every sordid detail she is willing, and only once her sobs overtake her words do I drop down by her knees.

"What happened to him, Mary Ann? The King. Where can I find him and cut the dick from beneath his pot belly and feed it to-"

"It's not...you won't find him. He's dead. After...after I miscarried, he went mad. He wanted to impregnate me again, that very day and I just, I just snapped. I grabbed the letter opener from his bedside table and stabbed him in the neck until he stopped moving. And then some more," she ducks her head, an ashamed blush coating her cheeks. I lift her chin back to face me, drying her tears with both hands.

"You did good, sweetie. So damn good," I reassure her. Just then, the hatch above is cranked open and the bitchier of the two fox-tenders drops straight down, landing on her feet.

"We're out of white rabbit wine." She shoves Mary Ann backwards off the barrel and kicks it towards the steps. I grab the fox's tail and yank her backwards, my temper already at the end of its fuse. Linking my arm around her neck, I twist and drag her to the floor, leveling a punch to her snout.

"Try some fucking manners next time." Releasing her, I help Mary Ann to her feet and ease her behind me for when the fox-tender stands to brush her fur off.

"Figures the two rejects would seek each other out. I'm surprised you'd be willing to miss the show though. It's heating up on the stage," she bops her orange eyebrows at me. I scowl, not giving two shits if Cash was doing a fan dance with a lettuce leaf. Some things are more important than my libido.

"Do you know why she's been enslaved?" I ask, throwing a thumb back in Mary Ann's direction. The fox chuckles.

"Of course, the entire realm knows. It was our first voting poll when the democracy was introduced. A beheading seemed too...swift for her punishment." The fox narrows her eyes and hisses through her sharp teeth at the girl over my shoulder. I step-side in the way to regain her focus.

"So, you all turned her into a slave for killing a rapist asshole? I'd have given her a medal and a public holiday." I cross my arms.

"To kill a member of the royal family is treason of the highest order. And she's guilty of it twice, or did she miss out the part where she murdered her own child too." The fox barks a sneer. I falter in my stance, peering behind me.

"It wasn't a miscarriage," I mutter, seeing the shadow of Mary Ann's small head shake. Understanding dawns and I stiffen in front of the fragile girl once more. Reaching back, I take Mary Ann's fingers in mine. "How far along was she?"

"Does it matter?" the fox growls. "She took a drug-induced oyster from the Walrus and in doing so, eliminated the life of the future heir. For that, she will forever be a slave." A slender claw is jabbed in my direction and I whack it aside.

"It matters to me. Mary Ann, how far along were you?" I snap, my patience waning. Not at her, at always having half-truths.

"Four, maybe five weeks," she steps closer to my back, molding herself against me for comfort and I roll my fucking eyes. You've got to be kidding me. Without moving too quickly, trying not to spook the misguided girl at my back, I glide us forward a step and then stamp on the fox's foot.

"You've got your wine, get the fuck out of here before I really lose my shit." The fox-tender yelps, holding her sneaker and shuffles over to the barrel. Rolling it into a small dumbwaiter, she hops on top before slamming her claw on the red button. Both glide upwards until out of view, the muttering of me being a crazy bitch trickling through the shaft. Now is no time for compliments. Turning, I keep close and take both spindly hands in mine.

"Mary Ann, look at me," I order with just enough of a sharp tone. She immediately complies. "What you did was prevent another innocent life from being born into the abuse you were suffering. You also stopped another tyrant following in its father's footsteps and repeating the pattern. Do not feel ashamed for taking back control of your body and life. You did the right thing, and I'm so sorry you've been punished for it."

Tears well in her eyes, the urge to look away making her head tremble.

"It's-it's what I deserve. I killed my baby; I need to be punished. To be unhappy."

"What?!" I shout and she flinches. I blow out a calming breath. "No. No, no, a million times, just no. You may have been scared and acting out of fear, but you're here. You survived and it was bravery that pulled you through. You're so strong Mary-Ann...on the inside at least. Promise me you won't let anyone make you feel ashamed again. It's your body, your choice. The most insignificant thing in the world is other people's opinions. You got that?"

She doesn't respond and I can already see I'm wasting my breath. One different opinion isn't enough to rewrite the scorns she's heard for years. If there's something I know, it's overcoming ridicule, and this girl hasn't got the balls for it yet. She's too fragile, too innocent. Not a lot riles me in day-to-day life, but this sort of shit makes me fierce with rage.

"Wait here, I'll be right back."

Moving away, Mary Ann grabs my arm in the weakest hold I've ever felt. My grandma could have squeezed me harder, and she's dead. I pat her hand and sit her on a crate. "It's fine, I'm going to fix this. I promise."

Waiting for her faint nod, I climb the stairs and throw the wooden hatch open, uncaring of who might be behind it. Hopping up on ground level, my feet are moving. A woman on a mission. I cut through the rows of seats, barge between the crowd now gathered in front of the stage and jump up onto it. Cash spins around the pole, his pants dangerously low on the horizontal length of his thick cock and stops suddenly at the sight of me standing there, arms crossed and lips pursed.

"I need a favor."

"Can it wait?" he narrows his eyes, a tick beating in his jaw. I don't move. Clicking his fingers, the music dies and house lights go up. A groan of disgruntled customers follows until one observant bean shouts "oh my gawd! Look, it's Alice!" A shudder rolls through me but with my task in mind and anger already burning, I manage to shove an impending episode to the background for now. The women whisper and gossip, Cash's eyes fixed on mine.

"Well? What the fuck do you want?"

"Mary Ann is to be released from her binds and set free," I nod matter-of-factly. A smirk graces Cash's face, joined by the laughter of the crowd watching on. I scowl at them all.

"What makes you think-"

"You have power," I cut Cash off and gesture to the crowd, "and...*connections*. I believe you have the leeway to get whatever you want. And you. Want. Me." I jerk my chin, challenging him in front of his adoring fans to deny what he said in his bedroom. It's like a double test, wrapped up with a ribbon and tag that says, 'I dare you to back down now.' Smirk slipping, fury seeps across Cash's face, his nostrils flaring but with one smooth stroke of his hand through his hair, it's gone.

"As you wish," he mutters for my ears only. Swooping low, Cash drops to one knee and silence falls around us.

"I declare the slave, Mary Ann, is to be released from her eternal sentence. Consider this as a gift of the Queen of Spades to her newest ally," Cash announces loudly and those watching gasp once more. His blond eyebrows raise, the cunning smirk back in place. Whatever. I got what I wanted. Turning to stride down the stage steps, his arm bands around my front and Cash tucks my hair behind my ear to talk into it.

"You may have freed her, but there isn't a soul in this land that won't be out for her head. She won't make it through the night."

"Is that a threat?" I ask, twisting my head to the side. Hot or not, Cash does not want to be on my shit list. If he so much as touches Mary Ann, I'll sever his fingers and fuck him with them individually.

"Not by me, Crazy One. I'm merely giving you all the facts. She was protected at the farmhouse. Not all fights need to be fought." I frown, ignoring how his fingers trickle over my shoulder and patter towards my cleavage. Batting him away, I push out of his hold. Now's not the time. Through the club, I see a tiny pale face peering out from the curtain of dark hair reaching her shoulders. The fox-tenders are creeping up behind her with a hammer and spanner in their hands.

Jumping from the stage, the females dive aside, giving me a wide birth as I race through the club, grab Mary Ann and tug her into Fantasy Walk.

"So, I-I belong to you now?" she asks from behind me. I whip her around by a large wooden door decorated with vines and small purple flowers.

"No, sweet pea. You belong to you. I'm sending you somewhere you can find the help you need. A sanctuary for women like you, they'll give you a fresh start." Whipping a notepad and pen out of the pockets of her dirty dress, I write down the details I know by heart. If there's one thing a girl in the human world should have, it's options. Too bad for deluded psychos like me, the only option was to kill my father and dance on his grave. Oh well.

Handing her the notepad, I clasp Mary Ann's hands tight around it. A warm fuzzy feeling grows in my chest.

"I can't thank you enough," she says and for the first time, a small smile pulls at her cheeks. It changes her entire face, brightening her brown eyes to enticing pools of chocolate. I reciprocate her smile.

"No thanks needed. Go, live your best life." Pressing my hand to the door, I believe the room behind to be of the human world. Mary Ann throws herself into my arms, giving me her best version of an awkward hug and twists the handle, disappearing from view and my life. It's a shame - I reckon I could have used a girlfriend. Also, a tad ironic that the place I would rather see burn is her salvation, but life works in mysterious ways.

"Cook isn't going to be happy about this," Cash strolls up behind me. I fold my arms and give him my back, still pissed off. Sure, he may have allowed me to set Mary Ann free, but the fact she was enslaved in the first place – and for so long – irks me. I am *irked*.

"Yeah, well, I'm not fucking happy. How can you all be so archaic? How can I have spent so long wishing to return to a realm that sells and imprisons women for their freedom of choice?!" I huff. Those arms wrap around me again and this time, I don't fight him. I can't continually punish Cash for the laws he had no say in creating. It's all the power-hungry kings and queens who weren't told 'no' enough as children.

"Wonderlust is not what you once knew," Cash lays his head on mine. A layer of sweat and skin rests against my back.

"I'm starting to think I didn't know Wonderland either."

"Of course not. As soon as one believes to know the lay of the land, it alters. To know it is to claim it, and a land of wonder could never allow that to be." Turning me, Cash pushes his thumbs against my cheeks, forcing me to smile.

"Give it another day or so, and we should be safe to journey to Spade Castle. Lilliana will be so glad to meet you. Then we can start working together to set these wrongs right. It's all going to be okay. And if not, we will have each other." Easing his hands into my hair, Cash pushes my head back and dips his, putting his mouth merely centimeters from mine.

"Say it back," he breathes against my lips and I sigh. I'm a goner. Goodbye feminism, it was nice knowing you.

"We will have each other," I agree, and seal it with a kiss.

CHAPTER 31

MAL

S trolling behind the bar to join my new foxy besties, they snarl as I help myself to yet another round of shots. Watching Cash be fawned over by a crowd of randy females lost its appeal in the early hours of the morning, but the drinks have held my interest far longer. I tip the bottle of unlabeled, clear liquid over a tray of glasses, watching as each fill with a different color. Neon pink, green, yellow, blue and never mixing.

Setting down the empty bottle, I take the tray and hunt for somewhere quieter. Somewhere away from the screams that never cease, despite the hint of morning starting to peek through the gray clouds beyond the spade-shaped windows. Meandering into Evasion hallway, I spot a leather armchair and grin. That'll do.

Shoving aside the miniature bottles and tiny cakes upon a coffee table, they crash to the ground and my tray takes pride of place. I drop into the chair, drinking and reminiscing to myself all the while.

> *The boat sails dreamily beneath a different sky,*
> *Carrying aboard a spirit which refuses to die,*
> *The ocean is vast and reflected in her eye,*
> *On a never-ending evening of July.*

Kicking off my heels, I sigh and finish my round of drinks. With each color comes a different flavor. Blue - raspberry, pink - candy floss. Yellow is banana and green sends a burst of sour apple skating across my tongue. Soon enough, my head lolls back and my legs are both tingly and numb. Reaching back, my knuckles scrape across the suede wallpaper. It's mirrored on either side of the hallway, leading to a single door at the end. Dulled gray metal and a small grate stare back at me, enticing me to peek inside.

"So, this is where you've been hiding," a very sweaty, naked Cash smirks. He strolls closer, the long line of females leaving via the exit just visible past his glistening body. At first I thought the club lights were up, but in fact sunlight beams through the windows and declares the night over. Through my daze and mumbled response, Cash slips his arms under my arms and legs, and heaves me up. "Come on Malice, time for bed."

"No," I whine like a child trying to break out of his hold. "That way." Leaning back, I point behind. From my upside-down view, the dungeon door creeps closer as Cash chuckles and obeys my request. Easing it open,

Cash places me down on wobbly legs long enough to close the door behind us. Darkness falls. Without my sight, I sway further, holding my hands out to try to retain some balance. A wave of dizziness washes me aside and Cash catches me before I hit the ground. Blinking upwards, his emerald eyes are there, steadily glowing brighter.

"Welcome to Evasion, Crazy One." Those eyes glow vivid enough to make me wince, until the black of his pupil begins to bleed out and create a spiral with the green. Round and round, I follow the swirl, feeling myself sink further into his arms.

"Wha...what's evasion?" I ask, my head dropping back onto the ground. Cash lays the rest of me on the stone, untying the corset at my waist.

"A method of releasing the madness when it all becomes too much. I can ease your worries; help you see with clarity." The corset pops free and I inhale as if for the first time, filling my diaphragm and shuddering violently.

"Sounds awful," I groan, remembering a very similar pitch from Nurse Suzie and my antipsychotic medication. Cash chuckles, the sound filtering through the goosebumps lining my skin. His hands trail my arms, easing me up into a kneeling position. Freeing the puffy sleeves from my shoulders with a gentle caress, the dress pools at my waist. Sitting before me, Cash's eyes dip to my hardened nipples, a rumble locked in his chest. His hands rise to cup either side of my face.

"Open your beautiful mind, let me see what troubles you." I don't do anything, just sit in the dark and wait for whatever is next. A tense moment passes, Cash's thumb shifting to drag the pad across my bottom lip. "You have to work with me here. If done properly, Evasion can set your soul free of its woes."

"I don't have any woes," I half-shrug. "I can't open up anymore. I literally say what I want and feel no repercussions. Maybe it's you that needs to unload his troubles." Knocking Cash's hands aside, I grab his face and draw him down to meet my face. If he can see in the dark, he'll note how I widen one eye, squint the other and cross my vision to the bridge of my nose. "Is it working yet?"

"Not quite," Cash drawls blandly. He sits back, making a noise in the back of his throat. "No one has been able to resist my hypnosis before."

"Sorry to disappoint," I chew on my bottom lip. The sudden bloom of laughter makes me flinch and Cash shifts, his chest brushing mine.

"Oh Malice, you are many things – but disappointing is not one of them. Perhaps it is my brother's blood in your system that is saving you from me." His fingers trickle into my hair, his jaw brushing my temple. I brace myself on his chest, allowing my hands to explore his abdomen in the dark. He flexes beneath my touch, the coolness of his skin matching the low temperature of the room.

"How about a trade then?" I suggest. "I shall admit a truth for each one you offer me." Cash tugs lightly on my hair, exposing my neck to him.

"Very well." His head dips, fangs dragging over the vein throbbing in my throat. We both know he won't – not while Tweed is still tainted within me – but damn if I want him to. "I never lost hope in your return," he whispers and my mouth falls open. I didn't realize we were going in so serious right away. Cash's lips skate over my flesh, leaving a trail of fire in his wake as I scramble for something to admit.

"I've wondered why I was able to enter Wonderland in the first place. Was it a fluke, a freak accident?" His mouth closes around my nipple and I push into him, my head rolling back. Sucking, with the hint of danger scraping at my breast from his sharpened teeth, Cash switches between soft and hard, before pulling away completely.

"I don't believe so, but it doesn't matter either way. The second you fell into our realm; you became part of it. Part of us. We need you here as much as any other." His mouth takes mine this time, unhurriedly laying claim to the one part of my body his twin won't touch. Lips collide, tongues seek. We fall into each other, not an inch of space between us. Stealing my breath, he trails his hands down my spine.

"It's your turn," Cash breaks the kiss that was becoming feverish to place his forehead on mine. I nod, trying to pull my scattered thoughts back together.

"I can't have children," I blurt and instantly regret it. Cash's hands on my back freeze. My cheeks flare with heat. Shit, what a turn-off. "The drugs at Charmsfield. There was an experimental trial my family signed me up for. I mean, free test subjects are too good an opportunity to pass up. But by the time the side effects became apparent, it was too late...I can't...fuck," I stop blabbering and start to pull away. Cash refuses to let me.

"Did you think that would scare me away?" his deep voice asks, a hint of a dare in his graveled tone. "That I would find you defective? Look at me, for fuck's sake. No one can be judged by their misfortunes. In fact, I believe mine are what you regard as a main attraction." His eyes glow brighter and I roll mine.

"I don't want you because you're a vampire. I want you because you're...you." The blush returning tenfold, the urge rising to flay myself of skin and see if a new and shiny Malice is waiting underneath. But Cash doesn't care for a different me either. A wash of realization douses us and suddenly, we don't want to hold off any longer.

Our hands shoot to the dress at my waist, pushing it downwards over my ass. Cash holds me as I stand, kicking the dress away while he remains on his knees. Starting at my ankle, his long fingers trail up the backs of my legs in leisurely circles, his breath fanning the apex of my thighs.

"I hate that I've had to share you. That I'm not the only one in this realm to bring you to ruin," Cash groans his next confession. I push my hand into his hair and squeeze tightly.

"Then rewrite the story," I tell him, laying my thigh over his shoulder. He audibly inhales my pussy and shudders beneath me.

"I'm done talking."

"Thank fuck for that," I moan and drag his head the last few inches to my throbbing cunt. His tongue is quick to find my clit, his mouth closing around the small bud and worshiping it. My toes curl instantly, caught in the void between the icy chill of the dungeon and the coldness of Cash's devilish tongue. Like an icicle being dragged down my pussy and spearing me, I gasp and grab his hair tighter. I will take back from Cash what Tweed stole from me. My sweet dominance. My control.

Rolling my hips, Cash holds me steady. One hand on my thigh over his shoulder, the other stroking the length of my ankle to ass and back again. I shudder, barking at him to give me more. He immediately obeys. Two fingers thrust into my wet cunt with ease, powering in and out without pause. I cry into the abyss, only Cash's green eyes seeping through the everlasting darkness, anchoring me to this reality.

Working in time with his tongue, Cash wastes no time driving me to my first climax. I clench and writhe against his hold on my thigh, my nails dragging down the back of his neck. It's swift and full-bodied, exactly as he wanted it. A means to prepare me for what's to come. Preferably me, seven more times over. In a move too fast for me to track, my back is on the ground and legs pushed far apart. Cash settles himself over my body, his tongue dipping into my mouth so I can taste myself on his lips.

"Didn't take you for a missionary kind of guy," I smirk. Nudging his plump head at my entrance, Cash takes me in one swift, earth-shattering thrust. I moan, swallowing my words while his chuckle vibrates along my chest.

"Easy access to your pulse," he inhales the length of my neck. I turn my head away, giving him full access. I want Cash anywhere, everywhere.

Making a noise in the back of his throat, his glacial green eyes return to mine. I squirm, his dick sitting against my g-spot, making me ache for his next movement. Instead, a pair of fangs drag over my jaw and I freeze in anticipation. "The scent of his blood repulses me," Cash croaks and disappointment flares in my chest. "But you counteract him. So fucking sweet. You're...so much more than I expected." Withdrawing his cock, Cash eases back into me with less vigor this time. Still just as intense, especially with his eyes boring into mine.

"Expectations are made to be broken," I groan, my back pulling up to arch.

"Indeed," Cash agrees, building a steady rhythm within me. His mouth dips to nip and possess mine. I'm a stranger to myself, an implement of his pleasure. He could do whatever he liked to me in this moment, yet he doesn't.

"Cash," I beg, scouring my nails over his back.

"Yes, Malice?" he toys with me. I don't need to see that smirk to know it's there. I can hear it in his mocking tone. "You mustn't confuse me with my brother. I won't overpower you. I will fuck you just like this, until you instruct me otherwise." To prove a point, Cash retains the steady motion of his cock sliding into my channel, no matter how my ankles locked at his back try to rush him. "Tell me what you want, Crazy One."

"I want...to forget. Free my mind, as you promised," I muffle through my moans. My face contorts and I retract my hands to cover my expression from his all-seeing eyes. Taking my wrists, Cash pins them to the stony ground, his gaze fixed on mine. Each thrust forces my body to jostle, my breasts lightly bouncing and aching for his attention. "Bite me Cash. Drain my blood until I forget my own name, choke me until I'm about to pass out, and fuck me like it's the last time we'll be together," I attempt one last time, desperate but doubtful he'll listen.

"As you wish, my Malice," he nods once. I've barely inhaled when my wrists are pinned into one large hand and a pair of fangs drive into my neck. The first heady pull on my vein sends a beeline to my clit but there's no chance to groan. Not when Cash fucks my cunt with such ferocity, the sound of his groin connecting with mine drowns out all other sound. Reverberating around the walls, I drown in the wave of dizziness that claims my entire body. Unlike the alcohol I recently consumed, this feeling is filled with the bliss of release. My soul up and floats away, all notions of sense escaping my mind on an invisible breeze.

"Like that?" Cash groans, tearing himself away from my neck. I manage a single nod and he's gone again, attacking the vein on the other side of my neck. This time, he doesn't drink. Smoothing his fingers through the pool of blood exiting my body, Cash paints a picture across my breasts only he can see. His mouth hovers over mine, the slaughter on my pussy conjuring a climax I wasn't prepared for!

Ripping an orgasm from me, my lips part on a cry that isn't fulfilled. Cash pushes his bottom lip into my mouth, the bitter tang of his tongue prickling from self-made teeth marks in his flesh. I suck, hard, drawing a violent shudder from the body pining me down. Jerking his lip back, Cash's hand closes around my throat, as instructed. Blood loss, a lack of oxygen and an orgasm that pulses from one to the next does exactly what I needed. My thoughts are released, my sanity freed from its physical confines.

"You're all mine now, Crazy One. Only mine," he whispers in my ear. Dropping his head to lap up the bloodied pattern across my breasts, Cash misses the tear that falls freely from my eye, the upturn to my mouth and the slightest shake of my head. I orchestrated this. Fashioned it, maneuvered it. The ultimate control of who I am and what happens to my body is mine. Regardless to who is screwing me into euphoria, this is the epitome of self-preservation. It so happens, dear Cash, I've never belonged to myself more.

CHAPTER 32

MAL

"All set?" Cash hovers in the bedroom doorway as I finish strapping the laces on my boots. He's gone for the effortless look - tight jeans, simple tee, pushed back blonde hair and an easy smirk. Typical. When he'd told me to prepare myself for the Shadow Planes, I went full G.I Joe. Camo print cargos, army green crop top beneath a military jacket, two lines of eye liner on my cheeks. I even tamed my mane into a long French braid. Stan would have a heart attack at the amount of hair that came out in the fourth brush. The other three broke – not up to the challenge.

"Yep. Let's go." I follow with not so much confidence in my step. Swinging by the kitchen, I fill a backpack with bottles of water and some cream-filled snacks from the refrigerator. Tossing in a couple of apples for balance, I lift Mr. Budgerigar from the fruit bowl.

"Time for an adventure old chap, and if you feel like telling me something, I'm all ears." I pause, watching one beady eye blink open through the monocle. His feathery chest puffs out and as I hang on for any muttering that may follow, Cash urges me we need to leave. I ease the budgie into my jacket pocket with his walking stick and sigh.

Leaving Dirty Dee's and entering the Shadow Planes to meet the Queen of Spades is my only shot at finding Hatter. With her army and resources, it won't matter where Arabelle is hiding him, we will storm Wonderlust until his location is revealed. So why does each rung on the staircase towards Cash feel like the ringing of my own death warrant being called? Why, as I take his hand and exit through the front door, can I only see his twin's face staring back? Forming an allegiance with the Spades will be a giant middle finger to the rest of the realm, and an official goodbye to Tweed. Call me selfish, but I don't want to choose. I want to embrace both sides of my soul these vamps have awakened.

"Cheer up Buttercup," Cash half-smiles. "It always had to be this way." I nod, holding my head high to face the vast land before us. Then, we take the first step. And a few thousand more after that until my legs ache.

"Where's the portal glitter?" I huff, my boots crunching on the never-ending charred grass. Dark clouds loom overhead, the hint of an impending storm that never hits.

"Magic doesn't work out here." Cash's jaw clenches, his face too similar to Tweed's when he falls prey to his thoughts. "The Queen of Hearts has access to Wonderlust's central pool of magic, hence why her kingdom is blessed with warmer weather. The further away you travel, the more the magic wanes. With the exception of the Dirty Dee's built on sacred ground, the Shadow Planes are practically like the world you came from. Just...darker."

"Perfect," I grumble. Shithead could have told me to double sock back at the club, but no. Here I am – tired, cranky and sporting a blister on each ankle. Suddenly, I stop and narrow my eyes at him. I'm literally *walking* next to a vampire with enhanced speed. Holding my jacket pocket to not jostle Mr. Budgerigar into an early death, I leap onto Cash's back.

"Giddy up!" I kick his ass and smack the back of his head. That was for making me suffer unnecessarily for so long. Cash doesn't react aside from jolting forward, running faster than my eyes can track. Wind billows through my braid, puffing out my cheeks like a free appointment with the hygienist. Goodbye plaque, hello ominous mountains growing closer by the second. Cash skids to a stop before we cross the line of shadow separating us from the looming mountain range, grabbing my legs to stop me from vaulting over his head.

Placing me down, I peer up at the sheer cliff face hanging above. Melancholy gray stone, devoid of all color and fixed into a dripping effect stares back, casting a giant shadow over the land before us. Three guesses to where we are. Leading the way, Cash's shoulders grow tenser with each step. I follow, hugging the jacket around my front as a wind tries to blow it off. Silence falls over us, not even my sarcasm rearing its head to fill the stale atmosphere.

Arriving at the cliff face, Cash touches my shoulder, guiding me towards two, plain white doors amongst the rock. Setting me before the door on the left, then steps in front of the one on the right. Bracing his hand on the handle, he nods for me to do the same.

"I need you to do me a favor," he says too softly. I step away from the door and cross my arms. "Whatever you see or hear, remember the truth. You know me Malice. The Nightshade Trial will try to distort your beliefs, make you question what you know is right. I know you're strong enough to pass the test, and once we free the Queen, she'll-"

"Wait," I hold up a hand. "Rewind. Nightshade Trial? Free the Queen? I thought we were here to visit her. Have a cup of tea, talk strategy to find Hatter. I didn't agree-"

"She's banished, Crazy One," Cash's brows pull together and a rare look of desperation crosses his face. "Trapped in a prison that Arabelle created out of fear." Releasing the door handle, he closes the gap between us. Stroking my shoulders, his forehead lowers to mine. "I can't do this alone. I need your help, please. Then I promise, I'll give you everything you desire." Without moving his head, his fingers tilt my chin upwards to meet his breathy whisper. "Malice, I need you."

Placing a featherlight kiss to my cheek, I taste his bittersweet desperation. A slice of despair cuts through me, despite the pretense of confidence I manage to retain on the outside. Cash has an attachment to his queen, the same way Tweed does to his. He's asking me to save her, to return her to his life. And where will that leave me?

The budgie in my pocket wiggles and I remember. Alone with Hatter, that's where. With my chosen father, living a life of tea parties and nonsense. Everyday will be filled with laughter and copious amounts of sugar intake.

"Okay Cash. Let's free your Queen." Breaking away from the safety of his body, cutting the tie as swiftly as I can, I brace myself before the door on the left. Cash smiles, that heart-stopping smile only the devil should possess. Never have I been so weak for a set of dimples.

"Ignore what you see and hear. One of us must find the Queen of Spades playing card. It's the key. The other must locate her cell, in that order. I'll find you as soon as I'm able. Everything is going to be okay," he places his hand on the handle before him. Doing the same, I brace myself and stare at the non-descript door.

"So you keep saying." On the count of three, we push open our separate doors and step inside, just as a rush of wind slams into my back and a hand wraps around my eyes.

CHAPTER 33

TWEED - EIGHTEEN YEARS AFTER ALICE'S DISAPPEARANCE

*S*tanding before me at the castle entrance, Arabelle lifts the head of her
decapitated mother high in the air. The crowd of mostly females, who
have flooded to witness this frabjous day, roar with cheers. Feather dusters
and brooms are pumped high, Arabelle's name becoming a chant.

At my side, Cash stands tall, fulfilling the prophecy Arabelle and I saw
in the magician's library. Catching his eye, noting his smirk with one of my
own. The Red Queen is no more. Our suffering is over, and the new monarch

before us has been raised by yours truly. Our future is as good as it was ever going to get.

The crowd create a spiraling conga line and begin leading a procession through the rose gardens. An ox bodyguard steps forward, offering an ice bucket for Arabelle to dump the remainder of her mother in. This, along with every other mounted head in the trophy room, is to be burned and spread at the Great Scattering.

Families who have been mourning for too long will finally be at peace. Another reason for the realm to celebrate, their faith in Arabelle's leadership cemented. She's only just turned fifteen yet has a realm of loyal supporters behind her. A feat her mother tried to manage through fear alone.

"Tweed," Arabelle turns her tamed mane of red curls to the side, keeping her body straight on. A heart has been painted over her lips, her face carrying enough make-up to age her by five years. "Did you notice-"

"I did," I nod, stepping into earshot. "Four males in attendance. The decline is too rapid."

"We need to do something. I have an idea. Wait for me in the study." Arabelle's eyes rise to my face at the same time Cash prods a finger into my back.

"Er, actually, I promised Cash I would assist him with an errand during the celebrations this evening, if you permit me freedom from Red Castle? Tomorrow morning after our run, we can decide on a strategy going forward." The heart on her red lips shifts as she smiles, ruining the façade.

"I'm not my mother, Tweed. Go, enjoy your evening. You've both deserved it." She makes a point to look over her shoulder at Cash too. Returning to the parade, Arabelle claps her blood-stained hands in time with the chanting, floating down the steps with her back ramrod straight. She'll make the best queen this realm has ever seen. And yes, I'm taking full credit.

Leaving Arabelle to her ox detail, I follow Cash inside the castle and up to his suite, not a word being uttered. His broad shoulders flex in a navy cashmere sweater, concealing the fresh tattoos underneath. I bear the same, roses down my right arm to keep our matching façade. Whatever Cash has done to his appearance for the sake of his stripping career, I mimic. Once an identical twin, always an identical twin. Entering Cash's suite, the Mocking Turtle, in a bandana with inked designs covering his shell, has just finished packing away his kit and bids us goodbye.

"Spill," I fold my arms once we're alone. "I'm not going on any errands unless you tell me what it is." Cash strides into his adjoining bathroom, leaving the door open so I can see him changing in the mirror's reflection. His skin is pale, paper white and I have to wonder if he's sick. My suspicions increase as I inspect the platter of food on his bedside table, wondering when he last ate a proper meal.

"What the hell is going on with you, Cash?" I mutter to myself, barely audible. Turning, I slam into Cash's chest, his eyes intently on mine.

"It's an honor the almighty Knave would take notice," he replies, then strides back to the bathroom half-dressed. I jerk my head back as if I've been punched. What the fuck?!

"What's that supposed to mean? I've noticed the change since you started stripping, but I gave you space to work yourself out. We went through hell and stormed out the other side. I know better than anyone that shit takes a toll. Somehow, you've managed to maintain the persona of the humorous boy you always were, until now."

I reserve the fact I depended on Cash's personality more times than I could count. Where I would only see dark, he would be the light at the end of the tunnel. The reason to drag myself back to the surface of my despair and power through another day. Strolling out of the bathroom, now fully dressed in black fatigues, he waves a flippant hand through the air.

"You went through hell and survived; I merely tagged along for the ride."
I scoff, crossing my arms and leaning against a high-backed chair.

"So we're going for jealousy then? You would have preferred to be the one
being beaten, tested and forced to fight beasts on a daily basis, just so you could
call yourself the hero?" Cash laughs bitterly, tossing a pre-packed duffle bag
over his shoulder.

"Let's just say, I see with clarity now," he mutters cryptically. My nostrils
flare but he pays me no mind, pushing a pocket watch into the pocket of his
cargos. "Back to the mission at hand. And side note - you're not going to like
it," he finally gets to the point and I huff. By the attitude riding him this
afternoon, I could have guessed as much. "But I know where all of the men
are disappearing to and what's happening to them. We're going to get them
back." My arms drop in time with my mouth.

"You have information, and you haven't divulged it?! How long have
you known? How reliable is your source?" The questions tumble from me,
frustration riding my movements across the room to grip his t-shirt in my
grip. The tightened short sleeves reveal the ink coating his left arm. Cash's
seemed to have healed almost instantly. Mine are in the itchy, peeling stage
no matter how much cream and cellophane I apply beneath my tweed jacket.
Shoving me back a step, a fluttering laugh leaves his lips.

"No use dwelling on the past, right brother?" His green eyes seem to sparkle
at me. There's an unspoken meaning behind his words, but I don't have the
energy to fight with my twin. Not when I have no idea how much I need to
reserve. Especially now the severity of our errand has been revealed.

Tracking Cash to his fireplace, he pulls a coffee table closer and stands on
it. A grand mirror I haven't seen before sits above the mantle; the flourishing
frame coated in black. Touching a finger to the center of the glass, it wobbles
like liquid and Cash jerks his head.

"Come on then. Let's save the realm from itself." Jumping, Cash is pulled into the mirror's reflection and disappears inside. My heart drops, my feet moving. Pushing a booted foot onto the table's surface, I vault into the mirror and tumble through a darkened tunnel to crash through the other side. Landing hard on the carpet, I groan and run a hand through my hair. Cash's hand hovers in front of my face, tugging me to my feet.

A suite, mirror-image to the one we just left behind splays before me. Except everywhere a heart should be, there's a spade, and all hints of red have been switched for black. The curtains, rug, large-backed armchairs – all positioned the same. Enormous bed coated in satin sheets, a painted canvas of my brother mid-strip tease hanging above the headboard.

"Cash?" I ask quietly, trepidation crawling along the inside of my throat. "What have you been up to?"

"Making myself at home," he quirks a smile. I shudder, creeping across the room to peer around the curtains. Spade Castle is vast, outbuildings spreading far beyond the balcony beyond the French doors I've found myself at. Rain pelts the glass, various thunderstorms taking place through the expanse of dark gray cloud. A zipping sound brings my attention back to the duffle bag Cash opens, dumping the contents out on the bed as the door clicks open.

"You made it!" a hushed voice exclaimed, Queen Consort Lillianna rushing inside. "There's no time to waste, the King will notice my absence soon." Oh no, no, no. I find myself shaking my head, edging back towards the mirror. I can't be caught conspiring in whatever the fuck is happening here. I've worked too hard. Suffered too much to lose my position now.

"Cash," I growl this time, anger bubbling beneath the surface. Catching my eye, my brother removes the queen who has run into his hold and closes the gap between us.

"*The King of Spades is luring men here under the pretense of safety. I've done my recon; I've seen them flocking here with my own eyes. But none leave, Tweed. They're either portalled away or killed, all crying out one word. 'Alice'.*"

I freeze. The image of a yellow-haired girl in a blue dress runs across the forefront of my mind before I manage to suppress it. My heart beats erratically before I can get a handle on my emotions, and Cash's eyes drop to my chest as if he can hear it. Flexing my fists, I exhale through my nose and think.

Unbeknownst to Cash, Arabelle and I located the last chrysalis a few months ago. It's safely hidden until the day we are to release the butterfly, but apparently, I'm not the only one keeping secrets. Lillianna steps into Cash's side, her fingers tangling with Cash's. Oh brother, what the fuck are you playing at?

"*Wh..Why would they want Alice?*" *I decide is the most important question in the shit storm taking root inside my mind. Cash releases Lillianna and folds his arms.*

"*I don't have all the answers yet. For some reason, Alice is tied to this land. The men are infatuated, yearning to the point of madness. Her spirit is being called back and it won't be long before she returns. I can feel it,*" *he pushes a palm into his chest. I don't respond. The matter at hand, and the only one of real importance, is the fact our realm has lost half its population in the past few years. Mostly all of them being male. The women are scared, little-to-no babies are being born. Snapping myself back into soldier mode, I steel my jaw and address Lillianna for the first time.*

"*The King of Spades is responsible for this anarchy?*" *I ask. She nods, fear in her golden gaze.* "*It seems the two of you have a plan. Fill me in so we can get this over with.*"

"*He's been poisoning them with his golden chalice,*" Lillianna rushes to stay, stepping behind Cash when my glare comes across too strong. *I don't know this Queen, nor do I trust her. But if I could present Arabelle with the solution to the realm's biggest problem on her coronation, no one could deny Hearts as the superior suit. A notion I was not interested in, until the old Queen lost her head this morning and my position just became worth its title in gold.*

"*If you can steal the chalice, prove his guilt to the high council, he'll be executed for his crimes.*"

"*Why can't you steal it? Surely you have more access to your husband's belongings than we do,*" I twist my lips, continually raising my eyes to my twin's. *They're sparkling again, filled with mischief to match the smirk at his mouth. Lillianna bristles.*

"*And what do you suppose I do with it?*" she pokes her head back into view, her brows furrowed. "*Send it to the Red Kingdom by pigeon and hope for the best? It's the only proof I have, and as soon as he realized it was missing, I would be next.*" *A shiver rolls the length of her body, shrouded in a ridiculous amount of black satin with large puff sleeves, a corset pulled tight on her slender waist and a full-bodied skirt which hides her short legs. Nudging Cash aside, I speak low, only for my brother's ears.*

"*If she's right-*"

"*She is,*" Cash interrupts, *his shoulders tense as if preparing for me to fight him on this. I sigh, placing a hand on his chest.*

"*What I was about to say is that I haven't built a bond of trust with the Queen of Spades, but I trust you. I will follow you wherever you go, as I know you would me.*" *Sharing a nod with Cash, I return to the Queen and lower my head.* "*For the purpose of saving our realm, I will aid you in this. Once the King's crimes have come to light and you're dubbed as acting Monarch, we will arrange a sit down with Arabelle to discuss the possibility of an alliance.*"

"You've learnt well. Never one to waste an opportunity," Lillianna quirks a brow. With my acceptance, her back has straightened and she's suddenly able to stand free of Cash's protection.

"It's my job to protect Arabelle," I state, devoid of all emotion. In particular, the resentment her words distilled in me.

"Yet you'd risk everything to protect your brother," Lillianna's head tilts to the side. She's assessing me. Testing my loyalty to the man she's managed to coerce.

"On the contrary. I've sacrificed everything to save my brother. I have nothing left to give but my word." A tense moment passes. Lillianna's golden eyes dip to my neck.

"We shall see."

Seeming satisfied with my intent, Lillianna moves towards the items dumped over the bed. I hang back, my chest heaving as I rein myself back in. No one in Wonderlust can even suggest I've worked my way up the ranks with anything less than my own soul. I secured myself and Cash a future with the very blood that runs in my veins and skin of my whip-scarred back.

"I hope she's worth it," I grunt when Cash moves to join her. He pauses long enough to smirk at me.

"She's real, unlike the one we refuse to acknowledge." Leaving me to my own devices, I shake out my arms and crack my neck side to side. This is just a mission, like countless I've done before. Get in, get out, leave no traces I was ever there. Limbering up, I stretch my arms, dropping into a lunge.

Cash and Lillianna discuss their plan, my ears picking up on the gist of it. The golden chalice is stashed in a cabinet, guarded by the witch who works in the lab. The type of magic she uses leaves a residue in the cup, discoloring the hue, and there's our evidence.

As ready as I can be, I make my way toward the pair. Standing behind their lowered whispers, I gain a rare insight to how Cash must have felt all these years. On the outside looking in while I conspired with Arabelle.

Blinking up in awe, Lillianna smiles at Cash the way Arabelle has done to me a million times, and now, I understand the appeal. To feel important to someone, like you're enough to alter the entire course of their lives with your actions – that's a concept I know all too well. Taking Lillianna's lead, we stride for the door she entered through on silent feet. Her hand touches the handle and I bounce lightly on the balls of my feet. Let's get this chalice and get back to Red Castle, still in time to celebrate with the kingdom. It's the least Cash and I deserve.

"Before we leave, there is just one more thing," Cash says. I turn my head just in time to see his hand coming down, a spike of pain flaring at my neck. I stumble, holding the tiny splinter not much bigger than a thorn. He stabbed me. My own twin has actually stabbed me with some unknown substance.

A wash of cold floods my veins, from my neck outwards. Seeping into my blood system, it races through me at an intense rate. My knees buckle, my head swimming with a burst of emotions. Holding the splinter in place, I lower myself onto the ground before I fall. Whatever I do, I mustn't remove it. My artery will bleed out within minutes.

A shadow falls over me, the sharp sting of a hand tapping my cheek. My entire body is alive, acutely aware of each sensation. The dimmed chandelier above burns my retinas, the sounds of heartbeats and heavy breathing making my ears pulse. The contents of my stomach rushes from me, the acidic burn clinging to my throat after I have nothing left to vomit. Tugging the splinter from my neck, Cash tilts his head into my view.

"The...fuck...done to me," I gasp, struggling to breathe. I can only just compute this is what complete organ failure feels like before my world fades to black.

"Don't worry, brother. It's for your own good."

CHAPTER 34

MAL

"You can't be here," a deep voice growls into my ear, a cold chest plate pressed against my back. My breathing is labored, my vision still concealed by the hand clamped over my eyes.

"Tweed," I grit out, betraying the elation blossoming inside. He's here. But if he feeds me his blood again, I won't be able to remain in the Shadow Planes and ultimately, find Hatter, so I press my lips together tight.

"It's not too late to turn around. My foot is jamming the door open. Walk back slowly and we can pretend you weren't stupid enough to fall for Cash's lies and leave." If there was ever something not to say to a stubborn woman, that would be it. Knitting my brows together, I grab ahold of Tweed's arm and hoist us both forward. The door closes with a soft click, sealing our fates.

"Fuck," Tweed groans, releasing my eyes. I blink against the harsh lighting, finding no hint of Cash anywhere. To my right, a wall of glass reflects my own image against a background of staircases. On the ground, walls and ceiling, in checkered black and white tiles that blend into each other. Behind my reddened cheeks and wide, blue eyes, Tweed stares at my reflection. The image of fury, his jaw is tight, his expression glacial. Oops.

"You have no one to blame but yourself," I shrug and take a step forward. One that I completely misjudge, not realizing there was a step amongst the checkers and I pitch forward. Tweed grabs the back of my jacket, slipping it straight off my arms and I tumble. Down, down, off to the side and then I'm free falling. A scream is torn from my throat, a sea of squares zooming towards me. Swimming my arms through the air, my fingers graze a platform and I somehow manage to grab ahold. Yanking my shoulders, I grunt, my fingers clawing at the tile and slipping fast.

Appearing over me, Tweed rolls his eyes and grabs my hands, dragging me upwards. Heaving me the last few feet, he drops me on the ground and kneels, his glare slamming into me with more force than the floor would have.

"You really think you could survive the Nightshade Trial? You couldn't even make it one step."

"Maybe I just wanted to prove you would save me." I throw the back of my hand to my forehead, using my talent to be overdramatic to cover the erratic pounding of my heart. Tweed purses his lips and strides away.

I groan at the pain spiking through my shoulders, rolling aside to see his military boots disappearing around a corner. My jacket, slung over his shoulder, flaps out of view and I scramble to catch up.

"Give me that," I drag the jacket from him and onto me, checking Mr. Budgerigar. He's asleep, I hope, nestled in a handkerchief bed I don't remember being there. Tweed leans against the side of a staircase, folding his inked arms out the chest plate on his front. The red heart printed on his left peck reflects the tattoo I know to be underneath, both mocking me with his allegiance to the enemy. Cargos cover the thick muscles of his legs, his ankles crossed.

"Tell me you have a plan by trapping us in here," he drawls, already knowing I never do. Plans are the foe of spontaneity, in the same way lists are an organizational construct I refuse to conform to. The day I sit and write a to-do list, I might as well take a gun to my own head and blast my bland brain cells all over the ground. But Tweed doesn't need to know any of that.

"Of course I have a plan. Find the damn playing card and use Lilliana's army to storm the Red Castle. You'd better kiss your bed-full of whores goodbye, since you can't hide Hatter from a girl on a mission." I flick my waist-long braid over my shoulder and stride on by.

"Still jealous then?" Tweed cocks a brow just before I pass and I curse internally. Not looking back, I trip up the rise of a step I couldn't see and huff at myself. Get a grip Malice, stop thinking with your heart.

Placing a finger in front of my nose, I stare at it until my eyes unfocus enough for the staircase before me to present itself. It's an optical illusion, and that's some funky shit I mastered in Charmsfield. We had a library section dedicated to them, until Nutty Jack decided there was a conspiracy in the hidden images and burnt it down. Seeing the staircase in its entirety now, I race up it, keeping my vision hazy until my eyes become strained.

Every turn I take, Tweed is right behind. His judgmental eyes waiting for me to fuck up.

"If you're so sure I'm not worth saving, then why the fuck are you here?" I whip around, being slapped by my own braid. Tweed stops a few steps back, leaning against a slanted staircase to look me up and down.

"You think too highly of yourself. I'm here to stop you from ruining everything Arabelle has put in place. Lilliana will not return as long as I am here to prevent it." I ball my fists and then outstretch them on an exhale. I did not spend nine years locked in an institution, dealing with diagnosed psychopaths on a daily basis to be riled up by a male. A gorgeously dangerous male I'd rather silence between my thighs than look at me like a piece of trash as he is now.

"Where is Chels when I need her? Chels!" I call out, hunting for the ceiling. I'm not even sure which way is up, but I continue to shout regardless.

"There's no magic in the Shadow Planes, or have you not been paying attention?" Feeling Tweed's presence close in on me, I spin to slap him, my hand in mid-air when I pause. His blonde hair has fallen free of its naturally pushed back position, covering his brows and shifting with each blink of his lashes. His eyes, as intense as they are, have dulled to seaweed green. His skin is creamy in color, smooth with a hint of pink at his not-so-hollow cheeks. When his lips part to exhale harshly, there's no fangs to be seen. "Paying attention now, are we?" he remarks. My heart stops. There's no magic in the Shadow Planes, which means...no vampires.

"You...you're human in here," I breathe, stepping backwards. My footing slips from the side of the staircase and Tweed rushes forward, grabbing the lapels of my jacket.

"Human, perhaps, but not completely useless." Returning me to safety, Tweed gives me a gentle shove away. Not enough to knock me off the other side of the platform, but enough to prove a point. He's mad at me for trapping him in here. Particularly in a weaker form. Taking the lead, he strolls up a staircase that turns on itself and cuts over my head.

"You know," I chase after him, "now you're human again, I'm surprised you can remain upright with such a chip on your shoulder." He ignores me, muttering to himself while counting his footsteps. Up and up we go, then a sharp left and back down, following an invisible path. Then it occurs to me. Tweed is Arabelle's right hand man. He knows exactly how to escape. "Hey, wait up. I'll cut you a deal."

"You have nothing I want," Tweed snaps, losing count on his fingers and groaning.

"We both know that's a lie," I snort. He pulls up short, throwing an arm out before I waltz off another ledge. Have these people never heard of railings before? Instead of refusing his chivalry, I marvel at the arm across my abdomen. It's warm. Despite myself, not that I'm a fan of making smart choices in my day-to-day life, I wrap my hand over his.

"Do you miss it?" I ask, my voice small. Tweed spares me a half-tilt to his head, his eyes watching me from the corners. Tugging his hand out of mine and walking away, something inside me sinks. What the fuck am I doing? Tweed will be hunting for the way out, back to his precious queen, and since the moment he showed up, he's done nothing but prove exactly why I shouldn't hate him. I'm not leaving here without the Queen of Spades. She's the answer.

Turning in the opposite direction, I unfocus my eyes and rely on the only person I can depend on. Me. Each checked square I step on, my heart jumps further up my throat. The platform I'm on is high up and narrow, the bottom of the room not visible. Spotting myself over an arched pathway, I hurry back to the mirrored wall and press my back to it. Goosebumps prickle my skin, my breathing hot and heavy.

Mortality doesn't scare me. But falling to an early death and having an open casket all smushed up and mangled does. What kind of horny ghost sex can I have with the living hotties if I can't stand the sight of myself? Nope, that's not how I'll appear for an eternity.

Remaining against the mirror, I feel my way with my foot before each step. It takes forever, but at some point, I manage to get a scope for the room. The door we entered through is at the highest point and reachable by only one flight of stairs. From certain vantage points, the staircases across the unending room intercept each other and create a pattern. A diamond at first, then a heart. Moving down several steps, a cubic spade comes into view, complete with a black door hidden through the center. My breath hitches and a smile crosses my lips. Gotcha.

Maneuvering the platforms, mostly on my hands and knees, I keep that door in my eyeline. Even when I'm forced to climb downwards, just to cross a pathway and run back up again, I never lose sight of my goal. My calves are burning and my throat is painfully dry, but eventually I'm standing at the edge of an opposite platform. The door is directly opposite, not more than twenty feet away, but there's no way to access it. Just a black door, silver handle and tiled doorstop. Peering over the edge, I spot a pile of forgotten bones seeping into the darkness. I swallow, stepping backwards and bumping into a chest plate.

"What are you still doing here?!" I jump, shifting away from Tweed before he can shove me over the edge. "I thought you would have left already."

"I have to keep you safe," he replies, also judging the distance to the door. I scoff, not falling for his shit this time.

"So, you can prevent me from releasing Lillianna and return me to my execution with Arabelle. Yeah, I bet the Red Queen's Champion has strict instructions not to return empty handed." I puff out my cheeks, totally done with being treated as a bargaining chip. I may not be worth much, but I know I'm more than an object to be claimed. Tweed rolls his eyes in that condescending way which belittles me long before he's opened his mouth.

"You don't understand what's right in front of you. Lillianna can't help anymore than Cash can protect you. All he's done is passed on his skewered views and in doing so, will get you killed long before any prophecy can come to fruition."

"Why? Because he's fucking her?" I purse my lips, having suspected as much. Mr. Budgerigar shifts in my pocket, alerting me that he is, in fact, alive.

"Worse," Tweed stands before me and grips my chin in his hold. "He's feeding on her, regularly. I wouldn't be surprised if he's been doing so even more since you arrived."

"Wait, how – isn't she banished? Locked up somewhere real tight?" Tweed's face is stoic but a storm is brewing behind his emerald eyes.

"Banished from everywhere, except Dirty Dee's. It's her only reprieve from the madness that plagues her isolated mind and the reason Cash built Evasion for her." All feeling seeps from my body. My stomach rolls, flooding my system with nausea. I do my best to hide the dreaded realization filtering through me, but Tweed's narrowed gaze doesn't miss a beat. "What is it?" he asks and I finally twist out of his grip. Wrapping my arms around myself, the door across the gap seems further than ever.

"Malice," Tweed tries again but it's my turn to ignore him. Visions of Cash's glowing eyes in the dark blare to life in my mind. He took me for hours in Evasion. His hands claimed my body, his tongue lapped up my blood. Raising a hand, I cup my own throat. He told me to give myself to him, and I did. More than I care to admit. And the entire time, it was in the sacred room he created for his Queen. Was he thinking of her? Pretending I was her? Fuck, I feel sick, and it's all my own stupid fault.

Tweed's hand wraps in my braid, forcing me to turn to face him but I'm done. No more dominating, no more games. Spying a staircase slanting overhead, I yank myself free from Tweed's hold and run towards the nearest steps. Fuck falling, fuck fear. Whether I make it or not, I've been used as a puppet since before I arrived in Wonderlust. These are my decisions. My actions. Tweed chases after me, ordering that I talk to him. That's cute. I'm sure that would work on his piglet servant, but I've stopped listening. Blood pounding in my ears, my heart thumping, I twist and race up the adjacent stairs. Peering over the edge and spying the tiny platform in front of the door, I don't think. I just jump.

Arms flailing, my legs braced for a painful landing. Grabbing my jacket before it flies off, I hold Mr. Budgerigar close and slam into the tiny perch of tile. Agonizing pain shoots through my ankles, a scream ripping from my throat. Hugging my legs to myself, I barely notice the shadow diving down over me until Tweed's hand smacks against the ledge at my feet. He's misjudged the jump, and despite myself, I grab his wrist in an attempt to help him up.

With no space on the platform and a deadly fall beneath him, I open the door and heave him upwards, over the ledge and through the threshold as I scoot back. Tweed pulls himself up more than I am of assistance, and soon enough he's collapsing on top of me, both of us gasping for breath and lucky to be alive.

"How about we use our words before acting irrationally next time," Tweed mumbles and I groan in frustration, shoving him aside.

"You're one to talk," I scowl down at him. Sitting upright, I pull the small, frail bird from my pocket and check him over. He's shaking, his beady eyes open and more alert than ever – but not for a good reason. I've almost scared the unfortunate thing into an early grave. Tweed also pulls himself into a seat position, shifting down to my feet and starts to massage my calf.

"You found Nigel," he comments, jutting his head towards the bird. "He's been missing for over a year now. Disappeared from his royal cage one day, none of the guards could find him. Arabelle was beside herself." Easing his hands down to my boots, Tweed unties the laces and slowly peels off one, then the other. He busies himself testing the extent of my injuries while I observe the budgie in a new light.

"You're the Queen's pet?" Mr. Budgerigar manages a weak shake of his head, but it's Tweed that answers.

"Not exactly. He was the Royal Adviser's companion." I hiss as Tweed squeezes my ankle, turning it over in his hands. "You're lucky. There's no breaks and the swelling should hold off long enough for us to leave and I can heal you with my blood. This one however," Tweed places down my left foot and eases up my right.

"Hold here," Tweed instructs. I place Mr. Budgerigar on the ground with his walking stick and bend my knee back to hold my calf, as Tweed instructed. Reaching over, Tweed takes my braid and pushes it between my teeth. That's not a good sign. Then, his fingers lightly peel my sock down, the warmth of his touch still alien to me. Bracing a hand on my shin, he quickly yanks, pushes and jerks my ankle with an audible 'pop.' I scream into my hair. Just before my vision begins to swim, my ankle is eased to the ground and a silhouette appears over me.

"What took you so long, beautiful?" a carefree tune drifts to my ears and I distinctly know Cash has found me, as promised. Spitting my braid free, I inhale sharply.

"I ran into...an issue," I push through gritted teeth, forcing my head up to find no sign of Tweed anywhere. Fucking typical.

CHAPTER 35

MAL

My eyes flutter open, a state of exhaustion holding me firmly in its grip. Speaking of grip, I'm currently in the strong arms of a handsome male, a slight jostle to his footsteps.

"I never realized how heavy you were," Cash peeks down and smirks at me. I grunt, bearing my weight downwards to make myself heavier.

"I never realized how human you were," I cock my brows right back.

"Nicely played." Cash gently places me down, his smile never slipping despite the sheen of sweat covering his flushed cheeks. Unlike the sexy glisten he had at the club, this particular perspiration hasn't been aided by the sheen of baby oil. This one is all physical excursion – something I doubt the twins have felt in an extremely long time.

Keeping my hold on his shoulder, I wobble and hiss at the pain on my right ankle. My boot is back in place and loosely tied, and it does little to support the swelling inside my sock.

"Do you think you can walk on it?" Cash asks. I assess the path laid before us. Rocky, uneven, winding through a forest that is identical to the Enchanted Wood. Long grass set between tree trunks offer no other route, a rustle coming from behind.

Looking over my shoulder, I note the shadow seeping back behind a trunk. On the edge of the path, two lengthy sticks with a V whittled into the tops have been laid on the ground. I narrow my eyes, wishing I was in a position to be stubborn. Following my eyeline, Cash rushes to retrieve the wooden crutches.

"Aha! Our luck is beginning to turn already," he grins, passing them over. I grumble about this particular stroke of luck starting with T and ending in Dick and accept the aids anyway. Keeping my right leg elevated, it takes a few tries to get the hang of swinging my body through the middle before I can start to navigate the path without Cash's assistance.

"Okay, explain. And this time, don't leave anything out," I growl. Talk about waking up on the wrong side of the bed. I woke up on the wrong twin in my opinion. Misery loves company and I'd feel a hell of a lot better if Cash's smile wasn't constantly in my face. He shrugs, pointing up the path which winds out of view.

"We complete the test, find the playing card, supposing it wasn't in the first room you entered. I wasn't privy to the creation of the Nightshade

Trail so for once, I'm as clueless as you are." Turning my face up to the sky, fluffy white clouds sit against a constructed blue backdrop. If I stare long enough, my vision warps and I can make out the curve of a dome concealing us inside.

"So it's a game?"

"More like a treasure hunt," Cash runs his tongue over his teeth, seeming to miss the presence of his fangs. "One that needs two beings to solve. Given Tweed's allegiance to the Red Kingdom, Arabelle knew I wouldn't be able to find an accomplice to join my quest, but she couldn't have banked on you." I pull up short, Cash gaining a few steps ahead before noticing.

"Is that all I am, then? An accomplice to return you to the one you really want?" Cash's eyebrows touch his hairline, his rush to continue forgotten. A look of hurt passes over his features and as he retraces his steps to me, his hand slides around my nape tentatively.

"Where did that come from?" he breathes, searching my face. Another rustle comes from the bushes behind, and I swallow thickly. Coming to some unknown answer, Cash sighs and lowers his mouth to my ear in the way that makes every nerve ending in my body come to life.

"I understand. Your world has trained you to hunt for betrayal. Taught you that there's always a hidden agenda. True, I want to free Lillianna and yes, I need you to do it. But only because she is the true ruler of Wonderlust, Arabelle stole her kingdom, enslaved her people and cursed all men that became infatuated with you. Isn't it interesting she doesn't paint Tweed with the same blood-coated brush?"

Confusion flitters around my mind on butterfly wings. Amongst it all, a riddle Hatter once told me slithers through, although it doesn't seem much of a riddle now at all.

'There are always three sides of the story. Theirs, yours, and the truth.'

326 DESCEND INTO MADNESS

Looking back without the mind of a seven-year-old, I reckon that was the most sane, solid piece of advice he ever gave me. Cash moves his mouth towards my neck, the place he so recently savaged with his teeth, only to place a soft kiss over the sealed wound.

"Wanting to free this realm and return it to what it is supposed to be is my only motive. Whatever happened between us, that was an unexpected turn of events I refuse to regret." My body molds into his, my hyper awareness of being watched withering away. Let Tweed see how it looks to truly care for someone. Cash's arms wrap around my back, slipping beneath my military jacket to touch my skin.

"I'm...sorry Cash. Nonsense I can understand. I've drove myself insane in the real world, desperate to fit in this time. But...I still fit out. I'm still not enough," I choke on my words. The truth slams into me like a battering ram, stealing my breath and knocking tears into my eyes. I hold them back by sheer will, the tiny girl crying inside for acceptance closer to the surface than ever before.

"You're everything we need you to be, and more. You're much enough." Cash nudges my chin up with his nose, refusing to release his hold wrapped around me. Willing me to agree with his steady green eyes, I relent.

"I'm much enough," I smile weakly. Placing a faint kiss on my lips, Cash wraps his hand over my arm and aids my next step of the crutch.

"No more tainted thoughts. Let's find our treasure before nightfall and be home in time for tea." Now that's a plan I can get behind.

***

Nightfall came and went. I turn on my side, followed by Cash who insists on spooning me. His warmth is welcome, even with the humidity circling us. I've heard no other evidence of Tweed nearby, although I've lost enough sleep listening out for it. Rays of reddish orange peek through the trees, another long day in this apparent jungle dawning.

We found nothing yesterday. No life. No food. Only a pathway cutting through long grass and the continuous pattern of trunks. As I lay in the nest of leaves Cash fashioned, I sigh over the rumble of my stomach. Quests aren't nearly as exciting as the movies depict.

"Okay! I'm done!" I shout, jerking Cash awake. His eyes are wide, his hair is wild. Wriggling out of his hold, I grab my crutches to stand and stamp them for good measure. "What kind of treasure hunt has no clues?! We can't just keep walking and walking and..." my eyes snag on a lamppost that definitely wasn't there last night. Two arrows point in different directions, helpfully labeled in sketchy charcoal.

Back to the Start.

Start to the Back.

Cash joins my side, sharing a shrug with me. We don't want to return the way we came, so we're left with one option. The start to the back. Typically, this way turns away from the path and is laid with dense grass that I struggle to maneuver, but it's better than walking blind. Somehow, my ankle seems more tender than yesterday, each movement making me wince.

"Here," Cash comes up behind me. "Jump on." Rounding to my front, he bends for me to hop onto his back, the crutches hanging loose over his shoulders.

"You really have no idea what we should be looking for? Aside from a playing card and a cell, in that order. No riddle to solve, no clues?" I purse my lips.

"Sorry, Crazy One, that's all I've got. Risked my life to infiltrate Red Castle just to get that much. Tweed has never come so close to killing me for real. Too bad for him, I'm not so easy to get rid of," Cash chuckles and I look around the foliage. No shadows to be seen.

"How does one kill a vampire for real?" Cash peers over his shoulder, his mouth in an oddly straight line. I kick his thigh with my good leg. "I'm not going to try to fucking kill you. Just out of curiosity." Returning to trekking through the grass, Cash spots another sign on a tree up ahead and diverts to follow it.

"A stake to the heart with a diamond spear. The Cave of Wonders is packed with clusters of diamonds jutting from every wall. Shards so thick, you'd need two hands to wield them. Ironically enough, only Tweed has access to the cave."

"Let me guess, in the Red Queen's Garden?" I scoff and Cash nods.

"Gifted to her 'Champion'," he scoffs. "Her first decree as Queen. She called it a peace offering from the realm. Giving access to the one way he could destroy his beloved twin for merely sharing his genetics." I frown in thought. Why would Tweed need a peace offering from a realm that clearly hates him? The females that aren't in his bed call him a reject and scorn him. But that's not the biggest mystery being unraveled here.

"There must be more to Tweed's hatred for you than that," I comment. The trees around us are unnaturally still, not a bird or squirrel in sight. Cash shrugs, bumping me around as I hang over his shoulders.

"What does it matter? Too much bad blood has passed. There's no way back." Sighing, I bend my elbow and drum my fingers on Cash's head. Tendrils of hair fallen free of my braid tickle my cheeks like the loose strands of my thought process fluttering around in the invisible breeze. Cash suddenly halts, his head flicking side to side. "You hear that?"

"Mmmm? Oh, it's the cogs in my brain turning. They could use some grease."

"No, listen," Cash urges. Silencing my mind of oddities and theories, I focus. A trickle at first, but once I've latched onto the sound, I can't unhear it. Water. Running water.

Bucking my hips on Cash's waist, I point him in the direction I believe it's coming from. Left, no, right. Wait, it's behind us. The noise moves each time we do, Cash running in all directions trying to catch it. I grab his hair and pull back to make him slow to a trot before stopping completely.

"Stop, let's be smart about this," I ease myself from his back. Standing still amongst the grass as tall as I am, I close my eyes. Mud latches onto my boots. Cash continues trampling back and forth so I grab his hand, forcing him to be still.

"Think. What runs yet never walks, murmurs yet never talks? A river," I provide the answer straight away. "And rivers run down. With the mountains southwest, we should be standing right on top of it." Cash doesn't respond but when I peek an eye open, I see he is facing downward. Now he gets it. The mud has crawled up to the rim of my boots, tipping over the edge to pool inside. Cold at first, the sludge bubbles and hardens around my ankles like two blocks of cement. Fuck, I hope I'm right about this.

Keeping Cash's hand in mine, I lower us to the ground. Finding a Malice-shaped slot between the blades of grass, I outstretch my arms and exhale into the dirt. Each steady breath seeps me further into its cold clutches, willing the clay-like substance to crawl over my limbs and draw me into the ground. My hair sinks, my head being pulled downward until the mud is invading my ears, nose and pressing against the tight line of my lips. I hold my breath, clinging onto Cash's hand like a lifeline. He struggles, his arm shaking as he refuses to relax. Come on, come on.

The longer the mud takes to seal over the light coating my eyelids, the more my lungs scream for air. Fighting against a convulsion, an alarm blares in my mind. Fuck, I was wrong. This was a suicide mission by mud and no one will find our bodies. Buried alive, I mumble an inaudible prayer to any god that may exist. Surely this will go down as the stupidest way to die in history, but at least I'd have accomplished something.

A heavy weight presses on top of me. Shoving me deeper into the ground, I sink beyond the point of return. My chest is crushed, my mouth clamped shut. Mud enters the back of my throat via my nose, and suddenly, I break free. Bursting through the other side of the ground, my slipping grip yanks Cash with me and we're tumbling. Although, we're not alone. The heavy weight remains on me, arms wrapping around my middle.

Still blind, my face caked in clay, I can't push out the scream building up inside. At some point, I loosen my grip on Cash and hit water with a giant splash. Washing away the mud, I shove the weight off my middle and kick my legs, forcing myself upwards. Those hands on my waist give me a final shove and fade away as I breach the water.

"Malice!" Cash roars, splashing and fighting the water to tug me into his arms. I splutter and cough, struggling to produce a full breath. Wiping at my eyes, I blink against the harsh sun, my body laid upon the ground and I scramble to get off it. Not again, no thank you. Jumping upright, I hold my hands out in front of me while Cash remains in the water. A glistening pool of blue surrounds him, rippling where the thundering waterfall across the other side rushes from a cliff face. Luscious green frames the oasis, a mirror image of the jungle above reflected in the world underneath.

"You're," Cash raises a finger to point at my ankle. "You're standing." My gaze drops to my boots. Both feet are planted on the ground, not a hint of pain to be felt. I rock back and forth, rolling my ankles and aside from a crack I've always had, they're as good as new. Smiling, I hunt around for a hint of Tweed. There's no sign, naturally, so I leave him to his game of hide and seek that no one agreed to play.

Stripping, I dive into the pool butt-naked and roll my body like a mermaid. The water is a blessing for the sweaty, muddy mess I'd become.

Pulling my hair free of its tie, it floats behind me all the way towards the waterfall. Coming up for air, I'm alone in the water until a hand grabs my thigh and tugs me underneath. Lips seal a kiss on mine before I follow the tweedle swimming around the edge of the waterfall. The clear water seeps into darkness but I don't lose sight, keeping up until we breach the other side.

Concealed in a cave by the lack of lighting and echoing pound of water, I fall into his arms. A relieved smile plays on my lips. If there ever was a time to celebrate not dying by dirt, this is it. Fingers brush through my loose hair, a breath coating my mouth before he crashes onto mine. A hard reminder of how close we came to the end, a fevered rush of need. My legs wrap around his waist, his erection never failing to press into my core.

Gripping at the wet t-shirt molded to his body, I drag him impossibly closer. Parting my lips, I permit entry of the tongue in a race to seek out mine. Every second is rushed, every opportunity seized to grind my hips shamelessly over his waistband. He savors my taste as if for the first time, committing the feel of my kiss to memory.

Climbing him like a tree, he yanks my head back and takes the full advantage of my exposed breasts. Sucking, licking, massaging. His teeth sink into the soft flesh around my nipple, sending a sharp sting of pleasure to my cunt. There's no denying the water lapping at my hips has nothing to do with the wetness between my legs. I give myself over to this moment, wholly and complicitly submitting to his desires. His hands can take me, his tongue can have me and his teeth. Fuck, those teeth evaporate any regrets and douse my senses in everything that is *him*. Scraping my fingers through his hair, he travels upwards and buries his face in the crook of my neck.

"I'm starting to see what all the hype is about," his deep rumble vibrates through the vein at my throat. Bringing my gaze back down to his, another quick kiss is pressed to my lips but I don't respond this time. My brows knit together, assessing the strange glisten to his green eyes.

"Hey Malice! Where'd you go?!" Cash calls from the other side of the waterfall. I gasp. Tweed clamps a hand over my mouth. Beneath his wet palm, my lips tingle with the forbidden rush of realization. Tweed kissed me. He also tricked me but I'm used to that by now. Looking towards the thundering curtain barring us from his twin, Tweed regards me with the recognition of an enemy. The one I know too well.

"Call it my parting gift, because the next time you do something stupid, I'm not saving you." I attempt to jerk my knee into his balls before he sinks beneath the surface, but all I connect with is water. Diving under, I hunt in the darkened depths with no avail. That asshole stole the kiss I'd already decided he didn't deserve. Hovering lifelessly in the pool, I press my fingers to my lips. Then why did it feel so fucking good?

"There you are," Cash grins when I swim back into daylight. Standing tall in the shallows, his t-shirt has dried in the warmth draping over my weary head. These boys are going to give me whiplash. Spear in hand, Cash closes one eye and aims directly for my head. The sharp point sails through the air as I yell and dive aside. Chuckling as he retrieves his weapon, Cash helps me to stand, observing my swollen breasts, and produces the strangest looking fish I've ever seen at the end.

"Lunch," he tells me. I bulk at the slimy gray scales, rows of razor-pointed teeth and opaque white eyes staring back, my heart still hammering in my chest. Fuck whiplash, these boys will be the death of me.

CHAPTER 36

MAL

Any hopes I had of this jungle being any different from the one above were dashed an hour into our trek. Aside from the animals present on this plane, and the miraculous healing of my ankle. Cash is still very much human, the shadow stalking us is as present as ever. Even more sloppy than before, I can hear Tweed rustling in bushes and stepping on twigs the entire way. It's almost as if he wants to be caught, and then I groan at myself for aiding his nonsense.

"I have something to tell you," I nudge Cash's arm. "Tweed has been following us this entire time."

"I know," he nods, continuing to stare at the snowy peaks on the horizon. Catching me staring, his smirk doubles. "I don't need super hearing to sense my own twin. We shared a placenta for nine months and he spooned me for several years after. I'd be more surprised if he'd actually cut the tie and leave me the fuck alone."

"You hear that? You might as well come out and join us!" I call into the tall grass swaying in the breeze. A sigh comes from behind a nearby trunk and Tweed steps into view, his shoulders hanging in defeat.

"If I had my magic, you'd never have known," he grumbles. Cash pats him on the back.

"Yeah, yeah. Come on. You know as well as I do once you've entered the Nightshade Trial; you can only leave via the exit. Show us the way out, then we can get back to killing each other," he prods his brother a few steps ahead. I also give him a shove, just because. The valley dips, leading up and down a red, rocky path and around the side of a mountain. Across a bottomless gorge, crisp white snow coats the land, but on this side, it's high season in the tropics. Peeling off my jacket, I place Mr. Budgerigar in the dip of my crop top to be my breast guard. Sweat prickles at my overheated skin, my tongue thick and dry.

Tweed, free of the amour he originally wore, takes the narrowing route, never once looking back over his shoulder. Not that I expected him to, no matter how many times I slap my hands on my thighs and exhale down the back of his neck.

"Something to say?" he asks after an eternity, passing beneath a precarious archway of crumbling stone. I narrow my eyes at the back of his head.

"Yeah, actually. You bit my tit, *without* permission." I growl, giving his shoulder blades another push. He spins, catching my throat mid-yelp and throws my back against the mountain. Rubble rains down his back, his expression deadly.

"Your body gave me permission, and you fucking loved it." Leaning close, his lips vaguely touch mine. A feather-light tease I refuse to acknowledge.

"Break it up," Cash warns, a lash of jealousy on his tongue. Tweed pays him no notice, too focused on trying to teach me a lesson by the hand tightening around my throat. My pussy clenches. He knows it, I definitely know it, and a curse tumbles from my lips. "I said that's enough," Cash tears us apart.

Tweed slams his chest into Cash's side, almost knocking him from the ledge, but his intense stare isn't on us. Following Cash's eyeline, movement shifts within the rocks above. Still trying to pick a fight with his twin, I grab Tweed's dick through his cargos and squeeze, halting his macho bullshit for the time being. Hundreds of tiny faces peer over the cliff face, tilting heads of pink and white set with beady black eyes.

"Move," Tweed warns, ripping his dick from my hold and darting down the path. Shuffling from its hiding place, a small bear wobbles into view, growling at us with a set of cute teeth. Vaulting from the ledge, it free falls, arms stretched out. Cash and I step aside, allowing it to splat on the ground in a puddle of pink fluff. Scooping up a portion of its head with my fingers, I assess the substance before sticking out my tongue to lick them clean. Sweet, sticky and light.

"It's marshmallow," I share an amused look at Cash. An army of marshmallow bears that saw Tweed running for his life. Grabbing a handful of bear butt, I share the confectionery with Cash, much to the other bear's stunned shock. Their loss. Strolling in the direction Tweed ran, we pass beneath another archway when the ground beneath our feet shudders.

Thump. Rocks free fall, cascading towards the small path and bounce into the gorge beyond.

Thump. Thump. Turning slowly, a huff of forced wind blows over me. Mr. Budgerigar flutters against my cleavage, his little heart pounding in time with mine. Glass eyes of fossilized auburn capture me in their narrowed glower, a pair of tusks jutting forward in the same polished resin. I step back, bumping into Cash's chest as he too stares upon the beast – a rhinoceros made entirely of amber with four marshmallow bears sitting upon its back. Okay, now I'll run.

A roar pursues me, the uneven ground quivering beneath my boots. Boulders tumble and crash, missing Cash and me by mere inches as we fly down the mountain as quickly as our feet can move. Tweed is already at the base, a stick in his hand which he's jamming into the last of the stone archways. Heaving all of his weight behind it, he tries to dislodge the rock attached to an overhanging portion of the mountain. He's trying to trap us with the beast.

Pressing his hand on my head, Cash forces me to duck and my feet slip from beneath me. Skidding on my ass, weapons rain through the air and litter the ground. Swords, spears, catapulted stones. Panic surges my limbs, disabling my movements until Cash yanks me up and forces me back onto my feet. His hand remains on my back, pushing me the rest of the way down the slope. Tweed spots us nearing, his jaw tense and efforts doubling.

Another howl from the beast rocks our foundations, the heavy breath of his snout nearing closer and closer. Rocks soar past my shoulders, a wooden blade skimming my head. Nearing the stone archway, a weapon sits upon the ground. One I didn't note as being thrown. Striking me as odd amongst my rush to flee, a hammer with the glint of an amber stone fixed into the rear lays ready for the taking.

Using my momentum, I crouch, skidding my biker boots along the path to scoop it up and sail through the stone archway just as it begins to tilt. Cash tumbles on top of me, sending us spiraling off the edge of the pathway. Collapsing stones pound against the mountain, shaking the clay-smothered side of the gorge as we fail to grasp it. A hand locks around my wrist, jolting me to a stop. Tweed's face contorts, his muscles tensing as he drags me to safety. Peering behind with my heart in my throat, I spot Cash hanging from a rogue root. My cheeks puff outwards and the second I'm back on land, I race for the staff Tweed used to almost kill us and offer it to Cash.

"Help me or I'll make your eternal life hell," I growl at Tweed. His jaw is still tight, his vest filthy. Gripping the staff either side of my hands, he gives one swift yank to toss Cash up onto safety and storms away. *Asshole.*

Dropping back, I lie under the unforgiving sun, cupping Mr. Budgerigar in one hand and the hammer in the other. The rhino, if he's still alive beneath the huge pile of rubble, has fallen silent.

"What you got there, Crazy One?" Cash tries to lighten the mood, his breath wheezing in and out as he collapses next to me. I lift the hammer, turning it over to inspect further. A symbol has been carved into the wooden handle, a simple spade that holds so much more meaning than I originally realized.

"I'm not sure, but I've learnt to trust my instincts." Pushing it into the baggy pocket of my cargos, I plant a kiss on the budgie's trembling head. Another instinct of mine. If this bird has something to tell me, he'd better start chirping soon. I doubt he'll survive many more life-or-death situations. "Take care of him for me, I have a score to settle," I tell Cash, handing over my feathered friend. Then I'm on my feet and speeding away.

"Hey fuckface! Get back here!"

Splashing through a shallow river, I catch up to Tweed amongst a field of white daisies. He hasn't answered a single one of my shouted curses. Knocking his shoulder, he spares me a bored look while I double over and hold up a finger. Almost a decade in an institution doesn't bode well for all this exercise. Thrusting my hand in his trousers to stop him from strolling away again, I heave from the uncomfortable burn of fresh air causing my chest to ache.

"You...you nearly killed us," I use his clothes to drag myself upright. Tweed peels back my fingers, freeing himself from my feeble hold.

"Regardless of what you continue to convince yourself of," he brushes himself down as if my touch were more tainted than the dirt covering his front, "I'm not your friend. I have a duty to fulfill and since you've trapped me in this trial to free Lillianna, I have no other choice but to kill her first. She will not be allowed to roam free."

I roll my eyes, tired of the dramatics. What happened to the good old days of smoking hookah and having threesomes amongst the mushrooms? Sure, it was only a week or so ago, but the cold, unfamiliar expression on Tweed's face suggests its long forgotten. No chance for a repeat then, even if this bed of daisies looks comfortable enough. Nah, we're way past make-up threesomes. Everyone in this trial has an agenda, and its time I got back on track with mine.

"I never cared for politics, but I have a mission of my own. You don't want to get in my way, Tweedle Dick."

"Oh yeah?" he almost chuckles, holding his arms out wide. "Or what?" My nostrils flare, never one to fail a challenge.

"Or this," I grab the hammer from my pocket and hold it high above my head. Tweed doesn't even flinch as I bring the sharpened stone downwards, making no move to defend himself. That makes his death his own stupid fault, right? It'll be a shame, a real waste of a good tongue and decent cock, but at least I'm free of the blame. The hammer sails through the air, nearing Tweed's silky blond hair as a glint catches my eye at the last moment. Diverting its path, my arm falls wide and I peer around Tweed while he chuckles for real this time.

"Knew you didn't have it in you." Without warning, I swing the dull side of the hammer underarm into Tweed's dick. He groans and sinks to his knees. I step on his back, following the light drawing me across the daisy field. Tree trunks stand side-by-side, creating a circular wall much like an arena. The only way out is the way we entered, directly opposite the tree that now has my full attention.

"Malice, wait," Tweed calls out. His hand is outstretched, a look of conflict warring in his features. Now I'm even more intrigued. Nearing the tree, a single spear of light through the canopy reflects on a pane of glass. Blinding at first, until I stand directly before it and note the contents. A glass box cemented into the bark, a playing card mounted on a stand inside and red lettering printed across the front. 'Break me.' My eyes fall to the amber-spiked hammer in my hand, a replica of those you'd expect to smash a fire alarm seal in the real world.

"For once, just *listen* to the words I'm saying," Tweed pleads, scrambling his way towards me. Another Tweedle appears in the entrance, falling still in shock. Cradling the budgie in his palm, Cash's smile stretches from ear to ear, pride beaming from his puffed-out chest. I can feel his delight from here, washing over me like a warm balm of fuzzy feels.

This is really it. I found it.

Swinging the hammer backwards, gearing up enough strength to smash through the frosted seal, the weapon is plucked from my grip. An arm winds around my waist, a mouth brushes my ear.

"Malice. If you do this, I can no longer help you." Softly placing the hammer back in my hand, confusing me with the free choice he's now providing, his hands skate over my stomach. Too soft, drawing a pull of yearning from me. Now's not the time, and I'm not stupid enough to fall for his trickery. Far too little, way too late

"Help me?!" I bark a laugh, shoving Tweed away. Of all the times he's been able to manipulate me with tidbits of affection, this will not be one of them.

"All you've done is push me away and boss me around. You offer no answers, only more problems. I've given you many chances to show me the real you, yet I've come to the conclusion there's no Tweed inside here." I prod his chest. "Just an emotionless shell of a minion who never cared for me. Go back to your Queen, warn her of the war I'm bringing her way. I will find Hatter, even if I have to kill everyone in my path to do it. Including you. Especially you."

Silence falls between us, reflected in the daisies that lean closer. Not a breath is passed. Not a word is muttered. Tweed stands a few paces away, tall and sure of himself. He won't bend to anyone's will. He won't be blackmailed or swayed. Not even by me, cementing the fact I never meant anything to him. He took what he wanted, what I willingly gave, and has offered nothing in return.

"Okay Malice. I wish you luck in your venture," he gives a single nod and turns on his heel. My jaw drops. Wha...I mean, what the fuckitty fuck?! That's it? After everything I've said, after the number of times I forgave his actions in favor of believing the boy I once knew still existed. He turned and left.

Fury rages within my veins. My hand tightens around the hammer, a splinter slicing through the wood. I feel less vilified than if he screamed in my face. If he'd shown me there's more to him than a duty-bound zombie.

I supposed that's settled then. He's made his decision and the next time I see Tweed; it'll be with the full force of an army at my back.

Visions for the times we had together flash behind my eyes as I turn my back on his retreat. The pleasure he made me feel, the small glimpses of ecstasy he showed me through withdrawing control. Despite his attitude, I never felt danger in Tweed's presence until today. Until right now, when he's abandoned me without a care in the world. I suppose my instincts were wrong this time. Our choices define us, and mine will set me free of his bullshit. So out of spite, I raise the hammer and smash through the glass barricade.

CHAPTER 37

MAL

A tremor shudders through my arm. The glass beneath the amber-spiked hammer cracks, then shatters into a thousand tiny shards. A fluttering rises at my back, not that I'm paying attention. Reaching my hand out, Cash screams through the whooshing filling the tree-framed arena. My name follows and a word that vaguely sounds like...Malfoy? I didn't know Cash was in Slytherin. I'm more of a

Hufflepuff girl myself. Cute and cuddly, brutally honest, complete lack of self-worth.

"Malice!" the shout comes with that strange word again. Ahoy...Deploy...*Decoy*. My fingers skim the playing card's surface a fraction, knocking it from the platform it was floating above. It topples, floating to the ground and the noise increases tenfold. All around, daisies have popped free of their confines and are spiraling through the air. The flutter of tiny wings fills my ears, blocking the view of Cash across the other side of the field.

"Aww, nifty trick," I hold out my hand to brush the rotating petals. The daisy closest slices the pad of my finger with its blades and I jump back, holding it to my chest. "Ow!" Spotting the playing card laying at my feet, I kick it into the midst of the fluttery fuckers. They go crazy, whipping up into a swarming tornado with the card in the center, shredding it into dust. That's when I truly realize my predicament and catch Cash's eye through the frenzy.

Hurrying me with a flap of his hand, I edge around the daisies while they're distracted, treading carefully to not disturb any of the remaining flowers still stuck in the ground. An odd mix of chrysanthemum and daffodils.

Halfway around the rounded meadow, eyes fixed on my only exit, a vine wraps around my ankle. I rip it free, only to be caught by another. The instigator wobbles, a yellow dandelion with a face hidden within. A weed, in its truest form. My mother always told me not to pick yellow dandelions, as the milky sap inside causes you to pee the bed. She also insisted on living an honest and truthful life while screwing the gardener behind my fathers back, but this time - I'll heed her advice. A third vine latches onto my boot and I bend to tear it away.

"I don't want any trouble, okay?" I whisper-hiss at the dandelion. "I'll just be on my way and you can keep your pee sap to yourself." Taking the vine in hand, a thorn stabs my palm as I toss it aside. Ugh, splinters are my biggest pet peeve, right behind snoring. Hunting for the prickly bastard, it seeps into my skin and disappears from view. No pain, no evidence it was there in the first place.

"Malice! Watch your back!" I turn at Cash's cry, dully noting the daisy tornado has stopped. They're hovering, gently fluttering their petals and all facing me. I swallow hard, then they attack. Covering my head with my arms, the flowers slice every patch of skin they can find. Due to the fact I ditched my jacket back in the mountains, that leaves a whole lot of skin around my spaghetti-strap crop top. Like a thousand paper cuts lashing me, I scream, running directly through the center and barrel out of the exit.

Cash is just ahead of me, the audible fluttering taking chase like an angry swarm of bees. Turning a sharp left to lead us along the riverbank, we race towards the frost-coated land in the distance. Searing pain burns at the lacerations across my shoulders, stomach and back. The thought of dousing them by making a snow angel is my best idea of the day. I don't need Cash's wide eyes continually peering back to assess the damage to know I'm bleeding. A lot. My wrists especially, dripping with heat and flooding my brain with unwelcome regret. Did I really come this far, survived multiple worlds, just to be defeated by a daisy?

"This way! Hurry!" Cash shouts back over the thrumming petals, a note of desperation in his voice. He doesn't know where the fuck he's going, nor what he's going to do with me. Vampires don't have a need to learn first aid. No doubt he's going to pack my wounds with snow and will me to regenerate as a snowwoman. *Wait.*

I skid to a stop. Several flowers slam into my back, cutting me to ribbons while I block out the pain. It hurts enough to merely think on any given day, but right now, the distraction is a blessing.

"I need to go back," I mutter. Cash forces himself to stop up ahead, ducking behind a boulder. "I need to go back!"

"Are you insane?!" Cash cries, bobbing his head popping aside from the boulder. Despite the lashing at my back, I jut out my hip and narrow my eyes.

"Well, I find that highly offensive," I grumble. One brave daisy circles my head and cuts a gash along my cheek. Snapping her closed in my fist, I squeeze tight as a message to the rest of them. It doesn't work. "You distract them! I need to check something out!" For a hesitant moment, I thought Cash was going to let his vanity win over our quest. But then he jumps onto the boulder, swings his arms around like a caveman and starts running again. Most of the daisies take notice and chase after him. Those that remain are a select few I take immense pleasure in kicking off my boot and whacking them to the ground.

Shoving my foot back inside the boot, I'm aware of the time restraint closing around me. My shoulders tremble as I force myself upright, my entire body screaming in agony. Even the parts that aren't cut to ribbons, waning adrenaline tugs on the last of my energy and I fight just to take a single step. Come on Malice, we've survived worse than this.

Chirp. I pause, my ear twitching. On a whim, I abandon my mission and hunt for the sound. Around the boulder, I spot Mr. Budgerigar amongst the grass, his monocle and walking stick missing. He must have fallen, his blue and yellow feathers ruffled. Another tiny chirp escapes his beak and I scoop him into my hands.

"What is it, little one?" I ask, stroking him gently with my thumb. His chest rises and falls with a hint of difficulty and I reckon the time pressure

I was already under just became tighter. Prying his beak open, I lean my ear closer to hear his croak.

"House." I listen for more, and when it doesn't come, I give him the slight judder.

"What house? Whose house?"

"H-Hatter's hou..." his old man's rasp grows quieter. The roaring of blood in my ears, however, is louder than ever.

"Mr. Budgerigar! Where is Hatter's house?! Please, I need to know," I beg. He's still in my hand, the cold fleeting his feathery body. Placing a finger on his chest, I tap lightly to perform CPR and restart that fluttering little heart. Gasping, a bitter cough comes from his throat.

"House...wherever you need," he manages, his beady eyes drawing closed and head falling aside. No. I shake him but it's no use. He's gone. In my grip, the budgie's carcass grows cold and hard, draining of all color. Stroking my thumb over his wing, he begins to expand before my very eyes.

Bang. Feathers explode amidst a yellow powder that covers me, not a single bone or innard in sight. Spitting the powder from my mouth, I dust the remains of my brief, yet old friend from my body. It's on my cleavage and everything - fucking gross. Remembering myself, I rush to stand, the sting of lacerations no longer present. In fact, everywhere the powder touched, nothing but smooth skin is present and I gasp in shock.

"Aren't you a sight for sore eyes?" a leisurely tone comes, Cash strolling towards me with his smirk back in place. The snowy landscape at his back is still, no trace of murderous flowers against the frosted jungle.

"Cash! You managed to lose them," I run into his arms. If there was ever a time I needed a damn hug, this is it. And not just because of everything that just happened. The sting of his brother's rejection is still the ache that remains. The one that cuts the deepest.

"Turns out they're not a fan of the cold," Cash tugs me closer. His face buries in my neck, our bodies molding into each other like jigsaw pieces.

Since the day he arrived at the institution, Cash's loyalty to me hasn't wavered. He hasn't lied or given selected truths. He doesn't deny me the base attraction we're both enslaved to. Cash is real, and in my lifetime, that simple attribute has been the hardest to come by. He gives without question, provides without reason. I'm indebted to the realness he's offered. Even if I lose him after it, returning his Queen is the least I could do. Speaking of which -

"Cell."

"What?" Cash pulls away just enough to frown at me. The expression doesn't suit him. I smile, bopping him on the nose.

"You said cell. Not prison or dungeon or cave. The playing card is the key to free Lilianna from her *cell*. Living organisms, photosynthesis, are you catching on yet?" The blank look on his face I've seen too many times in the mirror is comical to me now. I link our fingers, guiding Cash back towards the meadow. The playing card wasn't a decoy – it was the key to getting rid of the daisies. Entering the tree arena, my blood patters the trail back to the yellow dandelion peering up at us.

"Your majesty," I curtsey before bending to pick her. I'm definitely peeing the bed tonight, but Cash's expression of awe is worth it. Just before my fingers pinch her stem, he jolts me aside.

"Wait!" Cash warns, holding his hands up. "One has to find the key, the other must release the queen. That's the deal." I nod on an inhale. Good catch. Green eyes on me, Cash plucks the dandelion and stands, holding it carefully in his hands. "Woah. You did it, Malice. You've saved us all." My fingers brush his, my chest expanding. No one has ever looked at me the way Cash is right now. Like a savior, a hero. Like his heart's truest desire.

"Take her to the river. Watering a flower helps it to grow," I tell him, remaining behind as he walks away on wooden legs. Unlike the twin who strode from me, Cash looks back, a dimple-studded smile on his handsome face. My heart flutters. After the trials we've faced, the bonds we've sacrificed, I did something right. Running my palm over the back of my shoulder, I rub the residue of yellow powder over an unhealed nick in my skin. Now, about Hatter's house. 'Wherever I need' the budgie said. Well, I really need it-

Stepping forward, my face slams into brick. Invisible from view, my hands trace a windowsill, across a trellis free from vines to the front door I don't need to see to know. I grip the elongated handle and twist, the interior of a house becoming visible amongst the meadow.

Well, I found all the missing hats from his workshop.

Headwear is piled on every surface, covering the living area, dining room and open plan kitchen. Organized by color, I grin and rush inside.

"Hatter! Hatter – I'm home!" I shout, running from one room to the next. My chest heaves, my smile stretched wide. After all of this, I won't need the Queen's aid after all. I beat the trial, gave Cash back what he'd lost and found my missing piece. We can all go on with our happy lives. "Hatter! Where are you?" I call, racing up the stairs. His bedroom is empty, the bed a mess of rags and discarded material. The bathroom, study, and attic-converted art studio, all empty. Cobwebs are rife throughout each room, my heart squeezing for a whole new reason. He has to be here. It's the only stone left unturned. The only place that makes sense.

"Oh fuck," I groan, touching a hand to my forehead. Heat meets my palm, a cold sweat prickling at my skin. As I thought - I'm thinking in sense. I must be sick. Entering the side bedroom Hatter made my own, I drop onto my old bed. Dust shoots into the air, filling my lungs and I splutter. For the most part, everything is exactly as I left it on that fateful day. I hadn't wanted to leave. I was chased out, locked out and forgotten about.

My vanity desk sits opposite, an oval mirror mounted on the fine craftsmanship. In a wooden toybox, the teddies Hatter made for me peek out. I reach for my favorite, a red bunny with its bones stitched on the outside. Large, hollow eyes stare back, tear drops of fabric running the length of its cheeks. Hatter knew concealing pain is a fool's errand. There's beauty to be found embracing our true selves. The good, the ugly, the crazy.

Cuddling bunny to my chest, I observe a few additions that weren't in here last time. A large dollhouse, showing a perfect replica of Hatter's house back when I knew it. Filled with color and warmth. A wooden Hatter at the dining table serving tea and cake. It was always tea time here. My abdomen twists, my throat burning for a sip of sweet caffeination. But without him, it won't be the same. He's the father I always wanted. The man I forged myself to make proud.

My own tears fall heavily, unhindered. Falling into bunny's fur, I bury my face into the stuffed creature. All I have left of the love I once knew. Maybe this is my own stupid fault. Believing those I knew would last forever. Chasing fantasies that were never meant to leave my head. Movement blurs on the other side of my tears but I don't want to see it. I don't care for who has come to gloat in my pain. To convince me I'm the stupid little girl my therapist failed to fix. Wiping my face on bunny's head, I peer across to the mirror, noting the movement is coming from within.

"Hatter," I gasp, sliding across the space onto the short, wooden stool. He's sitting across from me, his head lowered on the other side of the mirror. I outstretch a hand, only meeting the cool glass, all the while calling his name louder and louder. The walls behind him are littered with drawings. The White Rabbit, Cheshire Cat and Tweedle Boys playing with a girl in a blue dress.

I look over my shoulder at the same illustrations, remembering the day I started drawing them. Hatter brought me a slice of cake and I'd flinched, dropping the crayons and holding out the back of my hands for punishment. He'd merely burst into laughter and picked up the crayons, filling in the characters I'd yet to meet. But whereas the drawings behind me are discolored and aged, the Hatter's are vibrant. His head lifts, a full toothy grin stealing the breath from my lungs.

"There we are," he muses, holding a tiny wooden version of me in his fingerless gloved hands. His blue and green eyes are laser-focused, applying one last strand of yellow thread to the doll's head with tweezers. Yet I can't take my eyes off his smile. Joy bleeds from him, even through the mirror's cold surface. "What do you think? She'll approve, don't you think?" he asks, twisting his head. A body lingers on the outskirts of my view, but I know the voice. The steely, graveled voice devoid of emotion.

"Somehow, after all this time, I don't think she'll care," Tweed states, a dagger rounding the Hatter's throat. "And you won't be around to find out." The Hatter stills, as do I. His differently colored eyes rise, locking with mine. Narrowing them slightly, a smile pulls at the corner of his mouth and he gives an indistinguishable nod. A message to the viewer of this apparent memory. Before I can grasp it, the dagger is whipped away and the handle is slammed into the Hatter's temple. He collapses before guards in full black armor drag him from the stool.

A scream is torn from my throat, my fist pounding the glass as I shoot upright. Memory or not, I'll climb through the mirror and rewrite history if that's what it takes. A crunch sounds beneath my shoe, only distracting me long enough to see what I stood on. Needing a double-take, I bend beneath the desk, lifting the cracked version of myself. The paintwork was perfect, the craftsmanship some of Hatter's best. Rising, I drop back onto the stool, staring at golden eyes amongst creamy peach skin that is a perfect match for mine. The mirror has fallen still, an emptiness peering back at me until a hand slides back into view.

"What are you doing?" a female voice out of view asks. I raise my head as a Tweedle sits on the opposite side of the glass. Blonde hair pushed back from his hard, emerald eyes. Straight nose, sharply chiseled jaw and upon his bare chest, the tattoo of a black spade.

"It's all in the breadcrumbs, my dear," he smirks. Those green eyes hold me hostage as he produces a tiny felt hat, complete with three feathers. "Our plan will take time to put in place. Can't have the Alice losing faith while she oh-so-patiently waits." I barely even twitch at the A-word, my body numb. Taking a gold pen in hand, a glittery spark ignites at the end and he proceeds to draw a line through the air. A mere slit, large enough to slot the felt hat through. Lifting his hand with a flourish, he writes letters in reverse, ones I remember all too well.

Find me.

Definition and punctuated, the gash in the air seals and I fall off the back of the stool. No. None of this makes sense. A female laugh comes from the doorway, the real one to my left as I draw in ragged breaths on the floor. Two figures block my escape, their features hidden with the shadows and cobwebs. But I see enough. The outline of a woman in a dress of black rags, cinched at the waist and dipped low in her creamy cleavage. A Tweedle on her arm. The one who's been lying to me this entire time. The bastard who's taken me on this quest to keep me from discovering the facts.

Not Tweed. *Cash.*

CHAPTER 38

CASH - EIGHTEEN YEARS AFTER ALICE'S DISAPPEARANCE

*T*weed *groans beside my face again, rubbing the side of his neck. Lingering over my crouched position, he keeps leaning into the spot behind my ear to inhale deeply.*

"Dude, fuck off," I shove him away but he comes straight back again. I peer around the corner of the hallway, watching Lillianna stroll towards the lab. Using the key in her hand, she unlocks and opens the door, quickly speaking to someone inside. Not even a beat passes before a woman rushes out, a black

cape with silver trim billowing at her back. Long hair of the same, black and silver streaks, flies in her haste, disappearing with Lillianna into another part of the castle. The key sits in the now closed door, glinting at me with a cheeky wink. The wetness of a tongue tip strokes over the vein at my neck and I jerk out of my hiding spot.

"What the hell, dick-face?!" I kick out, knocking him on his ass too. Realizing I'm out in the open, I grab Tweed's shirt and rush us into the lab with a burst of speed. He stumbles aside, dropping to the ground in the lab while I softly shut the door. Another groan seeps from him while I look at the pitiful display, no need for light. My enhanced sight is enough, and at this current moment in time, I wish it weren't.

"You need to snap out of it, Tweed. We have a job to do." I nudge him with the toe of my boot. He rolls onto his side, holding his middle with both arms. This isn't right. He was unconscious way longer than I was upon receiving the vampire venom last year, and here I was, thinking he was the stronger one of us.

Incoherent words babble from his mouth. I know he's hungry. I understand the ache of his insides eating away at the blood in his own veins, just to last that bit later before his first feed. But I can't let him drink blood yet. The hunger only builds after that first taste, becoming an insatiable thirst. Lifting him by his arms with the strength I've forced myself to conceal up to now, Tweed lunges for my neck. I dodge him at the last second, pinning him against the wall as his green eyes burst with a glow.

"You won't be able to drink from me. Focus, Tweed," I give him a rough shake. "I need your senses in tune for this mission. Once we're done here, I'll provide you with enough human blood to last an eternity." Slight exaggeration but my words seem to do the job. Falling still in my hold, Tweed closes his eyes and collects himself.

"What have you done to me?" he struggles to speak around his newly grown fangs. I place him on the ground, turning to face the lab before us. It has two levels, connected by a winding staircase. The lower level is clearly where all sorts of experiments take place, across two huge workstations of glass bottles and vials. On the platform up above, I note the outline of a cauldron, and given the female I saw recently exit, I shoot that way. Tweed fumbles around in a bid to follow, still adjusting to his heightened eyesight.

Tarot cards are scattered across the floor, the only one upturned being 'death'. Beneath an oval window, a fountain of shimmering water swirls, black wisps oozing just beneath the surface. Clumps of tied lavender line the windowsill beside a herb grinder. Opening a few cupboards, all I find are bags of herbs and jars of shifting eyes. Interesting, but not the treasure I'm looking for. If I were a poisoned chalice, where would I be?

"B-behind the f-f-f," I turn when Tweed topples on the last step, only remaining upright by his hold onto the railing. The color has fully drained from his pale skin, his finger trembling as he points towards a picture frame on the wall. An oil painting of a beast with white fur, drool-dripping sharpened teeth and yellow eyes. The Bandersnatch, who to my knowledge is imprisoned beneath Diamond Maze. Although as the painting moves, a silent roar blasts from the creature's mouth, I'm not so sure.

Trusting Tweed's instincts, I lift the frame free of the wall. True enough, a cupboard is concealed behind. No lock or handle, just a simple slat of wood pressed into the wall. Pushing on one side, it releases of its own accord, revealing a chalice inside. Colored jewels are embedded around the cup, a slender tail leading to the sturdy, golden base. The scent of poison hits my nostrils instantly, burning down to the back of my throat.

Sensing Tweed dragging himself along behind me, I remember the whispered instructions Lillianna gave in my spade suite. 'Tweed must be the one to retrieve the chalice,' she'd commented, offering me her wrist. I drank swiftly and greedily, the intoxicating taste of her essence filling my system. Incredibly sweet, overwhelmingly addictive, with the slightest hint of an underlying taste. Similar to licorice with a mix of woodsy pine and lavender, whilst presenting a mild bitterness hiding in-between. Nothing helps me to see clarity like a drop of Lillianna's blood, her innocence putting my jumbled thoughts into perspective.

"You should take it," I tell Tweed, stepping aside. "I'll keep watch." Ever the brave hero, especially when his body is in full-fight mode, Tweed grabs the chalice from its mount. He holds it close to his nose, sniffing and jerking back. I watch him adjust to his increased smell, wondering if he's trying to reject his new abilities through pure stubbornness. Surely if he accepted his modified fate, he'd have adapted by now. The door below opens and I duck behind the cauldron faster than the average eye can track. Expecting Tweed to follow, he stands on the platform, fully out in the open.

"Tweed," I hiss, but it's too late. His eyes illuminate to lime green and in a burst of speed, he's gone. A high-pitched scream explodes from below. Shit. By the time I've raced to the witch's aid, she's already dead. Tweed's fangs in her neck, he drinks every drop of her blood, draining her until crimson streaks are dripping from his lips. Sighing in contentment, Tweed drops her like she meant nothing, a pleasured shudder running the length of his body. Then, he smiles.

"You good bro?" I ask, uncertainty curdling within. A broad grin splits his face in two, stretching from ear to ear in an image I'll see later in my nightmares. Before my eyes, Tweed's body expands, each muscle pushing against his skin. Licking his lips lazily, my twin stands tall, the image of perfect health.

"Never better." Grin in place, Tweed strides from the room without care for sneaking. I know that look. I've seen it in the mirror multiple times, but on him, it's plain horrifying. Complete satisfaction. Blissful immortality.

Where I've kept my abilities a secret, Tweed embodies his. Running after him, I urge us to return to the suite but he's not listening. Bolstered by the power thrumming through his veins, Tweed storms through the castle with confident strides. So much for laying low.

"Tweed, you asshole," I hiss through my teeth. "You're going to blow our cover."

"To who? There's no one here," he responds aloud. I halt, standing straight to listen through the walls. No distinguishable heartbeats. No chatter, music...Tweed is right, there's no life anywhere close by. Aiding him in his hunt, for what I'm not sure, we begin to look inside each room. With the King's presence close by, I've never snooped around Spade Castle before, and apparently, I wasn't missing much.

Mildew combined with dust-covered furniture are behind each bedroom door. Unmade beds and unhung curtains lay folded at the foot of bare mattresses, ready for a visitor. Taking a grand staircase down, the lower-level presents much of the same. Derelict ballrooms, neglected games areas. My frown increases until we approach a closed door at the end of a corridor and Tweed's hand flashes out to halt me.

"You smell that?" he asks. I step by his side, inhaling deeply. Yeah, I smell it – the lingering scent of death. Rigor mortis has just begun to set in, Tweed's nose twitching as he adjusts to the foul odor. After a recent feed, his senses will be intensely strong, but it won't last long. Then he'll crave more blood, searching for the high he can't get enough of. The patter of a single heartbeat catches my ear as Tweed twists the old-fashioned doorknob and shoves the door wide.

Flies. Out of everything my mind tries to accept in that moment, flies are what it picks out. Stuck to the bright chandelier at the top of the heightened dining room. Crawling across an uneaten buffet stretching from one end of the main table to the other. Buzzing around the body of a bull-headed man who is face down in his own plate.

"Lillianna?" I step inside, holding a hand over my nose. "What's going on here?" The Queen Consort lifts a steak knife from the table, her golden eyes looking at me with such adoration, she doesn't fit the scene around her. Nudging up the sleeve puffing from her shoulder to wrist, she holds my gaze as the blade pushes against her skin and slices in a sharp, single movement. Her blood markers fill the air and I'm a slave to my own greed. Shoving Tweed aside before he gets any ideas, I shoot across the room and have her wrist in my mouth before I can think any more on the dead body beside me.

Lavender and pine skate over my tongue, a taste that's uniquely hers. Drinking her in, gulping the blood I need to live on, Lillianna invades my senses. The haze of satisfaction falls over me, drowning out the confusion in my mind. All that remains is peace and understanding.

"Cash," Lillianna whispers into my ear as I lick her wound clean. "The King tried to kill me. I didn't have a choice." My eyes seek out hers, my tongue still touching her wrist. "It was self-defense, but no one will believe me. They'll say I'm an outsider who killed her husband for his riches." Lifting my head, I cup her cheek.

"What do you need me to do?" Lillianna's gold eyes flick over my shoulder to where Tweed would be standing. Her lips lean into whisper in my ear.

"Tweed is holding the poisoned chalice. We can let him take the blame." My head jerks, knocking Lillianna's cheek but her hand slithers to my nape, holding me in place. "The new Red Queen is fond of him. She'll spare him the harsh punishment I would receive. I'd be dead by morning, Cash." Desperation leaks from Lillianna's tone and my eyes drift to the darkened window at her back. Rain continues to fall heavily, but underneath the thunderous sound, is another. Almost indistinguishable, but once tuned in, I can't unhear it. The repetitive echo of marching.

Soldiers storm the main entrance, turning for the dining room without need for instruction. Ox and Bison with heavy hooves, all dressed in armor and chainmail stamped with a heart. Arabelle is in the center of them, her nose creasing and brow furrowed. Tweed's head snaps back, the army parting for him as a member of their own. I anticipate his actions but make no move to stop him. Lillianna's hand curls around my arm.

In a flash, Tweed has gripped Arabelle by the neck and thrown her tiny body into the chest plate of a guard behind. Swords are drawn, only Arabelle's raised hand holding off the soldier's attack. My brother's name is a plea on her painted lips. His head jerks from her carotid to her face, a growl rumbling in his chest. This is where the bloodlust takes its truest form, mixing the man with the monster lurking inside. The Red Queen will be dead within seconds. Except when he pushes two words through his crazed hunger, my brows shoot to my hairline.

"Help me," he begs of her. The hand on Arabelle's neck shakes under the weight of his waning control, the chalice in his other hand cracking. Keeping her eyes on him, Arabelle pushes against Tweed's chest and through sheer will, he drags himself a step back and whimpers. Tremors rack his entire being, his head downcast like a scorned dog. He's fucked up, and he knows it.

"Someone needs to tell me what's happening here," Arabelle says when her throat will allow it. Lillianna is quick to race around the dining table, me hot on her heels.

"It was Tweed! He killed the King!" she points a finger to the half bull, half man laying dead on the table. I follow her point, grimacing at the flies crawling into his pierced nostrils. My heart squeezes at her words, but my body remains stoic, my mind uncaring.

"I didn't do this," Tweed shakes his head, his voice too quiet. Defeated. It doesn't matter if he did or didn't; my brother just made an attempt on the queen's life. He's utterly screwed regardless.

"He's holding the chalice used to poison my dear husband," Lillianna forces a fake tear. "Just look at him!" The soldiers glance nervously at Tweed, his face smeared in blood and shame. Arabelle doesn't shift her steady stare from the Spade King.

"Cash. What do you have to say about all of this?" she asks softly. Her large eyes lift, watching my emotionless face. Inside, however, indecision wars. My soul tugs towards my brother, but my mind speaks reason. Tweed will be fine. Even as Arabelle refuses to acknowledge him, I can tell she'll give him a far lighter sentence than Lillianna would receive. And besides, Tweed is immortal like me now. One day all these people will be a distant memory and we'll get our fresh start. Over and over until we do it right.

"Lillianna is telling the truth," I nod in resolution. "Tweed killed the King of Spades out of jealousy. He wanted..." my mind scrambles for the end of that sentence, "her." I nudge my head towards the woman at my side. The atmosphere thickens, only penetrated by the buzzing of flies hovering around. Amongst the army's worried expressions, Arabelle has yet to react and internally, I smirk. Tweed trained her well. Now he will receive punishment by her hand.

"Guards," Arabelle snaps her fingers. The bison and ox army raise their swords to Tweed's chest, his head hung and body unmoving. "Arrest Lillianna."

"W-what?!" the Queen Consort gasps, stepping backwards and bumping into a dining chair. "N-no! Tweed is a stone-cold killer, he committed treason!" she babbles, tugging me to stand in front of us.

"I stand with my Knave. I trust his word far more than yours, Lillianna."

"Don't be a fool, young Arabelle. Your Knave was caught red-handed and the rumors have already begun to spread," a bitter laugh comes from behind. The flies on the chandelier swarm into the outline of a spade before fluttering from the room, rushing to spread the word to the masses. "Once the realm hears how you let a murderer walk free, they'll turn their backs on you. Renounce you as Queen."

"They will not," Arabelle replies, instantly and confidently. I almost respect her in that moment, before the next order comes from her perfectly painted lips. "Arrest Cash too." My eyes widen as Tweed finally looks up, not a trace of regret to be found. Stepping closer, Arabelle doesn't refrain from raising a hand to my brother's shoulder, even though he could tear a chunk out of her wrist and kill her before the guards could even move.

"We'll get you the help you need," she tells him. My gut flips. Not only because the guards are closing in on me, the promise of an eternity imprisoned glinting at the end of their swords, but because of the love Arabelle and Tweed share. Love. The sibling-ship kind. The very same one I've been chasing all these years, yearning to share with my twin like we used to.

"Not today," Lillianna mutters. I peer back to see her eyes fluttering closed, a chant on her lips. Just as the first point of a blade eases into my chest, the room around me fades into smoke. Lillianna holds my arm, the carpet dissolves as my feet give way. We tumble, sailing through space until charred grass meets us at the other end. A light blares through the darkness and as I raise my hand, a neon sign labels the building before me as 'Dirty Dee's.'

"I made this for you," Lillianna rushes to say, dragging up her heavy skirt to stand. Her pulse is erratic, her blood already calling to me but there's no time. Taking my hands in hers, Lillianna's mouth opens as a claxon begins to chime across the land. The royal alarm for fugitives. Lillianna licks her lips and tries again.

"Remember who saw you when others only wanted to use you for your body. I gave you eternal life, and in turn you promised to protect me, so I know you'll do so again. Once Alice has returned, come for me. She's the missing piece to this." Beginning to run away, I shoot forward and Lillianna slams into my chest.

"The missing piece to what? What is happening right now?" I shout above the alarm ringing from the darkened clouds themselves.

"Bring her to me alive. Together, we will put an end to the Red Kingdom's reign. You shall be the King on my throne, and we will see that those who have ever wronged us both, suffer immensely." Leaning up on her tiptoes, Lillianna sinks her teeth into her bottom lip just before pressing a kiss to mine. As quickly as she placed it there, she's gone, and this time, I watch her go. Tongue darting out, I taste the increased essence of pine and lavender and my eyes roll back in my head. I'm sailing through the air, yet I barely feel as my back slams into the ground, a pair of spades dancing in front of my vision.

Lillianna is right. She saw me when no one else wanted to. She saved me from a life of being a mere possession. The club before me glows through the night, providing a safe haven. A place where I dance on my terms, for my own gain.

Suddenly, my mind begins to reel, calculating the ratio of women left to men. Soon, I'll be a rare commodity, and with that comes power. The power to create my own rules, decide my own fate. Even set my own currency. If there's one thing of importance I've learnt in the past year, it's that lust buys anything. Especially submission.

CHAPTER 39

MAL

"Pesky things, mirrors," a male chuckles, stepping into my childhood bedroom at the Hatter's house. "They retain as much as they observe," Cash muses, throwing something up in the air and catching it. Brass glints, a chain trailing behind and I squeeze my eyes shut. Hatter's pocket watch. He took it from me at Arabelle's castle and never gave it back.

My mind rolls and twists like a Rubik's cube, too many pieces slotting conveniently into place. The way Cash has hindered me, how he's always been too close. Behind my lids, I can envision him crouched behind the boulder, squeezing the life from Mr. Budgerigar. Shuffling closer, I open my eyes to glare at the Tweedle crouching before me. His smile is set in place, a simple shrug ready on his shoulders.

"For what it's worth, I really wish you hadn't seen that." Lifting his fist, Cash peels back his fingers to reveal a mound of gold glitter which he promptly blows into my face. I scramble aside, the room already disappearing as my hand closes around the splintered doll that reflects my soul a little too keenly. Laughter circles me as the glitter eats away at the room, replacing it with a hallway. Dropping in from a height, I manage to land on my boots just before Cash and his Queen follow suit.

Wallpaper made of crocodile skin. Doors of all sizes lining either side, towards a club at the far end. Above the archway, a neon sign blinks in mockery, one I know to say, 'Fantasy Walk.' The instant Cash materializes, he shoves my chest through a doorway that the Queen rushed to open. I fall back, my head slamming against a hard ground and my vision swims.

"If it's any consolation, you got what you wanted. Sort of," Cash chuckles, slamming the door closed and darkness falls. I shoot upright to bash my fists on the door, screaming every colorful way I'm going to make sure Cash suffers for this. A snicker sounds from within the shadows, a match being struck to glow upon a pale face with differently colored eyes.

"Quite the stir indeed."

"Hatter," I breathe, refusing to believe it. I've been tricked before. One more betrayal and I will crumple. Raising his flame, a hanging lantern flickers to life, brightening the space I'm now trapped in. A room, not much bigger than the single bedroom I so recently sat in.

A table divides the space in half, set with six chairs and I must wonder if we're expecting company. One side is decorated with empty photo frames and a medley of clocks that all say different times. The other has been scribbled on, in much the same way some of the inmates at Charmsfield would expel the contents of their brains over the walls via illustration. Words, pictures, scribbles. My eyes drop to Hatter's fingerless gloves, the tips are coated in smudged charcoal.

"You're late, young Malice, but always on schedule. Time for tea, don't you agree?" Hatter gestures to the tabletop. White doilies hold empty plates, cups on saucers holding dust as opposed to liquid. The teapot in the center shudders, Miss Dormouse popping her head upwards to wear the lid like a head piece. I sigh in relief that he's at least had company, rushing forward to take Hatter's hands in mine.

"Hatter. You've been right here, the entire time." Tears prick my eyes, a hitch in my voice. Hatter pats my hand, drawing me towards a drawing of a fireplace, much like the one in his home.

"I'm neither here, nor anywhere but exactly where I am." His smile is exactly as I remember it. A gap in his front teeth, a crooked tilt to his mouth. The blue eye watches me while the green one tracks Miss Dormouse hopping closer. She jumps from the table, landing on my shoulder and sniffs at the back of my ear just like Stan did. Oh, I can't wait to introduce the pair of them when I get out of here. If I get out of here.

"I've been so stupid," I slap myself in the center of the forehead. Hatter catches my hand, pulling it back when I try to do it again.

"Stupidity is a far cry from sensibility." He follows a thought with his eyes now in sync, his mouth parted to say something else. Then he smiles. Guiding me to a chair, Hatter waits for me to sit and tucks me towards the table. He takes the opposite side, blowing out his cup and using the handkerchief in his jacket pocket to bat the dust residue away. Leaning over, he does the same to mine, placing the cup delicately on the saucer and stares at me expectantly.

"I'm so glad you're okay," I breathe, slowly shaking my head. He tilts his.

"How else should I be?"

"Dead," I shrug. "Tortured, drained of your you-ness."

"Sounds dreadful," he shudders and I laugh through rising tears. Stark orange brows bob beneath the rim of his large hat, spiky hair of the same color flicking free at his nape. Amongst a purple and green patched jacket, a marvelous polka dot yellow bow bursts from his neck. Lifting his finger, he lifts the teacup and sips, a real slurp drifting around the room. I frown at my own, spying the full cup of tea which wasn't there before.

"Fantasies become reality in here," Miss Dormouse slides down the length of my arm and plops into my cup. "Whatever you wish for, except the way out. Only the club's owner can release the exit." Sinking her back down, she sighs in contentment, her tail flicking around the saucers as she takes her bath. Peering around the room, my mouth inclines to the side.

"Then why does it..." I stop mid-question at Hatter's shocked expression. I know, I know. Too much sense. The thing I've been trying to outrun my entire life, yet it found me in the one place it shouldn't be needed. But even as I try to quell the questions batting around my skull, an answer is produced. The room looks this way because it's exactly how Hatter wants it. He's been sitting here, mostly alone, waiting for me.

Closing my eyes, I puff out my cheeks. As pleasant as I'm sure it could be, I can't sit here for an eternity. Not when Cash is strolling around out there, his Queen on his arm. There's some notion of saving Wonderlust in that sentiment but I'm lucid enough to admit to myself my motive is spurred by jealousy. I freed that bitch. She should be kissing my feet while Cash is massaging my shoulders. Then there's Tweed...yeah, no, we're not going there right now.

"You're plagued," Hatter places down his cup. At first, I thought he was inferring to my mental state, but as I nod, my head wobbles and a rush of dizziness knocks me sideways from my chair. My hands are shaking and that cold sweat from earlier is back. Hatter drops on his knees before me, turning my hands over several times in search of something. "Black magic is at play here," he speaks gravely.

"Black...magic?" I repeat back. "Like, the Queen of Spades?" As the words leave my mouth, Hatter's jaw tightens and I wince. Yeah, I thought so. Hiding my shudder under his scrutiny, I continue on. "There was a trial. A quest of sorts. A lengthy journey, rough terrains, an injury, some problem solving, an ambush, a death, a betrayal. Couldn't be any more cliché if I tried. Anyways, the Queen was a weed and she attacked me with some vines. One of the thorns went in my hand and disappeared. I forgot about it to be honest." Sinking my head between my shoulders, Hatter holds my stare until I'm sure my eyes are about to bleed.

"Your hair wants cutting," he takes a strand of my mane in his fingers. Twizzling it, he returns to the table, sitting a seat on from where he was before. Fresh dusty cup for him to blow into and produce a stick of butter from his pocket to stir into the central teapot.

"Hatter," I say, a low warning in my tone. "What is the black magic going to do to me?"

"Magic attacks magic. You're perfectly safe, being moderately human." Rounding the table, I take the tea pot out of his hands before he is able to pour a cup of cancer into his cup.

"Stay with my train of thought," I tell him and he immediately looks for a train. "I can...conjure things. Whatever I believe to be true, is. Does that count as magic?" Hatter presses his lips together tight, as if he doesn't like the answer he's due to give. I'll take that as a yes. "And what would happen to one who isn't moderately human?"

"Worry is the disturbance of hope," is all I receive and I hang my head. Fuck, it's bad. Really bloody bad by the way Hatter avoids my gaze and produces a second bar of butter, just to chew on the edge. "As long as you keep your insanity intact, you shall prevail. My muchness has already taken hold. It won't be long now." Hatter gestures a hand towards the wall of scribbles and I tiptoe closer.

I appear in the drawings many times, always surrounded by a line of rainbow color, ranging in thickness. The word 'Malice' repeated often with an accurate definition circled below. '*Noun. The desire to harm someone; to mean ill will. Synonyms: spite, malevolence, animosity.'* All of the above I want to remind Cash of while I ring his fucking neck with my thighs. Clothes on. Let my sweet juices be the last his heightened sense of smell inhales, after he lost out on screwing me by screwing me over.

Speaking of which, my eyes travel the drawings as if re-watching my adventures. From the institution to the twins in the visitors' room and beyond. My return to Wonderlust, the town, Humpty Dainty, the maze, the wood. I sure know how to get around. In most, the twins are by my sides. If I hadn't been trapped in here by him, I'd never have guessed Cash was the twin with pointy-down eyebrows and a cruel smile in every deception. But Hatter knew.

"Who are you?" Hatter's voice comes close to my ear and I flinch. He tilts his head into my eyeline and I frown, looking back to the drawings.

"A gullible horny bitch?" I guess, not seeing what he's referencing. Hatter grips my chin and twists my head up to the top corner of the wall.

"Who. Are. You?" he repeats. I stare upon our first encounter in stickman form. Hatter stands beside a tree, the rainbow lines circling him thick as my four fingers pressed together. The small girl beside him has the same. Knowing better than to ask sensible questions, I point to the colors and wait for him to fill in the gaps. "Muchness," he nods, slinking back towards the table.

"I have muchness?" I peer over my shoulder. Miss Dormouse has left her beige bath and is drying her ass on the tablecloth. She pauses to nod at me.

"Tell me, young Malice. Why were you permitted entry to our world above all others? Isn't it obvious?" Hatter's smile returns, a full beam of teeth and joy, his arms raised high at his wall of doodled madness.

"Our skill is seeing through a kaleidoscope,
where others see shades of black.
Our magic is believing it into reality,
And our duty to bring the colors back."

Hatter's hand falls, his finger pointing to a hodgepodge of words, outlined, smudged and outlined again.

Successor. Progeny. Inheritor. In-hatter-or.

"You arrived in Wonderland because I called for an heir. I *believed* one into existence, and so you appear." His voice is full of wonder. Bursting with pride I struggle to accept. I can't...I'm just...a lunatic. An accident, falling between realms with no real sense of belonging anywhere. Right?

A shiver creeps down my spine as my entire world falls into place. Shuffling at my back, Hatter returns to his position peering over my shoulder, like his feet just can't stand still. Like he's been rehearsing this moment in his head a thousand times, and now it's here he doesn't know which version to play out.

"Arabelle's Champion promised me he'd protect you. That he'd stop you from entering the Shadow Planes. But I know you as well as I know myself. I'd have found a way too, no matter how well guarded we were under the guise of vampire blood."

Oh, it gets worse.

Tweed's image crashes into my mind like a wrecking ball. His stoic stare. His know-it-all attitude. He tried to force me to play the game his way, to cage me from the truth. Where Cash provided fun, I saw freedom. Chaining a bird meant to fly will always result in a chewed-off foot. Conjured by the thought, a sketch of Mr. Budgerigar catches my eye – sitting on Hatter's shoulder beside the Red Castle. The Queen I knew, pompous and round with a bright red face, lays at his feet, her head a few inches away.

"Young Malice, why is a raven like a writing desk?" Hatter mutters, giddy on his feet. I shake my head.

"I have no idea."

"Ahh. But why is this realm like a carburetor?" My body freezes, my mind already in overdrive. I know the sensible answer will earn me a slap but my mouth blurts it out anyway.

"It controls the air and fuel to the engine?" A gloved hand smacks up the back of my head for speaking sense, while Hatter commends me for being correct.

"We're the fuel," he spins me around with a swift jerk of my shoulders.

"The air is the air," Miss Dormouse pitches in and I give her a solid thumbs up.

"Yeah, I got the metaphor, thanks." This time, Hatter shoves me and I tumble back into a chair. His eyes wander in different directions, his mouth twitching between seriousness and a burst of impending crazy. Could be anything from animal noises to plain screaming, so I shrink back and prepare myself. His fingers jerk, drifting to the rim of his black hat. Four playing cards are fixed into the red sash around the center, a King of each suit. Lifting it from his head, he holds it high in the air.

"Our liveliness jump starts those around us. Provides the delight they need to thrive. I've been stuck in perpetual time long enough, waiting for you to be ready. You're ready." Bringing the hat down slowly, I jerk out of the chair and push it between us, my hand halting his movements.

"Woah, no, hold up." My chest rises and falls heavily. Hatter freezes, not a muscle moving, his face staring on expectantly. "If I accept, you're not going to...die, right?" A beat passes before Hatter releases a high-pitched laugh. His head falls back, facing the ceiling and even Miss Dormouse finds me comical.

"Of course not, you silly goose," Hatter wipes a tear from his blue eye. "I'm merely retiring. Hanging up my hat, so to speak. Sit, young Malice, be my hat rack." Exhaling loudly, I ease myself back into the chair. Miss Dormouse jumps onto my shoulder once more and I tilt my head to whisper into her ear.

"I can't fill Hatter's shoes." Her twitchy nose tickles my cheek, the hat above my head lowering.

"I see your point. He's at least six sizes bigger than you."

"I mean, I don't think I'm up to replacing him," I whisper-shout, sliding down in the seat to prolong Hatter's knighting. Maybe he'll change his mind, see sense and...oh, he'll never do that.

"Good gracious girl," Miss Dormouse tuts, "no need to fret. He's been grooming you for the past twenty years. You were never alone." The hat lands on my head and before I can respond, Hatter pulls me to my feet. Pure pride is projecting from his eyes, a look of relief capturing his entire face. Beyond the smile and vibrancy, a hint of dark circles hides beneath the white powder upon his face. I don't know how I missed it before, but now I can't unsee it. He's tired.

"Blood, sweat, and tea. That's what it takes to achieve all great and terrible things," Hatter reminds me. He told me the same as a little girl, and now I'm standing before him in his oversized hat, it's like no time has passed at all. "You're the Hatter now."

I chew on my bottom lip. My eyes travel back to the wall of stories I lived but looking at them now, it's like staring upon a stranger. I can see my mistakes, the clues I missed. Where my stupidity and blunt refusal to see sense clouded my judgment. I don't want to be tricked again, to let down the realm again. Lilianna is free because of me, her poison running through my veins. Not the best selection for an heiress.

"Believe it. Say it," Hatter urges. If I can even still call him that.

"I-" my voice wobbles. Never, in the past twenty years, have I felt this unsure. This...scared. A tear falls from my eye, caught by Hatter's thumb.

"Forget what you think you know. Trust your instincts. Believe you're worthy." Gloved hands cup my cheeks, the man I adore tilting my head up to face him. The pride is still there, unwavering and resolute. Twenty fucking years I've waited to see him again. Our perfect reunion was shattered, but I needed to see Wonderlust in its rawest form. To learn the ways of this world, to feel its sharp sting of betrayal in order to rebuild. As Mary Ann would say, bleeding out is necessary.

"How did you do it?" I ask, pushing the smallness from my voice. "Live in our own world, not caring about those who try to penetrate it? I wanted to return to this realm so bad, but it isn't a dream come true at all. This is a fucking nightmare."

"A dream is not reality, but who's to say which is which?"

"I am to say," I mutter and Hatter orders me to say it louder. Clenching my jaw, I cast one last glance at the drawing of the Tweedle boys. Identical on the outside, both assholes with vendettas. Obviously Cash is top of my shit list currently, but when I break out of here, Tweed will not escape my wrath either. There's a thousand ways our hate-filled relationship could have played out and he made his choice. It's my job to make sure he pays for it. Well bring it the fuck on.

"I am to say!" I shout, clenching my fists. "I am Mal Hatter. I'm a badass bitch and I'll bring this realm a level of crazy they've never seen." Hatter steps back, clapping his hands wildly. In the corner of my eye, the loose hair framing my face shifts. Pulling the rest of my mane forward, I splutter. Luscious curls, silky smooth and perfectly styled slip through my fingers. What's more, my blonde locks have molded into vivid orange, a shade brighter than Hatters. I believed it, and it's come true.

My clothes change next. Black leather clings to my body, supported by spaghetti straps from my chest to high thigh. Stockings meet the dress with a lace trim, a pair of checked ankle boots on my feet with a chunky heel. Starting from my back, a jacket expands and wraps around my shoulders. Pulled tight at the waist with a flair of under-netting, the collar high at my nape. To finish, a black bow with red dots slides around my neck and ties itself. Top heavy due to the hat, my head drops to the side.

"This absolutely calls for a tea to celebrate," I grin. Miss Dormouse has jumped free of my shoulder, her tiny feet scattering through the saucers towards the tea pot. Hatter moves the same time I do, jumping to catch her before she bathes in the only tea pot we have. Closing my hand around her, she nibbles at my fingers until I set her down in the sugar bowl and flick the lid shut.

Hatter settles in a seat at the top of the table, I take his left. Setting about making tea, he pulls various screws and cogs from his pocket, sprinkling them into the teapot. I don't even question it, seeing complete reason amongst the madness. Afterall, how else would you make a builder's tea?

"Your hair still wants cutting," Hatter winks and I incline my head to agree. If he offered to do the job with a butter knife, I'd let him. I understand now, clear as day. Since the moment I landed ass-first in this Wonderlust, the crazy has been seeping from me. A festering wound I didn't notice until it was too late to stitch closed. This was supposed to be my salvation. Where I would be liberated. Free to be myself. But I, too, had fallen prey to my personality being chipped away at, until all that was left is...logic. Pure, boring and reasonable logic. No fucking thank you.

Willing the clocks on the wall to all spin to six o'clock, chimes sound and I share a knowing look with Hatter. Believe and you'll receive. Before my eyes, the small room bursts to life. The lantern brightens, replicating the sun. A fantastical spread of tea, cakes and biscuits is laid before us. Hatter tucks a handkerchief into his tie and I do the honors, pouring the tea and passing Miss Dormouse a Cherry Bakewell the size of a pea. We may be trapped in Fantasy Walk, but for a while at least, I'm content to stay. I have so much to learn, even more to understand and the ideal guide to mentor me.

I know where I belong now. Hatter has passed the baton, retired from his reign of absurdity and gifted it to me. Luckily, I already had plenty of my own to spare.

I'm Mal Hatter. Wonderlust will bow to my insanity, or off with their heads.

AFTERWORD

I sincerely hope you are enjoying this chaotic duet so far, and why stop now? Embrace the Mayhem is out there and waiting! See the details below to continue this epic tale where nothing is as it seems. Until next time, happy daydreaming!

Embrace the Mayhem
Wonderlust Book Two
www.books2read.com/embracethemayhem

Blurb:

Fact: Malice always falls for the bad boys.
Another fact: This time may have been her last.

Confined to yet another cell, this one of her own creation, Malice has learnt a harsh lesson in thinking with her libido. The realm she loved is falling apart, and it's her job to save it. Newly appointed as the Mal Hatter of Wonderlust, she must maintain the balance of control and chaos, all the while resisting the drop-dead gorgeous Tweedle Twin vampires.

One holds Malice's heart, while the other commands her attention. This game of cat and mouse can't last much longer, although she'll do anything to preserve the lust which fuels her every waking moment. The prophecies are set, the future defined. Will Malice be able to play her role, or will she screw it up for everyone involved? Namely, herself.

Trigger Warning: Unlike the original, all characters in this spin-off retelling are very much adult. Expect steamy scenes, exaggerated episodes, ridiculous rhymes and apparently, alluring alliteration throughout.

ACKNOWLEDGEMENTS

During the course of writing Descend into Madness, I've faced many trials in my personal life. There were times when I thought I wouldn't find the words to finish it. This book is truly a testament to others around me who continue to boost and support my work on a daily basis. Family, close friends, encouraging indie authors and readers I can't thank enough. I hope Malice's wild ride has done you proud.

A special thanks to:
Jo for her incredible editing skills.
Kristina, Lou and Joy for being my Alphas.
Megan J Parker-Squiers for the cover and **Nautilus Visuals** for the illustrations which inspired this duet.
Lewis Carroll for the chaotic and limitless world he has opened up for so many imaginations.

And lastly, my readers.
It's plain and simple; I'm nothing without the readers who support me!
Thank you all for devouring my books, and also becoming my friends. I

love getting to know you, seeing your gorgeous book shelves and building connections with so many talented and wonderful people.

OTHER WORKS

If you're a new reader to Maddison – welcome to the Mole's Burrow!! Maddison is a married mum of two, and a serial daydreamer. As a huge fan of all romance tropes herself, it was time to pen the stories which consume her mind most hours of the day.

As a child, Maddison was a jet setter and has lived all over the world, only to return to the south east of England, where she is now happily settled. With a double award in applied arts and art history, Maddison is a creative with a dark passion for feisty females and spicy stories.

Join my Newsletter or on my website:
www.authormaddisoncole.com
Facebook – **Author Maddison Cole**
www.facebook.com/Maddison.cole.314
Facebook readers group - **Cole's Reading Moles**
www.facebook.com/groups/colesreadingmoles
Instagram and TikTok - **@authormaddisoncole**

Other Works:

I Love Candy
Dark Humor RH - Completed

* Findin' Candy (novella)

* Crushin' Candy

* Smashin' Candy

* Friggin' Candy

All My Pretty Psychos
Paranormal RH with ghosts and demons - Completed

* Queen of Crazy

* Kings of Madness

* Hoax: The Untold Story (novella)

* Reign of Chaos

Bound by Fate
Fated Mates Shifter Romance

* Moon Bound

A Deadly Sin
MMA Fighter BSDM RH - Standalone

* A Night of Pleasure and Wrath

A Wonderlust Adventure

A Twisted Menage Retellling

- Descend into Madness

- Embrace the Mayhem

The War at Waversea
Basketball College MFM Menage - Completed

- Perfectly Powerless

- Handsomely Heartless

- Beautifully Boundless

Co-Writes

- Life Lessons with Emma Luna

Standalone
RH High School Bully Romance

- Beautiful Delusions

Made in the USA
Columbia, SC
22 October 2024

44804488R00213